Ferris Wheel

The Ferris family's journey through their wheel of life

Ferris Wheel

The Ferris family's journey through their wheel of life

a novel by

Katie Jackson

Melissa,
Thanks for standing by
me all these years!

Best Wishes always

Katie Jackson

Cover and author photographers:

© Lauren Madeira, laurenmaderia.com

© Bruce MacPhail / Fotolia

© Jan Kranendonk / Fotolia

ISBN 978-1-257-04491-7

To all of our friends in the Huntington's community. Keep fighting the fight and hold tight to the hope that one day there will be a cure.

Contents

The Meeting

It all began the summer before high school.

I come from a small town where everyone knows everyone's business, and as school wound down that spring, there was a lot of talk about a new family moving to Pollock. Rumor had it that some big-time lawyer from Sacramento had decided he wanted to move his family to the country. There was an old, half-rotten Victorian mansion directly across the street from my house, and that was the place they chose for their new home. The Victorian was huge, but it was ancient and decrepit; the paint was chipped and peeling, and the rain gutters were sagging off the eaves. The rank vegetation surrounding it would have reached higher than my waist, if I'd dared to step onto the lawn. From the street, the place looked exactly like any creepy old house you might see in a horror movie-and I could only imagine what it looked like inside.

That soon changed. You could tell that the family had a lot of money, because they proceeded to rip the house apart and just start over. The work proceeded amazingly quickly, too. One morning I woke up to the smell of fresh paint, and found that the workers were just about done touching up the exterior. Others were laying fresh sod in the bare patches of the now-tamed lawn and planting flowers in the long-neglected beds. The former horror house looked enchanting with its new coat of white with cream trim. The grass, old and new, was vivid green and lush; and by that afternoon, the flowerbeds looked like a rolling sea of brilliantly colored blooms.

By then, the thrill of summer was in the air. My friends and I made a game of sneaking around the Victorian to see if the mysterious family had moved in yet. My girlfriends were hoping that some cute new boys would be arriving soon; they claimed to be "so sick" of the same boys we'd known since we were babies, and they constantly joked about who would get dibs on the new ones, if any. Me, I could have cared less at that point. I had too many worries as it was to have to deal with a boyfriend, too.

We'd been out of school for about a week when I noticed a moving van pull up to the front of the Victorian. My room was on the second story of our house, with the window facing the street, so I sat at my desk and watched the movers bring in a parade of grand-looking furniture. It was like nothing I'd ever seen before: royalty-quality stuff, huge, heavy, and ornate, obviously expensive. There was a lot of it, too, and it all seemed to match. The movers carried in the furniture for hours...but there was no sign of the new neighbors.

That night, after a long day of watching and not doing much else, I went downstairs to fix dinner for my Dad and brother. This was a nightly routine for me, since I was the woman of the house; my mother had passed away when I was very young, so it was just the three of us. My Dad did the best he could, but he worked full time at the firehouse in town, so he wasn't home very much. Most of the time it was just me and my brother...at least, when Cal wasn't running around with his friends. He was very social and had a ton of buddies—the total opposite of me, really.

Oh, sure, I had friends, but I wasn't the social butterfly type. I was your typical dorky, awkward fourteen-year-old girl. I didn't play any sports—I was way too clumsy for that—and I wasn't into the things most girls were into. I didn't wear make-up, and my plain, muddy-brown hair was usually tied back in a ponytail rather than teased into any noticeable style. I guess you could say that I was an authentic tomboy. I was raised without a female role model, so I was never taught how to be a girl. Add to that the fact that I was pretty much a by-the-book rule-follower, and my life was kind of dull...although I was very good at taking care of my family, I have to admit that. I kept the house squeaky clean and took care of the place with panache.

I was the oldest fourteen-year-old in the whole world.

About six o'clock, we all came together at the table and started eating. As usual, the guys talked about the latest sport scores and dickered over some football draft somewhere. After reaching my limit, I broke into the conversation: "Have you guys heard anything about the family moving in across the street?"

Dad frowned, and swallowed his latest forkful of mashed potatoes. "Heard there's three of 'em," he said. "A couple and their son, about your age. They lived in the city for years, but the wife got sick, and she always wanted to live in a small town. Sounds like she might not have much time left, and her husband wanted her to have what she wanted while she could enjoy it…so they packed up and bought the old Jefferson house."

"I heard the son's a total dweeb," Cal replied helpfully. "You two ought to get along just fine."

"Is that so?" I asked my Dad. He gave me an odd look, and said that he knew the kid was going to start at the high school next fall, but he really wasn't sure about much more than that.

After the boys stuffed their faces, my Dad settled on the couch to watch basketball on TV and Cal took off, as usual, to go hang out with his friends. Once I'd cleaned up the kitchen and kissed Dad good night, I went up to my room and got on the phone with Page Claremont. Page was my best friend: we'd been like sisters for as long as I could remember, and I had to fill her in on the info I'd gotten from my Dad about the new people. We speculated about the new boy for a while, then moved on to all the standard drama that teenage girls usually talk about. Towards the end of our conversation, we made plans to go to the community swimming pool the next day to lie out and get some sun.

I woke up early the next morning with that very sun heating up my face; it wasn't even eight, and it was already a blistering hot day. As I rolled out of bed, still half asleep, I noticed a car pull up into the driveway of the house across the street. A sleek black Cadillac, it looked like no other car in our town. A well-dressed man got out of the driver's side; he had jet-black hair, was incredibly tall, and radiated a sense of self-confidence. Moving briskly, he opened up the passenger door on his side, and helped out a stunning woman. She was very thin and tall, her buttery blonde hair piled high, with curls hanging down to her shoulders. In her long, flowing white dress, she looked like a fairytale princess, and was easily the most beautiful woman I had ever seen.

She was very refreshing, actually. It was extremely hot outside, but she looked as cool as a night breeze. There was something different about her; I noticed that she swayed back and forth as she moved, almost like she was dancing in place. It was a very fluid movement, and her hands were also making odd little twitches.

The man came around to the lady and took her by the hand. He looked at her with a big, heart-melting smile, the way lovers look at each other in the movies. His profound affection for her was plain; it was as if she were the only person he'd ever really looked at. They headed towards the door, and as they did, the man looked back to the car and beckoned to someone inside.

The back door swung open slowly, and there he was: the loveliest boy I'd ever seen. I simply couldn't take my eyes off of him; even now, that image glows in my memory. His hair was black, like his father's, and his skin was the most perfect golden brown. He was tall for his age, and had a solid build. His smooth walk as he strode up the sidewalk revealed him to be cool and confident. As he hurried to catch up to his parents, he pulled a set of headphones off his ears and stuffed them in a pocket of his jeans. He took his mother's other hand when he reached them and, together, the three beautiful people walked into their newly-beautiful home.

As I watched them, and thought about this mysterious new boy, I was overwhelmed by an emotional onslaught of a kind I'd never felt before. My stomach seemed to be stuffed full of fluttering butterflies, and I felt unbearably light, as though I were floating on air. A tingling feeling all over made me feel faint. I had no idea what was going on...I loved the whole sensation, but it also made me extremely anxious. And I most certainly wanted to see that boy again.

I clomped downstairs, where my dad was sitting at the kitchen table drinking coffee and reading the paper. "Hey Dad, the new neighbors just pulled up!"

"Really." Dad radiated indifference; clearly, he couldn't have cared less. But of course, my Dad was like that. He was your typical mountain man: shaggy-haired, bearded, simple, rough-edged, and straightforward, very hard-working but unimaginative and hardly touchy-feely. He never talked about feelings or anything like that; in fact, I'd rarely heard him talk much about anything. Our small town was Gossip City, but my Dad never got involved with any of that nonsense. He worried about taking care of his family, and let other people worry about their own business.

Sometimes, I thought he cared about work more than us...though I know better now. But that didn't change the fact that he often stayed at work for a day or two straight, leaving us to fend for ourselves. That's part of the reason I got good at taking care of myself and Cal. Sometimes it was lonely, of course, and I wished I had my Mom there; but for the most part I was used to my circumstances, and I had Page to keep me sane.

Ignoring my Dad's indifference, I ate some breakfast and then cleaned the kitchen before heading upstairs to get ready to go to the public pool with Page. I put on my bathing suit, a modest one-piece, and threw some shorts and a tee shirt over it. Since Page was going to be at my house in about a hour, I headed out front to water the grass. We used to have sprinklers, but they broke a couple of years ago…and of course, Dad never got around to fixing them. Well, it was my mission this summer to have some green grass. I swear, our place was falling apart!

I started spraying the yard down, and was out there for just a minute or so before I looked across the street and saw the elegant woman sitting on the front porch of the Victorian, drinking a glass of iced tea. I was still brimming with curiosity about the new neighbors, so of course I decided I would go over and introduce myself to them. I tossed the hose aside and trotted across the street. I have to admit that as I approached the newly-repaired walkway to the Victorian, I was a little intimidated, since I wasn't used to meeting new people. I probably wouldn't have ever introduced myself if I weren't so nosy.

I stopped at the bottom of the porch stairs. "Hi! My name is Kathryn Price. Welcome to the neighborhood!" I said cheerfully.

"Hello, dear, I'm Elisabeth Ferris," the pale lady said, smiling. She had a very soft voice, like a beautiful Sunday hymn.

"It's nice to meet you, Mrs. Ferris. I heard you guys moved here from the city?"

"Sacramento, yes. My husband, son and I decided we wanted a more peaceful life than the city could offer. Come on up here."

I clomped up the steps and stood on the verandah (well, you couldn't really call it a porch). She was even more exquisite up close; I saw that she had beautiful, sea-blue eyes, and was very pale. It wasn't like a sickly pale; no, she looked like an angel. She was still swaying back and forth, even though she was sitting in one of those wide-backed wicker chairs I'd always found so enchanting. It just added to the whole exotic picture.

Well, I didn't want to be rude and stare at her, so I decided that I should leave before she noticed the wonder in my gaze. "Um, Mrs. Ferris, I'd better get going—my friend will be here soon, so we can go to the pool to try to beat this heat. I just wanted to come introduce myself. My Dad and brother will probably come by soon to meet you guys. My Dad's a firefighter here in town, so he'll be gone for the next 24 hours or so, but when he's done I'm sure he'll be over." I realized I was babbling, so I shut up.

"That sounds nice, Kathryn," she said gently, carefully taking no notice of my *faux pas*. "How old are you, by the way, dear?"

"I'm fourteen," I said, suddenly feeling shy.

"Goodness, you're mature for your age. You know, I have a fourteen-year-old son; you two will have to meet soon. Carson's a lovely boy, and it would be nice for him to get to know someone this summer, so he isn't stuck in the house listening to his Walkman all day. I'm sure a responsible young lady like you would be a wonderful influence."

I wasn't sure I wanted to be Carson's influence, at least not in the sense of teaching him responsibility, but I said, "That would be great! Like I said, I'm going to the pool for the day, but maybe I'll come by when I get home, so I can meet him."

"That sounds lovely, Kathryn. I'll let him know, and make sure he's on his best behavior."

We both laughed, and I took off back to the house after we said our goodbyes. Mrs. Ferris—Elisabeth—seemed kind, and she was certainly captivating; I almost wanted to stay there and get to know her better. I wondered what was wrong with her. People around town had said that she was sick, and that's why her husband had moved them all to the country, where she wanted to be…but what could be wrong? She looked healthy; in fact, she was a striking woman, with rosy cheeks and the warmest smile. I would never have guessed she was ill. She had a very inviting air about her, and the only person I've ever seen who came close to her ethereal beauty was a princess from a Disney fairytale.

As I picked up the water hose and started trying to bring the lawn back to life again, I thought about the way she was swaying back and forth. Obviously, that had something to do with her illness. I also thought about her son. *His mother's illness must be hard on him,* I mused. Plus, it had to be hard to move to a new place right at the beginning of summer; if school had been in session, he'd have had time to meet at least a few people before everyone scattered. Seeing as how it was summer, though, that would be difficult. What a long, boring summer it would be, not knowing anyone our age!

That's when I decided I was going to take him on if he would let me. I'd show him around and introduce him to my friends, so he wouldn't be alone. And of course, I could get the first crack at him, if he just *happened* to want anything more than friendship.

After drenching the lawn in a way that was sure to have my Dad griping about the water bill, I ran upstairs and grabbed my bag, along with sun block and a towel. I was filling up a water bottle in the kitchen when my doorbell rang and the front door opened. "Hey, Page!" I called.

"Hey, Kathryn, you ready to go? Mom said she would drop us off, and then we could just walk home."

"Wow, that sounds wonderful! I love to walk in this kind of heat."

"Sarcasm will get you nowhere, Kathryn."

I grabbed my stuff and ran out the door, pushing Page ahead of me. I looked across the street, and there was Elisabeth rocking in her chair. I grinned and waved goodbye, and she smiled and waved back. I knew it would take all of two seconds before I was getting drilled on the new neighbors—Page was really nosy, like everyone else in Pollock—but at least she waited until I got into the car first. "Hi, Page's Mom!" I said brightly.

"Hello, Mike's Daughter," she replied, grinning at me in the rearview mirror. We always greeted each other this way.

"So the new people moved in across the street?" Page asked.

"No, that was a ghost lady on the porch," I told her grimly.

"Really?"

"No!" I bonked her lightly on the head with my water bottle. "Honestly, you can be so silly, girl. Yeah, they're the new people, just arrived this morning. Their last name is Ferris. I saw them from my window, and there's just the three of them. The mom's name is Elisabeth—that was her on the porch—and I don't know the Dad's name. Elisabeth says they have a fourteen-year-old son named Carson. I didn't meet him, but she invited me over to meet him later."

Page asked excitedly, "Have you seen him yet?"

"Yeah, from a distance. I couldn't really see too much."

"Was he cute?"

"Friend of mine said he's gorgeous," Page's Mom chimed in.

Not quite ready to go off on that topic just yet, I said, "Well, I really couldn't tell. It was from my bedroom window, you know... but can you imagine moving to a new place and not knowing anyone? He'll meet people when school starts, of course, but what a lonely summer!"

"Yeah...but you know this town," Page replied, batting her long lashes over her very blue eyes. "Everyone will be too curious to stay away too long. I'm sure people will be over introducing themselves in no time…especially the girls. It sounds to me like you *did* see him, so you must think he's cute. *You* seem to want to meet him really bad."

"Kizma, Page!" ("Kizma" was our code word for "Kiss my butt" so we didn't get in trouble from the parents.). I went on, "No, that's not it. I was really thinking about going to meet him just so he'd know somebody. I have no clue if he's cute or not."

Yeah, okay, so I kind of lied to Page. I *did* see him, and yes, he *was* really gorgeous. But honestly, that wasn't the reason I was eager to meet him. I'd never really been into boys the way most of my friends were, from about age 12 on. I *certainly* wasn't the kind of giggly girl who would sit around and think about a boy all day. Most of the time, I was too busy taking care of the household to do silly stuff like that.

Plus—worse—I was the plain girl in town. If all us girls were in a room together, I would definitely be the girl in the corner that the new boy would never notice. I was convinced Carson would want nothing to do with me, in any other way besides friendship. So why else would I be going over there than to offer him a friend, someone who could introduce him to people in town? It was practically my duty as a neighbor. I could only hope he would stay my friend for a while, at least until I was pushed aside by the more popular kids. I knew that Carson would soon join their clique, given the way he carried himself with such confidence...and, of course, all the other girls were going to try to sink their teeth into him, the first chance they got.

I wouldn't blame them. He really *was* gorgeous.

When we got to the pool, we waved goodbye to Page's Mom and tried to find a place to lay our towels down among all the kids scampering around. Mostly littler ones, since most of the older kids (and there weren't very many of us) considered the pool a less-than-cool place, even though it was a great place to *get* cool. As we got situated, I thought about how bored Carson would be here in Pollock. There was nothing here, really. In the city, there were bowling alleys and movie theaters and stores. Here we had a community pool and a whole bunch of wilderness. Ideal for someone who loved the outdoors; not so ideal for a teenage kid.

"So, Page," I said casually, "did you hear that the reason the new people moved here was because the lady was ill?"

"That's what I heard."

"Yeah, well, she looks healthy enough. But there's something different about her. She moves around a lot, almost like she's dancing."

Page adjusted her sunglasses and laid back, glancing around to see if any of the few teen boys around were watching. They weren't. "Really? I've never heard of anything like that."

"Yeah, me either. I wonder what could be wrong with her?"

From there the conversation drifted to other things, and after a couple of hours of swimming and lying in the sun, Page and I decided it was time to head home. We gathered our stuff and started on our long walk, hitting Page's house first. As we halted at her house, she said, "So, you're really going over to meet that new boy tonight?"

"Sure, once I hit the showers."

She grinned. "Well, make sure you call me and let me know all about your new *boy*friend."

I smacked her with my towel. "Don't be a smart-aleck. I'll talk to you later."

As I walked home, I tried to hold in my rising excitement. This was so silly! Here I was, trying to decide what I was going to wear to go meet the new boy across the street. I didn't know why I cared so much. There were girls in town who really cared about what they wore and how they looked, but I wasn't one of them. That's probably why boys never really noticed me; I mean, I was kind of plain, but I wasn't ugly. I guess I could have done something with what I had, but I never paid attention to that sort of thing…which was why I probably wasn't the right girl for Carson to meet first.

And let's admit it: back then, I also had no confidence in myself. I was actually a little nervous to meet this guy, who seemed to radiate confidence even from a distance. That type of person was intimidating for someone like me.

I reached my street, and noticed that the new family was sitting together on the front porch. I waved as I walked by; Elisabeth waved back, and the husband smiled at me. Carson didn't really have any expression on his face; he just sat there and looked at me. Maybe he didn't want to meet me. Maybe he thought he was too good to be around a small town girl. I couldn't blame him. What in the *world* could a country girl have to offer a cosmopolitan kid like him? I was sure he was used to a lot of excitement—and good luck finding that here!

After a quick shower, I sat in front of my closet and thought about what to wear. Girls in the city probably all wore name-brand clothes and fancy jewelry…and there was definitely nothing like that in *my* closet. After pulling everything out, I decided on a little pink sun dress that I'd always loved. I dried my hair carefully, then put on a little make-up and slipped on my fanciest flip-flops. That was about as good as it got.

The new family was still out sitting on their porch when I emerged, and I noticed there was another person with them now: an older lady, not dressed as elegantly as the other three. I gathered my courage and stepped lively up their sidewalk. When I'd reached the steps to the verandah, I said nervously, "Hello, Mrs. Ferris."

"Why, hello, Kathryn. Darlings, this is Kathryn Price, the young lady I was telling you about. Kathryn, this is my husband Bill, and my son Carson. Come up here and sit down with us."

As I got settled in, Bill Ferris got up from his chair and shook my hand gravely. "Nice to meet you, Kathryn."

"Nice to meet you too, sir."

I glanced at Carson and he instantly caught every bit of my attention. I felt like we were caught in amber, just the two of us, alone in this moment. Holy cow, he was *perfect*! I instantly felt my stomach drop to my feet, and my cheeks burned; I hoped my face wasn't as red as it felt. He looked at me with a smile, and I thought I was going to melt. My legs felt like Jell-O…but inside I was super-excited, full of nervous, jumping energy, and I couldn't keep up with all the feelings pouring through me. So this was what it must feel like to be attracted to someone!

He nodded at me. "Hi, Kathryn, I'm Carson. Mom says you're fourteen too?"

I didn't know what to say. He was like no boy I had ever seen. He was faultless, and his beauty simply kept me from speaking. I had been mistaken to think his hair was jet-black like his Dad's: it was actually dark brown, and now that I really looked at him, it was kind of wavy. He had big brown eyes, too. His skin was golden brown, like it had been kissed by the sun, and he was bigger than most guys our age. He looked like he could have been Cal's age, which is 17.

Wow, they must raise boys differently in the city, I thought. Most boys my age were awkward and weird, but Carson wasn't. He looked like he could be in the movies or something, and of course I was incredibly attracted to him right away. I felt tingly all over. I had so many thoughts running through my head that it took me a while to catch up with myself and realize that too much time had passed without me saying anything. I'm sure he noticed too, because he was kind of chuckling to himself. He must have been used to getting this response from girls.

"Umm, fourteen. Yeah, I'm fourteen." I completely stumbled over my words, sounding just like an idiot. He just looked at me and smiled. Oh boy!

Elisabeth broke the awkward silence. "Kathryn, are you starting at the high school next fall?"

I looked over at her so I could be brought back to this world—so I could act normal again. "Yeah...um, yes, ma'am. I'll be a freshman. My brother Cal will be a senior this year. I hear it's a good school…at least, that's what everyone says about it. It's small, though. There are 43 students in our class—well, I guess with Carson, it'll be 44. Most of us have been going to school together since kindergarten. There have been a few other people who have moved here, but not too many."

Elisabeth glanced at Carson, whose face now bore a shocked expression. I guess he was probably used to going to a much bigger school. "Don't worry, honey boy, it'll be nice."

Honey boy? I thought, and grinned despite myself. Well, it was an apt nickname.

He apparently didn't mind me hearing it; he just looked at her and smiled. I could tell he didn't really like the idea, but he was trying to act like he did, for his Mom's sake.

Elisabeth directed her regard to me. "Kathryn, you said that your father was a firefighter here in town. What does your mother do?"

I stopped grinning. "Oh, well, my Mom passed away when I was little, so it's just my Dad and my brother and me."

She put a hand to her chest. "Oh dear, I am *so* sorry. I hope I didn't upset you?"

"Oh, no ma'am. She's been gone a long time; I don't really remember her."

Carson was looking at me again. When I'd first gotten to the house, he was polite enough; but I realized that was all he was. He saw me, but it was kind of like he was looking *through* me. I could tell that he really wasn't too interested in me being there. Now, suddenly, he was looking me straight in the eye. He was truly looking at me…in a way I had never been looked at before, which was why I was able to understand that, before, he *had* been disinterested. He had this look on his face…well, it wasn't a look like he felt sorry for me, but almost a look of unfathomable sadness, like he understood me in some strange way.

The older woman, who had gone into the house when I was walking over, now came out and smiled at me. She addressed Elisabeth: "I'm getting ready to go now, Elisabeth. Is there anything you need?"

"No, Margret. You drive safe, and we'll see you tomorrow."

"All right. I unpacked all your clothes, and put everything in the right drawers. It's set up just like your old house."

"Thank you, Margret. It will be a real help knowing where everything is. We'll see you in the afternoon. Take your time getting here, since you'll have to be here a couple of days."

"Got it. Bill, what time are you leaving tomorrow?"

"Pretty early in the morning, since I have to be in court in the afternoon. But Carson will be here, so take your time."

Listening to this conversation, I began to put the puzzle pieces together. Margret must be here to take care of Elisabeth when Bill wasn't home. I couldn't figure out what illness she must have that she needed someone to be there when her husband was away, but clearly she did. If Bill was leaving in the morning and Margret wasn't going to get to the house till the afternoon, then Carson must have been designated to take care of Elisabeth in the time between. It must be awful, if Elisabeth could never be alone. Carson was a fourteen-year-old boy...and there was no way I would've trusted my seventeen-year-old brother with the responsibility for anything important, especially not another human being. Carson must be a wonderful kid, I decided, to be able to be trusted to be with his Mom when Margret and Bill weren't home.

Suddenly, my life didn't seem so bad. All I had to do was take care of the house and cook dinner. I didn't have to watch over my sick mother. That must be so tough-and I realized that Carson and I *did* have something in common. We both had a lot of responsibilities, compared to most kids our age.

A moment later, after exchanging a few more pleasantries, Bill spoke up. "Elisabeth, we'd better get inside and start getting ready for bed. I have to be up early to make it to the courthouse in time. It was really nice to meet you, Kathryn. We look forward to meeting the rest of your family."

He walked over to Elisabeth and helped her out of her chair. There it was again: she was moving oddly, like a weed in the wind, like a dancer. She looked at me and smiled. As his father drew her toward the door, Carson got up from his chair and gave his mother a kiss. One thing was clear: Carson adored his mother...and that was adorable in itself.

"You two stay and get to know each other," Elisabeth invited. "I'll see you soon, Kathryn."

"Thank you. It was nice to talk to you. Have a good night."

They slipped into the house; and when the door closed, I think my heart might have skipped a beat. I was alone with Carson Ferris! He was a completely unknown quantity, beyond his angelic appearance. I definitely wasn't used to that. All the other boys I'd been around I'd known since I was little. It's easy to talk to people you've known forever. I wasn't really used to meeting new people. I really didn't know what to say.

Fortunately, Carson took care of that for me. "So, what do you do for fun in this place?" he asked after a long moment.

I sighed. "Well, there isn't a lot to do, to be honest. There's the public pool, where everyone goes in the summer. We have a decent public library, and I suppose you could go downtown and watch the traffic lights change on Main Street. This place will probably bore you to death."

He shrugged. "Yeah, but this is where Mom wants to be—so if she's happy, then we're all happy."

He seemed to mean it, and I couldn't believe what I was hearing. Most boys my age couldn't care less about what made their moms happy: they were too worried about doing whatever made *them* happy. This boy really couldn't be just fourteen. I looked at him, and realized that I could get lost in those huge brown eyes.

"So...what are you doing tomorrow?" Carson asked.

"Well, my Dad's at work all day and we went to the pool today, so I was probably just going to sit around the house and watch some TV. Probably clean a little. But if you want, I can take you around tomorrow and show you the town. Everything's within walking distance, if you don't mind walking a lot."

He grinned. "I don't mind. In fact, that sounds good. Once Margret gets here, I'll be free to do whatever."

My heartbeat skipped again. "Okay, um, just come over and get me when you're ready."

"I'll do that. I'll see you tomorrow, then."

"Awesome!" I jumped up out of the chair I was sitting in, and turned for my house. Carson stood up too.

"Hey, Kathryn." I looked back; he was looking a little uncertain. "Uh, are you by yourself in that house tonight?"

"Umm, yeah," I admitted, "for now. My brother should be home at some point, but my big protector will probably be on the phone with some girl all night."

We both started laughing, and I waved goodbye as I all but skipped up the sidewalk and across the street, whereupon I flat-out ran up to my house and up the stairs. As I put some comfy pajamas on and laid down to read a bit, I couldn't stop thinking about what was going on with this new family. There was a Mom who was ill, and had to have someone with her at all times. Then there was Carson, who was responsible far beyond his years. I could *not* get his face out of my mind. There was something about him that made him so different from anyone I'd ever met...well, maybe not *some*thing. More like everything.

I decided that my mission the next day was to get a little more information about what was going on in that house. I was sure that I wouldn't be able to get Carson to talk about it all right away, so I decided I wouldn't ask any questions to make him uncomfortable. I wanted him to be my friend, not feel like he was being set up for an inquisition. I hoped he could clear up a couple of things, that's all; then my mind would quit running wild about what could be happening.

I woke up early the next morning and did the same old routine: breakfast for me and Cal first, then I called Dad at the firehouse to tell him that I had met the people across the street, and I was going to spend the day hanging out with their son, showing him around town. I cleaned the house a little, then went upstairs to start to get ready. I looked out my window and there was no car at the Ferris house, so I figured I had a while. Therefore, I took my time, making sure that each curl I made in my hair was just right, and I put on some pink lip gloss that Page and I had bought one day at the market and, until then, I'd never even opened it.

I was so excited that I was going to spend the day with Carson, to try to get to know this mystery boy a little better.

When I heard a knock at the door, I grabbed my purse and literally ran down the stairs. I opened the door, and there he was: young male perfection himself, wearing blue jeans and a white T-shirt. I'd pictured him wearing something a little more done up. Stupid, I know, but I was glad to see he was as casually dressed as me. The cute city boy looked good a little country, too. "Hi, Kathryn, are you ready?" he ask shyly.

"Yep, let's go! Good you wore your walking shoes, because this is one big town, so you'll need good shoes," I kidded.

Thank goodness he got my sense of humor; he just looked at me and started laughing. As we headed down the street, I pointed out every house I had a small town gossip story for, which was practically all of them. We walked for hours. I showed him the high school where we would be going to. We walked down the little strip of town, and I showed him the pizza parlor, the diner, the market, and our newest addition: the video store, where we could rent the latest movies. There was no movie theater in town, so of course whenever a new movie was released onto video, we all ran to be the first to grab it. In fact, come to think of it, that was about as entertaining as most of the movies.

I think it was kind of amusing to Carson to realize how little there was to do here. I told him about the small carnival that would come to town the week of Labor Day, and how all of us kids would stay there for practically the full four days straight (or as long as the money lasted, anyway), getting the feel of all the carnival rides for the one time a year we got to do it. We talked a bit about his old school in the city. He'd gone to a private school there, so I was sure he was ahead of all of us; our school would probably be a breeze for him. That worked out well for me. I needed to keep him around to help me, since school was hard for me most of the time. I figured he could tutor me if we were still friends when school started.

Well, that would be my excuse for being around him, anyway.

"So tell me more about you," I said, as we meandered down Main Street, hoping to get some answers to my questions.

He seemed pretty open about himself. "Well, what do you want to know? I was born in Sacramento. My Dad's a corporate lawyer there, so he'll be traveling back and forth a lot, at least until he wraps up his current case load. It probably isn't the best thing for him, you know, traveling so much—but Mom wanted to move to the country, so here we are."

I glanced at him. "You don't seem too thrilled about the move."

"What I want really isn't what matters." He shrugged and grinned. "Honestly? No offense, but it wouldn't be my first choice. It's hard moving away from all of your friends, and all you know. But what's really important is that my Mom is in a comfortable place where she wants to be."

"Why did she want to move here?"

"I don't know, exactly. I think she just wanted to live a simpler life. Ever since she started to get sick, her life has changed radically. She used to go to all of my Dad's corporate events, and she also coordinated a lot of charity events that Dad's firm hosted or supported. The condition she's in now, she's not able to do any of that. So I think she just wants to live the rest of her life simply, less demandingly."

I decided to be daring. "The rest of her life? Your Mom's so young! She should still have decades left!"

I could feel his gaze on me, and when I flicked my eyes in his direction, I saw that he was smiling...but it wasn't a happy smile. It was a doomed smile, like the one you use when you tell your dying friend that he'll be okay. "Well, we hope so, but we aren't sure," he said quietly. "My Mom has something called Huntington's disease. You probably noticed the way she moves."

"Yes." We walked along quietly for a moment, and finally I said, "Well, there has to be something the doctors can do, right?"

Carson looked into the distance. I could tell that this was hard for him to talk about; I felt his energy go dark, and a painful emotion stifled our conversation. We were passing a bench near the video store, so we sat and he just stared for a while. Then he looked at me and all but whispered, "No, Kathryn. There's nothing anyone can do. Huntington's disease is incurable. My mother is going to die...and it could happen at any time. That's why Dad wants to make her as comfortable as possible."

Oh my God. I had so many more questions to ask, but I didn't want him to think that I was as nosy as I really was. I could also tell this subject was one that brought him a great deal of pain, and I didn't want to hurt him any more than I already had. So I changed the subject pretty quick. I looked at my watch and said cheerfully, "Hey, I have to get home to start cooking dinner before my Dad gets back. But you know, there's a big waterhole with a rope swing about a mile down the way from our houses. Maybe we can go to it tomorrow and go swimming. I can invite some friends of mine, so you can get to know them. Everyone in town wants to meet the new kid, so once you get acquainted, all the rumors will stop about why you moved here."

He looked at me sharply. "What do you mean?"

"You know, small town. Everyone talks. I think at one point, there was a story that your parents had to move you here to get you out of trouble."

"Oh, really!" He laughed suddenly. "Wow, I've been here *one day* and I already have a reputation!" Carson shook his head. "Well, I'm sorry to disappoint you all, but I'm a born rule-follower. Although I do have a cousin my age who fits the story better. Brody comes and stays with us every once in a while—you'll probably meet him at some point. Now, he's a load of trouble. He'll definitely give your town something to talk about!"

I looked at him and smiled. "Ready to head for home, then?"

"Thanks, but you go ahead. I want to walk around and explore a little more."

"Oh! I wish I could stay, but I really do have to get going. I can call you later and give you the details about tomorrow."

Carson looked me in the eye and smiled slightly. "Kathryn Price, are you asking for my phone number?"

I blushed a little, but stood my ground. "Well, yeah, that would probably be helpful."

He reached into a shirt pocket and handed me a plain white card with a phone number written on it. I looked at it and said, "You had this ready?"

"I have a bunch of them. Mom told me it was easier than scrambling for a pen and paper when someone asked for my digits, and she was right."

"Your Mom's really smart. Okay, I'll call you in a bit."

"Good. I'll talk to you then." Maybe I was just hearing things, but it sounded to me like he was looking forward to it.

Feeling buoyant enough to float off into the sky, I ran home and cooked dinner: tacos, quick and easy. Then I started calling my friends—Page first, of course—to get plans together for the next day. I spent more time on the phone than I expected, because of course Page had to grill me about every little thing regarding Squire Carson Ferris. Teasingly, I didn't give her much.

I was just getting off the phone when Dad came home. Cal was a no-show, so Dad and I sat and ate dinner alone. While he worked his way through the meal, I told him all about the new family across the street. Mostly, he just listened patiently. I asked him if he had ever heard anything about Huntington's disease; he never had, but he told me he was sure there were some books about it at the library if I really wanted to know.

After a little more small talk with Dad, I cleared the plates and then ran upstairs, eager to call my new friend to give him the details about our plans. He answered right away. I outlined our plans for the next day, and then Carson and I started chatting…and before I knew it, we'd been on the phone for two hours. We talked about everything: families, his old school and old friends, what we liked to do, what we didn't. It was so easy to talk to him. I loved listening to his stories; he'd experienced so much more than I had. He had traveled all over, even to Europe. Me, I'd never really been out of this town.

He was so interesting, and I loved listening to his soft, sweet voice.

When we noticed how late it was, we started wrapping it up and firmed up our plans. We decided that Carson would come over in the early afternoon, and we'd go from there. I jumped into bed and thought myself to sleep. I thought about how easy it was to talk to Carson, how good it felt when we talked…and I thought about how I could not *wait* until tomorrow to get to see him again.

The next day, we all headed over to the swimming hole. Page got dropped off at my house, of course, and shortly thereafter Carson showed up at my front door. Then we trekked the mile down the road to the creek, chatting and laughing in the hot sunshine. Carson was very gallant; he insisted on lugging the bag full of snacks and the big blanket that I, ever the caregiver and organizer, had packed earlier. When we got there, everyone else was already there—and within minutes my friends were all over Carson, like they were flies and he was sugar. Everyone loved Carson: they grilled him with a ton of questions, though it didn't seem to bother him. As I'd already learned, he was a very laid-back guy.

After a while, Page and I left him to his admirers as we walked up the hill to the rope swing. "So…" Page said slyly, "you kinda like Carson, don't you?"

"What are you talking about?"

"Whatever Kathryn Mariana Price! Don't try to lie to me—I know you too well. You two are like magnets. You've been shoulder to shoulder all day."

"He's nice."

"He's very nice. But you really, really like him, don't you?"

I sighed heavily. "Well, okay, yeah, I like him. I like him a lot. But I can't imagine that he would like *me*. He's just so incredible, and I must be so boring to him. He's been so many places and has so many interesting stories. I'm sure he would never be interested in someone like me."

"Oh, really," Page said archly. "Because you know, I just looked back, and I don't think he's taken his eyes off you since we have walked away. Somehow, I don't think it's that old granny swimsuit you're wearing."

My heart leaped. "Really? No way!"

"Way. Look yourself."

"No! Quit looking! I don't want to look like a stupid giggly girl!"

It wasn't long before Carson and his retinue followed us up to the rope swing, where I could look at him all I wanted to without seeming too eager. We spent the whole wonderful day swimming and talking and getting to know Carson better. No one said so, but you could tell that all the girls with us were very interested in *all* that Carson had to say. I could also see that some of the more aggressive girls were already laying their plans for him, or trying to sneak their way closer so they could mark their territories. *Girls are so stupid in this town*, I thought, frustrated…but then again, Carson *was* the new boy in town, and he *was* gorgeous.

Eventually darkness started to fall, so my friends started, one by one, to head for home. As I started gathering everything up, I looked over and saw that Mellissa Chace was sitting on a rock with Carson, talking to him animatedly. Now, Mellissa was a girl I could see Carson with. She was beautiful, and always had herself done up to a T. Frankly, Mel was the girl that every girl wanted to be, and every boy wanted to be *with*. It was amusing to watch the boys all stumble over her, just to do something as simple as carry her books for her. She'd been the Aphrodite of the junior high, and I was sure she would be the same in high school. I sighed. She was a dancer, and would certainly start cheerleading when school started. I hadn't even bothered trying out; I was the uncoordinated, clumsy, plain girl.

I was stuffing trash into a plastic bag when I felt someone standing next to me. "What can I carry?" Carson asked quietly.

"Oh! Well, I think I've got it all," I said. "I'm going to head home. You can stay if you want. It looks like you've made some new fans…I don't want you to have to leave because I'm leaving."

"I came with you, and I'm going to leave with you," he said intensely. "So what can I carry!"

I looked up at him standing over me, and I wordlessly handed him the blanket. "Think you're ready to go?" Carson said to me with a smile.

"Yeah," I said, my heart fluttering. "I'm ready."

So we went and said our goodbyes to everyone who was still there. I could tell that Mel wasn't too happy that Carson was leaving…and call me petty, but I have to say that it made me feel delightful that he was leaving with me. It made me feel special, because I wasn't used to feeling that way. I was more the girl who stood back in the distance, the wallflower if you will, because for the most part, I didn't like to get too much attention. But with Carson, I *loved* the attention. I felt extraordinary around him.

As we walked home together (Page had left a half-hour earlier), we talked about all the people he'd met that day. Of course, I especially wanted to hear what he thought of Mel. "I think Mellissa Chace liked you a little," I ventured.

He smiled a bit. "Really? I kind of got that feeling too."

"You know, she *is* the most popular girl in school."

His smile brightened to about a thousand watts. "Is that right? Well, you know what I've learned about girls like that?"

"Um…no?"

"They're more trouble than they're worth," he told me.

You know, I've never considered myself to be especially stupid, but I sure was stupid that day. "Yeah, but she's pretty, don't you think?" I forged on.

He pursed his lips in thought, then replied, "Well, yes, I suppose so. But you know, she really didn't stand out to me the way that one particular girl did."

I suddenly felt sick to my stomach, and didn't dare reply. I didn't know what to say; I didn't want to assume he was talking about me, because how could he be? I was by far the simplest, plainest girl there. Maybe he'd noticed Page; maybe that was the reason he was staring at us as we were walking up the hill earlier.

This was going to drive me crazy; I had to stop thinking about it. But I couldn't. The terrible silence grew between us, and thank goodness Carson had the nerve to break into my thoughts: "So, Kat, what are we going to do tomorrow?" he asked lightly.

People tended to call me by my full name (at my insistence), but I decided I liked my new nickname. "Well, I dunno. What do you want to do?"

He tapped a forefinger against his lips in thought, then said, "My Dad will be back in town tomorrow, so let me see if he can take us to the first town that has a movie theater. There's a new movie coming out about a girl who goes crazy and kills a bunch of people. It looks pretty good to me, but I like horror and stuff. You may not want to see something so violent, so you can decide."

"Ha!" I snorted. "I live with two guys who think professional wrestling and football are tame! They figure if there's no blood, you're not serious. I've seen *Friday the 13th* like ten times, so violence really doesn't bother me. So call me later if your Dad can do it, and I'll ask my Dad."

He grinned. "Sounds good. I'll find out right away, and then I'll call you."

We were at the end of his sidewalk by then, so I said, "Okay, talk to you later!" and ran off toward my house to start dinner.

It wasn't until later that I realized that I'd been asked out on my very first date.

After dinner, I asked my Dad if it would be okay if I went to the movies with Carson and his Dad tomorrow, and he just looked at me for a long time before he said, "Okay. Let's just make sure I get to meet 'em both before you head out."

That was when the newsflash exploded in my brain. Holy cow, I was going on a date with Carson! *And his Dad,* some part of me reminded myself, but that was overridden by the fact said I was going on a date with Carson!

It got better, somehow. Carson called later on and said that his Dad was actually going to stay with his Mom, but Margret could take us to town on her way home, and then Bill and Elisabeth could come pick us up later.

Carson figured that we could go to that movie and then go walk around the shops downtown. I didn't care if we sat in the rain and played with snails. I was just excited about spending the day with Carson; I loved being around him. Today had been a little weird, with everyone around, and everyone wanting to get a little piece of the new guy. But tomorrow would just be the two of us... and I could not wait. This would probably be the longest night ever.

Have you ever just gone to bed early so you could get the night over with? That was exactly what I did that night, so the next day would come faster. I'd barely fallen asleep before my phone rang. I rolled over and picked it up. "Hello?"

"Hey, Kat."

"Carson?"

"Yeah. I couldn't sleep, and I was wondering what you were doing. You weren't sleeping, were you?"

"Uh, no, I was just lying down."

We talked on the phone for an hour, mostly just small talk. We talked about his Mom quite a bit, and I guess she had had a rough evening. I could tell he was upset and just wanted someone to talk to. I didn't have a problem with that. We talked about how Elisabeth sometimes had hard days and sometimes good days, and he told me how her disease was genetic—that is, passed on in the family. I guess Carson's grandpa had suffered from Huntington's disease, and out of his three children, only Elisabeth ended up with the disease. It turned out that only one of the parents has to have Huntington's for their children to get it.

A little scared, I asked him if he knew if he was going to get Huntington's, and quite calmly he told me he had a 50% chance, but that he really didn't want to know. Behind his brave words, it seemed to me that he was a little scared, after seeing what his Mom was going through; and that's probably why he didn't want to know. It would just be too terrifying for him to know his fate…especially since there's no treatment for the disease. If you get it, there're not a lot anyone can do, which was why, I gathered, Carson said he didn't want to know. But he admitted that if he did somehow have the disease, he'd know eventually, because he knew what to look for from watching and listening to his Mom.

As our talk stretched into a second hour, he said reluctantly, "Hey, I'd better get to bed. I have a big day tomorrow!"

"Me too!" I said merrily.

Just as we were getting ready to get off the phone, Carson asked me a question I wasn't expecting: "Kathryn, what's it like not having a mother?"

I sat there for a long moment, not knowing what to say, as my thoughts came to a jolting halt. No one had ever asked me anything like that before, and I certainly hadn't expected it of a considerate boy like Carson. But on the other hand, his mother was terminally ill, so I had to cut him some slack. On the other hand, my Mom had passed away so long ago that no one really talked about it with me. I didn't know what life would have been like with a mother, so I wasn't sure how to answer that.

"Kat? Are you there?" He sounded worried.

I said slowly, "Well, I really don't know, Carson. My Mom died of cancer when I was really young, so I never really knew her. My Dad talks about her once in a while, and I love hearing stories about her.

I guess I'm sad about it, because I never got a chance to know her. I don't know what would be worse—having a mother who's ill, or not having one at all. At least I don't know what I'm missing, while you're going to have to deal with knowing that she'll be gone one day. I…I can't imagine how horrendous that would be."

Right then my eyes filled up with tears, and I felt an overwhelming wave of sadness pass through me. I'd never really thought of how depressing my situation was. It was my life, and I just lived it every day and never gave it much thought.

Carson must have heard something in my voice, because he said quickly, "Kathryn, I'm sorry I brought it up. I didn't mean to upset you."

"No, it's okay," I said, wiping away the unwanted tears. "I really never think about it, you know? Just be happy you have your Mom right now, Carson. If there's any chance you'll lose her, just enjoy the time you have with her."

Silence.

"I'll see you tomorrow," I said.

"Okay, Kat," he said in a low voice. "Sleep well."

"You too."

As I hung up, I doubted that either of us would sleep well. I hung up the phone and laid in bed, staring at the shadowed ceiling, and tried so hard to remember my mother...but I was so young when she passed that I couldn't remember anything. I would have given everything I owned, or would ever own, for just the tiniest memory of her: but there was nothing.

I tossed and turned for about half an hour, then decided to go downstairs and work my way through a box of my Mom's stuff that my Dad still had. I went into the hall closet and pulled it out, then sat with it in front of me for a couple of minutes before I could bring myself to open it. I had always known it was there, and there was stuff in it that my Mom and Dad had decided to save, that they thought I would like to have at some point.

After taking a deep breath, I opened the lid and started going through the box. I pulled out a blanket first, a blanket my Dad had told me about before. My Mom was really sick when she was pregnant with me, I guess, and so she was in bed most of the time. So that she would have something to do, my Dad went out and picked up some yarn, and she knitted this blanket for me. It was green and yellow, probably because she didn't know yet if I was a boy or girl. I put the blanket up to my face and inhaled deeply, hoping that it would still have her smell on it. In fact, there *was* a faint but detectible scent of a sweet perfume or lotion. It was very faint, but it seemed to smell kind of floral. This must have been the fragrance that she wore, and I decided it was the fragrance of my mother.

Next I looked through some old pictures, which were in a loose stack under the blanket. Some I'd seen before, like the wedding pictures of her and Dad. He looked so happy back then, and you could tell they really loved each other. In every picture of the two of them together, they were either laughing or had huge smiles on their faces—the kind of smiles that meant you were more than happy, that meant that you were amazed and ecstatic to have found that one perfect person who completed you.

There were a ton of pictures of my brother and her, too, mostly from the little family camping trips they must have taken him on. There were pictures of Cal's first birthday, with him sitting on Mom's lap, cake all over the both of them. She was laughing in the picture. My mother had such a warm, caring smile; in all the pictures of her, she was laughing and seemed so happy. My mother had been a beautiful woman, much more attractive than I was; she was a natural beauty, too, and rarely wore any makeup. Her hair was a slightly wavy bright strawberry blonde, in contrast with my muddy mop, and her eyes looked like they were a light golden hazel. She had a huge smile that looked like it could light up any room; my brother smiled like that sometimes. Her face was very soft, and just about flawless. She was thin, but looked like she would be easy to melt into if you needed a hug.

I found a picture that finally broke me: me and my Mom at the hospital the day I was born. She was bent over, kissing the top of my head. Dad had always told me Mom had wanted a little girl more than anything. I was all dressed in pink, and she must have been so happy there, sitting with her brand new daughter in her arms, thinking of the day that she could braid her hair and put her in cute ruffly little dresses. Thinking of the day that she could help me get ready for my prom, or of the day we could go into town and she could help me shop for my wedding dress and plan the big event.

As I sat there and thought of everything Mom would miss in my life, I started to feel bad for both of us. I would never have a mother to talk about boy problems with, once I started having them. Up until now that wasn't a concern. But now I did like a boy. For the first time in my life, the general sense of loss I felt for my mother turned into a deep, longing ache, because I wanted to talk to her about Carson. This new boy that was generating weird feelings in me that I'd never had before, and I desperately wanted her advice on what I should do. How do you act around a boy you really like?

I took the blanket upstairs with me, along with the picture of Mom and me on the day I was born. I placed the picture on my nightstand, deciding that I would have to look for a frame tomorrow while Carson and I were walking through the shops. I curled up in a ball and snuggled close to the blanket.

For the first time in my life, I cried myself to sleep.

That night, I had a dream that I will never forget. I was in a meadow on a beautiful day, and all the flowers around me were in full bloom. There was a little creek flowing through the meadow, and it was all very quiet and peaceful. I could hear the rush of the water moving over the rocks and the faint sound of birds chirping. The sun was straight overhead, and the slight sting of sunlight on my skin felt good. I was walking casually through the meadow alone, just enjoying the beauty all around me…and as I walked, I noticed suddenly that I wasn't alone.

I looked over to my right, and there was a radiant woman in a flowing white dress walking with me. I stopped, and turned and faced her. There was a face I had seen only in pictures up to now: my mother's. She looked at me with the warmest, most comforting smile I have ever experienced in my life, and probably ever will. I thought to myself, *I should be scared. Mom died, and she's been gone for a long time.* But I wasn't scared: I was the complete opposite. I had never felt so happy in my life.

Mom was very sick before she died, but in this little slice of Heaven, she looked amazing, as if she had never seen a day of pain. As I looked at her, my eyes filled with tears; she smiled, then reached out and softly brushed an errant lock of hair out of my eyes. Her presence was so warm and soft and vivid, like a heated blanket on a brisk winter day. We never spoke a single word; we just looked at each other for a while, and then started walking together through this Heavenly environment, and despite myself, I hoped it would never end. I felt so complete; I had never realized, until then, just how alone I felt.

Suddenly, it all started to fade away. My Mom came close and kissed me on the top of my head, and then she was gone.

I awoke feeling like a totally different person. Yes, I was left in the world without a mother; but I'd gone to some other place that night, and she was there. For some reason, after that dream I felt worthy, more so than I had ever felt. I didn't know if it had been my mind making me feel better, or if my Mom really had been with me. I'm still not sure, but I've decided to believe my dream, and I know my Mom is with me, watching over me. Someday, I'll see her again.

I just wish she could have known Carson, and all that he's given me.

I got out of bed, still dream-dazed, and started to get ready for my day. After picking out what I planned to wear, I called Carson (this was getting to be a habit) and asked him what time we were going to leave. "Well," he said solemnly, "you and your Dad can come over in an hour. That way, our parents can meet each other, and we can leave from here."

Sounded good to me. After we got off the phone (which took longer than it should have), I took a quick shower, then trotted down stairs and made me and Dad some breakfast. "Dad, we're going to leave in about half an hour," I told him as he sopped up the last of his egg yolk with a triangle of toast. "So will you be ready to go over and meet Carson's parents?"

He smiled at me. "Are you kidding me? I've gotta meet the parents of the boy you've spent the last three days with."

"Dad! We're just friends! There's nothing going on."

"That's how it started with me and your Mom," he said, snickering.

I decided to ignore him, and started cleaning up the dishes. "You'll like him, Dad. He's been so many places, and has so many different stories."

"Uh huh."

"Dad, there's nothing going on," I said evenly, as I scrubbed the frying pan. "Carson and I are just friends, okay?"

"Me thinks the lady doth protest too much."

I stared at him, my mouth open. Where did my Dad learn Shakespeare? "Besides," I said sharply, "he has girls like Mellissa Chace who are *very* interested in him. What would he want with a girl like me except just to be friends?"

Dad stood up, and his smile was gone. "Kathryn, I am in no way encouraging you to have a boyfriend, or even like a boy—but you should *never* talk about yourself like that. You're a beautiful girl, you're smart, and you have a big heart. You're just like your mother that way."

I sighed, then put the pan down and slipped back into my chair at the table. "That's funny you would say that, Dad. I went through the old box of Mom's stuff last night."

He sat down too. "Oh yeah? What made you do that? You could have woken me up so we could have gone through it together, you know."

"I know, Dad, but it was something I wanted to do by myself...Carson's mom is really sick, and he asked me about Mom last night. I realized I've never really talked or thought of her all that much. So I went through all the stuff, and then I had a dream about her. I don't know if I believe in that life after death thing but it sure felt good to see her."

Dad looked at me steadily, and I could have sworn there was some dampness in his eyes. "If you ever want to talk about your Mom, I'll be happy to answer any questions you might have." I could tell this conversation was getting a little uncomfortable for Dad. He really wasn't good about talking about feelings.

I put my hand on top of his and said, "I know, Dad, and thanks. So go get ready, and we'll go over to the Ferris's house. Oh and by the way, Dad, Elisabeth—that's Carson's mom—she kind of moves around oddly. That's part of her illness. Just wanted to let you know."

"Okay, kid, I got it. I won't embarrass you too much. Give me a minute, then we can go."

Closer to twenty minutes later, my dad and I walked over to the Ferris house. I knocked on the door, and Margret answered. "Hello, Kathryn, are you excited to go to the movies?"

"Yes ma'am, and thank you for taking us to the city with you. This is my dad, Mike Price."

"So nice to meet you, Mr. Price. I'm Margret Lang, Mrs. Ferris's helper. Please, come in."

It was the first time I'd ever been in the house, and the interior was as amazing as the exterior. The entryway and parlor (and the whole house, as I would later learn) had dark hardwood floors, and it was decorated with old aristocratic European furniture. There was beautiful artwork on the walls, and an elaborate spiral staircase that Carson was currently descending. He saw me and grinned. "Hey, Kat! This must be your Dad. Hello, sir, I'm Carson Ferris."

Out of the corner of his mouth, Dad muttered to me, "Kat?"

"Yes," I hissed defiantly.

Aloud, Dad said, "Hi, Carson, I'm Mike Price." He approached Carson with his hand outstretched, and they went through the male ritual of shaking hands. "Welcome to the neighborhood."

"Thanks, Mr. Price, we like it here so far," Carson said briskly. He didn't seem nervous at all to meet my Dad. "Kathryn has been amazingly helpful in getting me settled in, sir. My parents are on their way down. Did you meet Margret? She'll be taking us today. My Dad and Mom will come pick us up later…"

Okay, so maybe Carson was a little chattier than normal.

Just then, Bill and Elisabeth appeared at the top of the stairs, Bill holding Elisabeth's hand and guiding her down. "Hello, Kathryn dear," she said elegantly. "And is that Mr. Price? The resemblance is striking, I must say."

"Thank you, but she takes after her Mom."

"Then her mother must have been a very beautiful woman."

"She was," my Dad said, almost fervently. I could tell that she'd already won him over in just a moment's acquaintance, and I was feeling somewhat confused. Yes, my mother had been beautiful…and if they thought I looked a lot like her, did that mean…?

I set that aside to look at later.

By then, Elisabeth and Bill had reached the bottom of the stairs, and she reached out to shake my Dad's hand. "Mike, we are so thankful for your daughter befriending our son the way she has," she said quietly. "It's hard to move to a new place and not know anyone, especially when you're young."

Dad nodded. "I work a lot, so it's nice that Kathryn's made a friend so close to us." With some difficulty, he transferred his attention to Mr. Ferris. "You must be Bill. Mike Price." They shook hands firmly. "Welcome to the neighborhood."

"Kathryn tells us you're a firefighter," Bill said cheerfully. He hovered close to his wife, holding one elbow, and we all ignored her swaying.

"Yeah, I work down at the firehouse on the outskirts of town. We're in our busy season now, what with the heat and dryness, so I find myself at work more often than at home these days. You're a lawyer?"

"I'm a partner in a firm in Sacramento. It'll mean a lot of traveling, I suppose, but it's worth it to get out of the city. It *is* nice to breathe fresh air."

They both laughed, and it was nice to see that it was more than just polite laughter. "Well, I won't keep you kids," Dad said. "I'll be going in to work today, Kathryn, but I should be home tonight. Have fun, and I'll see you when you get home. If you need me, call the station—I'll be there."

"Okay, Dad, I know."

He looked back to Bill Ferris. "It was really nice meeting you folks. If you need anything, we've lived in this town our whole lives, so there's really nothing we don't know about or how to get."

I gave Dad a quick hug goodbye. He looked at me and gave me the whole "be safe" dad speech, then headed for home.

Carson went over to his Mom and kissed her on the cheek, and we were off. Carson jumped into the front of Margret's car, and I got in the back. It took us about an hour to get to the city, and the ride was so long that I wanted to jump out of my skin. The anticipation of being alone with Carson in a dark movie theater was more than I could bear...but I made it, somehow.

Carson paid for both tickets; I tried to pay for my own, but he wouldn't let me. The movie turned out to be a little too violent for my taste, but I was just happy sitting next to him. I'll admit, I was hoping for a little of the old yawn-and-stretch pantomime that somehow got his arm around my shoulders, but it didn't happen. That's not to say that *nothing* happened. It may have been my imagination, but it seemed like he was leaning into me slightly the whole time...and his body, so close, felt so warm compared to the freezing movie theater. The feeling of his big warm arm against mine sent little shivers up and down my body that had nothing to do with the arctic air conditioning.

The movie ended much sooner than I expected, and despite its goriness, I wished that it had lasted longer. After staying to watch the credits (I soon learned that was one of Carson's little quirks), we walked out of the movie theater and wandered down the street, where there was a scatter of little shops. As we walked, I said to Carson, "So, last night after we got off the phone, I found some of my Mom's stuff in a box in the closet."

"Did you?" he replied casually, glancing at me.

"Yup. There was a picture of the two of us on the day I was born. I was going to try to find a frame for it, so it can sit on my nightstand."

"Hmmm. Sounds like a mission," Carson said in a very serious voice. "All right, that's what we'll do today: look for the perfect picture frame."

I grinned and curled my arm around his. He didn't object; in fact, he pulled me a little closer.

We went into all the little stores within ten blocks of the theater. I was amazed at all there was just on this one street...but then again, I was used to a much quieter, more sedate environment. One of the stores was perfect: it was full of picture frames, and eventually, Carson found the right one. It was understated, but it did say "Me and Mom" in block letters at the bottom. When we took it to the register, I pulled out my wallet to pay for it—and Carson stopped me. "If you don't mind, I'd like to buy this for you," he said, his eyes piercing mine.

"You really don't have to do that," I protested.

"I know, but I want to. That way, when you look at it you can think of your Mom *and* me."

How could I argue with that? Could this guy be real? How could a fourteen-year-old boy always know the right thing to say? I figured that all he had gone through must have made him so much older inside...just like me.

By then it was almost time for his parents to get into town; the day had gone by so quickly! We headed back to the movie theater, and when we arrived Bill and Elisabeth were waiting in their long black Caddy. Bill got out of the car to open the back doors for us—such a gentleman!—and asked jovially, "You kids hungry? We waited to eat so we could all go out to dinner."

"I could eat a horse, Dad. How about you, Kat?"

"I am starving," I replied.

We ended up at a nice Italian restaurant where Carson's parents knew the owners. We had a superb dinner, and we discussed all sorts of things, including how Elisabeth used to throw fundraiser dinners at that very restaurant back before she got too sick. She talked about all the different charities she'd volunteered her time to; she'd been very active in the community, and all the wonderful things she did for children and animals were just amazing. You could tell by the way she talked that she had a great love for both. She had volunteered weekly at an animal shelter, and had helped open a shelter for women who were in abusive relationships—a place they could go with their children, and get an education on how to make it on their own. There were so many ways she'd left her mark on the world. I could tell that Carson was proud of his mother and all she had done, and I wasn't terribly surprised to learn that she had him involved in the summer camps they put on for disabled children. They truly were an incredible family.

After finishing our long, cheerful dinner, we drove back to little Pollock, which now seemed so tiny after spending the day in the city. Elisabeth fell asleep on the way home; she clearly didn't have the energy that she used to, given the stories she'd told. Carson and I sat in the back seat and talked quietly, and I soaked up the wonder of his presence. By the time we got home, I was all abuzz. They dropped me off in front of my house, and I thanked them for taking me and then ran up to my room to talk to Page.

Then Carson called, and we talked for another hour.

By then it was inevitable, I suppose. For the rest of the summer, Carson and I spent almost every day together. We went swimming or on long walks, or just hung out at each others' houses. By the end of the first week, he was my best friend. Even though we'd spent most of the day together, we spent more time every night on the phone. I don't know how he felt, exactly, but Carson was like chocolate to me: I could never get enough.

The Ferris Wheel

Before we knew it, it was the last week of summer: the week the whole town looked forward to all year. That's when the carnival came around. I spent hours telling Carson about all the rides that we had to go on, and of course we made bets on who could eat the most cotton candy. That Saturday morning, nearly the whole town was out preparing for the carnival, with locals busy setting up their booths with all the homemade knick-knacks they'd made all year long. The rides pulled into town later that morning, and the people that worked for the carnival got busy putting them together.

Carson and I made plans with his parents to go to the local park in the afternoon and have a picnic, before we headed over to the rides for Suicide Night. That's what we called the first night that the rides were going, I guess because if any rides hadn't been put together right, we'd find out that first night. Carson and I headed over early to save a spot in the picnic area, and so we could get everything ready for his mother. Meanwhile, Margret was back at the Victorian putting together the perfect summer picnic lunch, slicing up watermelon and making big deli-style sandwiches. Once we'd staked a claim, Carson and I walked around the pond in the center of the park with a few of our friends, talking excitedly about which rides we were going to go on first. Page was there; I thought she would have been mad at me for spending so much time with Carson, but she'd been hanging around with a boy named Ben, whom she'd liked since the sixth grade. By the way they were holding hands, I had to assume they were together now.

When Carson saw his parents pull up to the park, we raced each other to the car—and of course he won, as usual. Our friendship was kind of an odd one: Carson and I were like two little kids together, laughing and singing and teasing each other constantly. When we reached the car, we grabbed all the picnic baskets and ice chests and lugged them to the place where we'd set everything up.

Dad made it there in time for lunch. He had to leave early to be on standby for the fireworks, of course, but at least he got to come eat with us for a little while. He and Bill sat and made small talk, and shortly after we were done eating, we heard the horn blow. That was an annual thing they did to tell us the rides were up and running. I kissed Dad on the cheek, and as I got ready to dash off toward the carnival with Carson, he yelled at me to be home right after the fireworks. Kids always hung out at the park afterwards and got into all kinds of trouble, so I was under strict orders to go straight home when they were over. Carson's parents called that he needed to come home then as well, and he agreed cheerfully enough.

He got to the rides before I did, of course. "Hey! Can't you let me win every once in a while, Carson Ferris?!" I yelled, a little exasperated.

He replied innocently, "If I let you win, you would *know* I let you win."

"I don't have a problem with that."

We saw a big group of our buddies a few yards away, so we met up with them. There were some girls there who were still being a little too flirty with Carson, asking him to go on different rides with him, which bothered me a little. But what could I say? He wasn't officially my boyfriend or anything, just my best friend…and I wanted him all to myself, at least when it had to do with other girls.

We went on just about all of the rides, and some that we really liked we went on three or four times. We switched partners, too, so that everyone got to go with everyone else at least once. One ride we kind of held off on, though, was Carson's namesake, the Ferris wheel. I wasn't a big fan, because I was scared of heights (as I still am). So when we exhausted all the possibilities with all the other rides, and we got ready to line up at the Ferris wheel, I started to feel a little sickly.

"You okay, Kat?" Carson asked, concerned.

Page answered for me; I was in no condition to talk. "Kathryn is totally scared of heights," she said helpfully. "She goes on the Ferris wheel every year, but she really doesn't like it."

They all started laughing, but I didn't find it one bit funny. I felt helpless as Mellissa Chace walked over to Carson and claimed him for this ride. Carson got in line with her, and I got behind them with Chris, another friend of ours. "Will you be mad if I rocked the chair?" Chris asked.

"I swear, Christopher Pepper, if you rock that chair, I'll get sick all over you—and then *your* night will be ruined too," I threatened.

As we were coming up to the entrance, Carson looked back at us. "Hey, Chris, if you don't mind, I'd like to go with Kathryn. I promised her earlier that I would. Plus, I have a strong stomach in case she does get sick." He lifted his eyebrows, and the two boys laughed.

"Yeah, man, she's all yours."

When Chris traded places with Carson, I could tell that Mel was really mad about how things had turned out—but I didn't care. I was so relieved that I was going up with Carson that I almost forgot the butterflies in my stomach. He made me feel safe in a way that no one and nothing else ever could...I also knew that he would never do anything to make me feel uncomfortable, the way Chris might.

He leaned close and murmured, "We really don't have to go on this ride if you don't want to, Kat."

"No, I do," I said nervously. "I know it's weird, but every year I feel like I have to beat the fear, and I feel better when it's over."

"Okay, then, I was hoping you would say that. I've wanted to go on this ride with you since we got here."

As we stood side-by-side, getting ready for our cart to arrive, I felt Carson's arm against my shoulder...and realized that he was kind of trembling. Was he nervous too, I wondered? Was he as scared of heights as I was?

Then, suddenly, I realized *why* Carson was a little shaky. I felt something wonderfully warm against my cold hand; Carson took his fingers and intertwined them with mine. I thought, *Oh my goodness, I really* am *going to throw up now*. I wasn't scared of the ride anymore, but Carson holding my hand...I had never held a boy's hand before, at least not that way. His hand was so warm, and my hand felt so small in his. Now my head was spinning out of control. I liked Carson so much it made me crazy sometimes, but did he like me that way? Was he just holding my hand because he was trying to make me feel better about the ride, or was it because he just wanted to?

I finally told my head to shut up and enjoy this moment, because if it was just a friend comfort thing, it would be over soon enough—and I needed to revel in the experience, just in case it never happened again. He was too amazing for me; I knew that. I was so plain and boring. Carson couldn't like me that way, because I wasn't good enough for him. I was so much less than he could shoot for.

Then the guy running the ride said we could get on, which broke my derogatory train of thought. Tragically, Carson let go of my hand to help me onto the ride...but only until the ride worker locked down the safety latch. Then he reached under the bar and grabbed my hand again, smiling faintly.

So weird…I felt so safe next to Carson. This ride was normally horrific for me, something I took on only to prove that I could handle it; but this time it wasn't scary at all. I felt like a little kid on Christmas morning as the ride started to lift us into the air, then jerked to a stop so it could let the next pair of people on. It kept doing that, and I looked at Carson to keep my mind off the jerking, nauseating ascent.

He was looking up into the sky. "Aren't the stars so bright tonight?" he murmured.

I followed his gaze up to the star-spangled night, to the faint splash of the Milky Way across the middle of the sky. The lights of the carnival muted their normal brilliance, but I supposed that to a city boy, the sky really was phenomenal here. I squeezed his hand in assent.

"My Mom and I talk about how much the stars shine here," he said dreamily. "In the city, there's so much light from the buildings you can't see the stars like you can here."

"It's really nice tonight," I affirmed, and only thought the rest of the sentence: *Because you're here with me.*

The ride kept lifting us higher and higher, a bit at a time, until we finally reached the top of the wheel. I felt Carson's hand squeeze mine a little tighter. "You were the girl, you know," he said softly.

Huh? "Which girl?"

"The girl who stood out to me that day at the swimming hole, right at the beginning of the summer. In case you were still wondering."

I started trembling like a leaf, and he looked at me with concern. "Kat, how are you doing? You aren't going to get sick or anything, are you?"

"No, I'm fine," I giggled. "More than fine, actually."

I looked over at Carson and started to laugh, and just like that, he let go of my hand. I felt a little rush of panic…until he put both of his hands on my cheeks, then leaned in close until we were practically nose to nose.

The universe stood still.

Perfectly motionless, I closed my eyes…and the next thing I felt were his warm, moist lips on mine, and I was lost in sensation. It all felt so natural as I started kissing him back, and I never wanted it to end, it was so mind-blowing perfect. I felt that Carson and I were levitating; I couldn't feel the cars pushing against gravity at all. We were floating, free as birds gliding through the clouds.

Then the ride jerked back into motion, and Carson pulled back and grabbed my hand again. He didn't say anything, and neither did I. The wheel whirled us around that vertical circle a few more times as we looked at each other, me noting the depths in his eyes and the flush of his cheeks and wondering what he saw in me, and then it started letting people off again. For the first time in my life, I didn't want this ride to end.

By the time we got off, just about everyone else in our group was waiting for us. "Come *on*, slowpokes! The fireworks are about to start!" Page called. She was wrong; they'd already started, there at the top of the Ferris wheel, and in my heart, they hadn't ended yet.

Carson and I glanced at each other, and somehow I knew he felt the same way; but we didn't say anything. We just headed over to the pond with the others to find a place in the crowd where we could sit on the grass to watch the show. I realized later that everyone was staring at us, because we were still holding hands, but at the time I didn't notice or even care what they thought. I was just delightfully happy, now that I knew he wasn't holding my hand just to make me feel better. He was holding my hand because he wanted to, and I was sure that nothing was going to break that contact short of death.

While we all sat together and watched the fireworks, Carson sat behind me and wrapped his arms around my waist, pulling my body in between his legs and tight against his body. I had never felt more comfortable in my life as I looked up into the sky and rested the back of my head on Carson's shoulder. He kept turning his head into the side of my face and kissing my cheek, and I couldn't stop smiling.

Somehow, the fireworks seemed more brilliant this year than they had in the past. I'm sure it was probably the same show that went on every year, but this year was special: I was watching it with Carson. When Carson was around, everything seemed better; he was like a spice that I had never known, something that improved every little thing about life. *So this is what it feels like to be in love,* I thought deliriously. This was what my parents had had, when Mom was still alive. This was what Bill and Elisabeth Ferris had. Everything felt, tasted, smelled, looked, and sounded luminous.

Growth

In our freshman year, Carson and I had two classes together. That wasn't too surprising, considering the size of our school; but he was in a lot of advanced classes that I could never handle. For Carson, of course, high school was a breeze. It was nice having a smart boyfriend, because he could help me with all my homework, and he never minded or ever made me feel stupid, as some boys would have. I still had to pinch myself, sometimes, to convince myself that he was real.

When we weren't together at school, we were usually together at home. Our parents got so used to it that they considered it entirely normal, and even Cal didn't tease us about it much. Elisabeth and Bill were always very gracious, and Dad seemed to love having Carson around. I think he felt better that I wasn't alone all the time, and of course he appreciated that Carson was helping me do better in school than I have ever done. After walking home from school together, we'd meet back up about a hour or so later to do homework together. We couldn't be apart for too long; personally, I started to feel a hole of loneliness in my stomach whenever he was away from me. That worried me a little, because it was probably a little bit out of control, but I was a teenager—and I think teenagers have a tenancy to be a little out of control with their emotions.

The school year went by amazingly fast, and before long it was summer again. Meanwhile, Carson and I had both celebrated the big One-Five, him in February and me in March. By then, it was like Carson had always been a part of the fabric of our lives. He was friends with everyone, of course; in fact, he was the most popular boy in school. As a result of that, I finally had a title: I was The Popular Boy's Girlfriend. It was silly, but it made me feel important.

That summer was more or less a carbon copy of the one before, full of visits to the swimming hole, occasional movies in the city, and explorations of the town and surrounding area. The only real difference was that Carson made the football team for the next year, so when school started again, he had practice all the time. I figured it was good for us to be apart at least occasionally, since I got to spend more time with Page and my other girlfriends. I loved his Friday night games, and Elisabeth and I never missed one, whether home or away. The nights that Bill was out of town, Margret would usually drop us off and the two of us would have a blast watching Carson kick butt.

I loved Elisabeth; she was a grand lady, and I spent as much time with her as I could. In a very real way, she was like the mother I had never had, and though Carson and I had never talked seriously about what would happen in our future, I suspected she would be the mother-in-law I *would* have. We loved to sit together and have girl talk whenever we were in each other's company, whereupon Carson would roll his lovely eyes and leave the room, if he happened to be there. It was nice having a woman to talk to, to explain to me what was going on with my body and how to take care of it. I'm sure that Dad was relieved that Elisabeth and I had created that bond, and frankly, so was I. I mean, how would Dad ever have been able to explain to me how to relieve menstrual cramping?

While I was reveling in my new life, my high school years slipped past...and suddenly, it was the summer before we started our senior year. Looking back, I had no idea how that had happened, because all I saw was a blur of happy days with Carson. We'd had our little squabbles, but they were utterly inconsequential, and soon forgotten in the face of all that was good and joyful. Even today, I can't really remember any of our spats in any detail, probably because it's too easy to remember the kisses, and the jokes, and the just being together.

Toward the end of that summer, our gang hit on the idea of going on a big group camping trip, and our parents agreed as long as a couple of our older siblings went. My brother Cal was back in town for the summer after two years at college, and he was more than willing to go when he found out that a couple of his high school buddies were going to be there. I really wished he *wasn't* going (he was still a great big pain), but I knew that his presence was the only reason Dad agreed to let me go. Knowing teenagers, he figured chaperones were necessary.

Page and I spent all day shopping and getting stuff ready for the big trip before we went and loaded up Carson's truck. It was a big, black lifted Chevy, a sweet sixteen birthday present from his parents— perfect to take off-roading to our camping spot. We ended up all meeting at Carson's, with five trucks and jeeps packed with goods and people ready to enjoy them, and off we went in a blare of goodwill and happy noise.

As it turned out, the perfect camping spot was in a local national forest, about fifteen miles off the county road east of Pollock. We set up camp near a large stream; Carson had a six-person tent for him and some of the guys, while my Dad let me use our old camping gear. Carson popped his tent up right away, but mine took us a lot longer to erect. Well, it took *him* longer to erect; I'm all thumbs when it comes to camping. My tent was just a two-person job, but it would be perfect for me and Page.

After camp was set, Carson and I decided to get away from the group and go hiking while there was still some light. We headed up a low mountain; it was a long way to the top, but when we got there the view was worth the work. We perched on a light blanket Carson had in his backpack, and just sat there for a while and took in all the fantastic things around us. To me, one of those fantastic things—*the* most fantastic thing—was the seventeen-year-old sitting next to me. It was a perfect day: it was a little breezy up on the mountain, but warm enough still that it didn't make me cold.

Carson wrapped his arms around me and kissed the back of my neck. Now, *that* sent shivers down my spine. His lips still against my skin, he murmured, "You know, Kat, I feel like the luckiest guy around here."

I turned my head to look at him and asked, "Really? And why is that?"

"Well, while all the other guys are down at the camp messing around with their tents, I'm sitting on top of a mountain, holding the girl I'm in love with."

This time the chill was complete: my whole body felt frozen. Carson and I had been together for three years, and he'd never out-and-out told me he loved me. We didn't talk about our relationship that way; I know that sounds odd, in this era of ready expressions of love, but it felt safer that way, somehow. I knew I loved him right off the bat, but I never knew whether he felt that deeply for me. He was always so sweet and told me how beautiful and special I was to him, but he never said those three little words.

When I could move again, I looked back at him. He put his hand around the back of my neck and started kissing me so hard, so deeply, that it literally took my breath away. When I finally caught my breath, I told him, "I love you too. I always have."

Isn't it funny how time can stretch to such an amazing degree? I swear that we sat forever in the same spot, smiling at each other and kissing; and I don't think our lips left each other's for more than a second at a time. After a wonderful eternity, he laid back and turned me around so that I was lying on top of him, facing him. I could feel a blazing heat pulsing between our bodies. Soon, it was almost more than I could take.

He brushed his hands across my face and said gently, "It's not time for that yet, Kat, but someday," and the heat damped down to a companionable warmth that I could accept, for now. I put my head on his chest, and he ran his fingers through my hair. "You know, I'm going to marry you one day," he breathed.

I jerked my head up, and looked at him to see if he was joking. He wasn't. He laid there and stared into the sky, his face a mask of...joy, I'd have to say.

He glanced down at my wide eyes, and brushed the hair out of my eyes. "I'm serious," he proclaimed. "I can't imagine my life without you in it. I've come to realize that there are things in life that are taken from you without your control and by God, there's *no way* I'm going to let anyone I love this much go, if I have any say in it."

I felt tears sting my eyes. "I love you too, Carson. I have from the moment I first saw you from my window, the morning you moved in. I can't imagine a day of my life without you in it. So let's get through our last year of high school, so we can really live!"

We both started laughing happily, and he leaned up and kissed me on the forehead. "We better start heading back before it gets dark," he noted.

Reluctantly, I climbed to my feet. "Yeah, Page won't be too happy with me if she has to cook dinner on the fire all by herself."

I helped him to his feet, and stared to step back toward the trail; but he grabbed my arm and spun me in towards him again, then gave me one of those kisses that, once again, left me gasping for air. "I love you, Kathryn Mariana Price."

I just looked at him and smiled. "And I love you, Carson James Ferris."

And then we walked down the mountain to join our friends.

Aside from the incidental growing up, not much had changed in those four years...except for Elisabeth. She grew increasingly ill as the years passed, and became less and less her gracious self. She seemed angry most of the time, largely because her short-term memory was gone, and she couldn't remember anything she had said or that we had told her. She was always mad at us, helplessly so, because she thought we kept forgetting to tell her things she needed to know. We did tell her, but she just didn't remember—and she kept forgetting that she couldn't remember. Some days she had a very hard time communicating with us at all, mixing up and stumbling over all of her words. She could barely walk without stumbling into walls, and fell all the time.

It was tearing up Bill and Carson both. Carson and I spent many nights talking for hours about Elisabeth and what might happen, what *would* happen, and more than once it ended with him sobbing helplessly on my shoulder. I just hugged him and gave him what comfort I could.

To keep from worrying all the time, he threw himself into athletics and applying for colleges all over the country. Naturally, he was accepted to every college he applied to; Carson had a perfect 4.0 through high school (the show-off!), and all the colleges wanted him to play football for them anyway, he was that good. Naturally, Elisabeth and Bill wanted him to go to an Ivy League school, but really, there was no school like that nearby, and I knew Carson wouldn't go far from his Mom or me; so he decided to go to California State University Sacramento, which was a very good school in any case. Ultimately, Carson wanted to go to law school and take over his Dad's firm. I didn't know if that would be right for him, though, because he really didn't seem like the arguing type to me. He was such a laid-back guy; not submissive as such, but not confrontational, either. We had been together for four years by then, and I could count on one hand how many fights we'd had. He usually just agreed with me, so our arguments wouldn't escalate.

The day before we graduated, my classmates and I spent the afternoon getting ready for the big day, gathering our caps and gowns and practicing for the ceremony that would take place the following night. By that evening, I was so tired I could barely keep my eyes open. Dad was at work, luckily, so I didn't have to worry about getting dinner for him; I just made a bowl of cereal and went up to my room to watch some TV and think about Carson. He was busy at home, getting ready for some of his family to come into town the next morning, specifically his grandparents and his less-than-stellar cousin, Brody. I had met his grandparents a couple of times, and they were really nice people. They were Bill's parents, of course; Elisabeth's had long since passed away, her father of Huntington's and her mother of a broken heart, a couple of years later.

As for Brody, it seemed he was always around. At one point, he was in trouble for something (as he usually was), and was sent to live with the Ferris family for a couple of months so that Bill could straighten him out. I guess his Dad ran off when he was young, and his Mom—who was Bill's sister—had always been more into her boyfriends than her son. Brody was your typical punk teenager. I couldn't say much to Carson, though, because he loved his cousin and they were really close. Several of the fights we'd had had been over Brody. I think Carson felt bad for him.

That's my Carson: always giving people the benefit of the doubt. I, on the other hand, was not as compassionate. I would always joke with Carson about how it was a good thing his Dad was a lawyer, because I figured he was going to have to represent Brody quite a bit in the future. Carson really didn't like the way I talked about Brody— like I said, he loved that boy—and to be honest, Brody was always really good to Carson and Elisabeth both.

I was lying in bed, thinking about that, when I heard something hit my window. I ignored it the first time, thinking it was the wind tossing a twig against the glass, but then it happened again. I pushed back my curtain, and there he was: the love of my life, throwing pebbles at my window like some lovesick kid from an old movie. I opened my window and called, "Hey! You're lucky one of those rocks didn't break my window, or my Dad would have your head!"

"Hey, were you sleeping?" For an intelligent guy, Carson could be awfully thick sometimes.

"Well, if I *was*, I'm not now, doofus! Why didn't you just ring the door bell? No one is home but me!"

He said guiltily, "Well, you know, I've seen this in so many movies, I wanted to give it a try. Can I come up?"

I rolled my eyes. "Yes, but how about I open the front door for you? I don't want you to get hurt trying to climb up a tree to get in through the window."

"Yeah, I'd rather walk across the field tomorrow instead of hobble."

I laughed and closed the window. I pulled my messy mop up into a ponytail, and ran out of my room and down the stairs. This wasn't a normal thing, for Carson to come over this late; I was wondering what was going on. When opened the front door, my perfect boyfriend stepped in, grabbed me by my waist, and pulled me tight into him. It felt like he was holding on for dear life. "What's going on, Carson?" I asked, concerned. "Are you all right?"

"*I'm* all right," he mumbled into my neck, "but Mom had a really bad night tonight. I think it's overwhelming for her that people are going to be at the house tomorrow. Her anxiety took over, and she started acting up. She was choking and gasping for air, Kat. I couldn't sleep. I can't seem to get the noises she was making out of my head. I don't understand why life is so unfair."

I reached up and put my hands behind his neck and gently kissed him. "Come up and lay with me for a while. My Dad is at work, and at this point we're both eighteen, so what are they going to say about it?"

He smiled sadly. "Promise you won't take advantage of me?"

"I'll restrain myself somehow." I laughed.

Carson grabbed my hand and pulled me upstairs to my room, where he jumped on my bed and propped some pillows behind his neck. I climbed between his legs and laid on his chest; and we remained quietly like that for a long time, doing little more than breathing, though I was playing around with his fingers in mine the whole time.

"You know, it scares me how much my Mom is going to miss in my life," he said finally. "The day I graduate from college. The day you and I get married. The birth of our children...Mom was so great when I was young. She would get on the ground and play with me for hours. When we would go to the park, all the other moms were on a bench, just watching their kids. Not my Mom; she was climbing around with me. It makes me sad that she'll never be like that again, Kat. I'm sad for both her and me at how *much* is going to be taken away from us because of this stupid disease."

"Do you remember that night years ago, when you asked me what it was like to not have a mother?" I asked him.

"How can I forget? I felt horrible when you started crying. You weren't just some girl to me even then, Kathryn. I knew I wanted you to be mine from the moment I saw you...and there I was, making the girl I wanted to be with cry, when what I really wanted to do was to make her happy."

I twisted around to look at him. "I never knew that."

"What?"

"That you liked me right away."

He grinned a little. "I guess all my hints these past few years were a little too subtle for you. So let me be blunt: on that day I saw you standing on our the porch, that first day after we moved in, I knew you were like no girl I had ever known. From the start, I couldn't help but smile when your name was brought up or when you were around. My parents knew they were in trouble from the very beginning. I think they were praying that you would feel the same way. I don't think they wanted to deal with a depressed teenager." He laughed.

I touched his cheek. "Well, sir, *I* learned something new tonight. I felt the same way when I saw you getting out of the Cadillac, the first day you came here. We were so young…and we still are. I wonder why we felt so strongly connected to each other so soon, and why we still are four years later. Maybe we *are* soul mates or something."

I said it lightly, but Carson hugged me into him so tightly I could barely breathe. I loved it when he wrapped his big arms around me like this, and my life was complete when he whispered in my ear, "Of course we are. What else could this be?"

I turned back and kissed him, much because I wanted him to loosen his grip just a tad and to show him how much I loved him, too. When we were done, and had pulled back into a more comfortable position, I said, "Okay, so back to what we were talking about with your Mom missing stuff. That night we talked about my mother, I went through my mother's stuff and then had an amazing dream about her."

I glanced up at him, and wondered if his heart was beating as fast as mine was. I was trying to dial this back before we went too far, and I'm sure he was too, so I kept talking. "I swear, babe, it was so real— like she was really there with me. I could feel her watching over me. From that night on, I believe that Mom has been with me, watching over everything I do. I honestly believe she's in a wonderful place…and that's where your mother will be." I grabbed his hand and held it tight. "Carson, she *will* be with you for all those things. She'll be watching over us and her grandchildren forever. It's just that we won't get to see her…and yes, that's too sad for words. It's a tragedy, but even when she passes, you have to realize that you *will* see her again someday. The times you need her the most, she'll be there."

I sank back in his arms, feeling safe and loved. "I feel my Mom all the time now. I don't know if it's real or not, but to me it *seems* real, and that's what matters. It makes me feel better, so that's what we'll run with."

"You are so incredible," he told me, and I could feel the gentle smile in his voice. "I knew you would have the right thing to say to make me feel better. And if you didn't, well, just feeling your body on mine instantly takes the worry away." He sighed and sat up. "I'd better get home. We have a big day tomorrow."

We walked down the stairs hand in hand, then stopped for a long moment by the door. He grabbed my hips and pulled me to him, rocking me back and forth for a minute almost like we were dancing. He leaned down and started kissing up and down my neck, then put his lips up to my ear and whispered, "I love you more than you will ever know." I pulled back, then put my hands on his hands and kissed his lips.

"I love you, too. Now go home and get some sleep."

He pulled me in and gave me one more of those passionate kisses that made my knees shake, and then he was off.

The next morning was absolutely crazy. Carson's family was having a breakfast for their family, and invited Dad and me. We went over about nine and had an excellent time, as always. My Dad got along well with Bill, they could sit and talk for hours. Meanwhile, Elisabeth and I sat together and talked about my plans for college. She was having one of her lucid days. Carson sat with Brody and made small talk. I don't know what those two could possibly have in common to talk about, but it mostly seemed to be about football. Carson was going to play football for CSUS, and I think Brody was really impressed with that. He started mouthing off about college girls, and not very politely at that, and then looked over at me. He was such a jerk. I looked away, not giving him any reaction at all; he really wasn't worth it.

After a couple of minutes of his comments, I couldn't stand it anymore. I turned and smiled at him and said, "So, Brody, where are *you* going to college?"

Everyone at the table, including Brody, looked uncomfortable. We all knew there was no way in hell that Brody would ever be accepted to any college; he hadn't even graduated from high school. Carson shot me a look, and I knew I was going to hear about this one later. "Well, Kitty-Kat, I'm not going to college," Brody said brightly. "I got a really good job working construction this summer."

I hated it when he called me Kitty-Kat.

No one said anything. You could have cut the tension with a knife, as the energy in the room completely dropped off. All we could do was keep eating.

I was infuriated at Brody, and more so with myself for stooping to his level and making everyone feel uncomfortable. My Dad left right after breakfast to go home and take a nap before the ceremony (and no doubt to recover from the shame), and I helped Margret clear the table and do the dishes. After we cleaned up, Elisabeth and I went outside together to get some fresh air.

"Elisabeth, I'm sorry for making that comment at the breakfast table," I told her, after watching the world go by for a moment. "It was totally inappropriate."

She laughed lightly. "Not really, dear. I would say he deserved it, the way he was talking about college girls with Carson. You aren't worried about that, are you?"

"I hadn't even thought about it before Brody brought it up," I replied truthfully. "Yes, I know Carson will be away during the school year. I always assumed we could make a long distance relationship work, though. I know I can't imagine being with anyone else. I think he feels the same way."

"Indeed he does, Kathryn," she said fondly, patting my hand. "Did you know, he was going to stay home and go to the community college in the next town to be with you? His Dad and I had to explain to him that his going to the University would be the best thing for both of you in the long run. Carson needs to get a good education, so he'll have a firm foundation for your future."

Elisabeth could have said, "his future," but she'd said "your future," and I loved her for that. "I couldn't agree more," I told her, my throat tightening. "I'd feel dreadful if he gave up his dreams for me. I know he's always wanted to work side by side with Bill. If it's meant to be, it will happen, and I think it'll be good for us both to focus on school and not be together every day. Though now that I think about it, Carson *will* be around beautiful, smart college girls every day..."

"Don't you even think about that, young lady. That boy of mine loves you. He loves you so much I think it scares him."

"Well, yeah, I'm sure everything will be fine. We're only two hours away from each other, after all. I'm sure he'll be home all the time checking up on us."

"I am sure he will be." She grabbed my hand, and squeezed fiercely.

I sighed, and stood up. "Okay, I'd better get home and start getting myself together. I know Carson is with Brody, so can you just tell him I'll be ready at four, so we can head over to the school then? They want everyone to be there at five."

"I'll let him know." She looked up at me, smiling like an angel. "Kathryn, darling, I'm as proud of you today as if you were my own daughter...and I know you *will* be some day. I know that if your mother were here, she would be *so* proud of your accomplishments, and of the beautiful woman that you have become."

I couldn't help it: a tear slipped out. Wiping it away, I went to Elisabeth and gave her a big hug. She kissed me on the check and told me she loved me. It was *so nice* having Elisabeth in my life. She was the mother I never got to enjoy, and I loved her dearly for that.

Four o'clock came quickly; and prompt as always, Carson was at my door, right on the dot. I told my Dad goodbye and said I would see him at the school; he was going to take us out to dinner after. We'd probably end up at the diner with everyone else in town, actually.

The drive to the school started a little awkward; it may have been my imagination, but Carson seemed a bit cold. I blurted out, "I'm sorry I said that to Brody. I kind of got my feelings hurt by his rude college girl comments."

He nodded, not taking his eyes off the road. "It's okay, babe. I know that upset you, and it was totally uncalled for." He glanced at me for a split second. "After breakfast, I told him not to ever disrespect you like that again. I told him I could put up with a lot from him, but I would never put up with him hurting your feelings."

He pulled over to the side of the road and put the truck in park, then looked at me seriously. "Kat, I'm only going to say this once, and I don't ever want to talk about it again. You're my world, and I know that. I would *never* do anything to jeopardize our future. You're going to be my wife, and the mother of my children one day. You are my forever. I know we started young, and yeah, some would say we should have experienced other things and people before we settled down. My response to that is that I got lucky. I skipped all the drama and bad relationship stuff. I found my soul mate on my first try. It's you I want forever, and it will always *be* you."

I felt so stupid as I felt the tears roll down my face—from relief, I think, that we were on the same page, and I didn't have anything to worry about. As he started the truck again, I slid over to the middle seat and put my hand on his leg. He grabbed my hand, and looked at me, a mix of concern and amusement on his face. "Jeez, are you crying? I'll never fully understand you girls. You'd better stop, or you're going to look like a clown for your graduation pictures."

"No way!" I said brightly. "I knew there would be some tears tonight, so this is waterproof mascara."

"Excellent planning." He kissed me on the cheek, and we pulled back onto the road.

The ceremony was over quickly, thank goodness. Our class was so small that it didn't take long to read all the students' names and have us parade across the stage. Afterward, we shuffled through the crowds, giving everyone hugs and trying to find our families. I finally found Dad, and we decided to get out of there right away so we wouldn't have to wait to be seated at the diner.

When we were walking out, we ran into Carson's family. I gave everyone hugs and told them I would see them tomorrow. Carson grabbed me and gave me a gigantic kiss in front of everyone. We never did that kind of thing in front of our families, and, well, you could tell my Dad wasn't too thrilled to see it happen. When Carson finally released the lip lock, I looked over at Elisabeth and saw that she was smiling. I gave her a quick hug, and told her that I would come over in the morning, and we could go for a walk or something.

"I'd like that," she said, touching my cheek fondly.

My Surprise

Carson and I spent every day together that summer, and the days tore by so quickly that I felt certain that time itself had sped up somehow. I was dreading the day we packed his truck up to move him to the dorm at CSUS. That day was fast approaching, and there was no way I could hold it at bay.

August 15 dawned: the day before we were leaving to take Carson to college. He told me that morning that he wanted just the two of us to go to the swimming hole and hang out for the day, so I packed us a lunch and threw my bathing suit on, covering it with my standard shorts and T-shirt. When I opened the door to him later that morning, he was a different Carson than the one I was used to. He seemed very distracted; he was normally so upbeat and happy, but today that wasn't him. I didn't know what was going on, and I dreaded not knowing. Maybe he was just nervous about tomorrow…?

As I bustled out the door with our things, I said to him, "Are you okay? You seem a little off."

"I'm fine," he replied shortly, and that was it. Normally Carson would explain to me what was going on with him, or at least jokingly make a case for me being crazy for thinking something was wrong. I just got a curt "I'm fine" today, and that worried me. He wasn't thinking about breaking up or something, was he? The very thought knotted up my stomach and made me want to cry.

We drove to the swimming hole in complete silence, and I desperately tried to calm myself. I thought about how this would be such a great day, how I wanted to make our last day together before the separation wonderful…and it wasn't going my way at all. Once we got there, I left all our stuff in the truck; I just stripped off my T-shirt and shorts, ran to the bank of the creek, and jumped in the water. If Carson wasn't going to talk to me, I decided, I would just go swim on my own. He'd come around.

My man sat at the edge of the water and just stared at me; he seemed almost to be shaking. Was he nervous about something? Why did he have a reason to be nervous? Suddenly, I felt like a knife was piercing my chest; it hurt, and I couldn't breathe. Panic gripped my entire body, freezing me in place, and I stared back at him. Maybe he *had* changed his mind. Maybe he'd brought me out here today to break it off. I could barely even swallow, and I started to feel sick down to my stomach. I managed to croak out, "Hey, Carson, I'm really not feeling good. Maybe we should just go home."

"Go home? No, we can't go home. We need to talk." He lowered his head and sighed. "I'm sorry. I had this all planned out, and it isn't going the way I thought it would."

I hugged myself, and started trembling. "What's going on, Carson? You're making me really nervous."

He laughed suddenly. "Get out of the water, Kat, and come sit with me."

Worried, I got out of the water and wrapped a towel around myself, then went and sat next to him. He looked at me and smiled gently. "Kat, I'm sorry—I didn't mean to make you feel like this. I'm just so nervous about what I'm planning to talk to you about."

"Well, why don't you just say it and get it over with?" I snapped.

"Get it over with? What are you talking about?" He looked confused.

I took a deep breath and stuck my chin out. "Carson Ferris, if you're going to break up with me, just do it!"

He stared at me for a long moment before muttering, "No, this really isn't the way I planned this at all." Taking a deep breath, he blurted, "I brought you out here to talk to you about the next year, and what we were going to do."

"Well, before this weird day, I thought you were going to college to study and play football," I said, "and I was going to go to the community college. I thought we could see each other on the weekends, and we could make it work like this for a while until we were done with school, and then we could be together all the time."

"That sounds good, Kat, but I was wondering if you could spend some time with my Mom over the next year…"

"Well, of course, Carson," I broke in, still a little annoyed. "I'll be with Elisabeth all the time."

"You didn't let me finish," he said softly, taking a small box out of his pocket. "I meant that I was hoping you could spend some time with my Mom planning our wedding."

Now I was *really* nervous.

At one level I was freaking out. At another, I couldn't believe that this was why he was acting so crazy. He was nervous because he was planning on asking me to marry him? I'd always known we'd be married someday, but, well, we were so young that this would be crazy…wouldn't it? We still had college and so much to do before we should even consider getting married, so what was he thinking? I didn't understand why he was doing this, when he knew I would wait for him forever. *Why is it so important to do this right now?* I wondered, my head spinning.

Then he opened the box, and inside was a beautiful golden ring. He got down on one knee, just like in the movies. "Kathryn Mariana Price," he said earnestly, "I promise to love you every day of my life. I will protect you when you need protection. I will make you smile when you're sad. I will be there next to you whenever you feel alone. I will be your partner, your lover, the father of your children, and your best friend until the day we take our last breaths. Kathryn, will you marry me?"

I looked into his big brown eyes, and all my questions melted away. "Of course I'll marry you," I told him, and he grabbed me and held me close to him.

"You know that ring?" he said in a low voice. "It was my Mom's original wedding ring. My dad got her a bigger diamond ring on their 15th wedding anniversary. When I told her I was going to ask you to be my wife and asked her if she would go look at rings with me, she told me she had something better. That's when she gave me the ring to give to you. She said that she would be honored to have you wear it. She loves you so much."

I pulled back to look at Carson, and was startled to see that he was crying; it just about broke my heart. "I love her too," I told him, wiping away the tears with my thumbs. "She didn't think you were crazy to ask me to marry you right now, while we were so young?"

"I told her last year that I was going to ask you," he admitted, "before we ever graduated. She talked me into waiting this long."

"Oh."

"We talked about it again a few days ago. I sat down with my parents and talked about what I was planning to do. I told them I loved you, and I knew you were the woman I wanted to spend the rest of my life with. You see, Kathryn, I always knew I would ask you to marry me one day. I've known since we were 14. We could wait, yes…but I decided I wanted to do it sooner than later. A lot of it has to do with my Mom, okay? I want her to be there for you and with you to plan the wedding. I want her to be a part of this. I want her to be there to see us take our vows and know her son is happy."

I had to blink to clear my eyes of the tears; all I could do was smile silently as he went on. "I don't know how much longer she'll be with us, Kat, and I want her to at least get to be here on our wedding day. I know how much this means to her… not just because I'm her son, but because she loves you so much that she wants you to be her daughter. I think she'll be happy that you can finally call her Mom, and it will be real."

That gave me goose bumps; I hadn't even thought about that. On the day we were married, I could not only call Carson Ferris my husband, but I could call Elisabeth Ferris my mother…and I couldn't imagine a more wonderful mother-in-law in the world. Swallowing against the lump in my throat, I told him, "Okay, so you convinced your parents. I think I'll leave it up to you to convince my Dad."

Carson grinned. "He already knows."

"What? How?"

"You know me. I wouldn't have asked you to marry me without asking your Dad if it was okay first."

I glared at him, lifting an eyebrow. "Really. You have to give me details."

"Well, at first he was a little shocked, and I don't think he liked the idea," he said, pursing his lips in thought. "I told him I would take care of you and be faithful to you. After a little, or maybe a lot, of persuasion, he gave me his blessing."

I giggled. "Wow! Now I *know* you're going to be an excellent lawyer!"

"Well, it *is* in my blood." He stood up, and helped me to my feet. "Now we'd better get back. I know Mom is probably looking out the window, eager for us to get home so you two can start planning."

"Okay…but what if I'd said no?"

"My life would have been over." He embraced me, and gently kissed my forehead. "We didn't consider that outcome, so thank God you didn't."

I smoothed a dark curl over his ear and murmured, "You didn't even swim at all."

"Okay, then, one swing into the water, you and me together."

"Let's do it!"

He stripped down to his board shorts, then we walked up to the rope swing and grabbed on to the rope together. We flung ourselves into the air, and landed together in a laughing tangle in the deep part of the hole before swimming back to the shallow area. I wrapped my legs around his waist and kissed him. I couldn't believe that by next year, I would be this man's wife. What a perfect life. As long as I had Carson, I knew everything was going to be perfect.

We drove back home where, sure enough, Elisabeth was waiting on the verandah for our arrival. She just sat there smiling, waiting to hear all the details.

Carson moped up onto the porch and groaned, "Mom, she said no. She flat out denied my proposal."

"Stop!" I smacked him on the arm, and we all started to laugh. I think Elisabeth was laughing with relief that her son's joking little comment was untrue. I ran over to give Elisabeth a fierce hug.

"So, it looks like we have a lot of planning to do, Miss Kathryn," she said. "We talked to your Dad, and Bill and I would like to pay for the wedding. Your father was very difficult about that, dear—he said he wouldn't let us. But we worked it out. He'll pay for your dress and all your other needs; we'll pay for the wedding itself. So I don't want you to think about money at all—I want this day to be exactly the way you want it."

Oddly enough, I'd never really thought about my wedding before. I wasn't like most girls, who had things planned out from childhood, so I had a lot of catching up to do. As it turned out, I could have any type of wedding I wanted; the Ferris's had more money than anyone I had ever met. A large, elegant wedding wouldn't fit me very well, I decided; so a small outdoor wedding would be best. I wasn't the type who liked to be the center of attention, so small would be good. The whole town would be there, because I'd known everyone in this town since I was a little girl. That was probably good, because given Carson's family and all the Ferris friends, if I left out the town, my guest side would be very small.

There was far too much to think about…but I had a whole year to worry about all the details, and for now I had to focus on my last night with my fiancé before he left for college. And I had to go home and face my Dad. I knew that he was going to work tonight, so luckily we wouldn't have too much time to discuss what had happened.

I was nervous as a cat from the second I hit the front door. Dad was sitting in front of the TV, vegging out. "Hey Dad."

He looked at me, expressionless. "Kathryn. And how was your day today?"

"Well...I'm sure you know that Carson asked me to marry him today."

Now he smiled slightly. "Yeah, that's what I heard was going to happen. And what did you say?"

"I said yes, of course." I sat down beside him on the couch. "Dad, do you think that is crazy? We're so young. Nobody gets married at 18 anymore, but Dad, I love him and I want to be with him forever. I know he'll take care of me and be a good husband."

He patted my hand. "I'm sure he will. Kathryn. And yes, you kids are young, and you'll probably have some challenges ahead. Your Mom and I were married young, too. I knew she was the one, and so I asked her to marry me when we were twenty." He sighed. "I *would* ask you guys to wait a couple of years, and I know you wouldn't mind that...but Carson's mother is sick, and she won't be getting any better. He really wants her to be a part of all of this, though that alone isn't any reason to get married. The reason I gave him my blessing was that when that boy talks about you, there's nothing else in the world for him. He's hopelessly in love with you, kid. It was like I was looking at myself all those years ago. That's *exactly* the way I talked about your mother. I guess when you know, you know."

I snuggled up to my father and put my head on his shoulder. He put his arm around me, and I felt like a little girl again, happy and safe. "I love him too, Dad. Thanks for being so cool about all this."

"Well, I *am* a cool guy."

I grinned. "Yeah, I guess. Sometimes." I unwrapped his arm from around me and sat up. "Now, cool guy, let me make you some dinner before you have to go to work. Oh, and remember—I'm going with the Ferris family tomorrow to help move Carson's stuff into his dorm room. I'll be back sometime tomorrow night."

I made Dad a quick dinner and then, as usual, he was off to work. He wasn't gone five minutes before Carson came over. After kissing me hello, he said in a rush, "Can I spend the night with you?"

I was surprised; we'd never done that before. Oh, we'd spent many nights talking until very late, sometimes together in my room, but he'd never spent the whole night with me. "What are you asking?" I said quietly.

"It's my last night at home. I want to spend every last minute with you. Let's go up to your room and just lie there and talk."

I pretended to consider it…but of course we were engaged, and it was his last night here for a while, and I wanted to be with him...so I of course said yes.

We headed up to my room, where we really did just talk. I felt so comfortable just lying in bed next to him, with him running his fingers through my hair and kissing me. I felt on top of the world; before long, I was going to be able to lay next to him every night. We talked about what we'd do after the wedding, once the first year of school was over, and how we would get a little apartment together. He could go to school at the university, and I could either go to the university with him, or go to a local community college. He seemed really concerned about what I was going to do… but I wasn't. As long as I was with Carson, I would be happy. Everything else was minor.

The next day was difficult, to say the least. We loaded up the truck with all the things Carson was taking with him, and headed out. It was a long drive to Sacramento; when we got there, the guys unloaded all the stuff while Elisabeth and I went to look around at the space where Carson would be spending the next several months. It was kind of drab, but that's dorm life for you. After everything was unpacked, we all said our goodbyes. Of course, I waited till last.

Carson grabbed me and held me so tight I thought I'd never be able to breathe again. Actually, I wasn't sure I would be, without him around; he was more precious to me than oxygen, and just as necessary. "Call me right when you get home, to tell me you got there all right," he murmured.

"With your Dad's cautious driving, I'm sure we'll be fine."

"Yeah, but will you call me anyway?"

"Of course." I kissed his cheek. "I'll miss you so much."

He stroked my hair. "I'll miss you too, my love." I could hear that he was choking up. "I love you more than you know."

"I love you too, Carson."

I gave him a quick kiss for the road, then turned unceremoniously and headed for the car. I had to get out of there before I started to cry. We all waved goodbye as we drove away, and I already missed him so terribly that I felt sick to my stomach.

The drive home was long and lonely. Elisabeth and Bill tried their best to keep up the conversation, to make me feel better, but nothing worked. I just wanted to get home, to be able to call him and hear his voice, and that's the first thing I did when we arrived back in Pollock.

The next few months were crazy, plain and simple. I welcomed college, though I didn't really like it much, but it gave me something to do and filled up most of my time. When I wasn't learning about a wide variety of things (I hadn't decided on a course of study yet), I spent a lot of time with Elisabeth, working out plans for the wedding. We were kept busy preparing guest lists and doing cake and food tasting. I didn't want to worry Carson, so I didn't tell him too much about his Mom.

The truth was, the last couple of months had been really awful.

I don't know if it was because Carson had left home and Elisabeth was miserable, or if it was just the disease, or some combination of both; but she became very depressed and got angry a lot. She would get really nasty with Bill, but thank Heavens he was such a good man; he would just take it and tell her he loved her. Her unrestrained movement also became shocking. She never had a still moment, poor thing, and she was getting to the point where she had a hard time eating. She would even gag on her food and water. I asked Bill if these were all new symptoms, and he admitted they weren't. He said they had all been there before...but now they were getting worse, and coming more often. I helped a lot with Elisabeth, whenever I could. Despite her odd behavior, I still loved her. When Bill was gone and Margret was working around the house I would sit with her, and marvel at how this once-strong, independent woman was now so weak and sickly.

We actually made it out to a couple of Carson's football games at CSUS, because Elisabeth just loved to watch him play. When Carson could, he would come home, usually about one weekend a month; otherwise, he was too busy with school. I loved it when he visited, because that's when I would update him on all the things Elisabeth and I were doing for the wedding. We'd finally decided on a date: September 7. Invitations and save-the-date notices had already been chosen and sent to the printer. Christmas was especially fun, because it meant having Carson home for a couple of weeks, but it also gave him a lot of time with his Mom...which let him see how bad she had gotten since he'd had been gone. He went back to school quiet, pale, and depressed.

Just a few weeks later, it seemed, the school year drew to a close. I still wasn't sure what I wanted to do professionally, but Carson had taken all his finals and was soon on his way home, his Pre-Law success already assured. I was excited to have him home for a couple of months, but I was also a little nervous. Things had changed over the past year, including my plans for what I would do once we were married. I wasn't quite sure how I was going to break it to him.

I'd come to the conclusion that I wasn't going to be able to move to the city with Carson after the summer so that we could start our lives as a married couple, as we had planned. Over the past year, I'd come to realize that I really needed to be in Pollock to help with Elisabeth. We were family now, and she and Bill really needed me. I imagined Carson would be disappointed, but relieved at the same time that I was staying...and I think he knew, as I did deep in my heart, that Elisabeth had very little time left. I could tell that the last time he'd been home, he hadn't wanted to go back. In fact, if it hadn't been for me staying, he probably *would* have returned home to help with his Mom. I didn't want that. He was so focused and doing so well in school that it would be silly for him to stop now.

The wedding plans were starting to come together, and by the beginning of the summer, everything was done. The hard part was going to be waiting until September. The wedding was going to be a little bigger than I was comfortable with—the Ferris's really had gone out with the spending. It was looking like it was going to be the picture-perfect day. We had everything planned down to the smallest details, which I'd had no idea were so elaborate. Elisabeth had thought of everything, right down to the wedding guest book and the pen to write in it with.

I was going through my final lists with Elisabeth when the front door of the Victorian swung open, and there he was: the most amazing man in the world. I jumped to my feet and melted into his arms. He held me tight, and we stayed there so long that poor Elisabeth probably thought we'd turned to stone. I think that we were both afraid that if we let the other go, one of us would disappear again. "Oh, man, I have *missed* you," he said fiercely, after kissing me thoroughly. "These last couple of weeks have been the longest weeks of my life. I know we've gone long periods of time without seeing each other before, Kat, but I think this last time has been the worst. I am *so glad* you'll be moving back with me. These long periods of time apart are killing me. At least we won't have to do that anymore."

Oh, dear. I pulled back and looked him in the eyes, and tried to smile. I decided just to be blunt. "Yeah, about that," I said slowly, "and a lot of other things. Carson, honey, we have to sit down and have a long talk about what's happened since you've been gone, and what I think we need to do from here. I think you'll agree with me when I explain it to you."

He froze. "You're not breaking up with me, are you?" he all but squeaked.

I hit him on the arm. "Are you insane? Or do you just think *I* am?"

He heaved a huge sigh of relief. "Okay, then. Let's go for a walk."

"Not until you go say hello to your Mom. She's been as anxious as I am to see you. Then we can go." I stepped out onto the verandah to give them some privacy.

Carson came out from seeing his Mom with a deer-in-the-headlights look. I knew what he was thinking: the last couple of months had been really hard on Elisabeth, and it was starting to show in everything she did. I snapped him out of his thoughts with a brisk, "Hey baby, are you ready to go?"

"…Yes."

We started to walk toward the swimming hole, one of our favorite places. It was a beautiful walk this time of year, so we just strolled for a while and enjoyed it as much as we could. "Has it been really bad?" Carson asked, about halfway there.

"She's been getting pretty sick lately," I admitted. "I'm only there during the day, so I don't know how she is at night, but I have to admit that your Dad is just worn out. He looks just as tired as she does. He tells me she has some nights that she's up every hour. She usually sleeps a lot during the day after those nights." I squeezed his arm. "Honey, her movements have gotten so bad she rarely feeds herself anymore. And now she has a hard time swallowing. She seems to choke on everything. She gets very angry with your Dad, too. She hasn't gotten that way with me…but sometimes the stuff she says to your Dad brings him to tears. I've tried to take him aside and tell him that it isn't her talking like that, it's the disease, but he knows it. He's pretty accepting most of the time…but sometimes, the things she says are so mean that I think he wonders if she really feels that way." I glanced up at him, and he was looking straight ahead, his eyes swimming with unshed tears. "Carson, I swear, he loves her *so much*—he's been so excellent with her. If you're half the man your Dad is, I'm going to be a very lucky girl."

I stopped, and he stopped with me, and we turned to look at each other. I touched his cheek and said quietly, "But Carson, he can't do it alone. Margret's really good about doing the housework, and she does a great job making sure all the right foods are prepared for your Mom, and she's been feeding her most meals. But she can't do it all, either. She needs my help, and I have to step in sometimes when the emotional stuff overwhelms your Dad and he needs to go into his room or for a walk to clear his head, so that he's always in the right mindset to take care of her. I sit with her and talk about the wedding. I get her water if she's thirsty. I do all this for a little while each day, to take some pressure off your Dad and Margret…and I think it takes pressure off your Mom too. So I really can't move to the city right now, okay?" He started to say something, but I overrode him. "Honey, you need to stay in school and keep going. Both of your parents would be so upset if you moved back and didn't finish school."

"I wasn't going to say I would move back…" he swallowed hard. "But Kathryn, none of this is your responsibility. She's my mother, and I'm the one who should be doing all of this for her."

I smacked him on the arm again. "Hey, don't be silly. She's almost my Mom too, you know. Heck, emotionally she *is* my Mom— and I'm her daughter. We have a really strong bond, and I think I am the best one for the job." I grabbed his arm, and we proceeded on our walk. "Plus, young man, you need to finish school, so you can go help your Dad. I have a feeling his business isn't too important to him right now, so it'll be nice when you can help him out with everything. So no more of this 'I'm staying here' business—you're going back to school."

"Yes, dear," he said meekly.

"Good! You've been practicing!" I grinned and glanced at him, and saw that he had his emotions in control now. "So. I'm staying here with her, and *you* are going back to school. For now, though, we need to wrap up our wedding plans. Elisabeth is so excited about it all." What I didn't tell him was obvious: that in her mind, this was the last big event of her life. "Trust me, you'll be amazed at the party she's going to throw," I went on smoothly. "It's going to be very detailed, right down to the napkins with our wedding date printed on them. You can tell she's planned a party or two."

He laughed happily. (Thank goodness.) "Yeah, I know she's loving this right now. And by the way things sound, it's good that we're doing it sooner rather than later." Now he sighed. "Kat, I can't imagine Mom not being at my wedding. It looks like I have to face the ugly truth that she won't be around for very much longer…that she's going to miss so much in our lives. I'm so glad she'll be at this event, the most important event that will ever happen to me…besides the children, of course," he joked, elbowing me gently.

"Hey hey, let's not get ahead of ourselves, mister! Let's just focus on the wedding right now."

"You mean you don't want to talk about what we're going to name our six kids?"

"Six? I don't think so, honey, unless you do really well in life, and I can have a live-in cook and diaper-changer. How about two?"

"Five."

"Four. I think maybe I could handle four, but that's my final offer."

"Hmmm…four. That might work. We'll have to see."

By then, we'd reached the swimming hole, which was unoccupied. I was glad we'd gotten past all the seriousness, but he had news to relate. As I leaned against a tree, he said, "Hey, I wanted to tell you about all the research I have been doing on Huntington's disease. There's so much to learn about it. I sometimes spend so much time reading all the new medical journals and books about it in the library that I forget I have other stuff to do in there." He leaned over and kissed me on the neck, which caused some serious shivers, despite the warm day. "You know, they found the gene that causes Huntington's."

"Really?"

"Yep. I could actually be tested for it—all they need is a vial of blood."

"I thought you didn't want to know," I said, solemnly.

"I don't," he told me, squeezing my hand, "but this isn't just about me anymore, or even about me and you. There's our kids to think of." He took a deep breath. "If they can find the gene, then someday, they should be able to figure out what goes wrong with it, and once they do, they'll know how to fix it. Look, I know it's too late for Mom. Medical research takes forever. I've found out about some things we should be doing, but for now I think we just need to make the time she has left as comfortable as we can, rather than trying to fight the inevitable."

"But…" I began.

"But there might, someday, be something they can do to help me if I have it. You know I have a 50% chance of getting it. I could live with that if it were just me. The only thing that really scares me is that if I do have Huntington's, every one of our children will have a 50% chance of getting it."

"Well, let's hope you *don't* have it, so our kids have a 0% chance of getting it."

"Yeah, let's hope."

I pushed away from the tree and grabbed his arm again. "Now we have to get back home," I told him, "and that's when your real work starts. Your Mom gets kind of irritated if things don't go exactly as she wants, so we'd better start getting things done on your wedding to-do list."

He groaned, and I punched him on the arm again, this time really hard.

The Wedding

After an amazingly speedy summer, I woke up one morning to find that my wedding was just days away. I couldn't believe it was all coming together so smoothly! Already Carson's family had started to arrive…and of course Brody was coming. In fact, Brody was Carson's best man. I'd pouted about that for a while, but what could I do? He was like Carson's brother—his dysfunctional, horrible, black-sheep-of-the family brother, and I wasn't going to be able to make Carson change his mind. I just told Page, who was my maid of honor, to keep him under control… and if anyone could do it, she could.

The rehearsal dinner was held at the Ferris house, of course; there was really nowhere in town as nice as the restored Victorian. Elisabeth hired a catering company to handle the food, and all the decorators bustled around that morning getting all the tables set up and decorated. The living room looked amazing. It was already about ten times bigger than most living rooms, and with all the furniture moved out to make room for ten huge, round tables, it looked like a banquet hall. The tables were covered in white linen with violet trim, and there were tons of candles on each table, along with violet rose buds scattered all around. There was a chocolate fountain going on the first table, too, with every type of fruit you could imagine. It was a beautiful, colorful spread; all the fruits were cut out like flowers, and placed on sticks in beautiful huge vases to form unique arrangements.

That wasn't all: Elisabeth also hired a string quartet to come play for background music. We choose Italian food to serve that night for dinner; it was my favorite, so I had to squeeze it in somewhere. I was so clumsy, though, that I was afraid to have red tomato sauce around me when I was wearing a beautiful white dress…so regretfully, I decided it would be better for the rehearsal dinner, opposed to the actual wedding dinner.

Basically, it was perfect, and everything was going along on time and exactly as planned. I'd been praying it would be like this; I didn't want anything to go wrong and put stress on Elisabeth.

After scanning the house and making sure that everything was there and in good order, I ran home to get ready. I threw on the little white lace sundress that Elisabeth and I had gone shopping for months ago, and put makeup on—which, as Cal never hesitated to point out, meant something really special was happening. Finally, I curled my hair and tied a white ribbon around the curls.

As usual, my doorbell rang right on time. When I ran down the stairs, I found Carson and my Dad greeting each other. "So, are we ready to go do this?" Dad asked.

Carson just stared at me. Finally, Dad nudged him, and Carson said, "Wow, Kat—you look amazing."

"Thanks! I clean up nice, I guess. Let's get over there so your Mom doesn't worry." I put my arm through his.

He sighed. "Couldn't we just, like, make this the wedding and get it over with?"

"No! Your Mom has put a lot of effort into this, and we're going to do it." I batted my eyes at him and said cattily, "You're just going to have to wait one more day for the wedding night."

My Dad, who had been watching us with a bemused expression, said, "Too much information," and pushed us out onto the porch as we both laughed. I knew he'd be over in a few minutes himself.

We walked into a fairy tale. The whole room was lit by candlelight; the music was playing, and the cocktail hour had started. The air was heavy with a magnificent floral scent, from all the hundreds of fresh flowers placed all over the room. People were going to the bar getting drinks; Elisabeth had also brought in a bartender to help. It was great not to have to do anything! Everyone seemed to love the appetizers; it looked like everyone's small appetizer plates were empty.

When everyone noticed we had arrived, they all started clapping, which made me nervous: this was the night I was going to be put on the spot, and forced to talk in front of everyone. I had a couple of speeches that I'd written, that I'd read over and over again and hopefully memorized, so I didn't stumble through them when it was time to give them. When the music stopped playing, I knew it was time for us to get up and start giving our thanks. Oh boy.

I had gifts for the entire wedding party, of course, and thanked everyone for all their help. My Dad got a beer mug engraved with our wedding date, so I gave that to him and thanked him. That was a politically correct move more than anything, because my Dad didn't do much of anything to prepare for the wedding. But he *is* a guy, and Bill really didn't do anything, either—you know how it is. Weddings are more of a girl's thing. Then came Elisabeth's turn.

I didn't have to glance at my notes when it came to her. "Elisabeth Ferris," I said quietly, "thank you for all that you have done to make this dream come true. You've sat with me for countless hours, getting every detail just right, and I love you for that—and for everything else you've done. Thank you for being the mother I never knew, my supporter, and my friend. You've taught me so much in the last couple of years. You have taught me strength and unconditional love. It wasn't till I met you that I realized how sad it was I didn't have a mother growing up. I didn't know what I was missing until I met you, my friend Elisabeth. I saw what a superb mother you are to Carson, and I can't wait for tomorrow, when you actually will become my mother, by law...although in reality, we established that relationship many years ago. And last, but certainly not least, thank you for Carson. I know that Carson is the man he is today largely because of you. You taught him to listen, you taught him to love, you taught him to be honest and true to his word. You taught him to be a hard worker, but at the same time to enjoy every moment of life. I thank you for being so incredible and raising him to be just like you. I truly know how lucky I am to have Carson, and to have your family's love. I will never take it for granted, and will always be grateful to have you three be my family."

I could barely breathe by then; I was so glad it was finally done. I looked at Elisabeth sitting in front of me, her eyes welling with tears. She signaled me to come over to her, so I walked over and knelt next to her chair. She leaned over and kissed me on the top of my head and whispered, "Thank you. I'm so blessed Carson found someone like you. I know you'll take care of my son for me always."

That comment sent chills down my spine. For most people, this might be an empty phrase; but for Elisabeth, it was different. She knew something was going to happen to her, and she really did want me to take care of him after she was gone. It made me sad to think that one day she wouldn't be with us...but I was also honored that she trusted me with her son.

I really don't remember much more that happened that night. Like all wonderful things, it was mostly a happy blur.

Oh, but the next day, my wedding day...that day was wild, because everyone was running around like crazy, getting everything ready for the big event. Page was at my house first thing in the morning, which for her was nine o'clock, and her job was to keep me as calm as possible until five rolled around. With that in mind, we went to the small hair salon in town, a little shop that Kathy, a friend of the family, had built onto her property. She had a girl there who also did nails, so I got my hair done while Page got a pedicure and had her nails painted. Then we switched. My hair took two hours to do. I don't know if it was because it was a lot of work (wouldn't surprise me) or because all the talking that was going on slowed things right down. In a small town like Pollock, a trip to the hair salon was an event that let you catch up on all the town gossip...and Heaven knew, this wedding was a big deal in our town.

There had never been a wedding like this in Pollock; usually, people got hitched in what you think of as the typical small town barbeque wedding. Nothing wrong with that—it's how my parents did it—but this was much different. The little town lodge had been totally made over for the wedding, many thousands of dollars had been spent (I only found out how much later, and I was horrified and gratified at the same time), and a huge crew of people were brought in to create a very elegant scene. Elisabeth and I had decided that if we could have something done in town we would, and everything else would be brought in. I think that this event was a little over-the-top for the small florist and baker in town. We had a guest list of 400 people, which seemed huge to me. I don't think I'd ever had 400 pairs of eyes on me all at once, except maybe at graduation, and the thought of it was daunting.

Elisabeth pulled up to the salon right when we were finishing up. Her appointment was immediately after ours, so she came early to see the final results. By then, my hair was all pulled up, with curls pinned everywhere. I had a little headband with pearls on it that surrounded and accented the art that had just been perpetrated on my head.

"Hello, ladies, how is everyone this morning?" Elisabeth asked as she swept in. This was one of her good days, I was happy to see. In fact, I suspected that if it had been a bad one, she would have *made* it a good day by sheer force of will.

"Still breathing," I admitted. "How is everything going at the lodge?"

"We just drove by there and to the garden, where they're finishing up the altar. Oh, sweetheart, everything is so beautiful. You're going to love it!"

"And how are *you* doing today?" I asked gently.

"I'm feeling very good today, actually. I'm just so thankful to be here in the moment with you kids. My goodness, Kathryn, your hair is beautiful!"

"Yeah, Kathy did an amazing job," I said, blushing. "Now Page gets the challenge of makeup! We'd better get going, because we still have a lot to do—and the time seems to be flying by today!"

"Okay, dear, I'll see you at five o'clock."

"Can't wait! Just make sure that son of yours is there."

"I assure you, honey, wild horses couldn't drag Carson away from the altar. I think he's more eager to get married than you are, if that's possible." We both laughed.

Page and I flew home to do our makeup and get dressed. The photographer was showing up at four to take pictures of us girls, Dad and Cal before the wedding. Page was wonderful with makeup, so I knew she was the one for the job.

Dad came in right when Page was buttoning the back of my dress. "Hey, Dad," I said shyly as he stood in the doorway, staring.

"Wow, kiddo, you look stunning."

"Yeah, it's amazing what a little makeup and a poofy princess dress will do for a gal."

"Hey, Page can I have a minute with my daughter?" he asked quietly.

"Sure thing, Mr. P., I was just heading out to go get dressed myself."

My Dad sat down on the edge of my bed and just stared at me for a long moment; then his eyes filled up with tears. "Dad, what's wrong?" I asked, almost frantic. "You can't cry, because then I'll cry, and then Page will have to redo all this!"

He rubbed the tears out of his eyes. "Sorry, Kathryn. It's just...you look so much like your mother right now." He took a deep breath. "So, I came here to make sure all the final touches were taken care of."

"What do you mean?"

"You know: something old, something new, that whole thing."

"Well, I think I have the something new covered. Everything is new."

"Yes. I'm here for the something old." He reached into his pocket and pulled out a little diamond bracelet. "This was your mother's, Kathryn. I've held on to it for all these years...she wore it the day we were married. When your Mom found out she was sick, she gave it to me to give to you on your wedding day."

I felt a warm presence surround my whole body, and I had to remind myself that I couldn't cry yet. I was so glad that I had something of my mother's to wear on this special day. I had wanted to honor her in some way, but I could never figure out the right thing to do. This was unquestionably perfect. I had a piece of my mother to carry me and to carry *with* me through this day. I knew she was there, watching this moment with us, even if she wasn't with us physically.

I dug deep into my subconscious and pictured my mother for a moment. Silently, I told her that I loved her, and thanked her for bringing me into this world. I told her I was fortunate and truly happy, and that I would be very well taken care of as long as Carson was around. Then I opened my eyes to snap myself back to reality. "Dad, it's perfect. I hope it fits."

Dad reached out for my hand to put it on me, and lo and behold, it was a perfect fit. I could see the tears shining in his eyes again. My Dad wasn't a very emotional person; you could tell this was too much for him, and he wanted to make a break for it.

I grabbed his rough hands in both of mine. "Thank you, Daddy," I said fervently. "I know it was difficult raising us on your own. I want you to know that you did a great job."

He crooked a smile. "Thanks, kid, that means a lot."

"So, are you ready to go take a ton of pictures? I know how much you love getting your picture taken," I joked. Truth was, Dad hated this kind of stuff.

He stood up. "Laugh it up, little lady. I decided not to be too much trouble today, so I've been working on my smile." He grinned woodenly.

We both started laughing to ease the mood, and walked out of my room and down the stairs, hand-in-hand. I hadn't walked with my father like that since I was a little girl, but it felt right today. Out front, a limo was waiting to take us to the garden to get our pictures taken before the guests arrived. This was the first time any of us had been in a limo, and it was pretty amazing. There was even a bottle of champagne sitting on a little sidebar in a bucket of ice. We all filled our glasses, and toasted a new beginning.

After we took what felt like hundreds of pictures and it probably was, we had the limo take us to the lodge to wait. There was a little conference room off to the side of the huge banquet room, so Page and

I sat down in there and played around touching up makeup and hair to make sure everything was perfect. Dad sat in a corner with a beer in his hand. I could tell that he was nervous. We're alike in the fact that we don't like a lot of attention, and we both knew that in a couple of minutes, we were going to have to be the *center* of attention.

About the time I thought my nerves were going to fray right apart, the limo driver came in and asked quietly, "Are you all ready to go?" Without saying a word, we all got up and went to the limo. The drive to the garden was horrible; my stomach was all knotted up. I didn't get any better as we pulled up and I saw the 400 white chairs lined up in two sections. Every single chair was full. Somewhere in my mind, I suppose I'd been thinking that not everyone would show up, maybe only half, and that would be easier. But no such luck! There wasn't an empty chair in the place.

There was a long, white narrow rug laid out for me to walk down, with red rose petals artfully sprinkled all over it. The altar was beautiful: it was wrapped with white tulle lilies and white roses. There were twinkling lights in the altar, too, but it wasn't yet sunset, and you really couldn't see them well. At the end of the aisle was a small stage with the minister standing there. I heard the music start: Pachelbel's *Canon in D Major* was the song Elisabeth and I had chosen for the flower girls and Page to walk down the aisle to. I was so tense that I could hardly breathe.

I stood there, not sure if I was going to be able to take the first step. My whole body was shaking. Dad held me up; thank goodness we had to be arm in arm, or I don't know what I would have done. Just then, *Canon in D* faded out—I'd hardly even noticed Page and the flower girls march down the aisle—and the traditional wedding march swelled to grand life. Dad looked at me. "You ready?"

I nodded, afraid to speak, because I might lose it if I did. Just then, everyone stood up and looked straight at me. That didn't help any! Then I looked straight ahead and saw Carson…and suddenly, everything was just fine. I felt my nerves calm down, and I returned the gigantic smile on his face. It was indescribable, the affect this man had on me, even after all this time. I could be in the most terrifying situation, and as long as I knew he was there I felt at peace. I could do anything with Carson by my side, I decided, and today we were going to make a commitment to each other to be together for the rest of our lives.

My Dad and I started pacing forward, and an eternity later we arrived at the end of the aisle. Carson stepped down from the stage and shook my Dad's hand, and without my Dad's arm holding me up, I started to feel a little tipsy. Right then, I felt a warm hand wrap around mine, and Carson's warmth shot through my whole body, bringing with it all the strength I needed to step into this new life. He wrapped his arm around mine, and we stepped onto the stage.

The minister went through the entire traditional wedding introduction. I barely knew what he was saying, because I kept going over the vows I'd written for my man, hoping I would get them right. Suddenly, the minister got to our part. "Carson and Kathryn have written their own vows," he said, looking expectantly at my husband-to-be.

Carson looked at me, still smiling, and I got lost in his eyes. "Kathryn," he said quietly, "I knew I loved you from the moment I saw you. Today, I take you as my partner and my one true love for the rest of my life. I will stand by you forever. I vow to always be faithful to you, and to always be respectful and honor you. I will stand by you and laugh with you in good times. I will hold you and protect you in bad times. I will always be your best friend. I will always be loyal and honest to you. I will be the best man I can be for you and for the children we will one day have. I will always be honored to be your husband. You are like the air I breathe. I look forward to experiencing every bit of life with you, in good times and in bad. I will be your strength when you are weak, and your lover forever. I look forward to loving you more and more each day—for eternity."

I felt something warm and wet slide down my face; I couldn't hold back the tears anymore. This was the man I was going to spend the rest of my life with. I didn't know what I'd done right in this life to deserve him; even now, I don't. And now it was my turn to tell him how I felt. How was I going to compete with that?

I closed my eyes for a moment, and then opened them and looked into a pair of eyes that gave me more strength then I ever thought was possible. "Carson, you are my love and my best friend," I began. "I never thought that I would ever get a happy ever after until I met you on that hot summer day five years ago. Wherever you go, I will follow. I will always be faithful and loyal to you. I will make every moment count. I will always take care of you, in sickness and in health. I will stand by you through anything and everything. I will always be true to you, and to the children we will one day have together. Today, I give you all of me. I give you my hand and my heart, and promise to love you for always. I promise to stand by your side in good times and bad. I will kiss you every morning at sunrise, and love you every night at sunset. I will respect you and love you forever."

Carson leaned in and started to kiss me. We both started laughing when the minister protested, "We haven't gotten to that part yet!" Everyone in the audience laughed with us, and then we did the exchange of the rings. Finally, the minister said, "You may kiss the bride." I wrapped my arms around Carson's neck; he grabbed my waist and held my body as close to his as he could, and started kissing me like he had never kissed me before. I don't know if it was so intense because we were kissing for the first time as husband and wife, or what, but it was the most fervent kiss I'd ever felt in five years of practicing. We finally pulled apart, both of us taking deep breaths; it obviously had the same affect on him as on me.

Then the minister said the part I'd truly been waiting for: "Ladies and gentlemen, it is my great pleasure to introduce you to Mr. and Mrs. Carson Ferris."

Everyone started cheering. We walked hand-in-hand down the aisle, which was a lot shorter going up than it had been coming down. After the photographer took a thousand more pictures, we finally got to enjoy the reception. The lodge was beautiful: there were hundreds of candles lit everywhere, and the white linen tables were decorated with beautiful centerpieces of violet tulips and lilies, white roses, and baby's breath. The caterers did a wonderful job on the buffet; I can't imagine how they managed to make each dish look like a work of art. I filled my plate like everyone else (actually, my brother did it for me), but I really didn't get a chance to eat anything, because I was so busy talking to everyone.

The night went so fast. After we ate (or tried to), we danced our first dance to *At Last*, by Etta James. It was a perfect fit to how I felt. Then the champagne started to flow freely. Page gave a wonderful speech about us being more than just friends, and gave us her best wishes. Brody's speech was okay; he definitely talked about how much he loved his cousin, but that was really it. I don't think he really wanted this wedding to happen, but he wisely avoided bringing that out into the open.

Later, we cut our five-layer cake together. It was a true work of art: white with red petals scattered all around the white linen-covered table it sat on. All the layers were square. The fondant made it very smooth, but the cake decorator had included tiny detailed flowers bordering the edging. Luckily for Carson, he was good, and didn't shove my first slice in my face.

The night was coming to an end, and it had seemed to fly by.

For Carson and I, the night was far from over: we were leaving straight from the lodge for the airport. We were flying to Texas that night, where we were planning to spend the night in a hotel. The next day, we would fly into Cozumel. I had never been anywhere exotic in my life; well, I'd never really been anywhere. I was so excited; I could hardly wait to get there. But there was one thing I was sure was on both of our minds.

As you might have noticed, Carson and I were kind of traditional. Unlike most kids in this day and age, we'd never been intimate with each other. Oh, we'd spent the occasional night together...and trust me, it was difficult for both of us. But we'd decided right from the beginning that we wouldn't take our relationship to the ultimate level until we were married. So believe me when I say that I was very excited about that night...but I was nervous, too.

Suddenly, it was happening. The whole flight to Texas was pretty quiet. Before we left, we dressed down in our sweats to be comfortable for the flight. I was reluctant to leave my gorgeous dress behind, but it just wouldn't have been practical to take it along. On the way, we lifted up the little armrest separating us, and I curled up on Carson's chest and laid both my legs over his leg so I could be closer to him. He kept picking up my left hand and kissing my ring finger, and the golden ring that shone on it. We were both so happy. I was his wife, he was my husband, and it felt so good.

When the plane landed in Houston, we wasted no time in recovering our bags and skedaddled to the hotel. Elisabeth and Bill had booked everything for our honeymoon, so I was sure everything would be amazing. We were staying that night at the Hilton a couple miles from the airport. We had to be back at the airport the next afternoon, so it was good that we were close.

We pulled up to an absolutely beautiful hotel, and after a minor amount of hassle, we checked into our room and threw our stuff down. We were so tired—but I wasn't going to waste this time. Humming happily, I went into the little overnight bag I'd brought with me so that I wouldn't have to dig through my huge suitcase, and pulled out the nightgown I'd brought to wear for this night. I thought it was way too sexy for my style, and before then, I would have been too embarrassed to wear it, even just for myself. But now I was married, and I wanted everything to be perfect.

I took a deep breath and walked out of the bathroom. Carson was lying on the bed watching something on TV; when he saw me, his eyes widened and he jumped to his feet.

"Wow! You have to be the most perfect thing I have ever seen in my life!" he breathed.

I blushed rose red. "Perfect? I don't know about that, Mr. Ferris."

"I assure you, Mrs. Ferris, I meant exactly what I said." He walked over to me and put both hands on my cheeks, then started kissing me softly. Then he literally swept me off my feet and walked me to the side of the bed, never taking his lips off mine. Very gently, he laid me down on the bed...then, as I watched, he took off his clothes and laid down beside me. His hands slipped down my legs; then he grabbed one in his strong hand and wrapped it around his waist.

By then, everything was happening in slow motion. I felt my blood boil as his fingertips gently explored every part of my body. I was so in the moment that I wasn't nervous at all anymore. I reached behind him, and ran my hands up and down his back. His lips then left mine, but only so he could kiss my neck. I could barely breathe; it felt so good, so right! I'd never felt this way before, not even when we'd gone a little further than we should have in our playing with each other games. Chills started to race up and down my whole body. The moment that our bodies became one, I thought I was going to die of sheer pleasure. I gripped the pillow behind my head, squeezing it as tightly as I possibly could to slow my shaking. I loved the way I felt, and I had no control over what was going on with my body—which was fine, because it felt so good I didn't *want* to have any control. I could feel my toes curl up; the feeling was so amazing that my mind didn't know how to respond anymore but my body did.

I could hear Carson breathing heavily in my ear, and I could tell he felt the same way. I was so glad that we had waited. I wrapped my legs around his waist and pulled him in to me. I never wanted this to end; I wanted our bodies to stay like this forever. I had never felt so close to Carson, and I don't mean just physically. Not only were our bodies becoming one, I could feel something so much deeper, so much more intense than that.

After a hour or so, it was over.

He rolled off me, and curled his body tight beside mine. We laid there, cuddling, and didn't say anything for a while; just smiled and touched each other. He ran his hands through my hair, and his touch made me tingle; I couldn't get my body to calm down. I had absolutely never felt anything so amazing in my life; I could still feel it, all the way down to my toes. It was a feeling I couldn't describe, but I *liked* it—and I was pretty sure from the look on Carson's face that he felt the same way.

"Well, I think we did pretty good for our first time," Carson said, an eternity later.

"Oh my God, I can't believe we waited," I replied. "It's a good thing we didn't realize what we were missing, or this might have happened a lot sooner."

"Yeah, but I think it was like this because we *did* wait until we were married."

I laughed happily. "Thank goodness we're married now, so we get to do this all the time!"

I woke up on the first morning of marriage not even remembering having gone to sleep; we were so tired that I think we were both out before we even knew it. I rolled over to face my husband; he pulled forward and kissed me. "Good morning, my wife," he whispered. I loved the way that sounded and couldn't help but smile, thinking, *I am now Carson's wife.* It still seemed unbelievable to me...but so right at the same time.

I rolled on top of him, and we began kissing enthusiastically. Now that we knew what making love felt like, we couldn't get enough. We were in bed for the whole morning, making up for lost time.

Eventually, however, reality beckoned, so we reluctantly rolled out of bed and jumped in the shower...together, of course. Afterward, we got all our stuff ready and headed out to grab some breakfast before we went to the airport. I walked a little higher that entire day. I don't know why; I was the same person, but for some reason, I felt more like a woman than ever before. I don't know if it was because I was married now, or if it was because of what had happened the night before...but something in me had changed.

Our honeymoon was nothing less than perfect. We had lots of sun and beach time—and us time, of course. Cozumel was the most beautiful place I had ever seen; the images I'd seen of the Caribbean did it no justice. The white sand beaches and teal blue waters were magnificent. I couldn't believe that there really were places like this…but of course, what really made it perfect was the man I was with. I was sure the next place we went together would be just as special. It wouldn't be too long before it happened, either—Carson loved to travel, and he already had vacation after vacation planned out for us. I was sure we would both be big travelers someday. I couldn't wait to travel the world with Carson.

It was sad on the way home, though, because we both knew that Carson would be on his way back to school soon—and we would be separated again.

His Surprise

Carson was gone again, and I was taking a couple of classes at a nearby community college—but I was with Elisabeth every day. The poor thing had become so frail that she could barely eat, and we had to force her to drink water. Her movements were completely out of control now. She couldn't walk without falling and running into things; we had to be with her every minute. She had a hard time doing everything, in fact. It was getting so bad that we had to take her to the hospital all the time to deal with all the different things that were happening to her.

She was also starting to be constantly ill with other sicknesses on top of her Huntington's, particularly pneumonia and various bacterial infections; and it finally got to the point that the doctors felt that she needed 24-hour care, with a medical professional present at all times. I knew that this would be the hardest decision that Bill would ever have to make. Their love was so true and strong; how do you give up on that? How do you make the decision to institutionalize your spouse, a woman who's been the most important thing in your life for more than 30 years? But Bill knew that he had to make the right decision for Elisabeth… and that was to put her in an assisted living home.

Before he made the inevitable decision, Bill did a lot of research on the best possible facility to place Elisabeth in. He wanted it to have the best medical care around, but it also had to be close enough for us to visit her anytime we needed to. The care home that seemed to make the most sense was a place called Greenbrier. It was located in Sacramento, not that far from CSUS, a careful examination proved that it was one of the best facilities in the country.

The arrangements were made, and I packed up my stuff as well. If everyone was moving to the same town as Carson, then I was going to go live with my husband. He was hurting so badly about his Mom, and I knew he needed me with him right now. He seemed eager to have me, or maybe he was just his well-prepared self: within hours of me asking, he'd found a small rental house with three bedrooms, so there would be a place for his Dad to stay when he was there…which we knew would be most of the time. Bill Ferris was going to stay close to his beloved until the very end.

We never wanted Elisabeth to be alone, we all took turns hanging out at Greenbrier with her. It was nice there, considering what it was. We spent almost two years this way, as his mother slowly but inevitably got worse. They had Elisabeth on a variety of medications, most of which were intended to take care of her secondary problems. They worked…but she always seemed to be on an antibiotic for one infection or another, and they also had her sedated pretty much all the time by that point. It didn't matter; we were there for her no matter what.

It broke my heart sometimes; but even so, I would sit and talk to her for hours. She wouldn't respond, but I knew she could hear me. I talked to her about how good Carson was to me, and how well he was doing in school. I told her how he had passed all his classes already, and how he was going to graduate with his bachelor's degree at the end of the next semester—a full year early. I also told her about all the law schools he had been accepted into...every single one he'd applied to, no surprise there. Sometimes she would cry when I would tell her these things, and I'm sure that it was because she was so very proud of her son.

For his part, Carson was being superhumanly strong…or so it seemed to most of the people around him. I knew better; I was the one who held him at night, when he shivered and struggled not to cry, and sometimes lost the battle. He was devastated over his mother's condition, but he doggedly remained strong and kept up with his studies. That was what his Mom wanted, so he plugged away, and would be graduating at the top of his class. I think he was relieved that this part of his schooling was finally almost over.

As for me, well, I was still taking classes here and there—but most of my time was dedicated to Elisabeth. Carson had school to occupy him, and Bill was still trying to keep his firm running. So I stepped in to do the cooking and cleaning, keeping the house together just as I had when I was a kid, for Dad and Cal. The rest of my day, I was with Elisabeth.

It was nice, being with my husband every night, and going to sleep next him…but I wasn't feeling so well myself. I didn't want to worry him further, so for more than a month, I didn't say anything. Then one night, while I was lying next to Carson after we'd made love, I finally broke down and told him. I kissed him and caressed his face, and said, "Honey…I've got something to confess."

He lifted an eyebrow. "What's wrong, Kat?"

I sighed. "Well…there's so much going on that I just don't want to be a complainer…but I really haven't been feeling well lately. There's something going on with my body, and I just don't understand what it is. I've been feeling so achy lately. I thought it was a bug or something like that, but it's not going away. It's been a few weeks now."

His eyes widened. "Babe! A few weeks, and you're just now saying something?"

"I didn't want to worry anyone."

He sat up in bed. "Kathryn! You're my wife! I don't care *what's* going on, you need to let me know about things like this!"

I sat up myself, and leaned back against the bedstead. "Okay, so what do you think? Should I go see the doctor?"

He rolled his eyes. "Yes, of *course* you need to go see the doctor! You might've caught pneumonia or something from Mom. Make a appointment in the morning, and let me know if you want me to go with you."

"I really don't think that's necessary," I said.

"It's necessary to me! If you've been sick that long, I'm going to make sure we get answers!"

Carson was right: he was far more assertive than I was. As far as I was concerned, they could have given me some type of pill and sent me on my way, and I would have just been fine with that. But Carson wouldn't settle for a pat on the head and a placebo. So the next morning I called our family doctor and made an appointment, and was happy to learn that he had time to see me that afternoon. Carson had classes that entire day, so I called him on his cell and told him not to even think about taking time off school. I'd go on my own, and then call him right when I got out of the office to tell him what the doctor had said.

On the way, I stopped to see Elisabeth for a while before my appointment. She was doing pretty well that day, so I sat and admitted to her that I was on my way to the doctor, because I hadn't been feeling very good. She didn't really talk these days; she would mumble sometimes, but it was usually impossible to make out what she was saying. In any case, she was so heavily medicated that I wasn't sure if she understood what I was talking about. I told her everything anyway. I don't know if it was just my mind protecting me, but I thought that she really did comprehend everything I was talking about; she just couldn't communicate back. As it got close to my appointment, I kissed her on the forehead and went on my way.

When I left her suite, she almost seemed to have a smile on her face. I think she knew already.

At the clinic, I checked in with the front desk at the office, and wonder of wonders, I was called back right away. The nurse asked me about all my symptoms for my chart, and as she was writing them down, she was chuckling quietly to herself. Dr. Creswell entered the examining room. "Hello, Kathryn!" he said cheerfully. "So, what's going on with young Mrs. Ferris today?"

I swallowed and recited my symptoms. "I've been sick for the last few weeks. Nausea fairly often. I also have a headache I really can't kick. My whole body is pretty achy. My breasts hurt. At first I thought it was the flu, but it's not letting up."

He nodded, half smiling. "Have you been out of the country at all?"

"Not for a while."

"Any fever? Any excessive vomiting or anything like that?"

"No, not that I know of with the temperature, but I haven't really taken it. I haven't thrown up at all, but a couple of times I thought I was going to."

"Hmmm. Still having your periods regularly?"

I nodded. "Yes, actually, I'm bleeding right now. Started this morning."

"Really? Is it heavy?"

"No…just spotting, come to think of it. I do have some pain on my right side. I figured it was just menstrual cramps."

He grinned, and I swear, I had absolutely no idea why. "Well, let's do a urine test and see what's going on in there."

"Okay."

I went to the bathroom and did the whole pee-in-the-cup thing, then returned to the exam room to wait for the doctor to return. Now I was starting to get nervous. What if I was sick? Then another thought struck me: what if I was *pregnant*? That was the last thing we needed. We really didn't do anything to prevent it, though…. I cussed myself for an ignorant little county girl. Why being pregnant never crossed my mind I don't know. I decided that I really *should* call Carson, because this was something he needed to know. But then I stopped: this was news I didn't want to tell him over the phone, if in fact I *was* pregnant. So I just sat there with my stomach in knots and waited for the doctor to return.

About ten minutes passed and there was a knock at the door. The doctor stepped in and smiled. "Well, we found out what's going on! Kathryn, you're going to be a mother in a few months."

I sat there for a minute and didn't say anything; it all seemed so surreal. The doctor waited patiently for me to say something, but nothing was coming out. I was in shock, I suppose; I just sat like a statue waiting for some feeling, but nothing was coming. I felt frozen emotionally. I knew I should be ecstatic…but how could we deal with this on top of Carson's mother dying, and him trying to finish out his degree?

"We need to talk about the bleeding and the cramping in your side," Dr. Creswell said gently. "Where exactly is it?"

I pointed to where it had been hurting, and he looked a little concerned. He told me he was going to send me down the way to have an ultrasound. "There's such a thing as a tubular pregnancy," he explained, "and they can be dangerous. To be on the safe side, we need an ultrasound done to check the baby's position." As I listened silently, he explained to me where to go, and what I needed to do. Afterward, I walked out of the door of the exam room, I decided it was time to call Carson.

I really didn't want to tell him any of this over the phone…but I had to tell him something, even if it would worry him. So when he answered, I just told him they were going to have to do some more tests before we found out, exactly, what was going on with me. "But I would really like it if you could come meet me here," I told him in a small voice.

He agreed instantly, saying he was on his way and he would be there in a couple of minutes. When I managed to shuffle down to the ultrasound office, I put my name on the list—and they once again they called me right back. These people were good; I couldn't believe how fast this was all happening. So I went back to the room, and got onto the examination bed. The lady doing the ultrasound asked me if I wanted my husband to be back here, and I told her he was on his way—and could she please tell the people in the front to let him back here when he arrived?

That's when I called Carson back to tell him exactly where I was. He just absorbed it without any questions, and vowed that he was on his way.

The ultrasound tech spread a cold gel on my stomach and sides, and started moving the ultrasound wand around, focusing on my right side. I told her I was pretty scared, because my doctor said it could possibly be a tubular pregnancy. Right then was when she found the heartbeat. There was nothing there that I could see, except a little dot pulsing. Smiling, the tech said, "No, honey, it's not a tubular pregnancy. But the baby's on the right side of your uterus, which is why you've been feeling little cramps there."

I sat there, staring at the little pulsing heart on the monitor. I was going to be a mother! Suddenly the excitement overwhelmed me, and I started to laugh and joked around with the ultrasound lady. She asked if we had been trying to have a baby, and I told her we hadn't—that this was all a wonderful surprise.

That's when the door opened, and there was Carson, stopped in the entrance, eyes wide, with a look of wild surprise on his face. No one had to say anything: my husband was a very smart man, and he knew exactly what was going on. He walked over by my side and grabbed my hand. "Hey, baby," I told him. "I didn't want to tell you over the phone. You're going to be a daddy."

He leaned down and kissed me, but still didn't say anything; I think he was shocked, like I was when the doctor first told me.

"Want to hear the baby's heartbeat?" the ultrasound tech chirped.

Of course we did! She pushed a button on the machine, and the audio started. You could hear a lot of stuff going on in there, but then she found the perfect place to pick up the flutter of our baby's heartbeat. It was so fast! "The baby has a very strong heartbeat," she told us.

Carson and I both just sat there, hand in hand, staring at the little monitor. We didn't have to say anything, because we already knew what the other was thinking; that wasn't unusual, because we'd been together so long. I knew that we were thinking the same thing: we were lost in wonder at the fact that we were going to be parents, both a little shocked and a lot ecstatic. We sat in that way for a couple of minutes, lost in the moment, just listening to our child's heartbeat.

It was the most astounding sound I had ever heard. I had a life inside of me, a little one who depended on me to take care of him or her. I said, "I could sit and listen to this all day," and Carson grinned. He knew just how I felt.

"Oh, this machine can record audio," the tech told me. She went into the drawer and pulled out a blank CD, which she slipped into the machine so that she could record a couple of minutes for us.

I looked up at Carson and said quietly, "This would be a great way to tell people. Have them listen to the CD, and figure out what our big news is!"

We went straight to see Elisabeth after leaving the doctor's office. Hand-in-hand, we entered her room where she was sitting up, watching TV. I felt a pain as I always did, upon realizing how lonely she must be when none of us were there. All that time to sit and think…it must be horrible for her.

Carson walked over and kissed his mother on the hand. "Got some big news today, Mom," he said quietly. "We decided you should be the first to know."

Carson put the CD in her little alarm clock that we'd bought to play her music with; he pushed play and then sat next to his Mom and held her hand. The CD played a very clear audio of the baby's heartbeat. I looked at Elisabeth, and watched as a tear flowed down her face. Carson leaned over and told her gently, "You're going to be a grandma."

He related the whole story about me being sick and how we'd found out. As he did, I went over and sat on the other side of her and rubbed her arm. My heart hurt so badly right then; I realized that I'd been so excited to tell her that I hadn't even thought about how she would take it all, and what it must be doing to her. Even if she lived to see our child's birth, she would never be able to hold her grandbaby. She would never be able to tell the child stories, and run around after her.

I also realized, suddenly, that this baby wasn't going to have any grandmothers. All she would know were stories about two amazing women that she would never be able to meet in this life. As I thought about how wonderful it would have been to have Elisabeth and my own mother in this baby's life, I started to cry myself. When I looked Carson in the eyes, he knew exactly what I was thinking.

After close to half an hour of listening to a loop of our baby's heartbeat, Carson leaned over and said to Elisabeth, "Mom, we'd better be going. It's been a long day for Kat, and we'd better get her some dinner." He grinned. "Seeing as how she's eating for two, now." We both kissed her and told her we loved her.

The car ride home was different than the car ride to see Elisabeth had been. I confessed to Carson that I had been so excited to tell his mother about the pregnancy that I hadn't bothered to wonder how it would make her feel. We speculated about the reason she had been crying, maybe because she was so happy for us, or maybe because she was sad, given all she was going to miss. We decided it was probably a little of both. Carson and I talked about our child not having a grandmother, but we also talked about how we were lucky we have two very healthy fathers who would be around for a long time. They would keep their wives alive in memory; they would pass down to our children the stories about the amazing women whose blood ran through them. It wouldn't be the best-case scenario, but at least there was something.

After talking about it for a while, we decided to change the subject. The weight of the conversation was so heavy neither one of us could handle it anymore.

"So, Mom-To-Be," Carson chuckled, "what do you want? A boy or a girl?"

I realized that I hadn't really thought about it until then. "It's so funny," I mused. "I wouldn't have guessed in a million years that I was pregnant. I was thinking in the doctor's office that I must be pretty stupid…that I must have had a mental block about it. All the signs were there—the morning sickness, the fatigue—I still can't believe I didn't think about it." I slid my hand into his, and squeezed tight. "Carson, are you happy, nervous, excited? How do you feel about it?"

He grinned. "All that. I guess I feel a lot of stuff right now. I'm nervous about all you're going to go through, but you know I'll be there every step of the way, making you as comfortable as I possibly can. I'm as thrilled as ever that you're my wife, but it feels more intense to know you're carrying our baby. We're going to start our own little family, and that makes me very happy! How do *you* feel, baby?"

"Beside sick?" I giggled. "I'm overwhelmed. I'm relieved to know what the heck's going on with me. I'm *very* excited. I'm nervous, because I've never really been around babies, so I'm not sure what I'm doing. From what I hear, everything just kind of comes naturally…but of course, I'll read a lot of books to make sure that what comes naturally is what I'm supposed to be doing. So I guess I have something new to study for now."

He nodded solemnly. "Maybe you should take a break from school, and just focus on this. It's your decision, and you know I'll back you on anything you decide. I just don't want you to have any unnecessary stress. Really, think about it; the most important job in the world is being a mother. You need to take some "you" time and get ready for that."

I swear, I love my husband; he's always looking out for me. He has to be the most unselfish person I have ever known, and I knew that would make him an amazing father. I was so excited to share this whole experience with him.

Bill practically jumped for joy when we told him the news that night, and we stayed up for hours, talking about how it was going to be so nice having a little one around to make everyone smile, and how Carson had law school yet to deal with, and how we were going to handle everything. We quickly concluded that I would take a break from school after this year and just take care of the baby, while Carson continued to plug away at law school. Honestly, I think that Bill may have been concerned that Carson would be distracted from school, with all that was going on. I knew he really counted on Carson passing the bar and coming to work with him eventually; he could have hired a new partner by then, but he wanted to keep it a family affair, so he was trying to hold off until Carson was done with school.

The next day, of course, we took a trip to see my Dad. We wanted to tell him about his first grandchild face-to-face. We called him up early to let him know we were on our way, and that we wanted to see him while we were in Pollock. Our excuse was that we needed to check the Ferris house, to make sure that everything was okay, since it had been shut up for so long. It was nice pulling into the old town. Ever since we'd moved to Sacramento, things had been crazy; this place brought me back to a simple time. Back then, I didn't have a worry in the world. Back then, before Elisabeth was so sick, we were able to sit on the porch and have long talks together. Now poor Elisabeth couldn't communicate anything. I'd left here a young, newly-married woman, and hadn't been back since. It had been up to Dad and Cal to keep up the family visits; otherwise, I had kept in touch with everyone over the phone, so there was really no reason for me to visit. But being back was nice. Now, having lived in the city, I could see why Elisabeth had wanted to move her family here.

I rolled down my car window and took a deep breath of the clean, piney air. We'd brought bedclothes so that we could spend the night in the Victorian, and Bill had given us a list of stuff to check around the place. We'd talked about getting it ready to rent out to someone until we were able to return and live there, but the house was full of all their belongings and memories, and moving it all into storage would be more work than we were prepared for at the moment. So we went to the Victorian and dropped our stuff off, and walked across the street to my childhood home. Dad was very glad to see us, especially back on his territory.

As we walked into the creaky old log house, I looked around and realized that Dad had been getting along fine without me. I hadn't been sure how he'd handle everything when I left, but it seemed he was doing well. As he welcomed us into the house and we entered the living room, I saw someone sitting on the couch: Izzy (short for Isadore) Davis, who lived on the other side of town. I'd heard through the small-town grapevine that she was in the throes of a divorce, which frankly was pretty rare in our little hometown. The story was, her no-good husband had left her and moved out of town, leaving her with two boys to raise. So what was she doing at my Dad's house?

Then it hit me all of a sudden why Izzy was in my Dad's living room, I felt like someone had punched me in the stomach. Well, that explained why the house was neat and my Dad was still alive; he was being taken care of. Everything I used to do all seemed to be in good order. I wondered how long this had been going on...and my goodness, couldn't he have warned me somehow, so I wasn't blindsided by the whole thing?

I stood in the entranceway to the living room for a moment, round-eyed; Carson had all ready gone in, and taken his place on the other side of the couch. Noticing my confusion, Dad looked at me and asked, in a slightly sarcastic voice, if I might like to sit down for a bit? I snapped out of my daze and sank down beside Carson, then I looked at Izzy and said hello. She said hello back, and asked us questions about our new lives in the big city.

We chatted for a few minutes, a little self-consciously on my part, until Carson said brightly, "So, Pop, we've got something for you to listen to. Can we borrow your stereo for a little bit?"

He nodded, so Carson went over and popped in our special baby CD. "You start a band or something?" my Dad joked.

"We've started something," my husband affirmed, as he turned up the volume.

Dad's face got serious as the patter of the baby's heartbeat filled the room; and after a few seconds, he looked at me sharply. "That's right, Grandpa," I told him.

At first he had no response; his face was blank, probably in shock, like everyone else's when they first found out. Then he stood up with a whoop and shook Carson's hand and told him, "Congratulations!" He came over to me and gave me a big hug.

"You're gonna be a great Mom," he said fiercely. "You had a lot of practice taking care of me!" All of us laughed, even Izzy.

Speaking of Izzy, she turned out to be a pretty nice lady, and I was glad that she and Dad had found each other. After we revealed our news, Izzy and I sat and talked for a little about it, chitchatting the way women do about how far along I was and when my due date was (seven weeks, as it happened). At first I wasn't sure why she was still here, but Dad seemed happy about it; if he was, so was I. After we'd all chewed it over for a while, Carson and I told them we had to head over and do some stuff around the Victorian before we lost all the sunlight. We made plans to meet for dinner, and left in a chorus of goodbyes.

As we walked in the door of the Ferris house, Carson looked back at me and smiled. "So, did it bother you seeing Izzy at your dad's?"

"Why would that bother me?"

He snorted. "Yeah, right, babe. That look on your face when you first saw her…well, you didn't look okay with the situation."

"I was just a little surprised. I wish I'd known she was going to be there." I sighed. "God, I probably looked so shocked. Do you think I made them uncomfortable?"

"Nah, I just know your mannerisms. I don't think they noticed anything, really. So, do you think something's going on between the two of them?"

"Well, of course…" I began, but stopped to reconsider. "Maybe not. I don't think she's his housekeeper, but maybe they're just friends. They're both alone, so maybe they're just keeping each other company."

He smiled again. "Uh huh…well, remember that movie *When Harry Met Sally?* When a man and a woman start keeping each other company, it usually means they're more than just friends."

"So maybe I'll ask him tonight." Nonchalantly, I walked over to pick up an empty cardboard box, which I intended to fill with some items that I thought Elisabeth would enjoy having in her room at Greenbrier.

Carson just about had a heart attack. "Whoa, whoa!" he said, taking the box away from me. "You're not supposed to lift anything!"

"An empty box?" I asked, lifting an eyebrow.

"You're going to fill it up, aren't you? You shouldn't lift heavy things!"

"I'm not made of china, Carson."

"Well," he grumbled as he started putting things in the box for his mother, "you can't be too careful."

"I guess I need to jump on those baby books to see what I can and can't do," I told him, a little sourly, "but you need to calm down a little. For the last two days you've been watching over me like I'm due to break any second, and I won't."

He put down the box and enveloped me in one of his warm, safe, life-affirming hugs. "I'm new to being a dad," he said softly, then kissed me tenderly on the forehead. "Gimme a break."

"Hey big guy, I know this is all new to both of us, but you're walking on eggshells. Women have been having babies a long time. I know a lot has to change now that I'm pregnant, but I can't stay in a box… and honey, you can't protect me every minute."

"I can try."

Later on, we went over to Dad's house for dinner. We talked about Carson's school and how Dad would have to come to the city for his graduation, and of course I talked with Izzy a little about the pregnancy. She really was a nice lady, and she gave me some good pointers on how to prevent morning sickness and when to take my prenatal vitamins. It was good talking to a woman about this stuff, because I was surrounded by men who knew nothing about it…and Elisabeth was just too far gone to help, though I knew she desperately wanted to, just as much as I wanted her to. Ironically, I was the first of all my friends to have a baby, just as I'd been the first to be married. They would all be excited to hear about it, but they wouldn't have any first-person advice of their own. Izzy would have to do for now.

When Izzy left after dinner, we exchanged phone numbers, just in case I ever had any questions. It was actually nice having her there, but I have to admit that I was excited for her to leave so that I could find out what was going on with her and Dad.

As we were cleaning up, I said casually, "So, Dad, have you been spending a lot of time with Izzy?"

"Oh, Kathryn, here we go." He put down the dish he was drying and sighed. From across the kitchen, where he was putting away the leftovers, Carson shot me a grin.

"No, no, I'm not going to grill you. I was just wondering what was going on."

"Hmm." He put the plate away in the cabinet. "Yeah, we *have* been spending a lot of time together. Look, kid, I really like her. She's a very nice person."

"I'm sure, Dad. She seems very nice. Are you two serious?"

"Well, it seems to be getting that way," he admitted.

"That's good, Dad!" I patted him on the arm. "You've been alone a long time. I know you're totally capable of taking care of yourself, but it makes me feel good that you have someone here. Cal and I are so far away most of the time, so I'm sure it gets lonely."

"It did at first, but knowing you kids are doing so well makes it easier. But hey, what's going on with you making me a grandpa already? You know I'm way too young for that!" We all started laughing. I could tell that Dad was happy about the baby; it would be fun for him to have a little one around once in a while.

We all said our goodbyes, and Dad told me to take care of myself and the baby. On the ride home, Carson and I talked a lot about Dad and Izzy. Carson told me he was proud of the way I'd acted when I'd seen Izzy with my Dad.

"Yeah? What was I supposed to do, throw a fit like a little brat?"

"Well…it was a possibility." I slugged him in the shoulder, and he laughed. "Owww! Hey, you never know—Pop's never brought a girl around before, right?"

"Hmm." I crossed my arms and said, thoughtfully, "Well, no, he never has. I'm not sure what he did when we were gone, but when we were at the house we never saw anyone. I always wondered how Dad went without companionship, but I guess I thought he was just so busy with work he never thought about being with someone."

"Or maybe he had a girlfriend at the fire station the whole time!" Carson said dramatically.

"Oh, hush!" Actually, I felt better knowing that Dad was spending time with someone. I was always worrying about him, there in the back of my head, and now I didn't have to worry about him being alone anymore.

Goodbye, For Now

The next few months were a real trial. I was constantly sick, and rarely got out of bed before the afternoon. I was scared to get out of bed, in fact, because invariably, the first thing I'd do was run straight to the bathroom and throw up. I learned that if I lay still in bed for a while, though, it wasn't so bad when I did try to get up. I soon came to realize a home truth about pregnancy: that if we women ever really remembered what it was like, we'd never do it more than once.

I was so tired all the time. I would go over to see Elisabeth and just crawl into the chair next to her bed and sleep. We were quite the pair these days.

Fortunately, the worst of it seemed to taper off as my due date approached. I didn't feel sick as often, and towards the end I felt a huge burst of energy, so I took advantage of this reprieve to shop for the baby. Bill gave us a card to use for everything—whatever we wanted—so I stared loading it up. Because I'd spent a lot of time in bed for the first few months, I'd already made my list…though I couldn't buy everything quite yet, since I didn't have all the pertinent data. It would be a few weeks yet before I found out the baby's gender. Instead of worrying about pink or blue, I bought a lot of things in yellow. It didn't matter; I loved buying baby things.

I was in a store filling my cart with stuff like baby soap and diaper rash cream when my phone rang and the real world came crashing back in.

It was Carson, and his voice sounded very shaky. "I just got a call from Greenbrier," he told me. "They've taken Mom to the hospital, so we need to get there right away."

I abandoned my cart in the aisle and rushed home. When I got there, Carson was waiting, his face as pale as a ghost's. I rushed over to hold him, and he broke down in my arms. I wanted to ask him what was going on, but I knew he needed a while.

After a few long moments went by, he pulled back and looked at me. His expression was that of a helpless child. "Carson, what's going on?" I demanded.

"Her whole body is starting to fail," he said in a monotone. "She's in the ICU. They don't think she's going to make it this time."

I looked at him. Not knowing what to say, I just wrapped myself around his body, and we both stood there and cried for a while. After we pulled ourselves together, we got in the car and went to the hospital. We found his father sitting in the waiting room, his face gray with strain and worry; we sat down on either side of him. After a long moment, he looked at Carson and told him, "It's not looking good. You need to go in and see your Mom, spend some time with her. She'll know you're there. When you're done, I'll fill you in on all the details."

I looked over at my husband, who put his head down and took in some deep, heavy breaths before looking at me and choking out, "You want to go with me?"

My heart breaking, I reached out and grabbed his hand. "No, honey, you go in first, so you can have some time alone with your mother. I'll see her later."

Bill rose, and held out a hand to his son. Carson took it, looking like he needed the support, and got up and walked down the hall with his Dad, so Bill could check him in with the nurse. I watched Carson walk through the doors back into the ICU…then my head fell into my hands and I started sobbing. It felt like someone was ripping my heart out, little by little, and she wasn't even my mom except through marriage. So much pain…I could only imagine what my poor husband must have been going through right that minute. Finally I sat back, leaning my head against the wall, and wondered what Elisabeth must look like, what Carson was seeing right then. I thought about what he must be saying to his mother. I never got to say goodbye to my own mother, so I couldn't even imagine what it was like.

Bill came around the corner and sat next to me. We talked a little about what was going on with Elisabeth. It sounded like it had started out with a virus, like all those she'd already fought off so many times…but this time, instead of recovering, her body had started to shut down. Death was inevitable at this point, short of a miracle; all they were doing was keeping her comfortable. They had told Bill that they were going to be moving her to her own room soon, because they were beyond the point of doing her any good; now it was just a matter of waiting.

Bill said he thought that that would be good, because only family could go back into the ICU to visit. At least if she had her own room, people could come and say their goodbyes. They'd already called in the pastor to pray for her, and he would be back for any family members who needed him.

I couldn't believe this was happening. Intellectually, I'd known it *would* happen eventually, but I don't think you're ever ready for something like this, even if you know the person is deathly ill.

After about an hour, Carson came through the doors of the ICU. He had no expression on his face; he just looked blank. He walked over to us and sat down, and no one said anything. After a while, Bill looked over at me and asked me if I wanted to go back and see her. I sat there for a minute and thought about that. Would it be better if I did, or would she prefer for me to remember her as she had been? Not that I'd ever remember her as anything other than the happy, carefree woman I'd first met, the wonderful woman who had nurtured me in my mother's absence...but would she want me to see the shell she was now?

I decided that none of that mattered; I had to say goodbye, and I knew it. Yes, at some level, I wanted to run out of the hospital like a coward and act like none of this was happening; but it *was* happening, and it wasn't going away. Sometimes I hated being an adult; I wanted the innocence of a child back. I wanted to have not a worry in the world, to be sheltered from all the pain that real life holds.

But I wasn't a child, and now I had to do a very grown up thing. I got up and told Bill I was ready.

We walked over to the nurse's station, where Bill told the nurse I was Elisabeth's daughter. She told me to go on back to the fourth room on the left. I walked very slowly down the long, white hall. The fluorescent lights nearly blinded me, and I felt stifled by the horrible sense of sadness and illness in the air. The smell of antiseptic was thick and omnipresent, and I could hear the constant *beep beep beep* from all the heart monitors.

When I walked into Elisabeth's room, I found her lying in a deep bed, like some kind of high-tech coffin, with tubes and monitor leads all over her and an oxygen mask obscuring the lower half of her face. I walked over and sat next to the bed in a hard chair. Her skin was ghostly grey now; the rosy checks were gone, but I could remember, and that's how I saw her. I reached out, and took her hand in mine; in memory it was pale and elegant, with manicured nails painted a delicate pink, her favorite color; in reality, it was a gnarled stick studded with IV needles, and her poor veins looked like might burst from all the fluids being pumped into them. I rubbed her hand, and sat there with such a huge lump in my throat that I simply couldn't talk for a long time. I didn't know how I was going to do this! But then a thought struck me: this was Elisabeth Ferris, the lady I had spent countless hours talking to and laughing with.

It was still her, still Elisabeth, my very dear friend.

"Elisabeth, it's Kathryn," I said quietly. "I want to thank you for a couple of things. First of all, I want to thank you for Carson. He's such an amazing man, and I know that behind every amazing man, there's an amazing mother. You taught him to be a hard worker, a caring person, and how to love unconditionally. I know he's learned this all from you. I only wish I'd known you sooner…but from the stories I've heard, and from knowing you for the time that I have, I know you're the most special woman I've ever known. Your heart is so big, so open. Your love for your family is like nothing I have ever seen."

I took a deep breath, and realized that my face was streaming with tears. Somehow, I went on. "Elisabeth, the time you've dedicated to people and animals in need is so wonderful, and lives have changed because of you. I have learned from you that one person really can change other people's lives, because you've changed mine. Your love and passion is so strong…and now I get to see it in your son's eyes. When I was young, I always felt that there was something missing in my life. I didn't realize what it was till I met you. You stepped in and took me in as your own. You filled that space labeled 'Mother'. You listened, and gave me wonderful advice. You taught me so much, and for that I am truly grateful."

I hitched in a deep breath. "I promise you that everything will be taken care of. I will love and take care of your son until the very end. I will raise your grandchildren with love and care, and give them everything they need, and hope that I can do that job half as well as you did it with Carson. I will work every day to be everything I can for them. You don't have to worry; we will *all* be taken care of here. We will miss you more than you can ever know, but I believe that you will be watching over us everyday. I know my Mom is with me, and I know you will be too. I will work on following in your footsteps. Thank you for all that you have done for me; I will forever be grateful. I love you, Elisabeth—my mother, my best friend."

I stood up and kissed her on the forehead, then walked out of that horrible room. The tears were still flowing down my face, and all I could think, as I made my way down that sterile white hall, was *Why is life so unfair?* I wanted this all to go away. I wanted this to go back to the way it had been last year, before she went into the home; or better yet, before she had gotten so noticeably ill.

I walked out of the ICU and headed straight to the bathroom, because I didn't want Carson to see me like this. I had to be strong for him, and strength was definitely something I didn't have right then. When I got into the bathroom, I started sobbing; I just couldn't hold back all the emotions. This was unquestionably the most awful thing that I had ever felt. When I heard the knock at the door, I figured someone probably had to use the bathroom, so I rubbed my face with a paper towel before I opened the door.

Carson was standing there, and I ran into his arms, where I started babbling incoherently, telling him I was sorry over and over again.

I was shocked out of it when I heard the alarms go off, and a voice cracked over the speaker: "Code Blue! Code Blue!" I didn't know what "Code Blue" meant, but it was obvious from Carson's reaction that he did. His whole body stiffened up.

"What does that mean?" I asked him.

He just held me and murmured, "It means someone's not doing very well back in the ICU. In fact, they're dying."

"It—there are a lot of people back there!" I cried out. "It may not be her!"

When we returned to the waiting room, Bill Ferris was sitting there with his head down, and I could see the tears falling from fifty feet away. Carson went over to him, and knelt down and put his hand on Bill's shoulder. "Dad. It may not be her."

Bill looked up at Carson, and his eyes…I have never seen anyone look so devastated, and I hope I never will again. "It's her, son," he said, almost inaudibly. "She was my soul mate. We were connected…and I felt that part of me die when she went."

There was nothing left to say after that. Bill and Elisabeth had been like Carson and I were becoming now; not really two people, but one being with two bodies. As long as I had known them, each knew what the other was thinking without saying a word. How else could that be possible, if their souls weren't intertwined?

We sat there for a subjective eternity, united in our grief, before a doctor came out from behind the doors of the ICU to confirm. There were several families camped out in the waiting room, and we all looked up with desperation in our eyes, hoping the doctor would go talk to someone else.

The doctor walked up to us.

He asked us if he could speak to us elsewhere, and we all got up and trooped to a little conference room. I shut the door behind us. The doctor started by saying to Bill, "I'm sorry, sir, we tried to revive her...."

After that I couldn't hear anymore. It was like I was in a tunnel, and there were echoing voices all around me, but I couldn't understand what they were saying. It was as if I was having an out-of-body experience, I thought vaguely; this couldn't be real. I started to feel very dizzy; I grabbed Carson's hand, and fell into a chair. Thank God it was there, or I would have fallen to the floor. The doctor kept talking, but I couldn't make out what he was saying, and I had no idea what Carson or Bill had to say in response, if they said anything at all.

Alone in my limbo of misery, I just sat there, not knowing what to do. The doctor finally left, and I realized that Bill had said he was going to see her. That snapped me back to reality and I sat up suddenly. "Bill? Do you want Carson and me to go with you?"

"Yes," he whispered hoarsely, "We should all go see her, to say goodbye."

When we entered her room this time, it had a different feel to it. The monitors and oxygen were turned off now, so it was quiet, where before it had been noisy. We all gathered around Elisabeth, and with a blank feeling inside, I looked at the body that had once been filled with so much spirit. There was an emptiness about her. This was a shell...our Elisabeth was gone. I held one of her hands; it was still warm, but the feeling of life, the warmth of the soul that radiated from her every time we held hands or embraced each other, was gone.

I looked at her face, which was still crimped in pain, and brushed an errant strand of once-golden hair out of eyes. Now it was a drab gray, the life drained from it by her suffering. I thought about how much pain her physical body had been in while she was still with us, and I felt a little frisson of happiness, almost of joy, that she had finally been liberated from the pain and suffering of this physical form. Her soul had never been sick—just her shell. Her soul was free now.

All three of us stood there for a while, in pain and shock. Finally, Bill bent over and kissed her forehead. He whispered, "Goodbye, my love, for now—until we meet again."

I kissed the hand I was holding and told her I loved her. Carson didn't say anything; he just kissed the top of his mother's head, and then walked over to me and grabbed my hand. We all left the room together.

That was the last time we would ever see Elisabeth in her human form.

The car ride home was silent. I had never thought, when I left the house that morning, that the day would end like this. I was so livid at the world; I just wanted to crawl into bed and never get out. And basically, that's what I did. When got home, I took a shower and got in bed; Carson was busy making phone calls with his dad, and I knew they would be up all night handling the various arrangements. As I laid in bed without my husband that night, I whispered into the dark, "God, why is the world so hard? Why do horrible things happen to good people?"

Then a thought entered my head, calming my roiled thoughts like oil on water. I don't know if it was God answering my question, or if it was finally me gaining some clarity in my bleak place. I thought of how much Elisabeth had been suffering. I thought of the woman she'd been when she was young and healthy—running around with little Carson at the park, keeping up with all of her household affairs, planning those huge charity events. The condition that had overwhelmed Elisabeth in her final years had destroyed that life, made it so that she could no longer do most of the things she loved so much. Who would want to live like that? The only thing that had kept her going since then was the love she and her family had shared, and I cherished the fact that I had been a part of that. If there was a Heaven, Elisabeth was certainly there now, dancing with joy, savoring the ability to live the way she had before her body had made that impossible for her. The spirit had always been willing; it had always remained happy, joyful, alive with wonder.

If there is a Heaven, and I know there is, then Elisabeth is there, and she is at peace. She's no longer in pain; she no longer feels the weight and hurt of this world the way she was forced to for the last half-dozen years of her life. She's up there smiling down on all of us, and she's fine; more than fine. I honestly believe this is true, and it was the only thing that brought me peace on that horrible day when my surrogate mother died. It gives me peace still, and has helped me through all the days that have followed since, whether beautiful or dark. I know that Elisabeth Ferris will always be here watching us, protecting us. The fact that I mourned at all, I realized with a thunderbolt of clarity, was a result of my inevitable human selfishness. I simply wanted her here with me, Carson and Bill; and above all else, I want her to be here to meet my child when he or she was born.

After thinking all this through, I felt an odd mix of relief and irritation at myself. Relief because I knew in my heart that Elisabeth was in a much better place. I felt irritation because I was being petty and selfish. Elisabeth was beyond pain now, so why should I want her to be here, suffering, for my own selfish reasons? I understood that it was a perfectly human reaction...but it wasn't helping anything, and it wasn't reasonable.

I pushed away my selfishness and put my mind to rest. I started to think about Elisabeth being here, not in her last, fragile human form but in a spirit form that was healthy and happy. That seemed to make the rest of the pain go away.

The next couple of days were hectic for all of us, as we made arrangements for the funeral and called our friends and family. When we went to the funeral home to settle all the arrangements, it was the first time I had ever been to one. A feeling of death enveloped me the moment I entered the place. The air had a funny smell: a strong disinfectant stink with another underlying odor that I didn't recognize. It was nothing like in hospital's, and after I thought about it for a minute, I realized with a chill that it must have been the smell of the chemicals they used to preserve the bodies.

The thought of that made me ill.

Near the office, there was a showroom full of caskets you could choose from. I walked around among them, and looked into one of them, taking a deep breath. It was a cherry-wood color, with silver bars along the long sides for the pallbearers. I had never looked inside a casket before, and was surprised to see that the inside was lined with beautiful white silk.

I stood there for a long time, my eyes misting up as I stared into the coffin. After an eternity, Bill walked into the room and looked me over. "You okay, honey?"

I looked at him and said quietly, "I don't think so." This had to be one of the saddest places I had ever been.

He nodded. "Well, I'm going to need your help with this. Elisabeth never did pick out her casket. I think that made the inevitability of it all too real." He walked over and put a comforting arm around my shoulder, and I leaned into him. "You know, we paid for the plots years ago…but this part we never took care of."

I looked up at him, sniffling, and said, "Bill, it really doesn't matter what we bury her in. That's not Elisabeth; it was just the shell her soul was wearing."

"You're right." His voice breaking, he said, "It feels so different now that she's passed. Everything's so empty and cold."

"That's because her soul was so warm and powerful," I murmured.

Bill eventually decided the casket I was looking at would be fine.

I couldn't believe what we were having to do in this time of deep mourning, but I suppose it's something every family has to deal with. It was hell on all of us, and frankly, I would have given anything not to have been there…but Bill needed our support, and Carson and I were a unit. We'd be there for him for every step through this nightmare.

When I had time alone to be with my husband, all I could think about was how fatigued he was. This couldn't have happened at a worse time; he was right in the middle of his finals. He had talked to all of his professors, and they all seemed to understand; they gave him what he needed to study and complete for the next couple of weeks, and he would just have to go back one day to take his finals, and then he would be done. That and calling relatives and friends, and arranging all the myriad financial details of the funeral, was draining him.

For my part, I was calling caters and rental companies to get everything together for the dinner after the service. We were having the service at the church that Carson and his family had gone to before they moved to Pollock. We rented the clubhouse at the golf club for the dinner, though, because we needed somewhere that could hold a lot of people. We weren't sure how many to plan for; that's the problem with things like this. It's not like there's a guest list, like there is with a wedding. Elisabeth had a lot of friends and colleagues from the charity organizations, so we were expecting a lot of people.

The morning of the service, Carson and I went to grab breakfast together before heading over to the club to make sure things were starting to come together. We also had a car full of flowers that people had been sending that we wanted at the church. Our house was full of flowers and food, so I was glad to get some of it out; I was starting not to be able to see my floor or the counters. We also stopped by a homeless shelter on our way and dropped some of the food off for them. There was no way we'd be able to eat it all, and it would go to waste if we didn't. Elisabeth would have never wanted that much food go to waste; she would have taken it somewhere for someone to enjoy, so that's why Carson and I went to the shelter. So we weren't without food by any means…but we went and ate breakfast anyway, because we had to get away from everything. The only times we could get away and not feel guilty was when we had to eat, you see, so we took advantage of that as often as we could in the days immediately after Elisabeth's death.

After we made our deliveries and ate, we went home and prepared for the service. I put on a black cotton dress that I'd found in the maternity section of a local department store a few weeks back. I didn't know why I'd bought it then, except that it was a good deal…but my subconscious may have had its own reasons. It looked like it had a purpose now.

When Bill emerged to meet the limo that arrived to pick the three of us up at noon, he looked like he wanted to die himself. He had a very somber look on his face; he told us he'd prayed this day would never come, and he couldn't believe it was here. I gave him a hug and walked out front by myself. I wasn't sure if Bill needed a second with Carson or not, but I didn't want to stand in their way during this very personal time. So I went outside, and was met with a beautiful day. Spring was in the air, and all the flowers were starting to bloom. They were lush and vibrant from all the rain the previous winter; everything was so green and perfect. The sun was out, without a cloud in the sky. The warmth of the sun touching my skin felt good.

I stood there and enjoyed it, until the guys came out of the house, and we all went on our way to pay our last respects to Elisabeth.

The service was very nice. The church was packed; all the seats were full, and there were people standing outside. After the choir sang *Amazing Grace* and the pastor spoke, they did an open mike session, where people could tell stories and talk about the moments they'd shared with Elisabeth. That part was astonishing. People I'd never even seen or heard of got up and talked about what a giving, generous, loving person Elisabeth had been, and how she had always been there to listen and support them. But I think the stories that touched my heart the most were those from the people Elisabeth had helped. Several people got up and talked about how one of her charities had changed their lives, and how they wouldn't be where they were right then if it wasn't for her. That made me even prouder than ever to be her daughter-in-law.

I learned something special that day, something that has guided my life since: that the smallest gesture can change someone's whole life. The tiniest thing can sometimes make a huge difference. I was astounded by the difference that she had made in so many peoples' lives; during the time Elisabeth Ferris was here, she changed the world.

After the service we went to the county club, all of us feeling a lot better about Elisabeth, finally able to get a handle on her death so that we could move on. While Carson and Bill were walking around talking to people, I went over and made them both plates; otherwise, I knew, they would never eat. So many people wanted to talk to them, and tell them what they thought of Elisabeth. Otherwise, I just sat there next to my husband the whole time, and dealt with what seemed like a million people touching my stomach and telling us congratulations. It went on hours longer than we had expected.

It took a couple of weeks after that before things finally started to calm down. Carson had his finals, and thank goodness he passed them all. Meanwhile, I was planning his graduation party. He didn't want to walk at the graduation, but I convinced him to do it anyway for his Dad. During that busy time, Carson and I also went together to our prenatal care appointments. Everything was looking good, they told us; everything was there and in its right place. We got pictures of the baby from the sonogram—and we found out that we were having a little girl. That scared me. Now, a boy I would have been good at; I'd always been a kind of tomboy. But I didn't know how to raise a girl.

Carson was absolutely thrilled. I didn't get it, and wondered if he was masking his disappointment somehow. I thought all men wanted boys. When I asked him about it, he said, "Are you kidding? I couldn't be happier! Mom always said boys are closer to their mothers, and girls are closer to their Dads—you know, the whole daddy's little girl thing."

The one thing that was good about having a little girl was that we wouldn't have to go back and forth with names. Of course, we both agreed to name her after her grandmother: Elisabeth Lee Ferris would be her name. And now that I knew I was having a girl, I could really start shopping! It became my daily thing to do a little something in the nursery. I started by painting the room pink and brown. I ordered all of my baby furniture right away, so it was exciting when a box would arrive at the front door. I washed all the baby clothes, too, and hung them in her closet, and I stacked the diapers in perfect rows on the changing table. Carson would laugh and ask how long I thought all that stuff would stay so perfect, and I would tell him I was *always* going to keep her room in order. He would just shake his head and walk away.

I think he was probably more realistic about the baby than I was. I was expecting this fantasy of the perfect baby that never cried, sleeping in her perfect little bedroom all night long. Carson knew better, but he let me keep thinking whatever I liked. He knew the truth would come out soon. He was so right.

Carson's graduation and the attendant party went well, and it wasn't long before he was getting ready to start law school. We'd talked about him taking a year off and just spending some time with the baby, which we both thought was a great idea…but we also knew it was best for Carson to keep going. After all, he was so sharp that it wouldn't take him long to complete his coursework and pass the bar. The law school he chose to attend was the Lincoln School of Law in Sacramento, which was only about a half an hour from where we were living. Now, we thought long and hard about staying in the rental house where we lived, because in some ways, the place was still ideal for us. It was near enough to Bill's work and Carson's school, and it was close to Elisabeth's resting place, too. We didn't really need to be there anymore, but Carson said he didn't want to move me because I was so close to having the baby...and he knew how much work I'd done to the baby's room. Over dinner one night, Bill and he both agreed that we should stay.

I stepped in and told them flat out, "I'd rather move right now than move after the baby comes."

Carson looked at me oddly. "How come?"

"Well, there wouldn't be that much stress on *me*. You guys would be doing all the work."

"You know," Bill said thoughtfully, "you could buy your own house. Carson inherited a lot of money from his mother." That was a fact. Carson had been Elisabeth's only beneficiary; she knew that Bill would be fine if he outlived her.

"I guess," Carson said; he sounded unenthusiastic about it. "My financial advisor was talking to me recently about how I really need to make some investments, so buying a house is probably a good idea."

"Well, I really don't want to be stuck in the city for good," I told him. "I want to move back to the country as soon as we can."

He nodded. "Yeah, but it's a good investment. We don't have to stay there forever—but it'll make a great tax write-off, and eventually we could rent it out and live where we wanted."

Now the situation became stressful. When we were just going to stay where we were, it didn't seem so bad; but buying a house was different. I had heard that buying a house was rather painful, in fact. I was sure that Carson would take care of all of the paperwork and stuff like that…but this was going to be my first house, and I wanted to make sure it was something I loved.

So we spent the next couple of weeks house shopping. We were going to have Bill stay with us for the time being; he was never really home, but he needed a place to keep his stuff and sleep sometimes. So we had to keep that in mind when we were looking…and we looked at a *ton* of houses, because frankly, the houses in the city were so weird. They had huge homes on little tiny lots, and the homes had no backyards. It was something I wasn't used to and didn't want, and I began to think we would never find a house. Finally, we decided to go look in the older part of the city. Our real estate agent said that the homes out there were older, but they were on bigger lots.

I wanted a backyard for our kids to run around and play in.

We pulled up to the first house, and I was excited see an enormous front yard. It was a two-story house with five bedrooms—and it was perfect. It was older, so it had some character. It had hardwood floors and a huge kitchen, too. But the thing that sold Carson and I on the house was the backyard. It was huge and had a big pool; the pool already had an iron fence around it, and there was thick green grass everywhere. Rosebushes and petunias crowded the flowerbeds, and there was a quaint little pool house next to the pool that even had a little living room and a bedroom and bathroom. We figured it would be perfect for Bill; that way, he would still be with us, but could have his own space. It was going to be hard with a new baby in the house, and I don't want him to be kept up by the baby's crying.

After we'd been there half an hour, Carson pulled me aside. "Do you like it?"

"It's perfect," I told him.

"I think so too. Let's try to get it." Carson immediately talked to our agent about writing up an offer on the house.

It took a couple of days, but our agent eventually called back and told us that the sellers had accepted our offer. We had thirty days, and then we would be moving! So for the next month, we spent every single day packing. We also went to the country house back home, and picked up some stuff from there for the new place. I was beginning to wonder if Bill would ever go back there…and of course, I also had to rethink the baby room. The new room was much bigger, so I could buy some more furniture. Everything was going great!

Meanwhile the baby was growing, and so was I. I was very big, and very uncomfortable. Elisabeth Lee was going to be a big girl from the start, it seemed.

Right on schedule, the movers came and started moving all the stuff out of the old house and into the new, and of course I had to be there the whole time directing traffic and organizing things. I wasn't suppose to lift anything, so I had to resort to just pointing. Carson was getting ready to start law school in a couple of weeks, so our goal was to get all of our stuff moved in and organized before he started school. From what Bill had told Carson, law school was quite intense, and he would have to focus constantly and study hard. We were already going to have a baby in the middle of the first session, which was bad enough, but Carson was so smart and determined that I was sure he would get through it just fine.

Soon, we were getting settled into the house; by then, Bill was all moved into the pool house. The rooms in the big house were starting to be organized…or at least, they were unpacked. We still had to paint and hang pictures, but everything was coming together. I did paint one room immediately: the baby's room was all done. I'd already had Mommy Mode kick in, and I wanted make sure everything was perfect for our little girl when we brought her home.

The doctor said the baby was close to arriving, and Carson had hit school head on. He was taking all the classes he was suppose to, and more. It was indeed intense: he was at school five days a week, and then he would stay up really late studying. I was so tired from being pregnant and working on the house that I always fell asleep before him, and he was always up before me. I kept telling him I was a bad wife, going to sleep early every night and not even waking up in time to make him breakfast.

"You're the best wife in the world," he would tell me. "You're doing something more important than making me breakfast." Then he would tenderly touch my stomach.

Hello, Elisabeth Lee

One morning I woke up early to a series of odd aches, unlike any I had ever felt before. It didn't hurt too badly, so I figured it couldn't have been contractions, though it was about time for them. Everyone had told me that I would *know* when I was having contractions, because they're really painful. These sensations were making me feel uncomfortable, but they weren't overly painful.

I woke up and kissed Carson on the forehead, and he opened his eyes and looked at me, worried. "You okay, Kat?"

"I'm fine," I said brightly. "I just woke up early for once. I'm going to go down and start making coffee."

I walked down into the kitchen, where I packed Carson's lunch and started the coffee. Carson came down the stairs just as I was finishing up. "Why did you get up?" I asked. "You still have another hour before you have to."

"I know, but I'm kind of worried about you, and I couldn't go back to sleep. So I figured I'd get up and study for a while as I drank my coffee."

I chuckled. "You're funny, babe. I'm fine."

He slipped up behind me and embraced me. "You *seem* fine," he murmured, "but you haven't been up this early in a long time."

"I know. I couldn't go back to sleep either." I decided to come clean. "I have these funny pains in my lower stomach. It's funny because they're coming and going just like they say happens with contractions, but they really don't hurt. I don't know—maybe I'm lucky and my contractions won't be too bad."

He drew back. "Well, do you think I should stay home from school today?" he asked, with concern in his voice.

"No, no, I think I'll be fine. I'll call you if I start to feel worse."

I went over to get Carson's coffee. As I poured him a cup, I asked him if he wanted milk for it. He said he did, so I walked over and opened up the refrigerator…and heard a splash of liquid hit the floor. Carson stood up suddenly. "Kat, what happened? Did you spill the milk?"

I had no idea; I was in a daze, standing there in the door of the fridge. When he pulled the door open wider, I saw that it wasn't milk on the floor...and realized that the entire bottom of my night gown was wet. I was standing in a small puddle of water.

It took me a moment to realize that my water had just broken, and that's when my stomach tightened and I fell to the ground in pain. Those light, clenching aches had transformed into the most horrific, nightmarish agony I had ever experienced, now that my water had broken. It was a kind of pain I couldn't explain even if I tried.

I couldn't get up off the ground. Carson stood there for a second with a terrified look on his face, babbling that we had to get to the hospital, and he kept asking me if I was ready to get up, because we had to *go!* I told him to go into the bedroom and grab the bag I'd packed in advance, and put it in the car. I knew that another one of those God-awful pains was going to hit any second, and I wanted him to go away so he wouldn't have to see my reaction.

Carson ran up the stairs, found the bag, and went outside to put the bag and the new baby seat in the car. We'd never gotten around to putting the car seat together, so I'm sure he just threw the box in the back. Right when Carson walked outside, another one of those pains started to come. I rolled up into a ball, braced myself, and started to breathe heavily. It hurt so bad that I wasn't sure how I was going to make it through this! It was too late to go back, but I wished like hell right then that I could.

By the time Carson came back for me, the pain had eased. I started watching the clock, because I knew the doctor would want to know how far apart the contractions were. I asked Carson to run up stairs and get me a change of clothes, and just when he came back down, the pain started up. I rolled into a ball again, and Carson started rubbing my back. Poor Carson. I know he felt helpless, so I tried to hide some of the pain...but it was *hard,* because I wanted to just start screaming at the top of my lungs.

It turned out that my contractions were about eight minutes apart. I stood up when the contraction was over, and hurriedly changed my clothes. I knew they were going to make me change when I got there anyway, but I wanted that gown soaked with all that amniotic fluid off of me.

As I was walking to the car, I felt another contraction start to come. I fell and rolled into a ball of pain in the front yard. What the hell had I gotten myself into? This was horrible! Why hadn't anyone told me that having a baby was like this? If they had, I never would have done it! By the time I'd cussed out all of womankind for not totally warning me about this crazy pain, it was almost over. Growling, I got up off the ground and climbed in the car, and we were off to the hospital, the buildings on either side of the road were flying by. Everything was in complete chaos: I was blinded and enraged by the pain, and my unflappable Carson was nowhere to be seen. I could tell he just wanted to get me into a doctor's care as soon as he could; he was shaking like a leaf, he was so nervous.

"How are you doing? How are you doing?" he kept asking me, frantic.

"Okay! I'm okay!" I kept telling him. I didn't want to talk too much because I was scared of what I would say.

I had two contractions on the way to the hospital. During the last one, we were at a red light. I looked over, and there was a car parked next to us. The man in the car was looking at me with a complete look of panic on his face. I can't imagine what I must have looked like in that much pain; that poor guy must have thought I was dying. By then, I was to the point that I wished I *would* just die—anything to make this pain go away!

We finally got to the hospital, and Carson ran into the emergency entrance to get me a wheelchair. "Try to stay in the chair," he huffed as he bundled me into the thing. "If one of those contractions hits again, the hospital floor probably isn't the most sanitary place to lie on." Then we were off at a frantic pace. I didn't know what scared me more: Carson running down the hospital halls like a maniac, pushing me in that stupid chair, or having this baby.

He took me right to the entrance of the maternity ward, and I could hear women screaming from the rooms. I was a bit out of it, so I wondered where the hell I was and what was going on here. I just wanted to rewind time and make all of this go away.

Well, they took one look at me and got me into a room right away. The nurse helped me get into a hospital gown, and then they started hooking me up to all these machines. The nurse checked me, and said I was dilated to about seven centimeters.

"I need pain medicine!" I shouted at her.

She just peered at me owlishly. "It may be too late for that, honey," she warned. "But I'll get the doctor, and he'll be able to tell you more."

I went into a complete panic at that news. I grabbed Carson by his shirt and dragged him to me, begging him to talk to the doctors and make them get me medicine. Right then another contraction started, and at that point, I couldn't hold anything in. I started screaming that I wanted medication. "I can't do this!" I wailed.

The doctor came in at the wrong time, and I looked straight at him and told him that he'd better get me something to make this pain go away right now *or else*. You could tell he dealt with this kind of thing all the time, because he just smiled pleasantly and calmly walked over to me. "I have to check you over first," he advised, "and then I should be able to get you some medicine. Now, I need your help, because if you want medicine we'll have to do this right now—you're moving along really fast."

After a quick check, the anesthesiologist came in and offered me some options. "Just give me the strongest stuff you have already!" I yelled, and she smiled and left to get things ready, leaving me with some release forms to sign. I didn't even read them: I just told Carson to get me a pen, because I didn't care what those stupid forms said, I needed some relief!

I signed the papers as soon as he pressed the pen into my hand, and right then another contraction came. I did the breathing I'd been taught to do (I had finally remembered), but it didn't matter: nothing was helping, the pain was too strong. The anesthesiologist came back in with a tray of stuff. "When was your last contraction?" she asked, taking in my wild eyes and tousled hair.

"I just had one!"

She put her hands in mine and said, "Okay, stay perfectly still. I need to wait till after your next contraction, and then I'll insert a catheter in your spine. Okay?" I couldn't believe they wanted another one of those horrible things to come, but I knew the sooner it came the sooner I could get my medicine.

The contraction came less than four minutes later.

After it was done, the doctor went to work. The anesthesiologist pulled out the biggest needle I have ever seen in my life, and I felt like I was going to pass out just from looking at it. The doctor told Carson to hug me from the front and arch my back; she told me to stay very still. It went pretty fast, thank goodness, and it didn't hurt anywhere near as bad as the contractions. The world started to be a better place about two minutes after the medicine began dripping through the IV. The next contraction came, and it hurt, but it wasn't nearly as bad as it was before. For the first time, I told myself, *I can survive this*.

It takes a long time to have a baby. After a couple of hours I felt something poking me down there. I called in the nurse, and told her I felt something funny; I couldn't feel much, though, because of the epidural. The nurse checked me and everything went crazy. The baby was doing something called "crowning." I didn't know what that meant, so I asked the nurse and she told me the baby's head was starting to come out. Well, I started freaking out then. I felt myself starting to breathe very heavily, just as the doctor burst in and ordered me to push.

Suddenly, everything went dark. I could hear what was going on, but I couldn't see anything. I kept hearing the nurse's voice saying, "Kathryn, stay with us," and I could feel her tapping me on the face. I didn't know what was going on, but by then, I was starting to get pretty scared.

When I was finally able to open my eyes, everything had changed. When I'd gone under, the room had contained only me, Carson, the nurse, and the doctor; now there were a ton of people in the room, and I was breathing through an oxygen mask. I looked at the end of the bed, and Carson was standing right there; he looked so scared and helpless. I looked at him and blinked my eyes, to try to show him I was okay.

The doctor cleared his throat and said quietly, "Kathryn, your blood pressure keeps dropping to scary levels. We flushed all the painkiller out of you, and now we need to get the baby out. It's going to hurt, okay? But we need you to push hard on your next contraction. We're close, so let's try to get this done so we don't have to put you into surgery."

Suddenly, that horrible pain was back! Well, believe me: I was bound and determined to *not* have to go in for surgery, so I was going to take all that pain I was feeling and push my hardest. Having made that decision, out of nowhere I got a sudden surge of strength. I bore down and pushed with all I had. The doctor said, "Excellent! If we can get a couple more of those, the baby will be out soon."

Actually, I pushed three more times. I was in so much pain that I would have given anything for this to be over…and by the look on Carson's face, he felt the same. He was terrified; he wanted to protect me and he couldn't, so I knew this had to be driving him crazy. I wanted to be strong for him…but the pain was just so enormous.

"Give me one more big push, Kathryn!" the doctor said. "The baby's head is out!"

Carson looked down and his eyes widened; then he came back to my side and held my hand in both of his. "She has a ton of hair!" he said, in a voice filled with awe. Somehow, that amused me and helped me get through the rest of that torture session. Oh, I was still scared; if it was this hard to get the head to come out, what was the rest of the body going to take?

I only had to push one more time, and my baby girl entered the world completely. I heard a lot going on over at that end of the room, but I couldn't make out what was happening. I was waiting for the baby to cry, but it seemed to take forever to come; after a minute, though, I finally heard a tiny wail. I was so relieved, and kept asking if everything was all right.

"Everything is fine," Carson said, his face bright, tears in his eyes. "She's a little angel. She's beautiful."

Beaming, the doctor walked over to me and put this tiny little person on my chest. I looked down at her. She was, in fact, the most perfect being that had ever been. I wondered how it was that God had chosen to give me the most gorgeous baby the world had ever seen. She had so much dark hair—she really did! She had beautiful pink skin, too…as far as I could tell, with all that stuff all over her. She was perfect, and she was mine. I was entirely in love, I bonded with her in way I had never imagined, a way only a mother could bond with her child.

"Hello, Elisabeth Lee," I whispered. "I'm your mommy, and I love you."

I kept telling her I loved her and kissing her on the top of her head. Carson came over to me, smiling and crying, and laid his head on mine, telling me what a great job I'd done and that our daughter was so beautiful. I wrapped my arms around our baby and held her close. When the nurse told me she had to take her and weigh her and clean her up, I felt a surge of panic; I didn't want my daughter to leave me. Carson could tell I wasn't happy about it at all, but the doctor was still working on me, and I knew I was in no condition to go with her anyway.

"Can *I* go with the baby?" Carson asked the nurse.

"That would be fine," she replied, smiling. "You can watch everything through the window that looks into the nursery."

"Good." Carson patted my hand. "Don't worry, Kat, I'm going to go with her, so I will keep my eye on Elisabeth Lee every minute. Okay?"

I knew then that Carson felt the same way about our daughter that I did, so I nodded mutely, and they left.

While they were gone, the doctor finished cleaning me up and putting the stitches in place; and after he did, the nurse asked if I needed to go to the bathroom. I told her that if I did, I would go on my own. When you have an epidural, you can't walk on your own for a while—and I suppose they thought my legs would still be numb. But I knew different, because I was feeling *everything*. Once they'd flushed all the drug out of my system, it had all come back in a rush, which was one reason I was glad Miss Elisabeth had finally arrived. Since I could feel my legs, I thought for sure that I would be fine going to do my business on my own.

It seemed like they were gone forever with Elisabeth, and I began to wonder if they were ever going to come back with my baby. Just when I thought I couldn't stand it anymore, just when I was about to get out of bed and go find them, Carson and the other nurse came in with little Elisabeth.

The nurse had washed her up and put her in the pink outfit I'd packed in the bag for her. She was adorable! Carson was so good; I hadn't even told him to get that outfit, but he knew what he needed to do, and went in and got it. The nurse picked her up out of her little crib after they wheeled her in, and as she gave me my baby, the empty feeling instantly went away. I just sat there with her in my arms; I couldn't take my eyes off her. She was so perfect. I had been so worried about how I would feel towards this new baby. Everyone told me there was an instant unconditional love, and they were right. I loved this child more than I could ever imagine possible. It was like I'd known her forever.

She made these little baby grunting noises trying to get closer to me, and I held her tight against my body. I asked the nurse if I was holding her too tight, as I didn't want to smother her. The nurse had the perfect answer: she said, "You've been holding her tight for nine months, so why stop now?" She was so right: we had been bonding for nine full months, and I hadn't realized it until then. I *had* known her for a while now.

Carson came over and got into bed next to me, and we just smiled at each other.

"Kathryn, she's so beautiful," he whispered. "Just like her mother."

I tried not to cry. "She's the most amazing thing. I can't believe she's ours."

"I know! Can you believe you're a mom?"

I leaned over and kissed his cheek. "Yes, and it's the most wonderful feeling ever. Do you want to hold her?"

"Yes, of course. You just seem so at ease when she's in your arms, and I don't want to take that from you."

I giggled. "You are so funny! Well, I guess I can give her to her Daddy for a couple of minutes, but *I* am watching the clock."

We both laughed at that, then Carson took Elisabeth and began walking her back and forth across the room. I was so proud right then; I couldn't believe how perfect my life was. I just sat there in the moment and watched my husband walking my daughter. I could have stayed in that moment forever.

***

After two days in the hospital, the doctors cleared us to go home. Carson walked beside the nurse who was wheeling me, Elisabeth in my arms, to the parking lot. I could have walked, but I guess that was part of the hospital's policy. Carson went to go get the car, and the nurse checked out the car seat to make sure everything was placed just right. This made me laugh; she obviously didn't know my husband. He was the most meticulous person I knew. He was also very protective of me, so I couldn't even imagine how protective he would be about little Elisabeth.

On the way home from the hospital, I sat in the back seat with her, holding her little hand. I had read stories about the whole postpartum depression thing, but there was no way, I thought, that it was going to happen to me. Yet as we were driving home, as I was looking at my baby, I started crying. Carson glanced back in the rear view mirror, worried, and asked me what was wrong. I just told him that I was so happy, and he smiled at me and let it go at that. But the truth was, I was crying because I was terrified. I was suddenly terrified of everything. God had given me this perfect baby, and I realized how precious life was. Suddenly I started thinking of everything that could happen to her: getting in a car accident, falling from a tree, or being stolen by some terrible person. I'd heard horrible stories about child abduction. And here I was with the most perfect child in the world: why *wouldn't* someone take her? Then I started thinking, *What if she stopped breathing*? I totally became a crazy woman. My head was spinning out of control. How could I protect my baby from the world? It was all so overwhelming!

We finally got home, and I grabbed Elisabeth and walked her into the house, where I sat down in the recliner and just started rocking her. Carson came over and asked me again if I was okay; he said he knew something was going on. That's when I broke down and told him everything. "This may be part of that whole postpartum depression thing," I sobbed, after I told him all my fears.

"Yes, I did some research on that." He sat down on the floor next to me, and put his hand on my leg. "Kathryn, listen. I will never let anything happen to you or Elisabeth. You two are the reason I live, all right? You don't have to worry about anything while I walk this earth. I will protect you both, and you'll both be fine. I promise: nothing is going to happen."

I trusted Carson with all my heart, and I think that was all I needed to hear. Oh, I still had the feelings; but Carson brought the fear level down. I knew that he would always be there for both of us.

I got myself together, and realized I had to feed Elisabeth. All of this was so new! When she was done, I asked her if she wanted a tour of her home. I explained to her that we had just moved here, so things were still a little crazy. I walked her back to her room and told her this was her place, but she could sleep in Mommy and Daddy's room anytime she wanted. Carson walked around the house with me; he laughed as I talked to our new daughter as if she could understand everything I was saying.

Bill brought dinner home for us, so Carson and I sat at the table and ate while Bill sat and rocked Elisabeth. He also had the instant bond, grandpa-version; you could tell he was so proud to be her grandfather. As we ate, Carson and I talked idly about how he had to go back to school soon. At one point he asked, almost hopefully, "So, do you want me to go talk to the school about taking some time off, to be here for you and the baby?"

"Absolutely not," I said in a determined voice. "You need to keep going so you don't lose your momentum. I'll be okay. This whole thing is overwhelming now, but in a few days I'll have the hang of it."

He reached over and caressed my face, smiling that heartwarming smile.

My brave words notwithstanding, the next couple of weeks were hard. The baby was up every few hours, and Carson was back in school. Despite his need for rest, he would get up with Elisabeth all the time. He was such a good Dad, and he considered it a privilege to get up with her and take care of her, so that I could get some sleep. I tried to put my foot down; I'd point out that he had school in the morning, so I should be the one to get up with her—but he insisted on getting up. He wanted me to sleep, so that I would be fresh enough in the morning to take it all on while he was in school.

He must have been exhausted, but he never said a word about it.

Soon we settled into a routine, and the first year of little Elisabeth's life seemed to fly by. It wasn't long before Carson was wrapping up his first year of law school, having done very well in all of his classes. At first he was going to continue on to summer school, but he decided to take the summer off, as he really needed a break.

I was looking forward to having some time with him, too: it seemed I was seeing my father and Izzy more often than my husband, because they were always coming down to see Elisabeth. I had never in my life seen my Dad like this before; he loved spending time with her, and he was just this big puddle of goofiness when he held her. Izzy was great with her, too. Apparently, she and Dad were getting really serious, and I was happy for them both.

When the summer finally rolled around, Dad and Izzy offered to take Elisabeth overnight so that Carson and I could get away together alone. I really didn't know how I would respond to being away from my baby overnight, but I also knew that my marriage was very important—and we really hadn't had very much time lately to focus on it.

The Coast

Eventually, Carson and I decided to have Dad and Izzy over to watch baby Elisabeth. We planned out a night at the coast, since we both loved the ocean. It was a fairly long drive to get there, but that would give us sometime to talk during the car ride. Dad and Izzy came to our house to pick up Elisabeth, which was great, because we didn't have to backtrack. Carson and I left right when they got there, so I didn't have time to freak out about not having the baby in the house.

The car ride to the coast was nice. We talked about school a little, but of course like all parents, most of our conversation was about our child. The hotel we were staying at had a spa, and Carson surprised me by booking a couples massage. It was so nice, lying there together getting the tension rubbed out of our bodies; it was a great way to start our little trip. Carson knew that I would be stressed out about leaving the baby, so he thought he'd do something to calm me down right off the bat.

We followed the massage up with a very romantic dinner at a restaurant that sat right on the beach. We ate outside, and listened to the ocean. As we were sitting back with a glass of wine, Carson asked quietly, "So, Kat…when are you going to give me a son?"

That question totally caught me off guard. I couldn't believe he was thinking about having another baby right now; Elisabeth was only a year old, and he still had two years of school left. After that, he was going to be working long hours with his Dad getting his career off the ground. "I don't think this is a good time to talk about having another baby," I told him honestly. "I think we should talk about it more after you graduate law school, all right?"

He flashed me a grin. "I just love being a father."

I knew that Carson wanted a lot of children, and I think he figured that if he was going to have a family of the size he wanted, we had to keep going.

"We agreed we'd have four children, at most," I reminded him.

"I know. But it would be nice if they were kind of close in age."

We came to an agreement that we would neither try nor prevent anything right then; we would let whatever happened happen. That was an arrangement we could both live with.

After dinner, we took a moonlight walk on the beach. It was a beautiful night, and I loved the feel of the ocean breeze caressing my bare skin. The sound of the waves crashing down on the sand was so peaceful, and the moon made a perfect reflection off the ocean water. We found some huge rocks on the ocean edge, and climbed up on them. I sat in between Carson's legs, and he wrapped his big arms around my body. I felt so safe and protected that way. After sitting there for a while and stealing kisses here and there, we decided to head back to our room. After I changed into my pajamas, Carson picked me up and kissed me, as I wrapped my legs around his waist. He still could take my breath away.

It was a perfect night, just being there with Carson.

We both woke up early the next morning, eager to get back home to our baby. After breakfast and a quick walk on the beach, we started on our long car ride home. I called Dad on the way, and he said he would bring the baby home, again so we wouldn't have to backtrack. When we pulled up to the house, Dad's car was already in the driveway. I could barely wait for Carson to stop the car to leap out and go get my baby.

Dad did a good job taking care of my baby, though I'm sure Izzy had a lot to do with that. Elisabeth was dressed in the clothes I'd left for her; her dark hair was in a little bow. She seemed very content. It was a nice feeling, knowing that we could leave her with her grandpa and everything would be all right. I should have known it would be fine; the man raised me on his own, after all, and I turned out okay. I asked them to stay for dinner, but they were anxious to get home. I'm sure they were ready for some alone time themselves, after their two days of caring for Elisabeth.

The next month was hard on all of us. Carson was getting ready to start his second year of law school, and Elisabeth was at the age where she was getting into everything. I was constantly running around after her, trying to keep her out of drawers and cabinets and out from under furniture. Poor Bill was working like crazy. He would joke with Carson and tell him that he didn't have to worry about finding work, that he had plenty for Carson to do—and the truth was, Carson could have worked with his Dad right then, doing some minor things around the office. But thank goodness, Bill never asked. Carson had so much on his plate with his own family and school that I think working would have done him in for sure.

On top of everything else, I started to get that sick feeling again—the one I'd experienced almost two years ago. I couldn't believe it, but I was sure I was pregnant again. This time I decided I wasn't going to go to the doctor; I would just go get one of those home testing kits and find out myself. Sure enough, when I took the test, I had two lines show up. I sat in the bathroom and just stared at the little stick. I knew Carson would be ecstatic over the news, but I wasn't sure how I felt about it. We had so much going on right now that I couldn't imagine having another baby. Then I decided that what's done was done, and I'd better get excited about it, because I was having another baby, no matter what.

I tracked my last period, and then sat there in disbelief for a minute. I was pretty sure I'd conceived on our little get-away trip to the coast. "Carson will be so proud of himself!" I muttered. He was the one who had been talking about wanting another baby on the trip…and it looked like we'd made that happen.

I called Carson on his cell phone and asked him if he wanted to go out tonight for an early birthday dinner. His birthday was in a couple of weeks, and I thought this would be the perfect present for him. I knew I couldn't keep it from him for another two weeks, so we would just have to celebrate early. He asked, "Why tonight?"

"Because your birthday present came early, and I can't wait to give it to you," I said in a sultry voice.

"Well, count me in!" He seemed amused by the whole thing, and agreed to dinner.

"Just the two of us," I said.

"I'll call Dad and see if he can watch Elisabeth," he replied eagerly.

I got off the phone and started getting everything ready for our date. Grinning, I took a little box and put the pregnancy test in it, then wrapped it all up in birthday paper. I had Elisabeth all bathed and in pajamas before everyone got home. After hopping in the shower, I slipped into a little dress and artfully applied some makeup to disguise the pale green tint to my skin, which had come along with the pregnancy.

The guys got home right about the same time, and I told Bill all about Elisabeth's nightly itinerary. Carson came over and gave me a kiss immediately after getting home…then took one look at me and asked if I was *sure* I wanted to go out. "You look like you may be getting sick," he said, still completely without a clue. I told him I was fine and I didn't know what he was talking about.

The great thing about men is that when it comes to the way we look, they never really want to get too into it. So when I told him I was fine, he totally dropped the subject. Carson went in the bedroom and changed, and then we were off.

We drove to one of our favorite little restaurants, the perfect place to give him the news. It was a dark little Italian place with dripping red candles in Chablis bottles on every table. We sat down and ordered drinks, and Carson looked at me, a little confused, when I ordered water instead of my usual glass of wine. I told him it was because I wanted him to have as many glasses of wine as he wanted, so I would stick with water and drive us home.

After we ordered our food, I pulled the little box out of my purse. "Happy birthday, baby!" I said cheerfully, as I handed him the box. He looked at it curiously; I'm sure he was wondering what I'd gotten him that could possibly fit in such a tiny box. He opened the box and, arching an eyebrow in confusion, pulled out the little test stick. He looked at it, looked back at me, looked at it again…then dropped it on the table and flew from his chair, kneeling on the ground next to me.

He kept saying, "Really?" and I kept nodding my head yes. He grabbed my hand and then leaned up and kissed my lips. Tears standing in his eyes, he said, "This is the best birthday present I've ever gotten."

I was happy to see him so excited, and it was his reaction that made me really excited about this baby. We didn't really eat much that evening; we called my Dad while we were still at the restaurant and gave him the good news. He was very excited, and asked me to try for a boy this time. We all started laughing at that, and I told him I would try. Carson had to call his father, too, even though we would see him when we got home. Bill was also ecstatic. Everyone was on board, and in about eight months there would be another addition to our little family.

This pregnancy was just as tiring as the first, and this time, there was no time to sleep! I was kept busy running after Elisabeth. Carson was well into his second year of law school, so he was constantly busy, but otherwise everything seemed to be going pretty smoothly. I kept up on all my doctor appointments; the baby was healthy and quite the mover, much more active than Elisabeth ever was. It made me worried about how active it would be.

When Carson and I went in for the five month appointment, we found out we were having a boy. "Perfect!" I joked. "One boy, one girl! We have all we need!"

He laughed and kissed me on the cheek. "You promised me at least four. I'm going to hold you to that."

We decided to name the baby Dylan James; James was Carson's and his Dad's middle name. We had to keep the family name traditions going!

The full nine months went by more quickly than I expected, probably because we were so busy. Fortunately, everything came together right in time. As my due date approached, the baby's room was done, my bag was packed, and Elisabeth's bag was packed. We decided that it would be best if Elisabeth, who was almost two by then, stayed with Dad at our house. Izzy and Dad would drive down when I went into labor, and would take care of Elisabeth for the couple of days that I would be in the hospital.

I went into labor in the middle of the night a couple of days before my due date; and this time things went smoothly, because I knew what to expect. Dylan James Ferris entered this world just a few hours after I started labor. It only took me just two pushes this time, and he was out. Carson joked and said that I was a pro at this now. He was so good with his son; he walked him around so proudly, and showed him to just about everyone in the hospital. I couldn't have asked for a better husband and father for my children. With my two kids and Carson lying in bed with me in the hospital, I thought, *Life can't get much better than this.*

The next few years went by surprisingly quickly. Carson finished law school and easily passed the state bar, and soon he was working long hours at the firm—but it wasn't nearly as bad as law school, thank goodness! As for me, I was kept busy running around after my two children. Elisabeth eventually started preschool, which was nice, so I had a couple of hours with Dylan by myself. I would usually take advantage of that time to clean the house or go grocery shopping. Not a second of my day wasn't filled with something to do.

It was crazy, but I loved it.

Three

Carson groaned and let his head fall back against the headrest of the couch. "I need a vacation!"

It was the first time in a while that we'd had time to ourselves; we had just sent the kids off to bed, and were snuggling with each other on the living room couch. Five minutes after Carson made his pronouncement, I was online looking over the possibilities: in particular, places with beautiful beaches where we could just go sit in the sun with the kids for a couple of days. The place that grabbed my attention the most was Cancun. When I was surfing around the Web, looking at all the stuff to do around Cancun, I somehow ended up on a site chronicling the poverty of that region of Mexico. It turned out that a lot of children there were unable to go to school, because they had to start working to help support their families at a very young age.

Then I found the website of a children's home in the Cancun area. The home was called La Casita, and it housed about 60 children who were orphans or had been removed from abusive situations. They were in desperate need of so many things, and were practically begging for items that my family took for granted everyday. I'd never thought that the Band-Aid I applied when Elisabeth fell and scraped her knee could be considered a luxury! These children not only didn't have Band-Aids, they didn't have enough shampoo or soap to clean their injuries with. They needed so much—and I decided that *this* was where we were going, and we were going to help.

I showed Carson the site and said, simply, "We have to help."

He smiled at me. "Of course we do. You remind me of Mom." And he was right: the elder Elisabeth would see something that pulled on her heartstrings, and she was off immediately, making a change.

"So…when can you get away? Because I want to book this trip as soon as possible."

He shrugged. "Pick a date, and I'll make it work. I'm so busy that if you leave it up to me, we'll never get away. If you book it, I'll have to take the time off."

I looked at the local weather and considered the best time to visit, and finally decided that we would go in January. It's always so gray and rainy in Sacramento at that time of the year, so I thought it would be great to get away to some sunny weather. Plus, that gave me four months to raise funds and get things prepared for my little project. Carson said that he would write up a letter about what we were doing, and send it to everyone involved with the firm. He would also talk about it in the office. "You'll be surprised at how many people will donate money," he told me. "A lot of our clients and associates are pretty wealthy, and they're always looking for charities to donate to for a tax write-off."

That seemed a little cynical, but I realized that it was reality; and the money would do a lot of good for these poor kids. So I started to make a list of everything I wanted to ship there, so it would be there when we arrived; and as promised, Carson typed up a letter and circulated it around the office. Money started to pour in to help with our little project. Every time I went shopping, I'd pick up items for the children. When I was at places like Target or Wal-Mart, I would grab a ton of crayons and coloring books, along with shampoo, body wash, Band-Aids, and Children's Tylenol. I also picked up all sorts of little toys for the children, along with various sizes of kid's clothes and shoes, diapers and diaper rash medicine, and anything I could think of. The children's home needed everything, so I was *buying* everything.

When I got home, I'd store the items in huge shipping boxes that I stacked up in corner of the living room. It gave me a really good feeling when I would look at those boxes, and think about how many people we were going to help.

When I had a nice supply ready, I contacted the children's home and told them that some big boxes would soon arrive there, full of the supplies that they had listed on their website. I also asked them if, one night when we were there, we could take all the kids out for a special dinner. During my web-surfing, I'd located a pizza place a couple of blocks from the home. The people who ran the home said that this would be fine, so I called the restaurant to ask if we could rent the place one of the nights we were there. They were delighted to accommodate us, so I booked it immediately and sent them a deposit.

It was all coming together perfectly, and the trip was getting close. Ultimately, I shipped 68 boxes of supplies in the weeks immediately before our trip. I imagined that the people who ran the house would be surprised when all those boxes started showing up at their doorstep; they probably thought I was going to only send a few boxes at best. Admittedly, I may have gone over the top just a little, but I had such a feeling of hope, peace, and happiness when I was doing things for the orphans.

I figured that once I'd started this, there would be no stopping me; I was sure that once we got home from this trip, I was going to be on the computer looking for my next project. I was so fortunate that I didn't have to work, and had all that I needed and more. This was going to be my new job...so I guess I was kind of following in Elisabeth's footsteps. They *were* wonderful footsteps to follow in, after all.

Meanwhile, Carson was arranging for his co-workers to take over some of his work while we were gone, and I was packing for all four of us. It took me a week to get everything together for us to go. This was the first time we'd traveled any great distance with the children, and it was turning out to be somewhat difficult—and we hadn't even left yet. Before we left, I called the children's home and asked them if the stuff had arrived yet— and they said it had. They seemed overwhelmed to have received so many boxes, and they kept thanking me over and over. I couldn't wait to get there to see the children dressed in the clothes, and playing with, and using the things we had sent them!

When Carson came home from his last day of work for two weeks, he immediately hit the couch; he looked so tired. I danced up to him and said, "So, sweetie, are you excited to be on vacation?"

He grabbed me and pulled me onto his lap, snuggling his nose in my neck. "You have no idea how badly I need to get away," he mumbled.

"Well, don't get too excited. Vacationing with Dylan and Elisabeth may be harder than you think." I winked. "And don't expect to get another baby nine months after *this* vacation, dear."

"It could happen. You still owe me two." He grinned.

"We'll see," I said, and quickly changed the subject. I told him that the boxes had arrived at La Casita over the past few days, and that the lady on the other end of the phone sounded so happy to have it all.

He looked happy as he replied, "I can't wait to go down and finally see all of this come together!"

"You and me both." I got up and made a quick dinner, while the kids attacked their father, crawling all over him as he tried to watched a ballgame on TV. This was Carson's favorite time of the day; he loved rolling around and wrestling around with Dylan and Elisabeth, because it relieved his tension from work. It was great for me, too; the kids needed me non-stop all day, but when Daddy got home, they wanted nothing to do with me. That was fine. I was grinning as I cooked dinner and heard the three of them playing and laughing. When I called for them to come eat, Carson came into the kitchen with Dylan on his hip and Elisabeth strapped to his leg. I wish I'd had a camera right then! After I'd organized the chaos a little, we sat and had a nice family dinner—an event that didn't happen much anymore, because Carson was always so late getting home.

It wasn't long before we were all in bed, since we had a seven o'clock flight the next day.

We woke up very early that next morning, and frantically ran around the house throwing things in the car. The real fun began when we parked in long-term parking at the airport and started packing the shuttle full of our stuff to take us to the terminal…and it just went on from there. Thank goodness there were two adults, because Carson was able to check us all in while I ran around the airport after the kids. Traveling had definitely changed from the sedate boredom of just me and Carson. All I cared about, from the point we entered the terminal, was getting the kids locked into their seats on the plane. We somehow made it through security; I think the officer let us slip by because he felt so sorry for us, having to deal with these energetic children in a busy airport.

We had a hour before our flight took off, so we went and got the kids breakfast, after which we let them run around and get some energy out. Right before we got on the plane, I gave both kids some medicine that my doctor had prescribed. I was so worried about their ears and the long flight, so the doctor recommended the drug; he said it would make the trip easier on them. We boarded the plane and put both Dylan and Elisabeth in their car seats on the seats, because I'd heard that would make them comfortable, since they were in a familiar place. It was all very exciting and interesting to them, but within an hour they were fast asleep. That medicine worked perfectly; now I just needed them to sleep another six hours. It was wishful thinking, but I'd be happy with whatever time I got.

The kids slept for about four hours, and it was wonderful. They woke up starving, of course; thank goodness I'd packed some snacks for them. They also served lunch on the plane while they were sleeping. I asked the stewardess if she could hold theirs for them till when they woke up, and she was fine with that; so when they awoke, she brought the kids out their lunch. Feeding them took another hour; and suddenly, we only had one more hour left till we were there. I kept the kids busy for the rest of the time by reading to them.

When we walked off the plane in Mexico, the humidity slapped us right in the face. It was really hot, too—but it felt great to feel the sun.

We took a cab to our hotel and got everything unpacked and situated. Carson wanted to go to the pool before we went out for dinner…and it was exquisite. The hotel we'd booked was an exclusive resort, and the pool basically sat right on the ocean. I took my book out to the pool while Carson swam around with the kids. Soon, I could see his face start to calm down; he was always very calm and soft-spoken with me, of course, but I could tell by his expression that he was really stressed out at work. Now, the constant stressed look in his face was gone. He was laughing and throwing the kids around and having a grand old time.

The next day, we made a trip to the children's home. When we pulled up, I couldn't imagine sixty children living in that house; it simply seemed too small! The owner of the facility came out immediately, and walked right up to me and gave me a hug. There was a huge language barrier, of course, but I could tell by her actions that we were very welcome there. When we walked into the house, I saw the things that I had sent all over the place, being used as they should be. The small tables were covered with crayons and coloring books, and I saw a number of the children wearing the clothes I had bought. It was wonderful, knowing I'd helped them in some small way!

And the children seemed happy. A child's spirit is so resilient; they don't need much, just a few toys and a lot of imagination, and they're content. These kids were full of laughter and play, and my own children took right to them. I remembered having felt sorry for these kids when I was back home; I'd thought about all that my children had, and felt bad that these children didn't have those things, so I was shocked at how content and well-adjusted these kids were anyway. I imagined that it was because they didn't know what they didn't have…and I suppose that's a good thing. They had all they needed.

I talked to Maria, the woman who ran the house, mostly through a translator: the multitalented Carson. He knew some Spanish from college; he wasn't fluent, but it was good enough. She told me that the children had some education; in addition to public school, they had a teacher who came to the house occasionally to teach the children basic skills. During the ensuing tour, I went into all the rooms where the children slept. In some cases, there were ten children in a room, split by age and gender. When I walked into one room, I found a little girl sitting on the end of her bed reading a book. She was such a gorgeous little thing, about five years old with beautiful long, curly brown hair and enormous brown eyes. When we walked into the room, she looked up and smiled at us. She had an exquisite smile, but her eyes seemed sad.

"What a beautiful little girl! What's her story?" I asked Maria. She told me that the little girl's mother had passed away, and her father was never around for her. Her grandmother had raised her until she was four; then her grandmother got sick and couldn't care for her anymore. Maria said she had a very kind heart. She pointed out that a lot of the kids didn't know what they were missing with family, because they'd been in the home since they were very young, and didn't know the difference. But this child was an exception: her grandmother had been good to her and loved her deeply, so she missed having that kind of loving family life. Maria said she spent a lot of time alone; and when I asked her what was the girl's chances were of finding a home, Maria told me the chances were pretty slim, because she was older than most of their residents.

I walked over to the little girl and introduced myself, sitting down on the bed next to her. She told me her name was Selena, and asked if I was the one who had sent all the stuff in the boxes. I told her I was. "You must be a very nice person," she said, regarding me with her big brown eyes.

"I try to be," I told her.

Selena smiled faintly, and her eyes tracked Carson while he followed our children as they ran around, shrieking with joy with their newfound friends. "That is your family?" she asked quietly.

"Yes."

The expression on her face made my heart thump; she seemed sad and happy at once, and I imagined that she was probably remembering how things had been when she'd had her own family. She probably wished for someone just to hug her, or kiss her on her forehead when she was sad. She probably wished she had a Mom and Dad to call her own. But she didn't: she was little girl alone in this big world.

I hugged Selena impulsively. I couldn't accept this as her reality.

We spent all day at the home. My kids played tirelessly with all of the other kids (I guess language isn't a barrier when you're tiny), and I read stories to them. Of course, language was definitely a barrier there. Most of the time, they would just stare at me, not understanding what I was saying, laughing at me occasionally; Maria said it was because they thought I sounded funny. Carson sat on the carpet and built things with Lego's and blocks with some of the little boys, and later, we all went into the yard and kicked a soccer ball around. Maria said that was one of their favorite things. The kids squabbled cheerfully over the ball, and they seemed to be having a good time.

After I'd worn myself out, I sat on a bench with Carson and talked about the children. "I can't get little Selena's story off my mind," I told him.

He looked at me knowingly. "So, what are you planning?"

"I don't know yet."

Later, we took the kids on their big night out. With the help of Maria and her friend, we managed to walk the whole gaggle of kids over to the nearby pizza place, and let them order whatever they wanted. Selena came and sat next to me at the table, constantly looking up at me and smiling. There was something so special about this little girl…she had such a beautiful spirit, and it just radiated off her. Carson kept looking at me, noticing how much attention I was giving her, and he looked at her and smiled a lot.

After dinner (and dessert, of course), we walked the children back home. I helped Maria get all the kids into their pajamas and their teeth brushed—somehow—and I decided that Maria was a very special woman for dedicating her life to something like this. When all the kids were cleaned up, I went up to say goodbye to Selena. I walked over to her bed and waved goodbye to her; we couldn't talk without Maria, so I thought gestures would be best. She looked at me with those big, sad brown eyes and waved back at me.

I gave her a hug and left before I started to cry.

It was so hard leaving La Casita. It was such a fantastic place, so full of love and children's laughter, and my heart ached as the taxi pulled away. Dylan and Elisabeth were happy and exhausted, and fell asleep on the taxi ride back to the resort. Carson just looked at me, knowing that something was coming; I was silent most of the way back to the hotel. He kept asking me if I was okay, and I kept telling him, "I'm fine." I was just reflecting on all that had happened that day, and it was a little overwhelming.

Finally, when we were almost back to our hotel, I asked him, "What does it take to adopt a child from Mexico?"

He grinned. "I've been waiting for that question, Kat. So…do you want to adopt *all* the children in the house?"

I laughed. "I'd love to, but I know I can't do that." I sighed, then looked down at my sleeping children. When I looked back up at my husband, my eyes were swimming with tears. "I want to take Selena home with me, Carson. I want to give her a family. We have so much to give, and I want to make her a part of our lives."

He didn't argue; Carson never did when I was serious about something. He made sure I got everything I wanted, and he knew this was very important to me. "I'll look into it," he vowed, "and see what's required legally." He looked at me solemnly and said, "You know, a lot goes into adoption, especially from another country."

"Is this…something you would like to do, too?" I asked hesitantly.

He smiled at me, in that special way that had made me fall in love with him in the first place. "Kat, if it'll make you happy, then of course it's something I'd want to do."

The rest of our trip was just as wonderful. When we weren't lying on the beach luxuriating in the warm sun or swimming in the lovely turquoise waters, we were enjoying excursions here and there; though most of our time was spent just relaxing. There was a camp at the resort that had a ton of activities for kids, which Elisabeth and Dylan loved, so Carson and I had plenty of alone time. I went back to the children's home a couple of times to see the children, and talked to Maria about Selena. Specifically, I asked her if there was a way that she could start attending a private school there, and I told Maria I would pay for the whole thing. I outlined what we were going to try to do—that we wanted Selena to start learning English right away, as we wanted to adopt her.

Carson stole a little time from our vacation, doing a little research and talking to an adoption agency while we were still in Mexico. We got all the necessary paperwork, and discussed how we would go about the legal process. It was fortunate that Carson was an attorney. Even if he didn't personally handle things like this, he knew lawyers who could handle the process for us.

The following year was a busy one; it seemed like that had always been the case since Carson and I had gotten married. Carson, as usual, was insanely busy; one of the perks of being one of the best at what you do, I suppose. Elisabeth was in kindergarten and Dylan was in the preschool program, so I had a little time to get things done around the house and work on Selena's adoption process. We finally got the okay for the whole thing almost a year to the day after our Cancun vacation. I talked to Maria regularly about Selena's progress, and was assured she was attending the private school and was loving it. I'd also hired a lady to come in and start tutoring her in English. I knew the whole process would be overwhelming for her, moving to a new country and adjusting to our family, and I wanted to remove the language barrier as much as possible.

One day, Carson came home from work and told me, "I have great news!" He put a huge stack of papers on the kitchen table and said happily, "The adoption agency has okayed everything! We can go pick up Selena sometime next month!"

I was beyond thrilled, and decided that when we went to get her, I'd book a week at the same resort we'd gone to the year before. That way, we could all have some family time together. There would be a lot going on when we got home: Selena and Elisabeth would be in first grade, and Dylan would be in kindergarten. I would have three children in school! My life was really going to change.

When Carson got the okay, I booked our trip to Cancun. While I was waiting for the day to come, I picked up more stuff for the children at La Casita.

When we arrived in Cancun, we went straight to the adoption agency to take care of the final paperwork. I was glad my husband was an attorney and knew how to handle all of this; just looking at all the forms would have driven me crazy. After we were done there, Maria brought Selena to the agency, and I went outside to meet them.

Selena had one little tote with her, which saddened me; I couldn't believe this little girl could fit all of her worldly possessions in one bag! It showed me just how spoiled my own children were. I walked up to Selena, not making any sudden movements; I wasn't sure how she was feeling. I knelt down to her level and said quietly, "Hello, Selena, it's so good to see you again. I was wondering if you would like to come home with us? We would love for you to be part of our family."

She started smiling, which I thought was a good sign; and when I opened my arms, she jumped right into them. I knelt there with her in my arms for a long moment, feeling an instant bond develop. This was my child now; our lives were intertwined forever. After holding her for a couple of minutes, I stood up; and, wiping tears from my eyes, I told Maria I had some things for the children in the taxi. I grabbed Selena's hand and walked over to the taxi driver, and had him load the boxes into Maria's car. Then we said our goodbyes to Maria. She gave Selena a big hug and told her something in Spanish; then, not looking back, she got in her car and left.

"What did she say, sweetheart?" I asked Selena.

In very good English, the little girl replied, "She told me to call her and let her know how I am in a while." Selena had learned so much since the last time I'd seen her; it's amazing how fast kids can learn.

We went inside the agency to finish up, then headed to the resort. I told Selena that we were going to stay there for a couple of days before we went home, so she could get used to everyone. It was incredible to see all our children interact. Both Elisabeth and Dylan took to her like they'd known her for years. Elisabeth in particular kept asking Selena a ton of questions, like any five-year-old would. Selena was very good about answering most of them. We all had an excellent time, swimming together and walking the beach.

At the airport as we were getting ready to leave, Selena shyly told us that she had never been on an airplane before. Carson replied, "Then you have to have a window seat, so you can watch the plane take off! Don't worry, I'll sit with you so you won't be scared." Carson was also getting very close to our new daughter; he was such a kind man, and it was obvious. Selena took to him quickly, as I knew she would.

When we got back home, we learned what busy really was. Dad and Izzy came down to meet their new grandchild; by this point, all my children were calling Izzy Grandma, and she was really good to them. We had very few problems adjusting to the changes in our lives, because Selena fit into the family like a glove. It was like we had always had her with us, and soon, I couldn't imagine life without her.

It wasn't long before the girls started school. Because I didn't want to have to deal with the school's bilingual program, I had Selena tutored privately in English; but in truth, she was already more or less fluent, so I was soon able to dispense with the tutor. When she wasn't studying, Selena and I got her room all decorated the way she wanted, and filled her closet with clothes.

Everything was working out perfectly. The house, which had felt so huge when we'd purchased it, was comfortably filling up with family. My time was filled with taking care of our children and the household; in my spare time, which was sparse, Carson and I did some charity work together. We were especially involved in charity events for a local organization that housed women and children involved in domestic violence. That felt especially wonderful to me, because Elisabeth had done charity work for the same shelter when she was alive. I knew now why Elisabeth had done so much for the community: it felt so good to give time to people who were in need.

We taught our children to give back as well. At Christmas time, we would adopt a family and bring in Christmas dinner and put presents under their tree. We also volunteered at the food closet on Thanksgiving, serving the homeless Thanksgiving dinner. I loved every minute of it, and I wanted my children to be loving and giving people. I wanted them to realize just how lucky we really were. I wanted them to be thankful for all we had.

I truly felt like I had the perfect life. I had three beautiful children. I was married to the kindest, most loving man alive. We were on top of the world.

Change

Several quiet years passed, almost without us noticing; we were too busy living our lives. All the kids were doing well in school, which was nice, because I was able to have sometime to myself. Carson, of course, was still working long hours; it seemed that he was never at home. He was stressed out most of the time, too, and the past years had really taken a toll on him. I tried to talk him into not working so hard, but he only wanted the best for us, and there was a constant call for the firm's services. I talked to his father more than once about hiring another partner to take some of the pressure off of them. Bill was getting ready to retire, and I knew that there was no way Carson could handle running the firm all on his own.

Over the course of several months, Carson fell several times for no apparent reason; it seemed that he was sometimes unbalanced. He also began to be irritated by things that had never bothered him before. I suspected that it was because he was under so much stress, and wasn't taking care of himself as he should. I again pointed this out to Bill, more forcefully than before, and he agreed that it *was* time to hire someone to take some of the pressure off them. Carson, of course, was a little irritated that his Dad and I thought he couldn't handle things.

One night I sat down with Carson and we talked about all that was going on. "Look here, pal," I said firmly, "There's a lot happening with the kids now. I know you want us to have everything we'll ever need, but you know what? You're one of the most successful men in your field, and I need more help around here, okay?" I really didn't, but I *wanted* him around—and I knew that if Carson thought he was helping me, he would be happier with the decision to step back a little at work.

He looked at me stoically, and I reached out and caressed his cheek. "Carson, let's cut to the chase. The kids and I miss you, and we want you home more."

"Well," he said thoughtfully, "There *is* a big stack of resumes on my desk from lawyers wanting a position with the firm."

"So hire some new people."

"Okay," he surrendered. "Dad and I will start interviewing some people next week."

Since that had been so easily taken care of, I pushed on. "Now: we need to talk about your balance issues."

"Stress-related," he said curtly.

"I think so too. I *hope* so. But you need to check with the doctor to be sure, mister."

He just sighed and agreed. Have I mentioned how smart my husband is? The next day I called our family physician and made an appointment, at a time when I could go with him. I was sure everything was fine—but if it wasn't, then I was afraid Carson might not tell me, not wanting me to be concerned. That's why I made sure I would be there: to hear everything firsthand.

On the day of the appointment, I dropped the kids off at school and then went to pick up Carson. We saw Doctor Creswell and told him about the balance issues. He suspected that it could be vertigo or an inner ear infection, but when he checked Carson's ears, they were fine.

As a preliminary step, the doctor wrote Carson a prescription for a medication to help his balance. "If this doesn't work," he said, as he handed me the prescription, "come back and see me, and we can do some testing."

I dropped Carson back off at work, then went and picked up his prescriptions before getting the kids. I tried to stay strong, ignoring the insistent thoughts at the back of my mind, but that unsettling feeling wouldn't leave me alone. I couldn't stop thinking about his mother, the elder Elisabeth, and how she'd had moved around so uncontrollably in the later stages of her illness. Her Huntington's symptoms had first manifested in a loss of balance and fine motor control... and I knew that Carson had a 50 percent chance of inheriting the disease.

Suddenly, a feeling of sheer terror welled up inside of me. Fighting to maintain control, I took the kids in the house and got them situated—and then I went online and started looking up information on Huntington's disease. I knew what I'd seen in Elisabeth, but I'd never really done too much research on the subject. Maybe it was a form of denial. Carson never talked about it either, probably because he didn't want me to worry about him possibly being diagnosed with it someday.

I found a huge number of websites regarding Huntington's: for a disease that most people had never heard of, there was a lot of information on it. The first one I opened was the Huntington's Disease Society of America website, because I figured that would be the right place to find correct information on the disease. The site laid it all out in stark, terrifying terms to me, explaining that Huntington's was an inherited neurodegenerative disease, most noticeable in middle-age people. It's caused by a higher repeat count in a protein called huntingtin that causes damage to parts of the brain. Apparently, there was a lot of research being done on different drugs and procedures to treat Huntington's—but there was no cure yet.

I was able to read about only a few of the symptoms of the disease before I gave up, because the thought of my Carson having this awful disease was more than I could handle. Those symptoms included mood changes, and I desperately told myself that I shouldn't read too much into that. Carson was under so much stress right now, what with work and family, and that would cause anyone to be moody. Sure, he'd always been a very laid back, go-with-the-flow type of guy, but he'd also never had as much to deal with as he had at the moment. I fervently hoped that once he pulled back from work, all this would calm down.

When I could look again, I read about the erratic movements that the disease caused in its advanced stages. That was called chorea, and it had terribly afflicted Carson's mother.

After Carson got home from work that night, I watched his every move like a hawk. I felt bad, because I thought I shouldn't be acting like this; but after everything that had happened that day, I couldn't help but to be very worried. We all sat down for dinner, and everyone talked about their days. Carson looked at me and smiled, because the girls were going on and on about kids we didn't know. Dylan talked about soccer, mostly, trying his best to get a word in over the girls.

After dinner the girls went upstairs to the play room, which was now more like a homework room. Dylan went and sat on his Dad's lap, and they watched a basketball game together while I cleaned up the kitchen. I couldn't stop worrying about Carson; my head would not shut up, so I decided when the kids went to bed, I would sit down with him and talk about all that was on my mind. It was a conversation neither of us had ever wanted to have—but we had to find out what was going on with him as soon as we could.

When I went and sat in the living room with the boys, Carson looked at me and said quietly, "Dad and I think we've found someone who we think will work well with the two of us. If everything goes well, we plan to hire him at the end of the week."

"That's great!" I was truly glad, because whether there was something truly wrong or his symptoms were just stress-related, Carson needed relief from some of the pressure at work.

When the game was over, I took Dylan upstairs and gave him a bath, and made the girls shower; when everyone was clean, Carson and I put all the kids in bed. As we left the girls' room, I told him I needed to talk to him about something that was on my mind, and he immediately grew somber. We went straight to our bedroom and crawled into bed, whereupon I demanded, "Honey, tell me the truth. How do you feel? Is there anything going on with your body? You're not yourself lately."

He sighed. "I'm just stressed, Kat. I think that's why I'm so tired and irritable."

"And what about your balance?"

"The doctor's on it," he said, sounding a little annoyed.

"Right. Well, I was online today, and I looked up some stuff that made me nervous."

He looked at me sharply, and I could tell that he knew exactly what I was talking about. "You know, they can test to see if you have Huntington's," I said gently. "It's a simple blood test. We could put this to rest once and for all."

"I know." He turned over on his back and looked at the ceiling. "I know I'll have to do it eventually…I'm just not sure if I'm ready to know. Shit, Kat, I'm not even 30!" He sounded very upset, and I reached out and caressed his cheek. He looked at me, his beautiful eyes hooded. "Do *you* want to know?"

"I really don't know," I told him truthfully. If he did end up with Huntington's, there wasn't much they could do for him anyway; and how would he feel, trying to move forward under what was essentially a death penalty? It didn't seem to make much sense to find out if there was nothing that could be done.

"Well," he said, "there are certain things I need to get in order before I find out."

I assumed he meant insurance-related stuff. "I know. I was just curious about whether you ever thought about it."

"I think about it all the time," he admitted, which surprised me. He never talked to me about it; I had no clue that this was on my husband's mind.

"Why didn't you ever tell me?" I asked, propping myself up on one elbow and glaring at him.

"Hah! I think about it enough for both of us. I don't want you to worry, so I never bring it up."

I smacked him on the arm. "You nitwit! I'm your wife, and you should never have to feel alone! You need to talk about this stuff with me." My eyes filled up with tears. "Carson, I would rather be standing next to you worrying than be in the dark, protected from reality!"

"I'm sorry, Kat." He was quiet for a long moment, then said, "To be honest, finding out the answer is just too much for me right now. Right now, when I feel something coming on, I have a lot of excuses for whatever's happening. If I knew I had Huntington's, then whenever anything happened, I would be worried it was because of the disease."

"Carson, still—"

Uncharacteristically, he interrupted me. "Kat, I watched my Mother progress with the disease, so if I *knew* that I had it, I would feel like a ticking time bomb—ready to explode at any minute! If I don't know for sure, I can act like its not there! I'm, I'm afraid if I find out for certain, I'll just go through life waiting around to die— and I don't want to think like that!"

He was getting worked up now, and I hated to wind him up more, but I had to know. "Carson, what will you do if the medication doesn't help your balance?"

"When work calms down and the medication has time to work, if there's no change, then I'll think strongly about getting tested." He turned his head to look at me, his eyes blazing. "For now we won't think about it."

So we didn't.

The next couple of months were much better, actually. Carson spent a lot more time at home, and it was nice having him around. He decided he would coach the girls' soccer team, something he could never do before because he was so busy at work. Meanwhile, Dylan started playing Peewee football; so with all three children involved in school and sports, we were always running around. I felt like we were never home; it was constant driving, here and there. I would joke with Carson often, asking him, "So, do you *really* want six kids?"

He would laugh and reply, "Your magic number of three is perfect."

"Oh? I thought my magic number was four?"

"Nope. Three is perfect. You were right, dear."

"And don't you forget it."

Every night we would sit with the kids and help them with their homework, and true to his nature, Carson was always very patient with them. In any case, the advanced stuff they were learning in school was more or less beyond me; I was glad that one of us had been good at the whole school thing. Me, I stuck with the cooking and cleaning during most of homework time, which I didn't mind at all.

Carson's lightened schedule gave the two of us more couple time, too, which we desperately needed. After the kids were fed, bathed, and put to bed, we would cuddle up and talk about everything. The medication for his balance issues seemed to be helping, so one night Carson told me he was going to stop taking it to see if it was just stress causing the symptoms. "Sounds good," I said.

As we were talking, a small movement caught my attention, and I looked over at Carson's hand. His index finger was twitching. I scooted closer to him and grabbed his hand, and saw that he had this worried look in his eyes like he'd been caught doing something bad. I held his hand perfectly still, and told him in no uncertain terms to hold it still too.

His index finger would not stop moving. "What's going on with your finger, Carson?" I asked, my heart filled with dread.

He closed his eyes for a long moment, then opened them and said, "It's been happening now and then. I, uh, can't control the movement."

"*How long* has this been happening?"

"Awhile." He tried to suppress it, but I knew him too well: there was a flicker of fear in his eyes. "But, hey, it comes and goes—it isn't a constant thing."

Like that made it unimportant.

"Don't you think you should see the doctor about it?" I asked fiercely.

Right then something happened that had never happened before, not in all the years we'd been together: Carson completely lost his temper. He ripped his hand out of mine, jumped off the couch, and started yelling at me. As long as we had been together, and as many confrontations and disagreements Carson and I had participated in, he had *never* yelled at me before.

"You're just trying to make me sick, Kathryn!" he raged. "I can't stand the way you're always watching me, like I'm going to become some kind of twitching wreck! I have enough to deal with—I don't need your crap to deal with too!"

It was a complete out-of-body experience for me; I couldn't believe what was going on. All I could say was, "Carson, I love you! I'm just concerned!"

"I'm *not* one of your children, Kat, so stop treating me like one!"

I stood up and stuck my finger in his face, angrier than I'd ever been in my life. "Carson James Ferris, I would *never* treat you like you're one of my children! I love you, and I'm concerned about your health! Now, I have no idea where this is all coming from, but you'd better stop saying hurtful things to me before you go too far!" That's when I lost it; I started crying uncontrollably, and ran to our bedroom and shut the door. I tried not to slam it, because if the kids weren't already awake, I didn't want to awaken them.

I crawled into bed and buried my face in the pillow, fully expecting Carson to come in and apologize for the way he'd just acted—but he never did. I cried myself to sleep that night, something I never thought I would ever have to do because of Carson. Usually, he was perfect in everyway; I simply couldn't figure out why or how this had happened.

Or maybe I did know, but didn't want to admit it to myself.

The next morning I woke up and started getting the kids ready for school, only to find Carson still asleep on the couch. Unfortunately, the kids saw him too. Little Selena looked at him solemnly and asked, "Why is Daddy sleeping on the couch?"

I smiled brightly and lied. "Oh, Daddy was very tired last night, honey, and he must have fallen asleep watching TV."

I took the kids to school, and when I got home, Carson was sitting at the dining room table. He looked at me, eyes filled with regret.

"Good morning," I said icily.

"Kathryn, I'm so sorry about last night. I don't know why I acted that way, and I feel awful for what I did." He hung his head. "It's just...I've just been feeling so bad lately. Things that have never bothered me before are really starting to get to me. I don't know why. I'm sorry I took it out on you."

I sat down at the table next to him. "Carson, I hope you don't really believe what you said last night. You're my life partner—and I never want you to think I'm treating you as anything but that. Yes, I've noticed that you've been very irritable lately. I said nothing about it, because I know we have a lot going on, and I'm irritable sometimes too. I was just concerned when I saw your finger twitching. I'm sorry if that upset you."

"Don't be sorry for anything, Kat. I was completely out of line last night. I know you're concerned…and after last night, so am I. I sat up all night thinking about what I was going to do." He blew out a huge sigh. "Magical thinking doesn't work, Kathryn. I think it's time to get tested. If I do have Huntington's, there are medications to control my moods. Mom was on antidepressants and anti-anxiety medications, and frankly, before she got on those pills she was very hard to deal with. I never want to act like the way I acted last night again, okay? Especially not around our children. I think it's time to find out for sure."

I got up and sat on Carson's lap. As he wrapped his arms around me and buried his face in the hollow between my neck and shoulder, I told him, "I love you, Carson, and if that's what you want, that's fine. But it has to be something you really feel like you want to know."

He looked up at me and nodded, not saying anything.

"I don't want you to get tested just because of last night," I explained. "Last night might have been something totally different. There are times when I kind of lose it, too. The stress of our household is pretty intense, and that may have been all last night was." I kissed him and continued, "But I also know my husband better than anyone, and the man I saw last night wasn't him."

"I know," he whispered.

"I'll support you in any decision you make. But do me a favor: give yourself a couple of days to weigh out everything, because finding out if you have Huntington's or not is a huge thing. I want you to be fully prepared for the outcome, either way."

He held me tight and said, "Okay. I'll do that. I'll give myself a couple of days to mentally prepare myself for this. But whether I get tested or not is no longer the question, Kat. It's time to find out. That's all."

I laid my head on his shoulder, and we just sat in silence, entwined there at the dining table. I had so much running through my head, and I'm sure he did too; I, for one, was overwhelmed. Among other things, I was seriously wondering if I really wanted to know whether Carson was sick or not. He was right when he said that if we didn't know, we could just go on as normal—and that's what we had been doing for a while now. Finding out about his fate could change our whole lives. How could it not? We had both experienced Elisabeth's final years, and while we didn't begrudge a minute of that time, it had been awful for her. Knowing that Carson might go through that same thing was monumentally scary.

This would change everything, and I wasn't sure if I was ready to take on that battle.

Answers

Carson called the doctor and made an appointment to be tested for Huntington's disease in three weeks' time. That was our agreement: to have three weeks to prepare ourselves. He worked quite a lot during that time frame; I suspect he thought it was all I was thinking about, so he didn't want to be around me too much. Well, if that was what he was thinking, he was right. I was so consumed with the thought of finding out that I had no idea how I would take it if he actually found out he had the disease.

Over the next three weeks, I tried to think "glass half full." Carson had just as much a chance of *not* having the disease as having it, after all; therefore, I could hope that everything would be fine. I thought of how wonderful it would be if the results were negative, and we would never have to think about it again. We could just go on with our busy lives from there, with one less worry, planning our future and growing old together—no longer being frozen in time by that horrendous "what if" factor. I prayed for that outcome every night.

The three weeks seemed to creep by. We kept up the normal schedule of school, soccer, football, and Girl Scouts with the kids, and I had enough going on to fill every moment of my day. Nights were the hardest time. I would lie in bed, thinking of the test and how much it meant. I would watch Carson while he slept. He seemed to be fine; he snored far too loudly these days, but besides that, he slept very quietly and still.

Then the three weeks were up, and I was driving Carson to his appointment. We didn't talk about it on the ride over there. Carson made small talk about the kids and what their schedules were, and I told him which sports were ending and which ones were starting up. Finally, I couldn't take anymore; I looked at him and said, in a no-nonsense tone, "When this is all said and done, we need to get away. Just the two of us." We love taking vacations with the kids, but Carson and I needed some alone time desperately. "I'm going to plan a trip, okay?"

"I think that's a great idea," he said. Then he grinned. "But what will we do with our time if we don't have to take the kids everywhere?"

"That's kind of the point. We're on such rigid schedules that we need sometime to do absolutely nothing."

When we saw the doctor, Carson told him hesitantly that he wanted to be tested for Huntington's disease. Dr. Creswell looked at him for a long moment, with an odd look on his face. "I've never tested anyone for that in all of my years of practice," he said.

"But you know what it is?"

"Of course. But it's a rare disease, and frankly, most family physicians don't come across it too often. So yes, I'll draw the blood for the tests, but we'll have to send it out to a specialist." The doctor hesitated. "You do realize that if the test is positive, I'll have to send you to a neurologist for further treatment?"

Carson just nodded, and the doctor wrote up the labs and said he would call us when the results were in.

We went to the lab and they took Carson's blood. When he came back from the little room, he said cheerfully, "Well, that's that!"

I grabbed his hand and we walked to the car. I could feel the tension in him. "Are you really okay?" I asked.

He shrugged. "I guess I'm doing all right. But…I'm afraid we just changed our lives forever."

"There's a fifty percent chance that you don't have Huntington's disease," I reminded him forcefully. "Don't give up hope."

We didn't say another word the whole way home.

When we got home, Carson came over and gave me a kiss goodbye. "Gotta get back to work," he said regretfully. "One of our clients passed away this morning, and I've got a ton of work to do to arrange everything for the wife and children."

"Oh, I'm so sorry for them," I said, and we both knew that I was worrying that I, Elisabeth, Selena, and Dylan might someday find ourselves in the same place.

"Well, me too. The man had a lot of money, and the whole case is kind of… sticky. I'll be at the office late, so go ahead and have dinner without me, okay?"

I hated that I had to let him go, after the day we'd just had. I wanted to lie on the couch with him and just hold him, to protect him from the world. But life had to go on, and there was work that needed to be dealt with.

I pulled out dinner to let it defrost, and then I was on my way out the door too: it was time to pick all the kids up from school, and then take them to practice. When we got home we ate dinner, then all the kids took their showers and got into bed. Carson still wasn't home from the office. I called his cell phone to make sure he was all right, and he told me that he was wrapping some stuff up and then he was going to go out with his dad for a drink. That was probably a good thing; he and his father were close, and Bill was so positive about everything, so he probably had just the right words for his son.

That was something I just couldn't do for Carson right now. I felt that everything I said was wrong, so I thought I'd let Bill have a crack at it.

When I felt Carson get into bed that night, I looked at the clock and saw that it was 2 AM. He curled his body up around mine, then kissed my check and quietly asked if I was awake. In response, I twisted my neck and looked up at him. "Sorry for being such a jerk lately," he mumbled.

I smiled, though I doubted he could see that in the darkness. "Don't worry. I understand."

"Yes, but that's still no excuse for the way I've been acting."

"It'll be over soon, Carson. We'll get the results, and the stress of that will go away, at least." I leaned up and kissed his lips. "Now, young man, you need to get some sleep, or you'll be a mess tomorrow."

"Good night, Kat. I love you."

"I love you too, babe."

***

It had been a week since Carson had given the blood for his test, and there still hadn't been a call from the doctor. That day, Carson had to go to a funeral for the client who had died. He called me in the morning, and told me his phone would be off for a while during the service. I told him to call me when it was done.

I put the phone down and had just started taking chicken out of the freezer for dinner when the phone rang again. I figured Carson had forgotten to tell me something, so I ran to pick it up. "Hello?"

"Hello, is Carson Ferris available?"

"No, he's not home right now," I said cautiously.

"Is this Kathryn Ferris?"

"It is." My heart started pounding. I knew what this was about.

"Hello, Ms. Ferris. My name is Dr. Carl Jenkins; I'm filling in for Dr. Creswell while he's on vacation. He asked me to call back the patients whose test results have come in."

"Oh," I said, my mouth desert-dry. "Okay. Well, Carson will be home late. He's, he's at a funeral right now."

"Well, ma'am, it says here that I can release this information to you as well. I can give you the results, and you can give them to him yourself if you'd like."

I stood there for a long moment, not knowing what to say. *Of course* I wanted to know the results—but only if they were negative. How would I ever be able to tell Carson the results myself if they were positive? I debated with myself which seemed like forever, but was doubtlessly only seconds, and decided it was better that he heard the news either way from me, rather than from some stranger.

I took a deep breath and said firmly, "That's fine, Dr. Jenkins. You can tell me."

"I'm afraid the tests came back positive. Mr. Ferris has Huntington's disease."

Like a marionette whose strings had been cut, I fell to the ground, nerveless in grief. When I could move again, I hung up the phone, while the doctor was still talking; I didn't care what he had to say. After that, I feel to the floor of our living room and cried. I felt so alone in the world, and I could not believe that this was our reality. Carson was such a good man; how could this be happening to him? This was the father of my children! What had they done to deserve this? How was I going to handle things on my own? Carson and I weren't going to grow old together! I was going to grow old alone! I was going to have to raise my kids *alone*!

I felt like there was a hole in my soul, a hole where Carson was supposed to be. As I laid there on the floor, my head was spinning out of control with all the what ifs, wondering what was I going to do now that most of my world had ended.

I sat up and grabbed control of my emotions, putting a stop to all those paralyzing thoughts. Carson didn't know the results of his test yet. He was sitting with a group of his client's family and friends, with all of them crying and saying their goodbyes…and now he had to come home to *this*. How on earth was I going to tell him something like this? How do you tell a man he is going to die? I'd thought that this type of news would be better coming from me; now I could see how wrong I'd been. Now that I'd actually have to tell him, I didn't know what I'd been thinking.

How was I going to do this? With all the recriminations, worries and emotions manifesting in my head, I started to feel dizzy, like I was trapped under a ton of bricks. Life was crashing down on me, and I was helpless.

I couldn't stand, so I crawled over to the couch and somehow pulled myself up onto it. I decided I had to focus right then on how I was going to tell Carson the news; everything else would have to go on the back burner. It all paled in significance, at least for the moment, compared to how I was going to tell my husband he was dying, in the gentlest way I could.

I couldn't do this alone. I knew that Bill would be with Carson at the funeral, so that was out; and in any case, he would be grief-stricken himself. I didn't want to call Page; I would definitely need her support later, but not yet. I decided to call my Dad and Izzy. I hoped they had some wise words to get me though this.

When Dad answered the phone, I blurted, "Daddy, I have some terrible news."

I felt my body start to go into full-fledged panic mode again; I was having a hard time breathing, and the room started to spin.

"Kathryn, are you okay?" Dad was almost shouting, he was so worried. "What's wrong? Are the kids okay?"

I sobbed, "Dad, the doctor called this morning. Carson was tested for Huntington's disease and his test results came back positive."

After a long pause, Dad said breathlessly, "Oh no, honey! I'm so sorry. How is Carson taking it?"

"He doesn't even know yet, Dad. He's at a funeral. The doctor called the house phone. How I am going to tell him something like this?"

"Is there anything I can do?" he asked quietly.

I loved him so much at that moment; I knew he'd be there for us. "I don't know, Dad," I replied. I continued, trying to calm myself down, "I don't even know what *I'm* going to do yet."

"What about the kids? Can I come and get the kids for a while?"

"That would probably be a good idea. I think we should probably deal with this for a day or so by ourselves, before the kids are involved. Are you off work?"

"Yeah. I have to work tomorrow, but let me call Henry Smith and see if he'll take the shift. After that I have two days off, so I can take them until Sunday if you'd like."

It was Thursday, which worked out pretty well. "Okay, then, if you came and got them today, they'd only miss school tomorrow. It…would be good if the kids weren't home for a while."

"Let me give Henry a call, and I'll call you right back. If he can take my shift, I'll head down there now and I'll just take the kids when they get out of school."

After I got off the phone with my father, I tried to call both Carson and Bill, but their phones were still off. I paced back and forth, not knowing what to do; then I decided it was time to call Page. I needed my best girlfriend right now. When she picked up, I instantly started crying; the news was so new that every time I mentioned it, I felt like I was reliving it again. Page and I talked for quite a while on the phone about how I was going to tell Carson the news. We both had a hard time figuring that out. Page said there would be no way to tell him and nowhere to tell him that would make the news any easier; she thought I should just tell him right away, that I should just come out and admit that the doctor had called with the results, and just tell him what they were.

She was right: no matter how I did this, it was going to be terrible.

I was hoping Carson would be home before I had to get the kids; I didn't want the three of them to be around when I told Carson the results. That didn't happen, right when I was getting ready to walk out the door to pick them up, my cell phone rang. It was Dad saying that he'd gotten the shift covered, and he was on his way to pick up the kids. All this timing was horrible: Carson would know that something was wrong when my Dad came to pick up the kids on a Thursday night. I didn't want to tell him the news around the kids at all. I decided I would just let Dad get the kids; and if Carson questioned why, I would just tell him it was because we needed sometime alone.

I'd barely made that decision when my cell phone rang again: it was Carson calling me. He said that the service was done, and he was going to just come home; he didn't want to go back to work after that. It was the first funeral he had attended since his mother's, and I was sure it had been emotionally wrenching, bringing back memories of that time for him.

"Dad's coming to pick up the kids for the weekend," I told him.

"When, tomorrow night?" he asked tiredly.

"No, right now. We need some alone time."

"What about school?" he asked, sounding confused.

"They all do great in school, Carson. They can afford to miss a day." He didn't have any response to that, so I forged on. "Now: can you afford to miss a day of work?"

"I can get it off," he replied cautiously. "What's this about?"

"I'll tell you later. Right now I'm about to go online and book us a room somewhere. We need to get out of town for the weekend. Where do you want to go?"

"It would be nice to go to the coast," he said, almost eagerly.

Carson loved going to the ocean; he wasn't questioning the spur-of-the-moment trip, I think, because he was just excited to get away. After we got off the phone, I jumped online and booked us a room on the coast, a room with a balcony and ocean view. I had a feeling we would be doing a lot of talking out there.

Carson walked in the door right when I was done, and it was a genuine struggle to keep myself together. I wanted to run to him and cry in his arms… but then he would definitely know something was up. Yes, I could tell him right now; but then I would have to get the kids, and I don't know how he would respond to the news, so I decided not to tell him at all until the kids were gone with my Dad.

"Good, you're home!" I said, all businesslike. "We've got a room waiting for us in Bodega Bay. Now, I've gotta go grab the kids from school."

"I'll go with you," he said, leaning over and giving me one of his heart-melting kisses.

As we pulled out of the driveway, Carson said reflectively, "You know, I felt terrible for the family at the funeral today."

"Of course you did."

"Death is so damn final," he replied, as if I hadn't said anything. "It was so hard for his wife; she could barely function, she was so sad about losing her husband. And the kids were all sitting there, crying their eyes out." He looked at me. "He was a good man, Kat, and I could tell how much their father meant to them. It was killing them to know that they would never see him again."

That did it: my eyes filled up. I tried to hold back as much as I could, but my emotions seemed not to care what my mind was telling them not to do. Carson just kept talking; he hadn't noticed the mini-breakdown going on next to him.

As I was blinking back the tears, he said, "You know, I wonder why Dr. Creswell hasn't called us back with my test results? I've been thinking about it all day today." I dared glance at him, and saw that he was staring out his window at the landscape. In a quiet voice he said, "Kathryn, I think everything will be okay. I've been feeling really good lately. Maybe it *was* all stress related, right? I'm feeling really good about it, so don't you worry. I have hope, and you should too."

I felt my throat swell shut, making it impossible to swallow and hard to breathe. I felt a fog surround my whole head. I felt sick about not telling him, and letting him go on and on. I couldn't lie to him anymore. He had to know the truth. I wished I could keep it from him forever, but he needed to know.

As soon as I safely could, I pulled over to the side of the road. I couldn't believe this was happening right now. I wished it wasn't. He was looking at me oddly, waiting for me to say something, and after several tries I croaked, "Carson, the doctor did call today. I tried to call you right away, but your phone was off for the funeral."

Carson's whole body stiffened. He looked at his watch, and then pulled out his cell phone. "Guess I should call and get my test results, then."

"Carson, the doctor said that you gave them permission for me to get the results if you weren't available."

His face was blank when he looked at me. "So you know?"

I couldn't speak anymore; I just nodded. Carson turned his head to look out his window. "I guess I know the answer," he said after a long moment. "That's why you wanted me to come home. That's why you planned for us to go away for a couple of days."

"Yes," I whispered. In a slightly louder voice, I continued, "Carson, I just didn't know how you would react to the news. I didn't even want to tell you until the kids were gone. I thought it would be good for the two of us to get away from all the stress we have to deal with, to have a couple of days to think without distractions. If you don't want to go, we don't have to. It is all up to you. I just wanted reservations to be made, if that's what you wanted." I reached out and touched his cheek. "I am so sorry, baby. I really don't know what to say."

He reached up and cupped my hand in his. Smiling humorlessly, he said in a wooden tone, "There's nothing to say, really. This is it: I have Huntington's disease, and somehow we're going to have to live with that. I think it *would* be a good thing to get away for a couple of days. I seem fine right now, but I think it's because I'm still in shock. I'm not sure how I'll be when it hits me…and I don't want the kids around when it does."

We didn't talk much after that; we picked up the kids, then took them back to the house. I packed their bags and told them that they got to miss a day of school to spend sometime with Grandpa, and of course the kids were excited, so they didn't ask too many questions. I think they just wanted to get out of there before I changed my mind. When Dad got to our house, he pulled me aside and asked me if Carson and the kids knew.

"Carson knows now, but we haven't told the kids," I said in a low voice. "That's something Carson and I are going to have to talk about first."

To be honest, I hadn't really thought about that until Dad asked. I had no idea what we were going to do about the kids; Carson and I were going to have to weigh the options of the children knowing versus them *not* knowing before we made any final decision. We had so much to talk about, in fact, that I didn't want to overwhelm Carson with all the details. I was scared myself, and I had no idea how he was going to react. He'd basically learned something today that he had hoped he would never hear, and he had to be going through hell…although to watch him play and interact with the children, you'd never know it.

Finally, I decided I wasn't going to talk about Huntington's at all unless Carson started the conversation. This weekend wasn't about working out all our problems; it was about him getting away and dealing with whatever he needed to deal with.

After Dad left with the kids in tow, I packed up the car and we were on our way. On the drive to the coast we didn't talk too much, though I did broach one subject with him: "Carson, have you told your Dad yet?"

I thought he wasn't going to answer; but after a full minute, he said, "No. I really don't know how to tell him. I know it'll bring up some bad memories for him. I can't imagine how devastated he must have been when he found out that the love of his life had this disease…and I can only imagine how he'll react when he discovers that the same disease that killed her is going to kill his only child."

His voice was shaking a little as he reached the end of that statement, but he took a deep breath and went on: "I…just don't know how he'll handle it. I don't even know how *I'll* handle it yet, Kat. I don't think there's an easy way to tell him…but I have to figure out the right way to do it. I also know that Dad will be very emotional, and I don't want my emotions to get in the way, so I want to make sure

I clear my head somewhat before I tell him, since I'm going to have to be strong for him."

I reached out and grabbed his free hand, clutching it tightly in my own. "Plus," he forged on, "I haven't seen Dad since I found out, obviously, and this isn't something you do over the phone. I, well, I have a feeling he knows something's going on, though." He glanced at me. "We never just jump up and go like this. I'm sure he's putting two and two together. So," he sighed explosively, "I'll tell him when we get home."

Swallowing hard, I said, "I'm sorry, honey, I guess I didn't think about how this would bring back memories for him of the day your Mom found out…much less the memories of what she went through. Now: I'm going to ask you another question. If all this is overwhelming you and you don't want to talk about it, just let me know. This weekend is about you and what *you* need. So if you don't want to talk about anything, just say it; I'm not going to be offended or upset." I took a deep breath and said, "But I do have one thing you need to think about. What are we going to do about the kids?"

He turned his head sharply and looked at me. I just stared at the road, both hands on the steering wheel, clenching hard. "What do you mean? We're not going to do *anything* about the kids. I decided when I wanted to find out if I had Huntington's; Dylan and Elisabeth can decide when *they* want to find out. I'd never force that decision on them."

"No, Carson, that's not what I mean. I'm still trying to deal with *you* having Huntington's disease! It hasn't even crossed my mind about the children." And it hadn't until then; now I was horrified yet again. "Oh my God," I gasped, "I don't *ever* want to talk about that. That's more than I can handle. What I meant was, what are we going to do about telling the kids about you?"

He shook himself. "Oh, crap. I'm sorry…your question kind of shocked me for a second. I…well, I don't know what we should do about telling the kids. I think the best thing is to not tell them right away. Let's absorb this ourselves before we bring the kids into it. For now, I want them to stay innocent and carefree. I don't want them to worry about anything while I'm around, especially not me, okay? We'll have to tell them eventually, but I don't think now's the right time. We'll know when the right time comes."

I dropped the subject, and I think that was a good choice. I didn't want the kids to worry about anything either. Eventually, they would figure it out on their own; after all, I'd known from the moment I met Carson's mother that there was something different about her. The kids would see the changes in Carson and start asking questions…so when that happened, we would take care of it then. But how about Carson and me—how were *we* going to deal with it? I hoped that Carson had all his legal affairs in order; I wasn't ready to talk about any of those matters, not at the moment. But if I knew Carson, everything was set into place well before he was tested.

It was quiet in the car on the rest of the way to the coast; neither of us felt like speaking. I wondered what was going on in Carson's head. His face was like a statue, showing no emotion at all. I wondered how long he would remain in this shocked state.

After we arrived at our hotel and unloaded our luggage, Carson and I decided to visit a winery next to the hotel. Although I wasn't sure, at first, if we should mix alcohol into this situation, it did seem to help us loosen up. The winery itself was very cute, featuring a large outside terrace with huge cushion couches. We sat out there and watched the waves wash onto the sand, and soon a young lady came out and brought us a wine list. We chose the seven types of wine we wanted to taste, and after a few moments she came out with a flight for each of us. We just sat there and watched the ocean as we sipped our wines. I kicked my feet up on the couch, and laid my head on Carson's shoulder. "I love you, Carson," I told him quietly. "Everything will work out."

"I know. I love you too, babe."

We sat there and watched the ocean for an hour, then decided that we should probably go and get something to eat. After we grabbed dinner and drank a bottle of wine, I told Carson that I needed some fresh air, so we went for a long walk on the beach. The sun had already set, but we could hear the waves crashing down, and we soon saw some benches up on a cliff. We climbed up the stairs to the top of the cliff, then sat there, quiet, as the cool ocean breeze swept over our faces. I could taste the salt air on my lips.

I cuddled up to Carson, and pushed the side of my face against his. When I felt something wet on the side of my face, I pulled back and looked at Carson…and at the tears flowing down his face. "Carson, are you okay?"

"I'm not sure," he admitted. "You know, I'm not so worried about me, and what I'm going to have to go through. I mean, I know it's going to be terrible and all, and I surely won't enjoy it…but what I'm really worried about is the kids. How are they going to handle not having a father? We have two girls who need a Dad to protect them. Dylan needs me around to teach him to be a man. There's so much that I'm going to miss, Kathryn. Think about it: short of a miracle, I won't be there to walk our daughters down the aisle at their weddings. I won't be there when Dylan graduates from college. I'll never be able to hold my grandchildren. And we'll never sit together as two old people on our front porch, rocking in our rocking chairs." He looked at me, his face a mask of grief. "I'm leaving you to raise the children on your own. I am so sorry, Kathryn." He looked away quickly.

My heart breaking, I said, "Carson, this isn't your fault! Don't ever apologize for any of this." I grabbed his chin and turned his face toward me. "Look: if I went back in time and someone told me, 'You're going to meet this wonderful man. He'll love you and take care of you like no one else. He'll be your best friend, and the best father that your children could ever ask for. The only thing is, you'll lose him at a young age. Your time with him will be cut short, but the time you *will* have will be special…' Carson, knowing what I know, I would do it all over again in a heartbeat. I would rather be your wife for the time we have together, than never to have been able to share all this with you because I ran from the pain."

His eyes full of tears, Carson said, "Kat. You don't want to deal with all this—it's too much. I'm going to be a burden, and I don't want to put that on you."

"Carson, don't talk crazy!" I was shaking by then; not with fear, but with something akin to anger. "When I married you, I took a vow that said, *in sickness and in health.* I meant that, and so did you. If the tables were turned, you would take care of me until my dying day. I know you would, and I can do no less. I *will* stand by you until the end. You've given me a life that most women can only dream of. You're a good, caring man, and your arms are always open. You love me and our children like no one else could ever. You're faithful and loyal to your family. You're an excellent provider. You've worked hard so that I could stay home and raise our children. I have the perfect life—and you aren't going anywhere. So don't even try to run away from us to protect us; that's out of the question. We love you, and we'll go on as a family." Breathing hard, I started to wipe away his tears.

He grabbed my hands. He wasn't crying now, but his eyes were filled with pain. "I'm worried about the kids…what they'll see. You remember how it was with Mom. I don't *ever* want my children to be scared of me, or of what's going to happen to me. You know how some kids who go through things like that end up doing drugs and going crazy. I…would hate if any of that happened to our children because of me."

"What are you talking about?" I gasped, a little exasperated. "Look at you, Carson Ferris! Look how you turned out! Our kids are going to go through the same things that you went through. You became a stronger person because of it. You always followed all the rules. You saw what your parents were going through, so you were careful never to rock the boat. You kept life calm for their sake. You took such good care of your Mom…because she and Bill gave you such a great foundation. You knew your mother loved you more than life itself."

I hugged my husband impulsively. "I think a lot of your compassion comes from what you went through, and honey, our children have that same foundation. They love you and they know you love *them*. We've taught them right from wrong. We're teaching them to be good, loving people. All three of them are going to be amazing, just like you. I promise you, Carson, that I am *not* going to let anything happen to our children."

He kissed me on the cheek and replied, "I know you're a great mother, and you'll do your best. But our kids need a father. Our kids need me. I don't want to fail them by not being there."

"Yes, our kids need you, and they have you." I broke out of the embrace and kissed him on the lips. "We just have to start living every moment to the fullest. Maybe something good can come out of this. We can focus on what's truly important, and use the years we have left to make wonderful memories with the kids—memories that they'll have for the rest of their lives and will pass on to *their* children. So many people go through life focusing so tightly on the future that they never live in the present, Carson…and when they're ready to live in the present, it's too late—their kids are grown and gone and their lives are almost over."

He looked at me, his eyes clear, and there was something like hope there.

"This is giving us an opportunity to live in the present," I continued, "to make every moment count. Life is precious; it can be taken away so fast. There's no guarantee of tomorrow for anyone. Most people don't know when and where they're going to die. It's almost a gift that we have at least some idea. Now, we can live life like it's supposed to be lived. We can live for today, give all we can of ourselves, know that at the end of the day, we did all we could to live life to the fullest."

Carson wrapped his arms around me, and held me very tight. He didn't say anything; I think he was absorbing all I'd just put on him.

After a long while of sitting in silence, we decided it was time to head back to our room, so we did that, then we both got into our sweats and went to sit on the balcony. I knew that balcony would come in handy! We stared quietly out at the faintly phosphorescent waves of the Pacific, and eventually Carson said quietly, "Kat, do you think there's a life after this one? I mean, take our mothers, for instance: where do you think they are now? Do you think that was it on the days they died, or do you think there's more to it?"

I smiled. "There has to be more to it, hon. Look at the ocean: it sends off an energy that's peaceful and tranquil most times…but it's also the most powerful thing in the world. Something really great had to create something so incredible. If you look around, Carson, God is all around us. Most of us don't take time to look. But when you do, it's overwhelming, really. A perfect sunset; a beautiful sunrise, the ocean, the forest, the sky, the mountains…it's all God's work. It would be awful to think that this is all we are: just temporary vessels of flesh and blood. That can't be it. We're so much more than that." I glanced at him. "I think we're spirits, just here to learn lessons. We come here for a short time and learn what we need to; then, in the end, we get to go home, to a place where there's no pain, no suffering, just…peace."

"My wife, the poet." He lifted my hand to his mouth and lovingly kissed the back of it. "But Kat, why would we *want* to come here? I know you and I live a wonderful life, and I wouldn't change any of it…well, except this disease thing. But it's so painful to know what we know. The future is scary now. If Heaven is so peaceful, why would any spirit want to come here and take this on?"

"Like I said, I think it's because we come here to learn. Think about it: if someone told you about pain and loss and you had never experience it, how could you know what it was really like? I don't think there's anything like that in Heaven. So a curious spirit would probably want to come here to understand what those words meant, since no amount of explanation can replace the actual experience. I could hear from a friend what it might feel like to find out that her husband was terminally ill, but I would never understand it the way I understand what I'm feeling right now."

"I suppose," he said, a little dubiously.

"I also think it's easier on us to know that we chose this life. It almost gives us some power in a powerless situation, doesn't it? We knew what was going to happen before we got here, even if we didn't know how it would affect us. There's a reason we chose this life, Carson. Right now we don't know why, but one day we will."

"How can you be so sure?"

"I dream about my Mom sometimes. Some might say that it's all just dreams, my mind making things up—but I refuse to believe that, Carson. It seems that I always dream about Mom when I need her the most, and it feels so real when I do. I believe she's there watching over me all the time, and I think your Mom is there, too. One day we'll see them again, and we'll enjoy eternity together. Every time I dream of my Mom, she seems so happy. I see no pain in her at all; the sickness she had is gone, left behind. I guess it's because our bodies are fragile—they can turn off or get sick at the drop of a hat. But our souls are always healthy."

I looked across the ocean. "I don't know if any of this is true," I said slowly. "But it's what I believe, and it makes times like this easier for me. Now, this is the most difficult thing I've ever had to deal with, even worse than Elisabeth dying. But knowing this life isn't it, and that it really *is* a short timeframe when you think of eternity; I think that makes it easier. So, sorry I went off on a run on that question…why? What do you think?"

He took a long, trembling breath and said in a rush, "I never told you this, but one night just after Elisabeth Lee was born, I woke up to check on her. I never saw or heard anything that was out of the ordinary…but while I was with the baby, I had a strong feeling that Mom was right there with me. It was a very warm, a very comfortable feeling. I felt her there, just checking up on her granddaughter. I never told you, because I didn't want to scare you or you to think I was crazy. But I'm pretty sure she was there."

"I'm sure she was." I smiled. "Your mother was the most perfect, caring person I have ever known. If she *was* there, I don't know what would be scary to me about that. I'm glad she's watching over us, Carson. One day we'll have all the answers…but for now, we're here. We need to live as much as we can, and experience as much as we can, while we are."

"I guess we *will* see, one day." He was quiet for a few moments before he said, "It's late, so I'm going to go to bed. Let's try to get up to make breakfast in the morning."

"Sounds good. I love you."

"Love you too. Goodnight."

I sat for a little longer outside. I loved the ocean; I could sit and listen to it all night, and in some odd way, it seemed to soak up my worries and apprehensions. Eventually, it started to get cold, so I went inside and joined Carson in bed. I fell asleep almost instantly, and it wasn't long before I was dreaming about walking through a long, dark tunnel. Everything felt so dim and lonely there; I didn't like that, so I kept walking down the tunnel, hoping for light. I finally did see a light at the end of the tunnel, and I hurried toward it.

Suddenly I was in a familiar meadow, walking alone down a pebble path. The sunlight felt warm against my skin, and the air seemed so pure that it was fantastically easy to breath. I felt the loneliness from the tunnel disappear immediately; now, I felt whole. As I walked along, I noticed someone walking by my side, and I abruptly realized where I was: I was walking with my mother, in the same place we'd met all those years ago before Carson and I had gotten together. I never stopped walking; we just accompanied each other silently down that heavenly path, and it felt so peaceful that I didn't want the feeling to go away. I didn't know if it was real or just a dream; but I decided to take a shot at talking to my Mom. I turned and looked at her angelic form and said, *Mom, I need help. I don't know how to deal with what my life has become.*

In a soft, ethereal voice, she told me, *Darling, everything will be fine.* Like everything here, her voice was beautiful; it was almost as though she was singing the words. I wanted to know more; I had so many questions that she might have the answers to—but I suddenly woke up.

I laid there grinding my teeth, furious that my dream was over. I wanted that feeling of bliss back; I didn't want to be shocked back to reality, somewhere I really didn't want to be right now. Fuming, I got up and walked out onto the balcony, just as the sun was coming up, casting long trails of shadow on the beach before me.

Mornings at the beach are so surreal. This wasn't as pleasant as the dream place had been, but I sat and watched the ocean, enjoying the moment, and thought about my dream. I thought about the tunnel and how it had felt: so dark, miserable, and lonely. Then I remembered how wonderful I'd felt when I was in the meadow. I thought, *This may be life. It's a dark tunnel, where we're constantly trying to find some light. How wonderful it feels when we finally* get *those moments of light.* I'd had that feeling when I met Carson. I felt that way when I had my babies. I felt that way when I brought Selena home. I felt that light when I was doing charity work.

These must be glimpses of what Heaven feels like.

I wondered what my Mom had meant when she said everything was going to be fine. Did she mean that they would find some miraculous cure for Huntington's disease, so Carson and I could go back to our normal lives? Or did she mean that when this life was said and done, everything would be fine then? Those were questions that only time could answer…though either way, I supposed, everything *would* be all right. I just hoped that I could bear all the madness and pain before we got there.

Well—I had to. I had no other choice. I had a husband and three children who depended on me to keep it together. I had to find a new strength that I had never needed before; I had to become bigger than what I was. I didn't know how I was going to do it, but I had no other choice. The kids and Carson needed me, so I would be there.

After an hour or so, I heard a light step behind me, and Carson eased into the chair to my right. "How did you sleep?" he asked.

"I slept well," I told him simply. "And how did you sleep?"

He sighed tiredly. "I was up all night. I couldn't turn my mind off."

"Would you like to talk about anything?"

"No, not right now. At the moment, I'm just hungry."

So we went and had breakfast at a little diner, and then decided to hit the beach. We set up our chairs and umbrellas and just relaxed all day long. We talked a little here and there, but never really got into any deep conversation about anything. Among other things, we discussed the need to find a neurologist to see what we should be doing. I told Carson that I would handle all that when we got home. The doctor had mentioned a referral, so I'd call him back and deal with it when we got home.

I was in no mood, at that point the doctor called and gave me the news, to talk about where to go from there. I wanted to deal with the news I'd just gotten before I tried to get a handle on the technical stuff.

All things considered, we had a good day, really enjoying our time together at the shore. We went out for a nice dinner later, and went to bed early that night; I think we were both exhausted from the night before. We woke early the next morning and headed home, both of us anxious to get home to see the kids.

My Dad was waiting for us with the kids when we arrived, and they came running outside to jump into our arms. There was something so soothing about our babies, I realized; in the worst situation, and this was one, they could give us a hug and instantly things felt better.

Dad headed home right away; he had to get home for work. Carson, however, had called his own Dad on our way home, making plans for them to go out to lunch that day so that he could give Bill the bad news. I could tell that he was upset to have to do so, but he masked it well; and I thought it was the right decision for him and Bill to go off on their own to talk about everything. I felt guilty, but I really didn't want to be there when Bill found out about the news.

After I made the kids lunch and heard about all the fun they'd had with Grandpa, I got them situated with a movie and went online to look up neurologists in our area. I was going to call our primary care doctor first thing in the morning, but I wanted to do some research before we got the referral. As I read over the information on the neurologists in our insurance system, I realized that there was nothing about Huntington's disease in what I read. Most of the neurologists worked mostly with Alzheimer's and dementia, and I saw a lot of mentions of Parkinson's disease, but there was nothing there about Huntington's disease.

After reading for a couple of hours, I had to walk away from it. I couldn't seem to find anything I was looking for, so I decided I would leave it up to our doctor. I was optimistic that they would refer us to the right person.

I'd just started cooking dinner when Carson came home from being with his dad. His eyes were pretty puffy, so I was fairly sure it hadn't gone well; it must have been terrible for both of them. "Do you need to talk?" I asked, pitching my voice low so the kid's wouldn't hear.

"Eventually. When I'm ready," he said, in a dispirited voice. "Right now I just want to sit down with my family and have a nice dinner."

He pitched in with the preparations, and soon we all sat together and ate. The kids talked our ears off, as usual; and their chatter was the medicine we needed to hold ourselves together. Carson and I would look at each other and laugh at the funny little things the kids were saying, and it was easy to forget, temporarily, the shadow that was rearing over all our lives.

Later all five of us crawled into our king-sized bed, where Carson read the kids a bedtime story. He was so animated; he had different voices for all the animals in the book, and the kids would laugh at their Dad whenever he changed his voice. I loved this kind of family time; I longed to stay in this moment forever. We did this sort of thing all the time, but tonight I realized just how important this time was. So I sat back and watched, as if I were watching a great movie, and enjoyed this little slice of time as my family interacted and laughed together. This was priceless; I loved it more than words can explain.

When the story was over, we tucked the kids into their own beds, and then tucked ourselves into ours. As I turned out the bedside lamp, I told Carson, "Honey, you don't need to tell me all the details about what happened today with your dad, but I do want to know if he's okay."

"I don't think he'll ever be okay," Carson said into the darkness. "He…took the news very hard, because he hoped this day would never come."

"I know. I'm sure he was hoping the gene would pass you by."

"Yeah. Well, I just told him that I'm going to live life to the fullest. I told him I was going to make every minute I had left count for myself and my family. I told him I was sad, but okay, and I think my attitude made him feel a little better." He turned toward me in bed. "Apparently, it took him and Mom a long time to get to that point. Dad said they were angry and resentful for a long time, before they embraced the disease and decided they needed to live differently." He sighed. "He said he was proud of me for getting there right away. He was very emotional, but I think Dad's going to have a lot of good advice for us."

Carson was very young when Elisabeth was diagnosed; he hadn't been aware of what his parents had gone through, those first couple of years, because they had masked it so well. I figured it would be good for Carson to have his dad to go to when he needed some advice on how to handle things, since Bill had already been through all of this.

"That's good," I told my husband, snuggling up against him. "I imagine you'll need him at some point, and I'm glad you're open enough to talk about it with me."

Bad Experience, Good Experience

The next morning, Carson went to work after he took the kids to school; meanwhile, I called the doctor to get a referral for a neurologist. Dr. Creswell gave me the name and number of a neurologist in their system, and I called the office immediately to make an appointment. "It's your lucky day!" the receptionist said cheerfully.

I was a bit less cheerful as I said, "Oh, really."

"Yes! It's normally a month's wait to see the doctor, but I have a cancellation for tomorrow. I can make an appointment for you if you can make it."

"Of course we can. We'll take it."

"That's great!"

After reciting my particulars I hung up, with sour taste in my mouth. A month? That was ridiculous. I didn't want Carson to wait another month before he could see the doctor. I called him right away, and told him I'd been able to get a appointment for the next morning. He seemed buoyed by the thought, and so the next day, we went to see the neurologist.

It was a fiasco. There's no other way to put it.

We were both anxious, of course, but also hopeful. We hadn't had to think about Huntington's disease for a long time, and we were sure that there had to have been some new medications approved or breakthroughs made in the intervening years. Surely.

We sat in the waiting room for two hours past our appointment time. This doctor was either in great demand, or just really slow and didn't care about his patients; I wasn't sure which, but there weren't that many people in the waiting room. In the interim, Carson called Bill and told him to be on call, in case we had to have him pick up the kids from school. We had no idea why it would take so long, but the nurse finally called us back. We had to wait in the exam room for another half-hour before the doctor came in.

Finally he walked in, tall and stooped, and introduced himself to us as Dr. Feinberg. He didn't spend a long time with us: he mostly sat and read the information that Carson had filled out during the long wait, and had Carson do a few tests to see how his reflexes and memory were. Frankly, he really didn't seem too interested in what was going on. I knew that this was his job, and things probably got a little repetitive—but this was our lives, and our doctor didn't really seem to give a damn.

After performing his stupid little tests, he looked at us blandly and said, "Well, you look like you're doing well so far." He started to get up.

"Wait a minute!" I burst out. "That's *it*?"

He glanced at me and said emotionlessly, "Well, it's Huntington's disease. There's not really much we can do for Huntington's disease." He shifted his focus to Carson. "Mr. Ferris, if you start to see any symptom you can't live with, come back and I'll try to give you some medicine to help." Then that ass just turned around and walked out of the room.

I sat there with my mouth wide open, unable to believe what had just happened. When I could, I looked at Carson; he was just sitting there on the examining table, his head down. I was filled with rage— so pissed I couldn't see straight. With just a few uncaring words, that idiot had crushed my husband's spirit!

"Obviously this quack knows nothing about Huntington's disease." I said icily, when I could trust myself to speak again. "We may have to see a lot of doctors before we find the right one. He isn't." With that, we got up and walked out of the room.

As we walked down the corridor to the nurses station, I saw Feinberg standing at the counter, reading some poor patient's file. I felt so sorry for whoever had to deal with this guy next. We brushed by him, but as we were walking out I turned around, marched back up to him, and got in his face.

"I have a question for you," I ask grimly. "Do you have any patients who have Huntington's disease?"

He seemed a little nonplussed. "Well, not right now, but I have in the past."

"How many would you say you've seen?"

"Well, really, I've had only a handful in all my years of practice," he admitted. "If you want to know more, I'm sure they have a society or something you could contact."

"They do. And I need to point something out to you, *Doctor*. You've forgotten something important."

He raised a supercilious eyebrow and asked, "And that would be?"

"A little something called the Hippocratic Oath, sir. 'First, do no harm.' You've made it clear that you really don't know shit about this disease, and you don't care to learn. My husband, that man right there, is a human being, looking for some kind of hope that will allow him to live to see his children grow up and graduate and marry someday. You basically told him to just lie down and die, to come see you if he got symptoms he somehow couldn't live with, and then *maybe* you could do something for him. I'm not going to let someone who obviously knows nothing and cares less bring us down. Maybe you need to check your patient's files before they come in, just in case they have something that you don't know anything about, so you can spare them from coming in here and getting cut down by your indifference. You are a joke, Dr. Feinberg."

I turned around, leaving the idiot gasping like a fish behind me, and grabbed Carson's hand and walked out of the office.

When we were in the hallway, he started laughing.

"What's so funny?" I snapped.

"Kat," he said, "you were so *scorching* in there. My calm, quiet wife, shaking a finger in that man's face and cussing like a sailor!" He laughed again.

"Ugh. Well, I wasn't going to sit around and let that quack make us feel the way he was making us feel. I refuse, in this day and age, to have no hope at all. When we were kids, leukemia was a death sentences. Now it is not, so why not Huntington's disease? Who knows how long you will live? I realize there's no cure right now, but there will be someday—and surely there's something we could do for the disease now— supplements, exercise, *something*. That was the worst doctor I have ever come across."

Carson just nodded, still smiling faintly. He tried to look chipper, but I could tell from his silence that that idiot Feinberg had really gotten to him—and I couldn't let that happen. I saw a bench beside the entryway as we exited the building, I sat down, and Carson sat with me, looking puzzled. I didn't say anything; I just pulled out my cell phone and called Information, asking if they had a phone number for the Huntington's Disease Society of America. The operator told me there were a couple of numbers, and I told her to give me the one for Sacramento. The call connected automatically, and as I listened to the burr of the ring tone I felt nervous, because I wasn't sure exactly what I was doing.

"Huntington's Disease Society of America," a chipper female voice answered.

"Good morning," I said determinedly. "My name is Kathryn Ferris. My husband was diagnosed with Huntington's a couple of days ago, and at the recommendation of our primary care physician, we just spoke to a neurologist in our insurance system. We just left the office, and it was a joke. The neurologist basically told us to lie down and die. We felt so bad after leaving that I immediately called you guys. I thought you might have some advice for me. We...we need to be with people who know more about this disease."

"Oh my goodness, ma'am, I'm so glad you called!" the young woman at the other end of the line said. "My name is Desiree, Kathryn. I'm sorry you went through what you did...but it's all too common unfortunately. Now, as far as the clinical stuff goes, I have a number that you can call to get some advice about all that. We offer plenty of support for Huntington's patients and their families, and we'll be happy to send you information on all of the events and conferences that are coming up in our area. We host an annual conference here in Sacramento, and we help with some funding of clinical trials. We have some things coming up soon. Would you like to get on our mailing list?"

I told Desiree that I would like that very much; I gave her my address and she gave me a number to call, which I had Carson write down. I thanked her for the information, and as soon as I hung up with her, I called the new number she'd given me. "Hello, this is Tami," a woman answered immediately.

"Tami, my name is Kathryn Ferris. My husband was just diagnosed with Huntington's disease a couple of days ago."

"I see," Tami said cautiously. "And who tested him for the disease?"

"We just went to our primary care doctor," I admitted.

"Oh, dear, I wish we could have done it instead," she said, sounding genuinely concerned. "We test a bit differently than your primary care physician would. Our neurologist takes the time to talk with you about all the pros and cons of getting tested, and then we have you talk to a geneticist. Being tested for Huntington's is a really big decision, and we try to prepare you here the best we can before you get tested. But it's done, so have you found a neurologist?"

"Unfortunately," I said. "We made the mistake of going to the neurologist our primary care physician referred us to, and it was the worst doctor's appointment I've ever experienced. He didn't seem to know anything about Huntington's disease and cared less—he just told us there was nothing he could do. I got the feeling he was telling my husband to just go home and die."

"Oh, no" Tami was silent for a long moment, then said, with something like a catch in her throat, "That's has happens to a lot of people, too." Sounding almost angry, she continued, "I'm so sorry you had to deal with that, because it's the furthest thing from the truth! Yes, admittedly, we don't have a cure for Huntington's yet, and there are no medicines right now specifically for Huntington's disease. But there's a lot of stuff out there that your husband should be doing. We have a physical therapist here at the clinic, and like I said, we have a geneticist you can talk to. We also have a lot of drug trials going on here, and there are plenty of things in the pipeline. There are drugs we can recommend that are proven to help with symptoms that may occur, okay?"

"Okay," I said, trying to take it all in.

"There are also plenty of vitamins and supplements that we think may help with the disease," she went on. "Mrs. Ferris, if you're interested, we can schedule you an appointment with our team here at the clinic. It sounds like you weren't happy at all with whoever you saw, so we would be happy to see you here—where you'll be welcome. Most neurologists don't deal with Huntington's disease very often. We deal *only* with Huntington's disease, so if there's anything going on, we know about it."

Feeling a bit more optimistic, I made the earliest appointment they had available. When I got off the phone, I immediately repeated to Carson everything Tami had told me. "It sounds like the clinic is the best way to go," I concluded.

"You're the boss, ma'am," he said, as we stood up. It had been less than 15 minutes since we'd seen the odious Dr. Feinberg, but it seemed like a lifetime ago. He hugged me impulsively, and said, "Now, let's get back home."

That night, I spend hours online, most of the time on the HDSA website. The site was amazingly informative, and when I read about their annual convention, I decided we would go. I told Carson about the conference, and suggested that Bill should go, too. It would be easy enough to arrange a babysitter for the day, so we could all three attend.

He agreed. He'd already decided to cut back at work to just a couple days a week because, as he pointed out, "I don't want to spend the time I have left just working." It wasn't like we were hurting for money.

We went to the Huntington's convention and, as I had hoped, Bill joined us. We spent most of the day in various workshops, though we parceled them out among us to take the best advantage of the resources. Bill went to a meeting about the financial benefits offered to people with Huntington's disease; Carson went to one titled, "Living positively with Huntington's disease." My workshop was for people acting as caregivers for those with Huntington's, and what I learned broke my heart and left me hopeful in turn. We each took notes for everyone else, and all the workshops proved very helpful. There was so much information, and so much of it was positive, it was a breath of fresh air for us all.

The second half of the day-long conference focused on the keynote speakers. One was a representative of company that was doing a lot of research on Huntington's disease; he made it clear that their mission was to find drugs that could increase the quality of life for people with this horrific disease, if not cure it. The final speaker, though, was a well-respected neurologist, Virginia Callender—which was particularly exciting for us, since she was the very doctor that Carson would be seeing in a few weeks. She was an amazing woman, soft-spoken but clearly passionate about the people she served. She had dedicated her career to helping people with Huntington's disease, and was incredibly knowledgeable about all aspects of the disease— the complete opposite of Dr. Feinberg. She gave us *hope*. Dr. Callender discussed the clinical trials that were going on at their facility, and outlined the various drugs and supplements they thought could be beneficial.

There was so much information, frankly, that it was overwhelming. Bill was especially happy after the convention, because there was so much out there now. "I wish all this had been available when Elisabeth was first diagnosed," he told me fervently that evening, "but I thank God it's there for Carson now."

For my part, I was anxiously awaiting Carson's appointment with Dr. Callender. I wished that this didn't have to be a part of our lives, but since it was, I was glad that he would be in the hands of this compassionate, intelligent woman. It was people like her who would cure this disease someday, not the uncaring Dr. Feinberg's of the world. I couldn't help but think of Bill's Elisabeth, and how hard it must have been to have no hope at all; it literally made my heart hurt to realize that when she had been diagnosed with Huntington's disease, just a few decades before, there really *wasn't* much research going on with the disease. How dark it must have been for her when she found out.

I realized that everything we'd heard about at the conference was still only in the trial phases, but this was how medical research was done; this was how cures and medication were found. There was a time when a simple infection could kill you, because no one had discovered antibiotics. At one point, smallpox ravaged whole societies; now it was extinct in the wild, due to medical science. Someday, Huntington's would be a footnote in a history book, no more. So I was still hopeful.

There had been no hope for Elisabeth.

As it turned out, Dr. Callender was just as wonderful in her office as she'd been at the convention. She was a tall, thin woman with a soft voice, and there was something about her that made her different from any doctor I'd met. Apparently, she had never managed to distance herself from her patients, as most doctors do to avoid getting hurt. Her passion for helping people with this awful disease radiated off of her like warmth radiates from the sun. It was intoxicating just to talk with her.

Cheerfully, Dr. Callender brought us up to speed on all the stuff we should be doing, which basically started with a healthy lifestyle. Carson needed to be working out, eating good foods, and trying to keep toxins (especially neurotoxins) out of his body. So no more alcohol and thank goodness tobacco wasn't an issue. There was a list of supplements and vitamins she wanted Carson to try, including fish oils and omega-three fatty acids. I'd learned that omega-three fatty acids were good for the brain. But some of the stuff I didn't understand, like creatine and CoQ10 enzymes. It was a wonder to me why they would think these things would be good for Carson; but then, I wasn't medically trained.

I kept waiting to hear what I needed to pick up from the pharmacy…but that answer never came, because there *was* nothing. Not a single drug had been approved for use against Huntington's disease at that point. So I knew the answer, but I still had to ask: "Is there any medication that Carson should be on?"

Dr. Callender looked at me brightly, then looked at my husband. "Mr. Ferris, would you like something for anxiety?"

"Not really," he grumbled. "No."

"Carson is very anti-drugs," I explained. "Not to a ridiculous extent, of course, but he's especially cautious about taking anti-depressants."

"I don't want to take medications for my moods," he told her, "at least not for the moment. I'm doing fine right now on my own, I think."

"Okay. If that changes, let me know, and I'll call in a prescription."

I was a little surprised, because most doctors forced their opinions on you. I should have expected this from Dr. Callender, though; she really did care about us, and about what we thought. Frankly, I didn't know why Carson was so dead-set against getting the prescription right then; his moods were the whole reason he'd decided to get tested in the first place, and we'd already had a talk about how the same medications had helped his mother. I was wondering if this was a common reaction for people with this disease: the stubborn "I can take care of it myself, I don't need any drugs" attitude.

This had to be causing him anxiety. I couldn't even *imagine* someone telling me I had a terminal illness and not having anxiety. In fact, in a way, I wished I could get on some anti-depressants myself: just the thought of him having to deal with this was almost more than I could handle. I couldn't even imagine how he must feel; even secondhand, the anxiety took my breath away.

I decided it was a pride thing. He thought he could handle this on his own; and if he thought that, I figured he should try.

"Now, you have to remember," Dr. Callender told him, as she leaned against the counter in the exam room, "The disease itself causes some anxiety and depression, so are you sure you don't want any medication?"

"I'm sure," Carson said adamantly. "I'm not ready for anxiety meds at this point."

"Okay, you got it. Now, how about some medication for your nerves?" He started to open his mouth to dismiss the idea, but she raised her hands and said, "Now, hear me out. When I say 'nerves,' I mean literally, okay? There's a drug call Neurontin, often prescribed to people with neurological disorders."

"No," Carson said flatly.

"Well, I can't force you." The doctor looked at him speculatively and then scribbled something in his chart; and that's when I decided

I would talk to him about all this when we got home. The doctor's office wasn't the place to have that sort of conversation, which could easily escalate into an argument.

I did step in and ask, "Would he have to take the Neurontin on a daily basis?"

"Nope, just as needed."

I looked at Carson, and asked him, "Honey, what's the harm of having at home, just in case it's needed?"

With an annoyed look on his face, he snapped, "I don't need it, Kat! If I do, it's easy enough to get!"

I kept my mouth shut for the rest of the appointment. There was obviously something going on that was making him very closed-minded about the medication, but this wasn't the time or place to explore it.

I didn't wait long before I buttonholed him about it. In the car on the way home, I asked quietly, "Carson, why did you refuse every medication the doctor suggested? She knows what she's doing."

"I'm not going to pollute my body with that crap if I don't have to," he said tightly. "When I need it, I'll take it."

I glanced at him. This time he was driving, so he couldn't take his eyes off the road for long; but he seemed withdrawn and unusually tense. Hesitantly, I said, "What about an anti-anxiety medication? I'm sure you need that now."

When he glanced at me, he was as angry as I'd ever seen him, but his voice was steady and low. "Kathryn, I'm not going talk to you about any of this anymore, okay? Let's drop it. When I need the medications, we'll talk then."

I shut up, though I knew he needed it right now. I also knew that it was his body, and it was *his* right to decide what he was going to put in it. On the way home, though, Carson stopped by the store to pick up some beer, despite the doctor's warnings. This seemed weird to me: Carson would have a drink here and there, but he never really drank at home, at least not when we weren't entertaining. And what was that he'd just said about polluting his body?

I figured he'd had a really bad day, having to see the doctor and talk about his fate, and that his nerves were ragged. Maybe he deserved a little chemical relaxation.

So I kept quiet.

Self Medicating

The next couple of months were difficult, because Carson started to drink constantly. I had heard about people self-medicating with intoxicants, and I was glad it was alcohol and not anything harder. It really did start to get out of control, though, so one night I sat down to talk to him about the whole drinking thing.

He sat quietly as I began. "Carson, Dr. Callender told you specifically not to put neurotoxins into your body, and you know that alcohol is a neurotoxin."

All he said was, "Yes."

Exasperated, I cried out, "Then I don't understand why you're drinking so much! Do you need to see a counselor, to talk to somebody about all this?" He certainly hadn't been talking to *me*, which pissed me off—almost as much as the way he behaved after drinking. He kept losing his balance, falling down, and running into things. Now, I'd never known any drunks, but I knew as well as anyone how people acted when they drank too much. This was different: he would have weird movements, eerily similar to those of his mother when I'd first known her. It was almost like he was speeding the progression of this disease…and he didn't even care.

Instead of answering, Carson got up and walked out of the room.

I could never understand what he was feeling, though I'm sure drinking made some of the worry go away….even though it was one of the things the doctor had specifically said not to do.

He was so unapproachable these days, I didn't even know how to talk to him about it. Once, he'd been so easy to talk to; now talking to him was like talking to a brick wall. I knew he wasn't listening to anything I was saying most of the time. I didn't take it too personally, however, because he was like that with everyone; he lived in his own world nowadays, one he didn't want to let anyone else into. Eventually, I talked to Bill about Carson's drinking; he didn't have too much advice for me, though, because Elisabeth had never self-medicated. He was concerned about how his son was acting, of course, and he said he was going to have a talk with Carson.

I know that would just piss Carson off. He wasn't very reasonable anymore.

I let everything go too far, because I didn't want to have to deal with Carson's anger. I'd never experienced it before in all the years I'd known him, so it frightened me to the bone. He was never physically abusive, but who knew when the combination of the disease and the alcohol might make him snap? I had no idea what I would do if that happened.

I was sure this was a just a phase, and I thought maybe Carson would get better after he'd dealt with it on his own for a while. He was moody and kept to himself, but he hadn't done anything serious to the kids or me, so I just went day by day.

At this point, I was doing everything on my own; I got no help from Carson whatsoever anymore. I'd just about reached my limit, but I held my tongue, hoping the situation would soon change—and indeed it did. One night after putting the kids to bed and cleaning up after dinner, I told an unresponsive Carson that I was going to bed, and I fell asleep for a while. I woke up a little when I heard Carson in the shower, and then I heard a big thump. I listened for a second; when I heard Carson moving around, I figured everything was okay, so I rolled over and fell back to sleep.

Later I woke up suddenly, tasting something salty on my lips. Half asleep, I got up and walked into the bathroom. I turned on the light and screamed in terror at what I saw in the mirror: the whole side of my face was covered in blood! I turned on the water and started rinsing the blood off with big double-handfuls of water, frantically searching for the source of the blood…but I had no injuries, no scratches or anything, and I wasn't in any pain. Eyes widening, I ran back into the bedroom, flicked on the light, and was presented with a horrific sight: Carson lying in bed in a puddle of blood, like some murder victim. I ran to him and frantically searched to see where the blood was coming from, and found a puncture wound in the side of his head. It wasn't big, but it bled like crazy. That's when Carson woke up and looked up at me.

The expression on my face must have shaken him, because he asked in a frightened voice, "Kat, what's wrong?"

"You cracked your head open, you drunken idiot!" I shouted at him. Eyes wide, he felt around his head and then looked at his red-stained hand. He jumped out of bed and darted into the bathroom, me following. "Do you even have any idea when you did it?" I asked him, nearly hysterical.

"I...I have no clue," he admitted. "I don't remember anything happening to my head."

I just stood there staring at him. I simply couldn't grasp how someone could fall and crack their head open, yet have no clue as to how they did it. It made no sense at all. I looked around the bathroom to see if I could find any clues about what might have happened. I opened up the shower door, and saw that there was blood on the shower floor, and a little on the walls. Light dawned. That thump I'd heard while Carson was in the shower—that must have been when he did it! We had a little stand in the shower that held all of the shampoos and soaps, and it appeared that that was what had caused the damage. "Look here!" I ordered, and he looked into the shower. "You must have done it when you were taking a shower earlier."

He just looked into the shower and said slowly, "I wonder how that happened?"

"I don't have to wonder," I snapped. "I know *exactly* how it happened. You lost your balance, as usual, because you were drunk!" His balance was going fast anyway, but when he drank, he would fall everywhere. Even if he only had one or two drinks, he would soon be crashing into walls and bumping into things, and this time he'd fallen in the shower and injured his head. He was so out of it at the time that he had no clue that he'd hurt himself, so he just crawled into bed and went to sleep.

Shaking, not daring to speak, I cleaned up the blood in the shower. Then I sprayed stain remover on the spots on the carpet where he'd shambled back into the bedroom, and pulled the bloodstained sheets off the bed and replaced them with clean ones. They were ruined; I just wadded them up and tossed them in the garbage. I wasn't even going to try to wash them. There was blood all over the mattress, too, but I really didn't know what to do about that right then. I replaced the sheets and got back into bed.

Carson just looked at me helplessly, and I glared back. "Kat, I'm really sorry," he said eventually. "I didn't know it happened. I would never have made a mess like that and not cleaned it up if I'd known it was there."

I felt my blood start to boil as I slowly sat up. I was a steam engine, ready to blow. I just sat there staring at him for a long second before I exploded. "Is that some kind of a *joke*, Carson? You've done nothing but make a horrible mess of your life ever since we saw Dr. Callender, and *I've* been the one who's been forced to try to clean it up—unsuccessfully, I might add! What the hell are you sorry for? Are you sorry that you've been ignoring this family completely while you wallow in self-pity? Are you sorry that you haven't given a shit about your own health? Are you sorry that you could have died tonight, and never have known what hit you? Are you sorry because your blood is all over the damn house? Or are you sorry that I had to wake up this morning *with the taste of your blood in my mouth?*"

He just stared at me like a deer in the head lights.

"I am *so disgusted* by you!" I yelled, something I never thought I'd say to him. "Please don't talk to me anymore right now. You make me sick. I'm going back to bed now. It looks like I have to get up in a couple of hours and start scrubbing my idiot husband's blood out of my carpet."

"But—"

"Shut up! You're turning into a joke, Carson. I don't even recognize the man I see in front of me. You need to look at yourself in the mirror. If you like what you see, then hell, go on and live this life on your own—because I'm not going to sit around and let my kids and I take the fall. If you *don't* like who you're looking at, then you'd better change, and damn quickly. You're very close to losing your family, Carson Ferris, and then where will you be?"

I threw his pillow at him and said, "Think about that as you sleep on the couch tonight. What's left of tonight."

I rolled over and pulled the covers over me, feeling sick to death. After a few minutes, though, my anger faded, and guilt kicked in. Carson was terribly sick, and I didn't know what to do. Now I was dealing not only with Huntington's disease but alcoholism as well; I should have been more forceful earlier on, long before it ever got this bad. I didn't know what to do. What if the kids had walked in and seen all the blood? What if I went to the store one day and something happened to one of them—and Carson wasn't able to help? I loved my husband more than life, but I was a mother first now. My number one job was to protect my children—not just their health, but their innocence as well. They were too young to have to deal with horrors like this!

I sure didn't want my children remembering their dad as a man who drank all the time and wasted what was left of his life. Carson had built so many good memories with our children, but the human mind is wired to remember the bad, often at the expense of the good. The intense situations are the ones that seem to stick in our minds forever, and I didn't want my children to have to deal with memories of a drunken father. It was bad enough that one day, they'd see him ill and have to deal with that, just as Carson had been forced to deal with his mother's illness.

Maybe the thought of that was what had driven him to drinking in the first place. It was a very difficult situation—the classic notion between the rock and the hard place. I'd vowed to Carson to stand by him in good and bad, sickness and in health; but when I had gave birth or adopted my children, I 'd vowed to take care and protect them, too. I had never, ever expected that I would need to protect them from their own father. He was their hero...and it would crush them for that to be taken away.

I never did sleep that night.

The next morning, I decided I'd have another talk with Carson. I had to let him know what I was thinking; one way or another, I couldn't let this carry on any longer. I needed to talk to him while everything was fresh in my mind, so I took the kids to school and told Carson that we needed to go out to lunch and talk. I know he knew what was coming; I think he was just wondering how it would be delivered.

We found a quiet little café and sat in a booth in the back, where we could talk—and I talked. He listened. I told him everything I was feeling, how I felt like I was in a horrible, hopeless situation. I told him I loved him and wanted to stay true to the vows I'd made with him so many years ago—and then I talked about the children, and about how it was my job to protect them. At that point, he tried to open his mouth and say something, and I said, "No, you listen. It's my job to take care of those kids, no matter what, but it's *your job too*." Eyes blazing, I leaned forward and said in a low voice, "Carson, you're an amazing father. All three of those kids idolize you. You're their favorite person in the world. Now, *what would have they thought if they could've seen you last night?*"

Carson hung his head, clearly disappointed in himself for what had happened. "Sorry. I'm sorry, Kat." I glared at him for awhile, and he just looked at me and kept saying how sorry he was and that he didn't know why he was drinking so much, except that it made him feel better about everything.

"Sorry isn't good enough, Carson. It's time you went to the doctor and got on some anti-anxiety medication. It doesn't make you less of a man."

"I don't—"

"I don't care what you don't want. You need something. You can't keep drinking like this. All you're doing is killing yourself faster, at the expense of all the rest of us. You already have a disease that's killing your brain and nerve cells, and now you're putting a poison in your body that will help speed up the process! Haven't you thought about your obligation to this family? The kids and I don't get to have you for another seventy years! Our time with you is going to be cut short as it is, and I need you here as long as possible! I can't imagine how I'm going to do this on my own as it is…and you seem determined to bring the day that I *have* to even sooner! I don't understand why you would want to shorten the precious little time you have!"

He just stared at me, his eyes wide, and seemed to try to speak; but no sound emerged, so I forged on. "You have to remember your children, Carson. Unless a miracle happens, in a few years all they're going to have of you is their *memories*. When you're gone, they're going to grab on to every one of them. Don't you want your kids to remember you as the man you truly are? They don't need any memories of you like this. They need to remember you like you remember Elisabeth: as a parent who loved them unconditionally. Our kids need to remember you as a parent who ran around with them, played with them, and laughed with them. And, unfortunately, as a parent who had this horrible disease, but was strong and fought it till the very end."

I reached out and grabbed his hand, squeezing until it hurt. "They don't need to remember you as a quitter. They don't need to think that Daddy got this disease and then just gave up. They don't need memories of you stumbling around and mumbling at them. This is a critical time in all of their lives. Don't rob them of a healthy, loving relationship with you. Carson, you also have to remember that Elisabeth and Dylan have a chance of inheriting the Huntington's gene. If one of our children ends up with Huntington's disease, they're going to remember you when *you* had it—just as you remember your mother's journey. Your mother took it on so gracefully; I'm sure the first couple of years were rough, but by the time I met her she was so strong. She battled it till the end, and that's how our children need to remember you. If they do end up with it, they can't think that the answer is to drink the problem away. You're their example, and you need to set a good one. Do you understand that? When we first found out about the disease, you were so fearful over what would happen to our children. You said you wanted them to always stick to the right path—you didn't want them to become druggies. Remember? Well, what are you teaching them? You may not be doing any illegal drugs—but you *are* doing a very toxic legal one. They're going to follow the example you set. You need to set the right one."

Carson's eyes were filled with tears. This time, when he tried to speak, the words did come. "I, I don't know why I'm acting like this," he whispered. "I've never been like this before."

He fell silent as a waitress finally noticed we were there, and took our drink orders. When she was gone, he looked at me and said, blinking hard, "I'm so worried about so many things, Kat. My mind just won't stop. When I drink…well, everything is quiet for a little while."

He hung his head, looking miserable. "It makes me ashamed to admit it, but, well, I never really thought of what I was doing to you and the kids. I was just trying to help myself. I am *so* sorry. It *is* my job to protect all four of you, and I've been doing a terrible job of it. I don't ever want to be a threat to you or the kids, so—maybe it *is* time for me to start taking something. I don't know why I haven't yet. I've never thought it would make me less of a man. I just thought I could handle this on my own. It's clear I can't, so I'll get on the medicine. Maybe it'll help my mind calm down."

I heaved a sigh of relief. "It's worth a shot, Carson. We have to figure this out. I love you, and I *will* help you through this. But you have to let me. Please don't fight me on everything."

"I won't." Carson got up out of his chair and came over and kissed me. It was clear that he felt bad about everything, and the talk couldn't have made him feel any better…but if I knew my Carson, he'd do his damnedest to fix this.

After a leisurely lunch in which things calmed down and we talked like an ordinary couple, we went and picked up the kids from school together. Later, we had a great family night. We all sat together for dinner, for the first time in a while, then we went into the living room and played some board games. It almost felt normal again. We all laughed and teased each other, and I wished I could stay locked in this moment forever. Carson seemed to be doing very well; he was very much his old self.

That afternoon, I'd called Dr. Callender and had her call in a prescription for an anti-anxiety medication, which I picked up early the next morning. He began to take it under my watchful eyes, and it took about a month for the medicine to really start to work. I noticed changes in Carson's moods; some things still bothered him that never would have bothered him before, but overall he seemed much calmer. Before he got on the medicine, he was snapping at the kids all the time; I'd had to tell the kids to leave Daddy alone when I could see that he was in one of his moods. The medicine seemed to be helping a lot with that. He also seemed to handle daily irritations a little better.

Carson also noticed the difference. He said that he felt much better, and that things that had been overwhelming to him before didn't seem so bad now. We seemed to have his moods under control. Before, he told me, he felt like he was standing still and the world was moving around him so fast that it was all a blur. Now, he was starting to move with the world again, because it seemed like it had slowed down a little.

Reunion

One afternoon when I went to check the mail, I found an invitation for our ten year high school reunion. I'd talked to Page a couple of weeks before and she'd mentioned that she had talked to Kristine Pine, who had been our class president, and that Kris had been planning a class reunion. We had had such a small, tight-knit class, and I decided it would be fun to see the other students we'd gone to school with. I wondered who else would actually go. Most of us had moved out of town, because there wasn't much to do in Pollock as far as a career. I knew a couple of people who had stayed, but not very many. Now though, with the wonder of facebook, you could kind of sneak around and see what everyone had been up to.

I asked Page if she was going, and she said she would if I would. By then, she was living in Texas, so a flight back to California wasn't exactly a hop, skip, and a jump; but she seemed game. She said it would be a great chance to get together with me and visit her parents, too. I'd only seen her a handful of times since school, although we talked on the phone all the time, so it would be great to see her. In a sense, it was only a few hours away, after all.

I told her that if we went, we would bring our kids and they could stay with my Dad. That way, Page would get a chance to see them. She hadn't seen the kids since Dylan was a baby, when she came down once and stayed with us for a week. I was excited for her to see the kids, and knew it would be fun to see everyone. I figured Carson would want to go, too—he'd surely love to see all his old football buddies. The only one he still really talked to was Chris Pepper. I was sure everyone we'd been close to in high school knew what was going on with us; it was such a small town, and good or bad, news traveled like wildfire.

When Carson got home, I told him about the reunion. "Yeah, Chris mentioned something like that to me," he said thoughtfully.

"Did he say whether he'd be there?"

"He wasn't clear on that. I'll ask him tomorrow."

I nodded. "Well, is it something you want to do? It's not like it would be a long trip for us."

He grinned. "Actually, that would be fun! I'd love to see everyone again!"

"Well, it's in a month. What do you say I call my Dad, and make sure it's okay if we take over his house for a couple of days? I know he'd appreciate a visit."

"Sounds good to me, darlin'." Quite to my surprise, Carson swept me into his arms and kissed me soundly.

"Wow! I guess I should RSVP Kristine to let her know we'll be there. I can't let you miss your chance to see Mellissa Chace, after all."

In response to my teasing, he just rolled his eyes and said, "Oh yeah, ha ha ha." Grinning, he released me and went about his business.

As I recalled, Mellissa had a huge crush on Carson from the second she laid eyes on him. The truth was, I think a lot of girls in school liked him, and I didn't blame them. But we'd started dating so young that none of them ever really got a shot at Carson…though I have to say that all the other girls had a little more class about it than Mellissa did. Mellissa would flirt with Carson right in front of me— mostly, I think, because she was shocked that he would choose me over her. She was the cute cheerleader that all the boys talked about, after all—and she was also the girl who went through boys like tissue. I think she liked Carson more because he *wouldn't* give her the attention that all the other guys did. Carson was also the best football player in the whole school, of course, which to Mellissa meant that they should be together and have that perfect cheerleader-football player relationship. I think it was very frustrating to her that he wanted the plain girl. Last I heard, she had married and then divorced a year or so later. I believe she was working as a waitress or something like that. Not that I had much room to talk, since I was a stay-at-home mom…I wasn't complaining, but it wasn't as if I had some great career to brag about.

Still and all, Carson and I knew that I was doing the most important job in the world to us. Staying home and taking care of babies might not seem so important and exciting to some, but I found it very fulfilling. Still, I couldn't wait to see what people had done with themselves. I had heard that a couple of them had kids, like us, and I was surprised that more didn't; but then again, Carson and I had started everything so young. I did know that we were the first people in our class to start a family.

As the date of the reunion drew closer, I decided I'd have to go shopping to find the perfect outfit. I'd also have to go get my hair colored and my nails done. I was a little irritated at myself for thinking about all that I was planning to do to prepare for this reunion. I told myself I was being stupid; it was a silly small-town high school reunion, and only a ten-year reunion at that.

The reunion date arrived quickly, and as planned, we loaded up the kids and headed to Grandpa's house. When we arrived, Dad and Izzy were sitting on the front porch, and Dad hurried out to the car to start in on his grandchildren time. He was such a wonderful Grandpa! After we brought our stuff in the house, I went to my old bathroom and started getting ready, and Izzy kept me company. We talked about everything that was going on with Carson, we talked about the kids, and of course I asked Izzy how everything was going with her and Dad.

"Oh, everything is good," she said cheerfully, but there was something wistful in her tone as she continued, "I keep waiting for him to ask me to marry him, but I'm starting to think that day will never come."

"Don't give up," I told her. "I'm rooting for you." Izzy and I had become very close over the past few years, and I'd long since decided that I would love to see her and Dad married. I knew he loved her, and she took such good care of him; I really didn't understand why they weren't married already. I had supposed that it was because they were older, and were just happy the way things were. It seemed that Dad was, anyway.

I stopped doing my makeup and sat down on the edge of the bathtub. "So," I said, looking at her seriously, "have you ever talked to Dad about it?"

She sighed. "Well, of course I drop hints all the time…but he just brushes them off."

Poor thing. "Izzy! You should know by now that Dad's terrible at this 'dropping hints' thing! You have to hit him on the head with it!"

After that, we talked for a while about Mom, and how devastated Dad had been when she died. I was so young at the time that I didn't go through it with him, but from the stories I'd heard, it had been very hard on him and Cal. Maybe his hesitation with Izzy was because he was scared of losing someone again; or maybe it was just that he was one of those "if it's not broken, then don't fix it" men. I was pretty sure

Dad hadn't dated anyone since Mom died…in fact, to my knowledge, Izzy was the first woman he'd dated in 28 years.

"Please be patient with him, Izzy," I told her. "I really don't think he knows what he's doing." I didn't say that to be glib; I really meant it, and I decided I'd talk to him later about it. I would hate it if he lost Izzy because of his fear, or just from not knowing what she was looking for. "I'm going to talk to him about it when I have the chance, okay? I won't mention that you and I talked, but maybe I can steer the conversation in the right general direction." I stood up and hugged her impulsively. "I'd love for you to be my new step mom, you know."

When she released me, there were tears in her eyes. "So…want me to curl your hair while you finish up your make-up?"

"I'm not going to do a lot more, but that would be great!"

So I sat there on the toilet while Izzy curled my hair and we chatted. After she was done with her styling, she fixed my make-up a little. "You have to remember," I told her, laughing, "I grew up without a mom, so I'm really not good at this kind of stuff. I was raised as one of the boys who cooked and cleaned a lot!"

She chuckled and said, "Well, if your Dad had been able to teach you how to use make-up, I'm not sure I'd want to marry him. Luckily, though, I used to love to mess around with make-up and hair when I was younger." When Izzy was done I looked in the mirror, and I barely recognized myself: she'd done a marvelous job. "I'm going to fool everyone!" I blurted, and we laughed together. This was far from the real me, but no one had to know that.

I slipped on the dress I'd bought for the occasion, and we walked down the stairs together. Carson was sitting on the couch talking with my dad, and when he looked over at me, he froze. When he could speak, he said quietly, "Oh, man. Babe."

I laughed and said, "Hey, I stay at home all the time. There isn't much going on for me to get all made-up over, so I turned up the volume today."

Dylan, who was on Carson's lap, looked up at his dad and said, "Mommy sure is pretty!"

Still looking at me, Carson said, "Oh yes, Mommy is *very* pretty."

Feeling a little self-conscious, I laughed again and said, "Okay, babe, we'd better get going." I kissed all my children and told them good night, seeing as how I was sure we wouldn't be home until after they were asleep.

Feeling like a couple of teenagers, Carson and I jumped in the car and headed for the hall where they were holding the reunion. We passed by our old school on the way, and that brought back memories of driving to high school every day together. We were high school sweethearts, and here we were, still together on our ten-year reunion. I called Page on the way, and she said she was there and would wait out front for us; she was bringing her fiancé, a man I hadn't met but had heard all about. They'd been dating now for about two years, and he had just asked her to marry him. I was so excited for her; she had been career-driven for so long, and I was glad that she was finally going to get a chance to have a family. I'd been afraid it would go the other way, since she was a journalist, and they have to be pretty dedicated to their jobs. Thank goodness she'd met Erik, or she might have remained married to her job for the rest of her life.

When we pulled up to the hall, I jumped out of the car and ran over to Page. In seconds we were like two schoolgirls again, chattering at each other a million miles a minute about how good we looked, and how good it was to see each other. Carson walked up to Erik and introduced himself, noting laconically, "This may take a while." Page smacked Carson on the arm, just like old times. Erik was very handsome; he looked like a well-to-do business man.

After the introductions were completed, we walked up to the sign-in area, where Kristine Pine gave us each a hug and our nametags. "Yeah, it's going to be hard remembering everyone, having such a big class and all," I said, laughing. But we put our nametags on anyway, and proceeded to the banquet room. Carson went straight over to some old football buddies he saw standing in a corner talking, and they all high-fived him and gave each other the whole handshake/man-hug thing. I walked with Page to get a glass of wine, and we sat at the bar area and talked about her trip here. Otherwise, we didn't have much to catch up on, seeing as how we talked on the phone all the time.

She did say that she had something to ask me, however: she wanted to know if there was anyway I could come down to Texas for her wedding, because she wanted me to be one of her bridesmaids.

"We'll absolutely be there!" I told her. "I would be honored." From the way things sounded, it was going to be a huge event.

While we were sitting there talking, I looked over at Carson. He was standing with Erik and a group of other guys, and as I watched two women walked up and joined them. I told Page to look over, and we glared at Mellissa Chace and Caitlyn Scully standing there, laughing and chatting it up with the guys. Page and I looked at each other, and I said, "Looks like my husband and your fiancé need our help right about now."

Casually, we got up and made our way over to the guys. I walked right up next to Carson, and said hi to all the guys and gave them hugs. Billy Roe, one of the guys Carson had played ball with, said heartily, "Carson was just filling us in on the kids and what you've been up to the last ten years. Sounds like you have a great life."

I leaned into Carson and said sweetly, "We do. There's been a lot going on." I noticed that Mellissa was just standing there, and I smiled and said brightly, "Hey, Mellissa!"

"Hello, Kathryn," she replied. "You look great."

"You too!" I said. You know, typical girl thing.

Shortly after, the two girls made up some excuse to dismiss themselves, and when they were gone, I looked at Carson and said, "Some things never change."

The whole group started laughing, and Billy said, "Looks like I'll have to take her off your hands," and walked off after Mellissa.

Soon, we all retired to a table that Page had found for us, so we could all sit together. It was so much fun, sitting and talking with our old friends. It brought back feelings of another time in our lives, a time that was simple and relatively worry-free. Of course, we'd had Carson's mother to worry about at that time, but we never worried about what the future would bring. Back then, Carson and I were young and in love. All I ever worried about was stupid things, like Mellissa trying to steal Carson away from me. That had seemed huge at the time, but it was less than nothing now, given what I *do* have to worry about.

I wanted to go back to that time; I suppose it's true that ignorance is bliss. Back then, I had wanted to grow up and be Carson's wife so badly that it hurt. I couldn't wait to be an adult, to be independent and able to love my man the way I wanted to. How ironic; now I wanted to go back. If there *had* been some way to go back to the worry-free, light life I'd had back then while keeping my children, I would have done it in a heart beat.

We try so hard to grow up so fast…and then, when we get there, all we want to do is go back to our childhoods.

I listened to everyone's stories, feeling almost jealous. I'm sure they all had worries, like not having enough money and finding the right person to share their lives with…but they had no idea what worry really was. I wished that all we had were financial worries; those we could overcome. This reunion really showed me how different our lives were, compared to those of most people our age. We had to worry about a terminal illness; we had to worry about how life would be once Carson really got sick, and I had to face becoming a widow at a very young age. I didn't have the luxury of thinking about how when our kids grew up and moved out, there would be time for just Carson and me. That would never happen for us; in fact, I would probably be sitting here alone at the next reunion. I wouldn't have the love of my life sitting next to me, joking with all his friends about the past.

I would give up all of our money and everything we had, just to have Carson live to be an old man.

After we ate, a DJ starting playing hits from back when we were in high school. Soon, people were getting up and dancing. I loved to dance; I wasn't really that great at it, but I still loved it. Carson, on the other hand, had what he called "white boy moves." He was a horrible dancer, and he didn't really like to dance, but he knew I loved it. So he looked over at me and said, "Come on, babe, let's show them how it's done."

Everyone still at the table immediately started laughing. "Oh, so you've taken dance lessons since high school?" Billy asked.

Chris said, "Yeah, Carson, we all remember how you used to dance. Let's see if things have gotten any better!"

I laughed and reassured them all that a lot had changed, but Carson's dance skills were pretty much the same. We got up and made our way to the dance floor, and everyone from our table got up to join us. We had a great time turning and spinning to the music we used to dance to at school dances. Carson swung me around and around (to take attention away from his terrible moves, no doubt), and after a couple of songs we all started to gather in a corner to talk again.

When all the guys started talking about going to a little bar in town, I looked at Carson with tired eyes, and he got the hint. "We're going to pass on the after party," he said regretfully.

"Yeah, we're pretty old now," I said. "Having three kids really takes a toll on your partying stamina!"

Carson and I said our goodbyes to everyone, and we all vowed to try to keep in better touch with each other. I told Page that we would meet her in the morning at the diner for breakfast, so that she could see the kids—and so we could talk about the wedding, too.

When Carson and I got in the car to drive home, he turned in the direction opposite from the house. "Where are we going?" I asked curiously.

"I want to go to the place where I first fell in love with you," he told me quietly. A few minutes later, we stopped at the path that led to the creek. He looked at me and asked, "You up to going to the old' swimming hole?" The truth was, I was exhausted; but I would power through anything to revisit the spot where Carson asked me to be his wife. We got out of the car and walked down the trail to our spot, stopping at the ledge where we used to jump off into the water, and sat down on the cool grass. I sat between Carson's legs, and he hugged me from behind. The moon made a perfect reflection on the water.

"Do you remember doing this?" he asked quietly.

"Do I remember? Carson, I *loved* coming out here with you."

"So did I! I remember the first time we came here together."

"Yep, this is where most of our friends met you for the first time. All the girls were so excited to have a new boy in town. Especially Mellissa."

"Ha!" I could hear the smile in his voice as he continued, "I really didn't notice them; I only noticed you. You were the only one I *ever* noticed. I don't think I would have ever believed in the love at first sight thing if it hadn't happened to me."

"And *I* remember thinking there was no way you would ever be interested in me. I thought you would be the new boy who would work his way through all the popular girls…I thought you were too perfect for someone like me."

"You're so silly."

"No, I'm serious! I'm glad you chose me. I couldn't have asked for a better life. I have you, and that's more than I ever thought I would have. I also have the three most amazing children in the world. My life is perfect…well, except for the whole Huntington's thing. I could do without that part."

"You and me both." He sighed. "I was thinking about that tonight. I was thinking about fourteen years ago, when you and I were together here, not having to think about what we have to think about now. I was a stupid kid, without a care in the world. Now… the world feels so heavy."

I patted his knee. "Yeah, heavy is a good word for it. But we'll get through it."

"I know we will. Now, are you ready to go home and go to sleep?"

"Yeah, we'd better go, or you're going to be carrying me home."

"I would carry you anywhere," he said quietly, and kissed me on the side of my neck. That still sent shivers all through my body.

We made our way back home, and went right to sleep the minute we crawled into bed. Quite the party animals, we were. The next morning, we took the kids out to breakfast with Page and Erik, where Page and I talked about all their wedding plans while, Carson and Erik talked about guy stuff.

After we returned home, Carson "volunteered" to take the kids over to the park to let them run off some energy before our drive home, leaving me alone with Dad for a while. I was eager to see where he was with Izzy, because she was such a perfect fit to our family. She was living with Dad now; I didn't really know what was holding him back from popping the question.

"Let's go for a walk." I suggested once Carson and the kids were away, and we went traipsing down one of the public trails near the house. We chatted for a while, before he asked me how Carson was doing. I think he thought that's why I wanted to go for a walk in the first place: so we could talk about Carson. So I played along. I told Dad about the new medication Carson was on for his moods, and how it seemed to be working. Then, after we fell into a companionable silence for a few moments, I asked suddenly, "And where are things going with you and Izzy?"

"Well," he said cautiously, "I wanted to talk to you about me and Izzy." I was a little surprised, but glad, because it seemed like this conversation was going to be easier than I expected. "So, kid, what do you think of her?"

"Are you kidding? I love Izzy, Dad. She's been a really good friend to me, and the kids love her too. It's nice to have a grandmother figure for them."

He looked at me and grinned. "I'm happy you think so, because you know, she makes *me* happy."

"Gosh, really, Dad? I never would have noticed." I rolled my eyes. "C'mon, I can *tell* she makes you happy. I know you love Izzy— I can see it in the way you look at her."

"I do love her," he said quietly, "and I've been thinking that it's probably about time I asked her to marry me."

I clapped my hands joyfully. "Dad, that would be great!" I stopped and put a hand on his shoulder. "But please do me a favor. Don't ask her like that."

"What do you mean?"

"Don't say, 'Well, I was thinking it was about time for me to ask you to marry me.' Please!"

He laughed. "Kathryn, I may be getting old, but I'm not *stupid*."

I made a big show of sighing and wiping my brow. "Whew! Well, that *is* refreshing. I was afraid…well, you *have* been out of the game for a while, you know."

"True enough. I haven't really thought about how or when I'm going to do it, but I'll ask her. I just wanted to talk to you about it first."

"Dad, I know I was the only girl in your life for a long time. I'm so busy now that I'm glad you've found someone you love and who loves you back. I'm relieved that you'll have someone to grow old with. Being alone isn't very healthy." I hugged him impulsively. "You've been the best Dad any girl could ask for. I know it must have been hard raising us on your own. You've been so selfless for so long, and it's your turn to be happy. Know what I mean?"

"Well, you kids always made me happy," he said, as we disengaged from the hug.

"I know, Dad, but now we're grown and gone. It's your turn…and I think this decision is a good one. Izzy's a good woman. I'd be honored to have my children call her Grandma. Even though I probably won't be doing the whole Mom thing with her—I'm a little too old for that now—she is a really close friend, and I give you my blessing."

We both laughed and started back to the house, where we spent an hour drinking coffee and chatting. When Carson and the kids got back, we packed up the car and headed home. Carson was pretty well wiped out from trying to keep up with three energetic children, so I drove, and told him about my conversation with Dad on the way home. "Great news!" he said enthusiastically.

"Yes, but don't say anything, because I'm not sure when Dad's going to ask her."

"Probably won't be long now," Carson predicted. "I think he was probably just waiting to talk to you about it."

"You think?"

"Sure. When us guys make a decision like that, we usually act on it pretty quickly." He grinned. "I know I did."

"Sounds like we've got a lot of wedding stuff going on in the near future."

After we made it home and put the kids to bed, Carson and I curled up next to each other in bed and talked about our trip home. "I miss that little town," he told me suddenly. "Now I know why Mom wanted to move there."

"I would love to move back there someday," I said drowsily.

"Maybe we can talk about that in a couple of years," he said. "I can't leave Dad and the practice right now, but someday…"

Life settled back to normal for the next few months—though I began to notice a clear change in Carson's movements. He seemed to be moving uncontrollably a lot more often lately; it would get so bad at times that he would knock things over. It got to the point where he'd broken more things in a month than he'd broken in his whole life previously, and he began losing his depth perception. He would be walking along, and just walk into a wall or door jamb. One day, when we were visiting Toys 'R Us to pick up something for the kids, he ran into the car next to us as he was pulling into a parking spot. Another time, when we were sitting down to eat at a restaurant, he hit the table and almost knocked the whole thing over. When we would go shopping, he would run into the displays. I could tell he was embarrassed when these situations happened, and I tried to tell him that it was okay and it wasn't his fault—but that didn't really seem to help. "People must think I'm drunk all the time," he'd tell me. "What else could they think?"

I'd just reply, "Who cares what people think? The only people who really count already know the truth."

The Getaway

We still hadn't fully explained to our kids what was going on with their father. Now, though, with things progressing and getting more noticeable, we decided it was time to sit down and lay it all on the line. It was better at this point for them to know and understand, rather than to just wonder why their Dad was changing so much. The kids were starting to get older, and they were all very observant; I was surprised, in fact, that they hadn't asked us yet about the changes.

After we talked about how we would go about the whole thing, Carson and I decided it was time for a family trip; we'd explain it to them then. His movements were getting pretty bad at this point, and we knew it was only going to get worse. He wanted to snorkel and hike around the Caribbean while he still could; we had no idea how much longer he would be able to do all the things he wanted to do. So we decided to book a cruise. That way, the kids could go to cruise camp, so we could enjoy things in our own way, and we wouldn't have to worry about anything. We booked the southern Caribbean cruise, it hit seven islands in seven days. I also booked four nights in an all inclusive resort in San Juan before we flew home.

Of course, I immediately started rushing around and shopping for all the things we'd need, and went to the school to tell them that my kids needed work for the next 10 days because we were going on a trip. Now, the principal at my daughters' school really didn't like it when kids missed school; he'd go off on this kick about how it wasn't good for the children, and the district would get involved if they missed anymore school, blah blah blah. I was so sick of hearing the same old song and dance. I knew why they wanted the kids at school: money. If the kids missed school, the state wouldn't send them as much cash. I really didn't care: my concern was that my children got to spend as much time as possible with their Dad before he couldn't do these kinds of things anymore. I was sure that my children would remember this vacation and the memories they made with their father much more sharply than whatever they would've learned in school that week.

This time when I went in the office, I was expecting the whole talk. When the school secretary started in, I slapped her desk and said fiercely, "I. Don't. Care. I'm sick and tired of you people being worried more about the money you'll get if my kids are sitting in class than about the mental health of my family. My husband has a terminal illness. My children are going to spend as much time with him as they can while he's still capable of doing things with them. That's all there is to it. Have their work ready in two weeks." Then I walked out.

Maybe I was pretty harsh to the secretary, but the one thing I was learning through this whole experience was to stand up to hidebound fools rather than be a pushover. I was the voice for my family in everyway. I was the voice for Carson to his doctors. I was the voice to protect my family. I had become pretty hard, I suppose, given all that I had experienced in the past couple of years.

I left the school and did more shopping; after all, I had just two weeks to make this whole vacation come together. If it had been just Carson and I, it would have been easy; but three active kids made it a lot more work. We were in the middle of winter, and it was freezing this time of year; I had all the kids' summer clothes packed away, so I had to pull all that out and buy replacements for what they'd already outgrown. I was also looking for some new things to take on the trip with us, but given the time of year, there was absolutely nothing summery on any shelves of any of the stores. Ultimately, I'd have to get a lot of the stuff we needed when we got there.

Personally, I was excited about the opportunity to get some sun. I got online and looked up the average weather on the islands we were going to, and found that it was sunny and in the high 80s this time of year. Seeing as how we had freezing conditions on some days, I just could not wait to soak up all the sun I could.

The trip came before we knew it, and we all piled on a red-eye flight to Puerto Rico. It was a really long flight, and I knew that it would be easier with the kids if we did the eight-hour flight while they slept. They seemed so excited when we got on the plane, though, that I was worried that they wouldn't go to sleep. I pulled down their little trays when we were in the air and put a page of homework down in front of each of them; I knew *that* would eventually put them to sleep. If it didn't, I had a ton of other work that they had to get done before they went back to school. I'd rather have them do it on the plane, so it didn't cut into any of our vacation time.

The plane landed in New York for a layover, so we all went and got something for breakfast and then waited for our next plane to arrive to take us to San Juan. As we were boarding our plane, I could see that Carson was having some trouble. He was wavering back and forth, and his eyes were bloodshot from not getting much sleep; he seemed to be in a fog. When we got on the plane, I gave him some Neurontin that I kept on hand for times like these. It put him right to sleep, and he was zonked out for the whole flight from New York to San Juan.

When we arrived in San Juan, we had a couple of hours before we boarded the cruise ship, so we did the touristy thing and walked around old San Juan for awhile. That was where the cruise terminal was, so we were able to stay close while still exploring a bit. When we were able to board the ship, we checked in and went straight to the pool. Luckily, I'd packed a little bag with our suits in it, since I knew we wouldn't have access to our luggage for a while.

Carson still seemed a little shaky. I figured the long flight and the horrible sleep was getting to him.

That night, we checked the kids into camp. They had so many activities for the kids, to keep them busy and wanting to come back, and to give the parents some adult time. Meanwhile Carson and I went to the formal dinner, and then we decided to go to the casino to do a little gambling. As we were walking to the casino, Carson's movement was a little unsteady, so I locked my arm around his. I don't know if he thought I was just trying to be close to him, or was helping him walk…it was a little bit of both for me, so he was right no matter what he thought. As we approached the casino Carson tripped; luckily, I had his arm, so I kept him from falling.

I was angry and mortified when one of the ship's security guards walked up to us and said sharply, "Sir, have you been drinking tonight?"

I couldn't believe what was happening; I thought, *What an idiot*, and I snapped, "Excuse me? My husband hasn't had *anything* to drink tonight. He happens to have a disease that sometimes impairs his balance. "By then I was building up a pretty fair head of steam, so I got in his face and hissed, "*How dare you* approach us like this. Look all around you, at all the people being loud and stupid—and you have the *nerve* to snap at us because my husband tripped?"

The guard swallowed and said, "Um, ma'am, I'm sorry, but it's my job to make sure everyone is safe and that no one is out of control.

I didn't mean to offend you in anyway. Can I, uh, just get your room number for reference?"

"Hell of a job if you didn't mean to offend us, because you just did. We're not out of control. And we're in cabin 1085, if you must know. Now, can I get your name, so I can complain about how you totally messed up tonight? You need to watch people a little more, mister, before you come up and start accusing them of things. This is unbelievable, and—"

Right then, I felt Carson tug on my arm. "Come on, that's enough, Kat. Let's not let our night be ruined."

"Sir, I apologize," the security man said quietly.

Carson, being the complete gentleman that he is, smiled and replied, "That's okay. You're just doing your job."

After Carson spoke to him, I think the guard realized that he was wrong. I saw in his eyes that he was genuinely sorry for putting us in a situation like this, but I still gave him a hard little glare before I walked away.

Carson and I sat down next to each other and played video blackjack. After a few hands, he looked at me and asked, "Is that what I look like to everyone? Like a drunk?"

"Don't worry about that guy," I said fiercely. "He was a complete idiot."

He sighed. "Hon, I'm serious. Is that *really* what people think when they see me moving around, especially when you have to support me?"

"I'm not sure what people think when they look at you, Carson." I looked at him; in the dimness of the casino, his face seemed gray and drawn. "And I don't care." I reached out and clutched his hand. "I admit, I feel a little bad about going off on that guy the way I did. I guess I just reacted, which is happening to me a lot these days. But let's not worry about that, okay? We're here to have a good time."

He smiled and went back to his game. So did I, but I was distracted. Of course the security guard hadn't known that Carson had a neurological disease; how could he? I was so used to Carson and his movements that I probably didn't notice them as much as everyone else did. I also knew about his condition, so I didn't have to wonder why it was happening. Other people had to guess why he moved the way he did…so I suppose people who had never been around anyone with Huntington's might think it was alcohol or drugs causing him to move like that. The problem was most people don't have a clue what

Huntington's disease is, and even fewer have ever been around someone afflicted with it.

After playing for an hour, Carson said he was ready to go pick up the kids and head back to our room for bed. I thought that was a perfect idea; I was sure the kids were just as exhausted as we were. The next morning we were going to stop over in Barbados, and we'd need a lot of energy to go exploring. So we went and gathered in our children, and all five of us were soon sound asleep.

Carson did much better the next day; I think his poor body had just needed a good night's sleep. The rest of our trip was fantastic. The camp the kids were going to had activities that they wanted to participate in on that day...and I was such a protective mom I couldn't imagine leaving our kids at camp and going onto the island without them. However, Carson wisely talked me into spending the first half of the day on the island with him, letting the kids enjoy themselves on the ship. There was a hike up to a waterfall he wanted to try, and we both knew that it would be way too hard for Elisabeth, Selena, and Dylan to handle. After the hike, we thought we'd spend the rest of the day shopping.

I was apprehensive about doing this, but in the long run I was so glad we did. Carson and I took a taxi to the falls and got there early, so there were only a few other people there. The hike wasn't as bad as I'd feared, and the view at the top was simply heavenly. I was almost overwhelmed: all my senses were struggling just to grasp everything that amazing place had to offer. It smelled crisp and dewy, like a fine spring morning, and was cooler than I expected. The trees, grass and moss surrounding us were brilliantly green; the water was vitreous and translucent. I could feel the moisture in the air coating my skin like a coverlet, as the birds around us chirped their enchanting little melodies. The monkeys swinging from limb to limb overhead were less enchanting, but still delightfully exotic. This virgin land was a place that I thought still existed only in our imaginations!

It was a perfect place for meditation, and I could have sat there all day and taken it in. There was nothing but beautiful nature surrounding us. The falls were in the middle of a rainforest, and all was quiet and tranquil. All we could hear, really, was the sound of the wildlife and the water falling into the pool underneath it. We decided to go back down and take a swim in the pool, so when we got to the bottom, Carson jumped right in. I got in much more slowly—the water was refreshing, but really cold! We swam around for a minute or two.

Then we went over to the falls, and Carson stood beneath the cascade as I wrapped my legs around his waist.

Life wasn't perfect, but there we were, in paradise. I couldn't imagine a more peaceful, beautiful place in the world.

While we were wading in the water, it started to rain. The rain falling from the sky was warm; it may have been because the water in the pool was so cool, but the rain felt magnificent. I lifted my hands and looked up at the sky, feeling the warm drops grazing my face, and a sense of euphoric tranquility and peace ran through my being. When I looked over at Carson, he was doing more or less the same thing; and we both started laughing. I did not want this moment to end; I knew it was a moment I would remember for always. Everything disappeared as the stress flowed out of my body; I felt so blissful, and wanted to stay there with my perfect man forever.

Too soon, the rain stopped, and the sun peeked through a break in the clouds. The sunshine felt so good against my cold skin, and I shivered in delight.

"It's probably time to head back," I said softly.

"Oh?" Carson hugged my body close to his, and his warm body felt delicious against my icy skin. "Let's stay here forever. Let's not go back. Well, we have to go get the kids, but after we do that, we can stay here, right?"

I looked at him and smiled. "Okay. I'll go anyplace with you, and stay there forever, if you like."

We maintained our embrace for a while, pretending that we really could stay there like that forever, before Carson said briskly, "Okay, let's get back."

We got out of the water and dried off, then headed back to our drop-off point. A taxi was waiting for us...and just like that it was over. I was so sad to leave that perfect place, that perfect moment, but one thing was for sure: no matter what happened, I would remember that magical moment with Carson forever. I had a place in my head that I could go back to whenever I felt overwhelmed.

If there's a heaven, I hope it's exactly like that.

We went to so many wonderful places over the next six days that I just couldn't keep track. I love the Caribbean; I decided that it would be a place I'd love to retire to with Carson someday, if we made it that far. Unfortunately, though, that dream would most likely never be our reality. If Huntington's disease had its way, we would never get to grow old together and spend our final years in paradise. As far as we knew, this was all we had—and we were both determined to enjoy it. Until this disease was cured or Carson died, it would always be day-by-day with us.

I guess if you had to live day-by-day, we were doing it right...at least for the moment.

Breakthrough

When we returned home after our Caribbean bliss, one of my first acts was to check my email, and one message in particular jumped out at me. It was from the HDSA, and the subject line blared in all capitals: TETRABENAZINE THE FIRST DRUG APPROVED FOR HUNTINGTON'S DISEASE BY THE FDA. Holy cow! I read the email with growing excitement: it seemed that the FDA had finally, *finally* approved a drug that helped people with Huntington's disease. It wasn't a cure, but it helped control their movements. This was such extraordinary news! I immediately called Carson into the room and showed him the email, and it wasn't long before he had a huge smile on his face. This was a drug that Carson really needed to be on, because his movements were growing progressively worse. Tetrabenazine should help with that—and it also gave us hope. Despite what the Dr. Feinberg's of the world thought, things were happening.

There were numerous drugs undergoing clinical trials for Huntington's, and it was so frustrating to know you couldn't get your hands on any of them unless you were in the trials. Even then, you might end up on a placebo instead. Yet Carson and I knew how important these trails were, and how important it was to participate in these trails, because it was the only way to see if the drugs worked—and it was the only way that they could be approved by the FDA. It seemed like such a long, crazy process…but this was such great news. A drug *had* made it through the trials! The drug really *did* help people with HD with their movements, and so the FDA had passed it.

"We need to call Dr. Callender and get a prescription right away," I said excitedly.

"I'll do it first thing in the morning," he vowed.

I thought about our trip, particularly the security guard who had accused Carson of being drunk. I realized that sort of thing was really hard for Carson; not only were his uncontrolled movements and the resulting clumsiness embarrassing at times, they occasionally prevented him from doing things he wanted to. He would get so frustrated trying, and I didn't know what to do when I watched him struggling; he was so prideful that he would never ask me for help. In the end, he would usually just walk away with his head down.

Thank Heaven there was now a drug that would help with that! It would be great to not have to wake up to see how bad Carson was on a particular day. I had learned to live with it, and sometimes I was blind to how bad it actually was. Carson, on the other hand, felt every little movement. He knew *exactly* how bad he was, and was conscious of the world as it was, he had to be acutely aware of everyone's stares, and had to wonder what people were thinking. He was also worried about the kids being scared. We still hadn't talked to them about his illness, except in the most general way…but he was worried that on the bad days, they knew something was very wrong. They were as perceptive as their father, and he feared that they were scared about what was going on with him.

This drug was a huge relief for Carson and I. Even if it only helped him with some of the movement, that would mean so much for us all.

When we went to see Dr. Callender a week later, she examined Carson thoroughly and proclaimed that Tetrabenazine was a good fit for him. She warned us, though, about the process we would have to go through to get this new drug. Seeing as how it was so new, it wasn't something you could just go the pharmacy and pick up; we would have to wait for the drug company to send it to us.

As Dr. Callender filled out the prescription, she said, "I'll send this in for you, okay? It'll be quicker that way. The company will be contacting you soon; they'll need to talk to you, Carson, and ask you some questions before they send it to you."

"Why would they do that?" I asked. "If you say Carson should be on the drug, why would the drug company try to step in on your orders?"

"Well," she said hesitantly, "there's a nasty side effect that worries both the company *and* me."

"Nastier than being unable to control your own movements?" Carson asked wryly.

"I guess that depends on your definition of nasty," Dr. Callender admitted. "You see, some of the people who have taken Tetrabenazine have had suicidal thoughts. A few have actually acted on their thoughts."

I gasped; I hadn't expected this. Oh, I knew that there were side effects to almost every drug; I always read the warning labels, especially for the antibiotics Dr. Creswell put the kids on when they got sick. There are always the usual suspects—upset stomach, drowsiness, dizziness—but suicide? That particular side effect was hard for me to swallow. Hesitantly, I asked, "Is that true? I mean, is it common? I know they have to list all possible side effects by law, no matter how rare, but are they doing this to just watch their backs?"

"It's not that simple," she said.

"Has it *really* happened?" I pressed. "How many people has it happened to? Are there any drugs that make it worse?" I had a million questions I needed answered.

She looked at me levelly and said, "Yes, Kathryn, it's happened. However, this is *not* a common side effect, okay? I assure you, there's no way the FDA would approve a drug that had that effect on most of the people who took it." She glanced at my husband. "Carson is already on anti-depressants, which is a good thing."

She looked at Carson searchingly. "Carson, have you ever thought about ending your life before?"

Carson looked startled. "Absolutely not! Even after I found out I was positive, the thought never crossed my mind. I have too much to live for."

"Good. Just be careful." She handed each of us one of her business cards. "I know you have some of these, but I want you to keep these on you at all times. Carson, if you ever have any thoughts that are out of the ordinary, call me immediately." She directed her attention to me. "Kathryn, watch him closely in the first few weeks after he goes on the drug. Keep an eye on his moods, and if there are any significant changes in any direction, tell me *right away*. I mean it."

When we left the doctor's office, I was terribly nervous. I'd been so happy when I'd first learned about Tetrabenazine, and now I was just scared. As we walked to the car, I asked him. "Babe, are you nervous about taking this drug?"

"Nope, not at all," he said matter-of-factly. "Kathryn, I'd never kill myself. I know how good I have it, and I would never, ever leave you and the kids alone. Not deliberately." He stopped and grasped my shoulder, looking deep into my eyes. "Honey, there are some things I can't control. If Huntington's disease takes me out, well, there's really nothing I can do about that, except prepare for it and make sure you all will be taken care of. I would never kill myself; I love my life too much."

Trembling I said, "I know that. I do. But drugs can do horrible things to your body chemistry. If you get on this drug, will you listen to me if I think I see any changes? Will you believe me and have yourself checked?"

"Absolutely I will! I don't want anything bad to happen."

About a week later, the drug company did call Carson. They asked him some questions, just as Dr. Callender had warned us, and in the end they decided he would be fine on the drug. They told him they would send it to us immediately, but before he got a refill, they needed to talk to him about how he'd done on it. If everything was okay, they would continue him on the medicine.

When the Tetrabenazine arrived and Carson started taking it, I watched him like a hawk. Thank God, he didn't experience any mood changes. The medicine made him a bit groggy, but aside from that, there were no other side effects. It wasn't a perfect solution, but it really did help his movements, and he seemed to be having a lot more good days now. There were still times when the chorea was obvious, but it wasn't a daily battle like it had been.

The medication also helped Carson with work. Carson and Bill were working on some pretty big cases at the time, and Bill really needed Carson's help, so he seemed to be at the office a lot more than he had been. This was fine with me; it almost felt better, knowing he was working and carrying on with his life, and I think working with his Dad kept his memory a little sharper. We were already starting to have some issues with Carson forgetting things, which was another result of the Huntington's disease. Dr. Callender put Carson on some medication they give to people with Alzheimer's, and he did seem to get better; I don't know if it was the medication working, or if it was him working his mind on these cases. In any case, the medications he was on seemed to be working well. Of course, I kept wishing for the magic pill that would cure him; but as long as his quality of life was better because of these pills we had, then I was happy with that for now.

Another annual Huntington's conference was coming up; it would be the fourth we had attended. The previous three years, it had seemed like we'd been hearing more or less the same things. There were some pretty cool new stories, though, like Tetrabenazine being the first drug approved for Huntington's, and the previous year we'd heard from a wonderful man who worked for a company called CHI, which was dedicated to finding new medications for Huntington's. They were testing so many new drugs, and it seemed like there was a lot of exciting news. I really didn't understand most of it, but it seemed wonderful.

The invitation for the conference listed all the keynote speakers and what they would be talking about—and this year, one would be discussing something called "stem cell therapy" for Huntington's. I wasn't sure what that was all about; it all seemed far too complicated for me, and they used a lot of terms that I didn't understand. When I called a friend of mine who was a doctor, she told me to check PBS.com for a site that discussed what "RNAi" meant. So I went online, and watched a cartoon explanation of the whole issue. While I thought that was a great way to handle it, I felt pretty stupid that it was the only way I understood it. But the truth was, watching it made the whole topic a lot easier to comprehend and digest.

It's amazing how our bodies can almost cure themselves, given the right opportunity. After learning a little about stem cell technology, I was excited to go to the conference and listen to this doctor speak. I'd heard a little about stem cell treatment before, on TV at least, and I knew they were already doing various flavors of stem cell therapy in other countries. Here in the United States, sadly, we were just starting to break into the subject. It seemed a very complicated issue; some religious groups were totally against it, claiming it involved the sanctity of life and that embryos were destroyed to obtain stem cell lines. I had never bothered to pay too much attention to the matter, since I didn't know anyone who needed stem cell therapy…or, at least, I didn't think I did.

After researching it for a while, I realized that stem cell therapy had promise to help a *lot* of people who were ill. It's a pretty amazing thing, actually. When I was reading about the stem cell for Huntington's disease, they mentioned extracting stem cells from adult bone marrow; they never mentioned anything about embryos at all. I also read that they could get stem cells from scraping human skin. It was exciting; I talked to Carson about everything I read, and how I couldn't wait to see what this new doctor had to say about what she was working on.

We went to the conference a couple of weeks later, and attended all the workshops we could that morning. After we took a break for lunch, the doctor we had been waiting for—Phyllis Harrington—got up to speak, and we were interested to learn that there was new state funding to create a stem cell research facility. Dr. Harrington displayed pictures of the facility that was being built in our city, and there were images of people walking around in labs wearing white full-body suits, testing and growing stem cells. She showed us slides of people working with mice and doing other types of research, then began discussing where they were heading with stem cells in regards to Huntington's disease. She was so wonderful, and I realized that it must be very hard for her, speaking to a room of people who didn't really understand much about science, especially medical science. Most of us, I'm sure, never took much biology in school—and if we had, it had been years ago, and we didn't really retain much. I, for one, was completely lost. During her PowerPoint presentation, she displayed a series of graphs that, mostly, made no sense to me—but I was thankful that there were people like her who understood it all.

Now, there was one part of the PowerPoint presentation that was very cool, and I understood it a *little*. These images showed a part of the brain that was dark, and then a stem cell appeared at that part of the brain and almost looked like it was attacking it; no, more like it was sending electric changes to that area, like it was trying to shock it back to life. After a while, the brain started to light up again. Dr. Harrington went on to talk about the different phases of stem cells that were being discovered, and would hopefully be in human trials in the next year. Apparently, it was very expensive to conduct this type of research, and of course the FDA needed all kinds of information before the research could go on to human trials.

It's so sad how long it takes for things to happen when the FDA is involved; sometimes, it seems that the FDA must be the scientist's worst enemy, given all they want from them. On the other hand, I know that the FDA is there to protect us and make sure that everything is safe before we go forward with any drugs; we don't need another thalidomide. As much as I wanted to jump on a plane and go to another country and pay for stem cell therapy for Carson, I knew that the best thing to do was to give it time here.

There was so much to take in; in the past few years, we had gone from having no hope at all to many exciting things going on. There was so much hope now, and so much to look forward to. The only problem was *time*. I knew the drugs were masking a lot of what was going on with Carson, but the bottom line was that he was still terminally ill with Huntington's disease, and that wasn't getting any better. Frankly, I wasn't sure that Carson would be around long enough to see the results of the stem cell research. One thing that I *was* sure of, however, was that given all the recent breakthroughs, there would be something there for my children by the time they got old enough to worry about Huntington's. Elisabeth and Dylan still had a lot of time before they would show any symptoms, if in fact they inherited the disease. I felt comforted thinking that my children would probably never have to live with Huntington's disease.

In fact, from what I had heard recently, it seemed that there were a lot of illnesses my children wouldn't have to deal with. What a world to live in—to be free of so many of the diseases that had plagued humanity from time immemorial! Stem cell therapy was being examined for much more than just Huntington's; it could also help various cancers and other illnesses, hereditary and otherwise.

The world was changing at blinding speed. I just hope that Carson would be around to see it.

A Wedding in Paradise

My Dad finally proposed to Izzy, and of course she accepted. They quickly decided they were going to do a destination wedding, which made me very happy, because I'd been afraid they'd just elope and get married without any of us knowing about it until it was all over.

I knew they wouldn't have a huge wedding; that didn't fit them. They did say that they wanted to have it on a beach somewhere, but they weren't sure where yet. I talked to them about maybe booking a cruise; that way, my brother Cal could come and bring his new baby and girlfriend, and we would all go, along with Izzy's kids. That was more reasonable for everyone, I argued, and they could decide if they wanted to get married at one of the ports, or even get married on the ship. They both thought that would be an excellent idea, and ultimately we decided to go to the Mexican Riviera. That way, we could all drive to the cruise port rather than pay airfare to get to there. We chose a seven-day cruise, and the happy couple decided they'd get married in Cabo San Lucas. I thought that was funny, because it was going to be our last port of call.

Dad ended up booking all of us together, so we were able to nab a group discount rate. When he emailed me our confirmation and itinerary, there were plane tickets included for a return one way flight from Cabo back home. I called Dad to see what that was about, and he said that Izzy had decided we didn't have enough time in Cabo before the ship left—so they'd decided to buy all of you kids return flights from Cabo! After we got off the ship in Cabo, it turned out, we would be staying there for a couple of days.

Now, my family and I had been on that cruise before, and Cabo was by far my favorite port. It would be great to spend sometime exploring the city and not being rushed to get back on the ship. Dad also said that they had reserved rooms in Cabo, so I told him I'd call and pay for ours. I knew Dad probably had to pay for everything for Cal and his family, so I wanted to make sure he didn't have to pay anything else for me.

When I talked to Izzy about all the wedding plans, I learned that they had booked a wedding service in Cabo that would do everything for them. It was a one-stop shop: they provided the dinner, cake, pastor, and photographer, and had a DJ for the reception and everything. All together, there would be eighteen of us for sure; Izzy had a few close friends she was inviting, but she wasn't sure if they could make it.

Carson and I decided we wanted to pay for something, for their wedding present, so I called the wedding planners and asked if there was a way I could pay for the photographer or the flowers. The woman I talked to said that Izzy and Dad had purchased it as a package, so everything was all priced together; but, she said, their facility did include a spa that offered a massage, facial, pedicure and manicure package.

It was perfect! I booked Izzy a spa package for her wedding day, and booked one for myself so I could do it with her. I thought it would be fun, a bonding experience for us both. I was the only other grown-up girl in the family, anyway—Izzy had two boys—and I thought she might appreciate some girl-bonding time. I called her to tell her what I'd done, because I didn't want her to call and book it herself, then have to deal with the hassle of getting her money back. She was so excited, and I knew I'd made the right choice!

When Carson got home from work that day, I outlined the whole game plan. By then, he was definitely looking forward to another getaway. He was home early, in fact, and he told me he wanted to take the kids out to do something when they got home from school. I suggested a jump-house playground, which was a great way for the kids to drain away their excess energy.

As usual, I sat and read a magazine while the kids and Carson ran around and bounced. As I looked around at the other waiting adults, it struck me how unique my Carson was. Most of the other dads (the few present) were on their cell phones, or reading a book or magazine like I was. Carson was the *only* father I saw running around with his kids. Once again, I was so proud to be this man's wife. He loved to play and laugh with our kids, which was a pure blessing. I laughed as I watched Carson and Dylan roll around, tackling each other in one of the jump houses. They were both belly-laughing, they were having so much fun. When the girls saw the fun that their father and brother were having, they ran to join in.

I didn't know what these kids were going to do when Carson wasn't able to wrestle and play with them anymore. It would be one thing if they had a dad like all the other men there…a dad who didn't really pay them much attention, who was too wrapped up in adult business to understand what they were missing. Thank God Carson wasn't like that. He loved being a child himself, at least with the kids. I wondered if it was because he knew his time was short, and so he focused more on the stuff that really mattered…but whatever the cause, at the end of the day, what really counts? The phone calls, the business deals…or the memories you make with your family? We only get one shot at them being young, and most of us just let it slip by us.

I was glad that Carson never hesitated to show them that they were more important than anything else in the world. He worked hard, but they were his most important reason for living…and whatever was going on, at work or in his personal life, he would be there with them in the moment. I knew that watching him enjoy his time with the kids was a memory that I, personally, would cling to, come what may.

I was right; I still do, and it still brings me joy, even in the midst of my sorrow.

I spent most of the next couple of weeks shopping, in preparation for the upcoming trip. After all, in addition to getting everything Carson and I needed, I had to get the children clothes appropriate for their Grandpa's wedding! We were thrilled to learn, in the last few days before we left, that Bill had finally decided that he was going with us; it was going to be the whole family. This time I didn't have to deal with the idiotic school administrators, because the kids were getting out of school for the summer just before we left. Finally: a break from homework, getting up early, and having to pack lunches! I loved summertime, at least at the beginning; oddly, there always seemed to be less work for me when the kids were home. Of course, I was always happy when school started up again…after three months at home together with no break; my children were ready to kill each other.

It wasn't long before we were headed to Los Angeles to start our vacation/wedding week. Our first stop was Puerta Vallarta, and we hired a tour guide to squire us around. Later, we went into the jungle and went zip lining, and all in all, we had a great time. We met up for the formal dinner aboard ship later that night, and talked about what was going on in each of our lives. This gave Cal and me a chance to get to know Izzy's sons (soon to be our step-brothers!) a little better, and I loved getting to hold my new niece. Her name was Claire, and she was just a doll! I held her every chance I got, which wasn't often, because Carson had her most of the time. Carson loved babies; he wasn't like most guys, who would just look at a baby and smile and walk away. Nope, he was getting in all the baby love he could. Cal and Karen, his girlfriend, got a lot of time to themselves, which they didn't mind, either.

I felt a pang of remorse as I watched Carson with Claire. I knew that he would have had a dozen kids if I'd let him. Now, knowing about the disease and the fact that he had a 50% chance of passing the gene on to them, having anymore children was out of the question. It would be impossible anyway: when he tested positive for the gene, he immediately had a vasectomy. If fate was kind, if someone found a cure and he lived a normal lifespan, there was always adoption, or any of a number of more complex options we could try. There was no way I would ever do any of that now; I was already terrified of raising the three children we already had alone. I couldn't imagine bringing others into the picture. Carson understood that, and he never brought it up, not once. I did know he would have had more children, though, if we hadn't been in the situation we were in.

It was amazingly frustrating, the way this disease had put so many limitations on our lives, hemming in our options. We were constantly saying, "Well, we would do *this* if we didn't have to deal with *this*." At least we now had a niece we could spoil and love…and then we could send her back to her parents for all the hard stuff!

The next day, we went on to Mazatlan. It was fun, but the obvious poverty surrounding us really got to me. There were so many children on the streets, and their parents were so poor that most of the kids didn't even have shoes on their feet. I watched over Selena closely that day, wondering if it was hard for her to see them like this. Did it bring back memories of when she was younger, and in a similar situation?

Later, when we went into the market, Selena came up to me and gave me a huge hug. I asked her, "Are you okay, baby girl?"

"Yes," she said, grinning. "I'm just so glad to be a part of this family!"

"There's no other place you could have been, sweetie," I told her, tears stinging my eyes. "You were meant to be my daughter… it just took a little longer for us to find each other than most mothers and daughters do."

The next day, we arrived in Cabo, and I spent the morning packing up all our stuff, since we wouldn't be returning to the ship.

Then I pulled out the dress I'd bought to wear for the next day, and hoped it would still fit, given all the rich food I'd eaten on the ship. They didn't stint on the meals, that was for sure; the gourmet food was one of things I liked best about cruises. Hopefully, all the walking around would burn off some of the calories I'd taken in.

We were staying at the hotel where Izzy and Dad were getting married, and it was simply beautiful; it sat right on the beach, which made it all the more special. Soon after we arrived, I went to check out the spot where the ceremony was going to take place. It literally took my breath away. It was a charming little garden area, with the beautiful turquoise ocean as the background. It made me wish that Carson and I had had a destination wedding; but it had been so much more important to have his mother there with us, so I had no regrets.

I stood there, staring out at the ocean and thinking my deep, sad thoughts for a long while before I felt someone standing behind me. I looked back to find my Dad standing there, smiling slightly. I hooked my arm in his, and we both strolled around for the next hour or so, checking to see exactly where everything was for tomorrow. "Can't believe I'm doing this again," he said more than once.

"You couldn't have picked a better place," I told him. "This is perfect. You can't help but smile the whole time you're here."

After we finished checking the place out, we headed over to meet everyone else at the pool. Most of the adults were relaxing, but of course my three kids were already in the pool with Carson. I sat on a lounge chair, and fondly watched him toss them into the air. I was struck, again, by how all three kids just hung on their father. After enjoying an afternoon of chatter poolside, we all went to dinner together, then went to bed early. The next day was going to be very busy, so we all had to get a good night's sleep.

The next morning, Izzy and I got up early for our spa day. We started with our massages. We got a room with double massage tables so we could talk, and that's what we did as the masseuses worked their magic. We talked about the day, and how excited Izzy was. She made it clear how much she loved my Dad… and how perfect and *im*perfect they were for each other. Then we went and got our nails done. It was so nice being pampered; I rarely did things like this. Being a stay-at-home mom, I rarely had the time to do things for myself.

By the time our hair and make-up were done, it was almost time for the ceremony. I went back to my room to finish getting ready and to get my kids all put together. When I arrived, Carson was putting on his tux. I love it when Carson wears a tuxedo; he looked so handsome I can hardly stand it. Luckily for my Dad, I knew how important this day was to him…because otherwise, with Carson looking the way he did, I would rather have sent our kids to the wedding while Carson and I stayed behind and…played.

"Hey there, handsome," I said, as I wrapped my arms around his waist.

Carson started laughing; he could tell by my actions what I was thinking. "You'd better be good, young lady," he cautioned. "Your dad's getting married in less than an hour, and we really don't have time!"

"Awwww…."

Right then, the kids came walking into our section of the suite. The girls had on their dresses and were swirling around proudly; Dylan looked adorable in his little three-piece suit. I took the girls in the bathroom and curled their hair, then squeezed into my dress, which was a little tight—but at least it fit.

When we were ready, we walked together to the wedding site. Dad was already there; he looked so dapper in his tux, being one of those men who cleans up pretty good (as I liked to joke). It wasn't long before the familiar strains of the wedding march swelled, and we all took our seats. I looked back to where Izzy was walking down the aisle; she looked astounding. She was wearing a beautiful white silk gown, the perfect beach wedding dress. I looked at Dad; he was just staring at Izzy with a smile on his face. They could not take their eyes off each other.

It made me so happy to see my father this joyful.

The ceremony was short and sweet, and afterward, we went back to the little reception room they'd set up with finger foods and champagne. The photographer started snapping off shots right and left, and I asked him to take some pictures of Carson, the kids and I on the beach; I figured this might be my last chance to get pictures of us all together all dressed up. I think Dad was relieved that I took the photographer away for a couple of minutes, because he isn't a center-of-attention kind of guy. I had to say, though, that he was doing better than I thought he would. He was doing it for Izzy's sake, of course, and I was proud of him.

Afterward we ate a wonderful dinner, and Dad and Izzy cut their cute little cake. Each of us kids got up and said a toast.

We were exhausted by the end of the evening. Dylan fell asleep on Carson's shoulder on our walk back to our suite, and the girls walked like little zombies. After we put the kids down in their room, Carson and I went to our room—and I shut the door and locked it. Carson looked at me, smiling, and then burst into laughter. I'd wanted to get him alone all night, and he knew it! When he began taking off his tux, I went over and helped him…and before I knew it, we were ripping each other's clothes off. I've heard that after a couple have been together for a while, they often lose their passion for each other. Thank goodness that hadn't happened with us! I was still as attracted to Carson as I'd been the first day I saw him, so we had a pretty wild night. It may have been all the romance in the air from the wedding, but all I know is, I just wanted to be close to him. The next morning I woke up early, feeling the same way. I grabbed both of his arms and wrapped them around me. I couldn't seem to get close enough to him.

When the kids woke up, we all headed out to explore the Cabo area. First we took a glass bottom boat tour, then went and saw the sea lions; the kids loved that part. Later, we walked around Lover's Beach. Eventually we stumbled upon a great swimming beach, and laid around the rest of the day. The next day, it was time to go back to reality—and I didn't *want* to go home. There were too many worries at home. When we were on vacation, we got to forget about everything that we worried about on a daily basis.

But I guess you can't run from your problems forever.

A Turn for the Worse

When all hope is lost, the world goes dark. This darkness was now my being. My hope had trickled away like sand through an hourglass…and my time had run out. When you feel your world start to go dark, hope can pull you through. It gives you light at the end of the tunnel.

Well, my life was a black tunnel, without a glimpse of light to reach for.

A year had passed since Dad's wedding, and Carson had taken a turn for the worse—much worse. He was starting to have trouble just eating and drinking; he would often spill things all over himself, and when he would take a drink of something, he would often choke on the fluid. I talked to Dr. Callender about his choking, and she assured me that it was one of the common symptoms of the disease. That didn't make it any better, but now I knew what was going on: Huntington's patients often have problems with their gag reflex. In addition to that, his movement was terrible again. I couldn't even imagine what it would be like without the medication. Even so, it was so bad, so uncontrolled, that we couldn't even sleep together anymore. Reluctantly, Carson moved into the spare bedroom down the hall.

His immune system also seemed to be deteriorating: if one of the kids brought home a cold, Carson would inevitably catch it…and sometimes it would turn into pneumonia. He was also having pain in his hands and feet. I would rub his feet and hands for him, and he said it helped, but I could tell he was still hurting.

We scrupulously kept up with Carson's doctor's appointments. When we had first started going to the Huntington's clinic, they told us we only had to go once a year unless we needed something. Then they had us coming to the clinic every six months. Now we visited on a quarterly basis, so I knew things were getting pretty bad. Carson had been in and out of the doctor's office for falls, too; he'd hit his head pretty hard a few times. Carson thought I was crazy to be always running him to the doctor; he said that things were getting worse, and if I kept taking him to the doctor every time he fell, we might as well set up camp in the office because we'd probably be there daily. We only had to take him to the emergency room once, when he fell down the stairs leading to our house. He broke his arm that time, and it had to be put in a cast.

His posture was also funny these days; he often stood with his back arched, kind of like he was pushing his rear out. He was always making funny movements with his arms, too, and would kick his foot back first every time he'd start walking. All these little things started to happen more and more often.

Carson was doing very well with his drinking; he hadn't touched a drop in a couple of years. His new addiction was gambling. Dr. Callender assured me that it was actually common for people with Huntington's disease to have addictive behaviors…but I don't know which one was worse, drinking or gambling. Carson spent a lot of money on it, anyway. Luckily, he mostly played craps; the money seemed to last longer that way than with slot machines or any of the other available options. He tended to make a lot of money when he played, so when he lost, it didn't bother me too much. The biggest problem was that it was taking him away from the family, since gambling wasn't something we could all do together. Either Carson would have to go alone or, if we went with him, I would usually stay in the hotel room with the kids while Carson was busy. I quickly got sick of the whole thing, and finally put my foot down and told him that his gambling could only be a couple-of-times-a-year thing.

Even though he wanted to gamble more than anything, he was really good at listening and responding positively to what I thought. He knew it wasn't healthy for the family or for himself to keep on like that…and he was also getting to the point where he really couldn't go anymore. In fact, there came a time when he really couldn't go anywhere without me. So it was horrible that he couldn't do as much on his own anymore, but it was nice that the gambling stopped.

His next kick was video games. I wished he would get addicted to something that was good for him! He was so full-force with gambling, and now those damned games! I told him that if he put all that effort in to taking care of himself, then he could be the healthiest person in the world.

Worse, over time, his memory started to go. He still knew who he was and who we were, of course, but there were so many things he forgot; he would get so frustrated sometimes, just trying to think of someone's name. I could tell it scared him, especially when I would ask if he remembered something from the past and I could tell by his expression he had no recollection of it. By this point, I couldn't depend on him for anything. He couldn't even remember what time the kids got out of school.

It was heartbreaking to see him go through this.

One day, when I was in the bedroom cleaning old clothes out of Carson's closet to take to Goodwill, I found a shoebox on the top shelf. I opened the box and found a ton of letters inside. They were all sealed, but had different things written on the front. Frowning, I started thumbing through the letters. One letter was labeled, "Elisabeth Lee, on her wedding day." Another read, "Dylan, on his graduation from college," and another was labeled, in his neat print, "Selena, on the birth of her first child." There were a couple of letters in there for me as well.

I felt a shock roll through me as realized what was inside those envelopes. Carson had things he wanted to say to us on the special days in the future when he knew he wouldn't be able to be there. He wanted the children, especially, to have special messages from their Daddy on those special moments in their lives.

I sat there in disbelief for several long minutes…and then I just broke down and started crying hysterically. The reality was that Carson would *not* be there for these events. It must have been so hard for him to sit and write these letters, to bring himself, in his mind, to those days, to think about what he would want to say to us. Though I was glad he'd done it, I couldn't imagine what he must have been going through when he wrote those letters. The thought of it made me so sick to my stomach that I ran into my bathroom and started to throw up. The anxiety of all this was too much for my stomach to handle.

Later, I flipped through the letters and read all the events listed on the front of the envelopes…and I couldn't imagine experiencing any of these things without him. Who was going to walk our daughters down the aisle when they married? I would be standing by myself the day our children graduated from college…and probably from high school. Who else would be as proud of them as me? The only person who possibly could be was Carson… and he wouldn't be there to share those moments with me. I felt so alone.

"I see you found the letters," a quiet voice said behind me.

I turned and looked at my husband, who stood shakily in the door. "I'm sorry, Carson, I wasn't snooping," I sniffled. "I was just looking for old clothes for Goodwill."

"I know," he said.

"Why didn't you tell me you were writing these?" I demanded, tears streaming down my face.

"I was going to tell you," he said, and I couldn't tell if the tremor in his voice was caused by the disease or by emotion. "I really was. I was just waiting until I was done writing them. I knew you would be very emotional…and I had to keep my mind clear when I wrote these letters. I had to make sure that what I said was right." He looked at me carefully. "Did you get sick?"

"Yes!" I cried. "Of course I did! When I was looking at these letters, my stomach filled up with knots!" I dragged a hand across my eyes, wiping away the tears.

"I'm sorry—"

"I'm *glad* you did it," I interrupted. "It will be very special for the kids, to know what you would've said to them on those days. It's just making me sick to think you won't be there with me. I don't want to be *alone*. I've been with you as long as I can remember. I can't imagine a day without you in it. I want this fixed. I want this to go away!"

He made his careful way into the bedroom and sat down on the bed beside me. "Baby, I want this to go away too. And hey, it might—there's a lot of promising research going on! And I'm not going anywhere today. I just wrote these letters while I still could. I thought about doing it for a long time, and I kept putting it off. Things have been so up in the air lately that…I didn't want to put it off anymore."

"It *was* a good idea," I acknowledged. "I should be doing the same thing. You know, I could be taken out in a car accident, or something else could happen to me. The kids need something to remind them of how much we love them, even if we can't be there with them. This lets us prepare for the worst…and maybe, someday, we can throw all these letters away, because we'll be there to tell them all these things ourselves."

He patted me on the back and made his way out of the room. I got myself back together, then picked up all the letters I'd spread out everywhere. I was just putting then back in the shoebox when little Elisabeth walked into the room and asked, "Mommy, what's wrong?"

"Nothing, honey, I'll be okay."

"Is it because of Daddy?" she asked gravely.

I looked at her sharply. "What do you mean?"

"You know, are you sad because Daddy's sick?"

I patted her on the cheek. "Yes, honey, sometimes I *am* sad because Daddy's sick. But it's okay to be sad and talk about it, if that's how you feel. If you're ever sad or worried about Daddy, you can come and talk to me or Daddy about it."

She nodded. "Well, I sometimes get scared when Daddy can't swallow. Why does that happen?"

"I don't know for sure why it happens, but it makes Mommy scared too. It's part of Huntington's disease, I guess. Daddy's nerves are damaged, so sometimes he does things differently than us."

"Will Daddy be okay? Will he get better?"

I sighed. I hated to lie, but I still clung to some hope, so I said, "I don't know, honey. Hopefully, there *will* someday be a medicine that will make Daddy better. There's nothing like that right now, but maybe someday. We just have to hope for it, someday."

"Will Daddy die?"

"Well, Elisabeth, we'll all die someday. No one lives forever. No one knows when they're going to leave this earth, which is why it's so important to spend as much time together as possible. We need to love each other everyday. If we live like that, than we have no regrets. I don't know if your Dad will die from Huntington's disease; only time will tell. But for now, we're all alive and happy, and that's all that matters."

I knew I was going to have a lot of conversations with my children about all this, and I had already decided that I was going to be honest with them. I 'd rather have them come to me and get the truth than assume that they knew themselves and have wrong information. Things were starting to get really bad with Carson, and I was afraid their friends would start asking what was wrong with their Dad. Kids could be mean, so I wanted to make sure that they could come to me if anyone at all was talking about it.

Of course, Carson really didn't leave the house much anymore, so the chances of the kids at their schools seeing him were pretty slim.

In fact, it was getting to be difficult to take care of the house and the children *and* Carson. I hated to leave him alone; I was afraid that when I was gone, he might choke or fall. I needed some help, and decided that it was time to start to look for an in-home care specialist to come in for a couple of hours during the day. I realized now that Margret, the elder Elisabeth's companion when Carson was a boy, hadn't been there to take care of Elisabeth as much as to ensure that Elisabeth didn't hurt herself while no one else was home. I consulted with Bill on how I should go about finding someone, and he said he would call Margret to see if she knew of anyone. Margret, with whom he'd maintained a relationship, was retired now, but she might have a referral. Both recommended someone with a background in nursing, if not someone with a full nursing degree.

"That'll be fine for awhile," I said to Bill, "but then what?"

"There's going to come a time when you'll have to put Carson in a care facility, just like I had to do with Elisabeth," he told me. "At some point, it's going to be unsafe for him to be under our care alone." He was right, and I knew it: we didn't know how to handle certain medical situations, so Carson needed to be in a place where there were nurses on hand, and a doctor if he needed one.

"When that time comes," Bill said, "We set up a long term care plan that will pay for the facility. Part of that plan will pay for some in-home care service as well. I'll call the insurance company and start dealing with that paperwork when I get a chance, okay?"

I agreed wholeheartedly. It sounded like Bill had already helped Carson set his affairs in order, well in advance, long before he got tested for the disease.

"Talked to your Dad today," I told Carson later.

"Oh?" He looked at me shakily, his eyes unreadable.

"It seems that you signed up for a lot of insurance benefits years ago, so we're pretty solid when it comes to your health care," I said.

"Yeah. I wanted to be prepared, even when I didn't want to know if I had the disease," he admitted. "Dad and I took care of a lot of things early on."

"Really," I said, putting my hands on my hips. "And why didn't I know about any of this? I thought it was important that I knew about everything we had."

"Well, I was afraid it would just worry you if you knew all the provisions Dad and I had made. I thought it might be too overwhelming for you." He hobbled over to me, and put his arms around my waist. "Dad will take care of that part, when the time comes."

"And what will happen if something happens to Bill?" I snapped.

"There are people at the office who know what to do."

I let my irritation drain away. In truth, it was nice of Carson to not want me to worry about all the details. I already had a lot to worry about...but at the same time, I didn't want to be ignorant about the whole thing, either.

As it turned out, Carson wasn't happy whatsoever that I was going to hire someone to come in to watch him for a while during the day, but I put my foot down and overruled him on that. I pointed out that I was worried that something was going to happen every time I walked out the front door—that I would come home and find him dead on the floor. He accepted that, but whenever it came up he would glare at me. He was very angry these days.

Over time, the children started distancing themselves from their father. It was heartbreaking to see, but I think that was probably a good thing, ultimately. Considering what was happening to him, it was hard for Carson to deal with the chaos that came with young children. He'd sometimes snap at them for no real reason...and I knew that if things kept getting worse, I'd have to find a facility for him. We couldn't live like that. My world became very dark; I was never happy anymore, and I felt so bad for Carson and the children. I missed *my* Carson, not the dying shell he had become, so badly it was an unbearable agony. It seemed that my whole life was falling apart, and I felt helpless.

I decided it was time to see a doctor for myself. I needed to get my head out of the dark cloud it was in, because if nothing else, my kids needed to me to be strong for them. So I went to our primary care physician, Dr. Creswell, and he put me on antidepressants. I was a bit hesitant at first, because I'd heard that you don't feel as much emotion when you're on such medications—that they kind of shut your head off, slowing those thoughts down. The doctor said that wasn't necessarily true...but I was afraid to suppress any emotions, in the fear that if I ever got off the medicine, I would go crazy as all the emotions came out. Still, I had to do something to help me through this, so I decided to give the medication a shot.

Meanwhile, I found a therapist who specialized in children with ill parents. The kids talked to me every once in a while about how they felt, but I think they were sometimes cautious about doing so. They were smart kids, fully aware of how much I had on my plate, and they didn't want to rock the boat; plus, sometimes I didn't know what to say to them. I tried to be honest and open, but how do you talk to your children about their father's terminal illness? It was something I didn't really know how to do, so I took them to a professional. I took part in the sessions with them, and watched how the therapist talked to them. I was shocked at how perceptive my children were; they were fully aware of things I didn't think they noticed, and they talked about them openly with the therapist. I had to remind myself more than once that Elisabeth and Selena were now 11 and 12. I had to face the fact that they weren't babies anymore, though I wanted them to be, so I could protect them from all this. But I couldn't. I couldn't protect them from the reality of what our world had become.

My father retired from the fire department that spring, and he and Izzy asked if they could take the kids for a week over the summer. I thought that would be an excellent idea, not just for them but for me; it would also give me a week to get my head straight and figure out my life a little. So a week after the kids got out of school, Dad came to pick them up. I made plans to go out to dinner with Bill the first night they were gone, because I needed his advice on when it was time to put Carson in a facility. I didn't want to give up on my husband, but I knew for his sake and the kids' that there would be a time in the near future when I *would* have to do that.

After the kids left I checked my email, and found a notice about the latest annual Huntington's conference. I wasn't going to be able to attend this year, given all that was going on, but I made sure I kept track of the event, and I read a little about what the keynote speakers were talking about this time. Apparently, enough funding had come through that they'd be starting the first phase of human trials with stem cell therapy. This was very exciting news, even though it was probably too late for Carson. But I had two children at risk, so the reality of it was that Huntington's disease would probably always be a part of my life, even after Carson's time here was done.

I thought about the families who had been chosen to participate in the first human trials of this new therapy, which offered so much hope in curing—or at least ameliorating—this horrible disease. How wonderful it must be to have hope!

Carson had a really rough day that day, so we gave him some strong medication that put him right to sleep. The nurse that we'd found, Peggy, had agreed to stay for a few extra hours while I was gone with Bill. At dinner, he and I talked about what the children had been talking about in therapy. "They're scared to death," I told him, "and not just about what's happening to Carson. They're scared *of* Carson a lot of the time."

Bill looked uncomfortable at that, but didn't have a lot to offer. "I'm sorry, Kathryn," he told me sadly. "Carson was older when Elisabeth got really bad, you know, and of course I only had Carson to worry about."

"I know."

He picked at his food a little and then looked up at me, his face drawn. "Your situation is so different," he said softly, "because the kids still depend on you so much. Back then, I was able to focus a lot of my time on Elisabeth, because Carson was off doing his own thing most of the time. And, of course, he had you."

"How am I going to do this?" I demanded. "I know that Carson doesn't want to go into a care facility. We had talks about it all the time when he first got diagnosed…and he understood that one day he would have to do it. He always told me, 'Don't make the decision based on what I want. Base it on what's best for the family and my well being."

"But he thought that the time when you had to make a decision like that would never come," Bill said quietly. "Didn't he?"

"Yes! I don't know if I can make this decision! How do you move your husband into a nursing home and then *leave* him there? I don't know how in the world I would ever be strong enough to do something like that. *I* would never want to be put in a home, either. I know Carson, and I know his character, and he would never put me in a home! He would fight until I took my last breath! How is it that I'm actually thinking of doing it to him?" By the time I finished, I was breathless, and my eyes were filled with tears.

"Don't make any decisions right now, Kathryn," Bill said. "Look, you'll know when the time is right. If you're questioning this decision so much, then now isn't the time. You're doing everything you can right now—you're keeping up with the kids, and keeping their minds right with the therapy." He put his hand on mine. "And you're taking care of yourself. I'm glad."

He meant the medication, of course. It did seem to be helping; I was no longer waking up in complete terror from the horrible dreams I was having. My downtime was always scary, since I would start to think about Carson's fate, which would usually throw me into a panic attack. Given that the attacks weren't happening as often anymore, the medicine *must* have been working.

I went home that night and got into bed next to Carson, and just sat and watched him sleep. He slept so soundly; I couldn't even tell he was sick right then. But the truth was, it was because he was so medicated that his body was in a coma-like state.

I kissed him on the forehead, then laid down next to him and fell asleep.

Carson woke up very angry, demanding to know where his children were and where I'd been the previous night. I reminded him that the kids had gone to my Dad's to visit for a couple of days; he'd known that's where they were, but because of the disease, he had forgotten. When I told him I had gone out with his own father the previous night for dinner, he didn't believe me. He accused me of having an affair.

I lost my temper then. "Carson, when would I have *time* to have an affair!" I shouted. "Every second of my day is filled with taking care of the kids and you!"

That made him madder than ever. "So I'm a burden, is that it?"

"I've never thought of you as a burden, Carson! But everything I do, no matter what, just pisses you off! I can't do anything right!"

He didn't say anything, and I decided just to stop talking. He spent the next half hour pacing around in a total funk, talking to himself and then to me. I had no idea what was going on, and he was only half-coherent at best. Finally, exasperated, I asked him, "Carson, do you want to go outside and go for a little walk, or maybe sit on the porch?"

"I don't want to do anything with you," he snarled.

"Fine," I said, cut to the quick. "I'm going to go sit on the porch, so I'll be out there in case you need anything."

As I settled down in the porch glider, I heard him stumbling around in the kitchen; and after a few minutes, he started coughing non-stop. When I went inside to check on him, he was shivering like he was cold. When I asked him if he needed to go to the doctor, he wouldn't even speak to me. I was still standing at the kitchen door when he fell to the floor.

I immediately called 911, then Bill. He made it to our house a couple minutes after the paramedics, who were working rapidly on Carson. As one slipped an oxygen mask on him, the other looked up at me and said, "Ma'am, we're going to have to take your husband to the hospital."

"What's going on?" I asked the paramedic.

"We're not sure yet," he said. "His blood oxygen levels are very low." They carefully positioned him on a gurney, then wheeled him to the ambulance and took off, with Bill and I following close behind. When we arrived at the hospital, they sent Carson back immediately.

While Bill and I were waiting in the waiting room, I called my Dad to let him know what was going on, and he assured me that he would keep the kids as long as necessary. Later, as Bill helped me fill out hospital paperwork, the doctor came out to meet us. He seemed cordial, if a bit distant, and I told him I wasn't sure if the paramedics had told them, but that Carson had Huntington's disease.

"We knew that," he said shortly. "We're running some tests."

"Well, what's wrong this time?"

"He has pneumonia."

"Again? He keeps getting pneumonia, and it seems like he can't fight it off." I sighed. "Look, he hasn't been coughing or running any high temperatures that I noticed."

That seemed to interest him, and he asked, "Has your husband been complaining of any trouble breathing, or anything like that?"

"It's hard to get Carson to talk about much these days," I admitted. I was just sodden with exhaustion and worry, and didn't know how I could go on any farther. "He never complained to me of anything like that."

"Well, Mr. Ferris's oxygen levels were very low due to the pneumonia, and that was probably why he passed out," the doctor commented. "We're also checking his heart because his pulse is irregular, and we're going to start IV treatment with an antibiotic to treat the pneumonia."

"Will he be okay?"

The doctor looked at me for a long moment and replied, "As of right now, he's fine, but we need to get his oxygen levels up."

After the doctor left, I asked Bill if he'd had to deal with this kind of stuff with Elisabeth. "Not really," he said. "But she would sometimes get bacterial infections that were really hard to shake."

It was like their bodies couldn't fight off this stuff on their own; somehow, the Huntington's shot down their immune systems, and certainly Carson's wasn't the same anymore. He got sick so very easily—all the time now, in fact—and it was probably from all the little illnesses the kids brought home from school.

"This is something you should get used to," Bill told me bleakly. "Elisabeth was in and out of hospitals."

He didn't have to tell me that; I could remember it all too well.

Change

What followed was a year of hell. Everyday seemed to be the same: Carson would just sit and stare at the TV, angry at everyone, constantly yelling at the kids and me. The kids and I turned to each other for comfort; we talked about what he was going through all the time. I assured the kids that it wasn't their fault for whatever their Dad was mad at that day, that he couldn't control how he felt most of the time. We also talked about how he no longer understood a lot about what was going on around him. Sometimes he would get mad at the kids for not being in school, and I would have to explain to the kids that Carson didn't realize it was Saturday.

He didn't think before he reacted anymore. The kids and I felt like prisoners in our own home, because we never knew how Carson was going to be from day to day. All four of us loved him so much...but by this point, we were scared of him.

Even when the nurse was there, I took the kids with me everywhere I went... I didn't trust Carson around the kids without me there to protect them. I talked to Bill and Dad, and told them that I couldn't live like this anymore. My worst fear was right around the corner: I knew it was time to find a care home for Carson. The kids didn't need to live in fear; and in any case, I couldn't take care of the three kids *and* Carson anymore. It was wearing on me. I swear I'd aged about ten years over the past year; I was so tired that I was living with my head in a fog all the time. I was afraid if I kept going like this, I would end up getting sick myself...and then what would my kids do?

When I took Carson to his next clinic appointment, Dr. Callender looked at him closely and said, "Carson's coloring is off. Has he been acting differently?"

Glancing at Carson, who was glowering at us both, I told her, "Well...I don't know. Every day is different. I, uh, I have a hard time knowing if it's something to do with the Huntington's or if it's some secondary illness."

Nodding, the doctor checked his oxygen levels, and then listened to Carson's chest. Stripping off her stethoscope hurriedly, she snapped,

"We need to get him to the hospital right away." She hustled to a phone and immediately called an ambulance.

Once again, I had missed something. It was becoming more and more obvious that I couldn't take care of Carson the way he needed to be taken care of. This was the second time he had almost died under my care. I just couldn't do it anymore; I had to face that. Carson was going to die if it was up to me to monitor him, and my children were terrified to be home with him anyway. It was time to make some changes.

Thank God for Bill. I don't know where he got the strength, but he called Greenbrier, the facility where Elisabeth had lived in the last years of her life, and set up an appointment for us to go talk to the owners. As I recalled, it was very nice, if you had to be in a place like that; but I didn't know how I would tell Carson that I was going put him in a home. I did *not* want to make that decision; despite all that was happening, who was *I* to tell Carson that it was time for him to be institutionalized?

On the other hand, Carson had medical needs that I couldn't handle, and I had no medical background whatsoever. Oh, I could have taken some classes to learn how to take care of him better, but I would never be as good as a real nurse or doctor—and where would I find the time anyway? I could barely keep up with life the way it was.

Despite that, I felt guilty giving up on Carson...and I often wondered what Carson would do if the tables were turned. As far as I could tell, he would do the exact *opposite* of what I was thinking of doing. Carson would stand by my side and take care of me until the bitter end. He would never put me in a care facility; his conscience wouldn't let him. So what kind of person was I? Not only was I going to put him in a care home, I was almost *relieved* that I was going to. I was a terrible person! Carson was my husband, and I was going to feel relief when he was gone. I couldn't even look at myself in the mirror, I was so disgusted. This was the man I loved. He was the most caring, understanding, loving man imaginable...or at least, he had been. And I was ready to just turn my back on him because times were tough.

Finally, I decided I needed to see a therapist—someone outside the situation who could help me. I chose a specialist in terminal illness and loss, this woman I figured must have heard stories like mine a million times. And, in fact, when I went to see Dr. Cabell, I seemed to answer all my questions on my own. I sat there telling her how guilty

I felt about putting Carson in a home, how he was my partner and life-mate, and here I was making an almost parent-like decision. I didn't want that responsibility! Then I started talking about how I would feel if something were to happen to my children, and how I couldn't trust Carson around them, because he would snap at them for the smallest things.

No matter what, I couldn't win. My children were still just that: children. Things would have been different if the children had been older and out on their own; then, I would have been able to dedicate myself full-time to taking care of Carson. Unfortunately, that wasn't the case; the children needed me for everything, and most of all, they needed me to look out for their best interests and safety. I couldn't keep putting my children through all of this. I didn't want them to be scared in their own home anymore. I didn't want to feel lucky at the end of the day that Carson hadn't done anything hurtful to me or the kids. He was a ticking time bomb most of the time, and I didn't want to have that in my home anymore.

Dealing with an illness that affects people's moods is terribly confusing. If you were married to a healthy man who was constantly yelling at you and calling you horrible names, who was denigrating your parenting skills and telling you that you were a worthless wife and then threatening you and your kids, you would leave him if you had a lick of sense. Well, it's a whole different story when that person is ill, when you know that there's a good, gentle, *real* person behind the illness. Before he was sick, Carson never said an unkind word to me. He never yelled and rarely raised his voice. He was so passive it was almost unreal; I would try sometimes to push his buttons, but he never lost his cool. He was constantly telling me what a great wife and mother I was, and always recognized my values and achievements. If he ever upset me by accident, he would be upset with himself. If I told him that something he said or did upset me, he would hug me and go on and on about how he didn't mean to, and how sorry he was. That was the *real* Carson. He couldn't help how he was now. It wasn't him; it was that damn disease.

I had found the most perfect man possible...and Huntington's disease took him away.

Carson was in the hospital again with pneumonia. He just couldn't shake it, and this time he was pretty bad off. At first, we thought he wouldn't pull out of it this time; but thank God, he managed to. While he was still recovering, Bill and I went to our appointment at

Greenbrier. We had talked about how we were going to have him go into the facility, it would be best to have him go straight out of the hospital. Bill told me bluntly that it would be too hard on everyone to bring him home from the hospital and *then* move him to the facility. He'd decided to have Elisabeth go to the facility right after she was in the hospital for a bacterial infection. "If I'd taken her home," he told me sadly, "I would never have been able to move her out again."

It ended up being a good thing he did, because after that infection, Elisabeth was never the same. She was sick constantly after that, in pain most of the time, and often sedated. All of her bodily functions started to go; she had trouble eating, swallowing, and even going to the bathroom. Bill would have had to do it soon after that hospital visit anyhow; and now, he told me, Carson was in about the same place that Elisabeth had been when he had to put her in the facility. Unfortunately, Carson was a lot younger than his mother had been, because Huntington's, affects each person differently. They thought it had something to do the repeat count of the Huntingtin protein. Carson had a higher repeat count than his mother; after he was tested, they told us that this meant that his life would probably be shorter than Elisabeth's.

That seemed to be exactly what was happening.

While Bill and I were at the facility, we arranged for a space for Carson, for when he was ready to leave the hospital. I asked them when I could get into the room, because I wanted to decorate it before he got there; if I could get it somewhat like his room at home, I figured, it might make things easier on him. They told me the room was ready right away, and I could go on in and do whatever I needed to.

I went to see Carson at the hospital that night, and to my relief found that he was doing much better. They had the infection under control; he no longer needed oxygen, and he was going to pull through just fine. The doctor confided that Carson's body itself was strong, no matter how compromised his nervous system, or how weak his immune system was.

Taking a deep breath, I went into Carson's room to talk to him about all the decisions that had been made. Despite the fact that they *had* been made, more or less, I decided that I needed to hear what he had to say. I knew he was on a lot of medication, so I wasn't sure how much sense he would make of all of it; but it still needed to be done. He was still my partner, and I thought he deserved a say in all of this.

I walked into the room and sat by his bed. He didn't say anything, but I could tell from the look in his eyes that he was glad to see me. I reached out and brushed his hair off his forehead. "Hey, honey, how are you doing?"

"I don't know," he whispered.

"You're on a lot of medications," I told him, "so it's probably hard to know exactly what's going on. But the doctor wanted me to tell you that you're doing better. The infection is under control, so you should start feeling much better soon."

He reached up and weakly grasped my hand. "Okay."

"I...I have to talk to you about something. I know it's hard for you to talk right now, so if you want to, just squeeze my hand or nod. I don't want to put any more stress on you than you already have, but Carson, there's a decision to be made...and I don't feel comfortable making it without you." I took a deep breath, and blurted, "I talked to Dr. Callender, and I've talked to the doctor here at the hospital, and it sounds like things like this are just going to happen more often. When you fell at home last year, I was so scared! I didn't know what to do to help you. I can't imagine what might have happened if I hadn't been there."

I glanced away for a moment, then looked back at him. "I wish so much that I'd gone to school to become a doctor, or at least a nurse, so I could take care of you the way you deserve, Carson...but I just can't. This time, Dr. Callender found out about your oxygen levels, and she sent us here just in time. I missed that, too. Can you imagine what might have happened if we hadn't had that appointment that day? We were lucky we had enough time to get you to the hospital. I talked with your Dad, and we talked about your mother, about when she got to this stage of the disease. I...I can't even believe I have to talk to you about this!"

I lowered my head and started to cry. I felt Carson's finger moving on my hand; he was trying to comfort me. How could I put him through this? He was lying in a hospital bed fighting for his life, and here I was, putting this huge new weight on him. I don't care what anyone said: Carson knew *exactly* what was going on. He was a human being and he had feelings. What I was about to do was going to break his heart; there was no doubt about that. I looked into his eyes, and saw that they were filling up with tears.

I reined in my emotions and said, "Carson, your father and I visited Greenbrier, the care home that your mother went to. I talked to the owner, and they have a room available right now. I don't know how I'm going to be able to let you leave our home…but I *also* know that I'm no longer able to take care of you the way you need to be taken care of. If you're scared in anyway of going to that place, just let me know, and we'll figure something else out. If this is the decision we're making, then I promise you that I *will* come and visit you everyday. The kids will be there everyday. I'll fix up the room exactly the same as your room at home. I just need to know: what we should do?"

He squeezed my hand and nodded sadly, as if he understood and was willing to accept his fate. My voice broke as I said, "Honey, I just need to know if you're okay with this. I know you don't want it—trust me, I don't want it either—but do you think it's for the best?"

Carson nodded, and I just laid my head on his stomach and cried quietly. I laid there for a long time, until I felt Carson's head kind of fall to the side. I sat up, and saw that he had fallen asleep. After looking at him for a long moment, my heartbreaking, I got up quietly and snuck out of the room.

I called Bill and told him, "I just talked to Carson. He wasn't able to say much, but he did push out a couple of words when I asked him how he felt. He seemed pretty confused by the question…I think with all the pain medication, he didn't really know how he felt."

"And Greenbrier?"

"I talked to him about it. He seemed to understand, and seemed to agree with me that this was the best decision for him."

After a moment of silence, Bill drew in a deep breath and said, simply, "Okay."

"Would you mind coming to the hospital? Carson fell asleep after we talked. I've got a lot to do, and I don't want to leave him alone. I want someone to be there when he wakes up."

"Of course, Kathryn. I've got a few things to wrap up at the office, but I'll be there soon as I can."

After we ended the call, I went and sat in the waiting room and waited for Bill. I'd put in a call to Dr. Callender, to schedule Carson an appointment for when he got out of the hospital; and I also had a question for her on one of his medications. When I checked my messages, I saw she had returned my call. Great, phone tag. I called the office and told them I was returning her call, and they sent my call back to her nurse. When her nurse realized it was me, she told me that

Dr. Callender was in her office, and that she wanted to talk to me, so she put me straight through to her.

We took care of the medication business, and I told her flatly about talking to Greenbrier, and my decision that it was time to put him there.

"Oh, you poor dear," she said sympathetically. "Honey, you may not have thought about this before, but the truth is that this may be the best thing for your Carson right now. It's hard for people with Huntington's disease to handle much chaos, and chaos is unavoidable with three kids, even if they're well-behaved like yours."

"Ha! You don't have to live with them! There are always kids running around, and there's always yelling and craziness."

"And I suspect you just block it out," she said, "because it's *normal*. But that's not so easy for Carson in his condition. He can't really deal with things like that. He needs a calmer environment."

She was right: I'd never really thought of it that way…but now that I did, I realized that our household was very demanding. I had thought Carson loved being a part of it all, and of course he had before Huntington's struck him down. It never occurred to me that it was overwhelming for him now! That was probably why he snapped all the time: he just couldn't handle it.

It was all clearer to me now. That didn't make it easier, though.

Carson seemed to be at ease with the decision for him to go into Greenbrier. It could be because of all the drugs he was on, of course…but maybe he was relieved that he didn't have to deal with the everyday pressure of being a parent to three young children. It was hard for me to comprehend, since I dealt with it all just fine; but then, I didn't have a progressive neurological disease. Carson's nerves were on edge already, without any stimulation; with all he got in the house, it must have been exhausting him.

When Bill got to the hospital, I talked to him about what Dr. Callender had said. "Well, that makes a lot of sense," he admitted. "Carson wasn't all that much trouble when Elisabeth got sick, since he was already a teenager, but she did get irritable when there was a lot going on in our house."

"So that must be it."

"I think it is," he agreed. "At this point, your household is just too much for Carson to deal with." He sighed. "Damn, I wish that wasn't true. He really loves those kids."

After I left the hospital, I picked up the kids from a friend's house, where they were staying while I took care of Carson; it was time to tell them what was going on. After we went to get ice cream, I took them home, and had all three come sit in the living room with me. "You all know how sick your Daddy is," I told them solemnly. "Well, I went to visit with him today, and the doctor said he's getting better."

"Yay!" Dylan cried, and we all smiled.

"But there's more," I said. "Now, I have to talk to you guys about a very grown-up thing. If you have any questions or concerns, please let me know. This has been really hard on all of us," I continued, "and I need to know how all of you are doing. It's my job to answer any questions and to take care you. Okay?"

They all nodded.

"I went and talked to Daddy today at the hospital," I said, and tried to keep my voice from trembling. "His pneumonia really is better, but the Huntington's disease, is going to keep getting worse. As it turns out, it's probably better that Dad moves to a place that can take better care of him. Grandpa and I found a really nice place that's close to our house called Greenbrier. They have nurses and doctors there who can take care of Dad better than I can, 24 hours a day."

"Can we go see Daddy there?" Selena asked dubiously.

"You can go see your Dad anytime you want to. We can visit him everyday, and we will! Now, I know it's hard for all of you to think of your Dad not living here anymore, but this *is* what's best for him. I know your Dad will miss being here watching you guys. He loves that! You three are the most important things in his life."

"Why can't he stay here then?" Elisabeth Lee asked, her eyes brimming with tears.

"Oh, honey, if we lived in a perfect world, your Dad wouldn't need to go into this care home…but we don't live in a perfect world. This is going to be hard on all of us, but I promise you that we *will* get through it. The five of us are still a family; we just have to do things a little differently than most families, okay? You'll still see Daddy everyday, but we can't be selfish. We have to think about what's best for him."

By then, all three of them were in tears, so I sat on the floor with them and pulled them all close to me. "It's okay to cry," I told them, and I started to cry with them. "Kids, we're lucky we have a family that has so much love for each other." I held my children close to me as we wept, and I kept kissing them all on the tops of their heads.

"Can we go see Daddy right now?" Dylan whimpered.

The doctor really didn't want Carson to have too many visitors, in case he caught something else, but I thought that with him doing better, it would probably be okay for the kids to go see their Dad. I called Bill to ask if Carson was awake, and he told me that my husband was dozing intermittently. "Well, could you go ask the doctor if it's okay if we all come to see him?" I asked.

"Of course. I'll call you back as soon as I track him down."

It took a while, but the doctor eventually assured Bill it was fine, so we all piled in the car and headed for the hospital. I'd made a promise to the kids that they could see their Dad anytime they wanted to, and I wasn't going to break that promise on the first day I'd made it; the truth is, I would have snuck them in even if the doctor had said no. Fortunately, when we got to the hospital, Carson was awake. I talked to the kids about how they had to be on their best behavior around Dad right now, because he was still really sick—and they were *very* good. They all kept their voices calm and quiet as they settled around their Dad's hospital bed. Elisabeth walked over and gave Carson a kiss on his cheek, while Selena held one of Carson's hands. I was happy to see that Carson held her hand back. Dylan sat on my lap.

During our visit, the kids told their Dad how much they missed him. The girls talked with him about what was going on in school, and Carson looked at them as they talked and just gave them a little smile. He must have had so much that he wanted to say to them…but he couldn't. I'd seen exactly the same thing happen with his mother.

Whenever he spoke these days, Carson sounded a lot like the elder Elisabeth had toward the end. It was hard for him to put the words together; I could tell he was frustrated with it, and he would just give up most of the time. When he didn't, his speech usually came out as mumbling. Most of the time, now, he would just listen and make some type of movement to show he understood. After about a hour I could tell that Carson was starting to fade, so I told the kids to say their goodbyes to their Dad, because he needed to get his rest. All three went and gave their Dad kisses and told him that they loved him. I gave Carson a kiss on the forehead and told him I loved him, too.

I desperately didn't want to leave; I felt like I was leaving the main piece of my soul behind. If I'd known that Carson was coming home at the end of all this, it would have been easier. But Carson wasn't coming home; so every time I left him to take care of the rest of the family, I felt the empty hole in my soul.

As I drove us home, I talked to the kids about their Dad and his fight with Huntington's disease. Selena and Elisabeth had a lot of questions, but Dylan really didn't talk too much about it. I could tell that it was affecting him differently than the girls, probably because he didn't understand what was going on like the girls did. Dylan wanted his Dad home, and he was a little angry that it wasn't going to happen.

The next day, after I dropped the kids off at school, I began to pack up Carson's things. I felt sick as I was doing it, and cried the whole time. I sat staring at the empty closet when I was done, hardly able to believe that I would never hang Carson's clothes up there again. I stored all of his suits in a hanging suitcase; I decided I wouldn't move those over to Greenbrier, because barring a miracle, he would never wear them again… since he would never set foot in a courtroom again. I recalled how incredible Carson looked in these suits, how I would just sit there looking at him in awe when he was all dressed up for court, and that made me cry again. What had we done to deserve this fate? Carson was the best man I had ever known!

When I ran dry, I took the pictures of me and our kids off the wall and put them with the rest of his things. These were what Carson would look at before he went to sleep in the care home: now, they were going to be as close as he could get to his family when it was time to say good night. He wouldn't be there to tuck his kids in and send them off to sleep, which I found infinitely sad.

When I went into his bathroom to start packing up all his toiletries, I really lost it: anger at the unfairness of the universe utterly consumed me, and I just started to throw things. Not even knowing what I was doing at that point, I hurled a glass jar containing bath beads against the bathroom mirror, sending soap and shards of glass flying in every direction. I glared at my reflection in the shattered mirror, and knew I was looking at my life before me. What had once been a perfect reflection was now shattered, ruined, and I had no idea how I was going to face that.

I wanted to wake up from this nightmare. This couldn't be real!

After I settled down somewhat, I called Bill and asked him if he could come over to help me, because I didn't think I could do it alone anymore. I was vaguely surprised to learn that Carson's cousin Brody had just come into town to visit Carson, and he said that they would both be right over. I really didn't want to see Brody: we were like oil and water, and I was a wreck right now. I was afraid I wouldn't be able to bite my tongue if he said something stupid. I hadn't seen Brody in years. When he would come visit, he would usually stay with Bill, and Carson would take the kids over to Bill's to see him. I always came up with an excuse why I couldn't go with them. Carson, knowing how Brody and I felt about each other, never questioned me about why I wouldn't go.

I'd barely gotten myself together when I heard a knock at the door, so I went downstairs and let the two of them in. Brody looked different than I remembered: he looked like a man now, not like the stupid punk kid I remembered. Without a word, he walked up to me and gave me a hug. I hugged him back, and after a long moment he said quietly, "Hey, Kathryn, long time no see." Thank God he hadn't called me Kitty-Kat!

"Hi Brody," I replied. "Thanks for coming."

He pulled away and held me at arm's length. "Kathryn, I'm so sorry about everything that's happening. I went and saw Carson this morning. I really didn't know things were so bad, or I would have been out here much sooner. Carson and I seemed to have lost touch, so, uh, I was kind of in the dark about all this."

"It's okay, Brody. Carson's lost touch with a lot of people. These last few years have been really hard on him. He hasn't even been able to talk to people like he used to."

"Well," he said uncomfortably, "I wish I'd known, Kathryn. I really am sorry."

"I know. You know now, though, and I could really use some help getting things moved over to the place where we're taking Carson, okay?"

"Yeah, Uncle Bill told me about that." He took a deep breath, then plunged on: "You're doing the right thing, you know. I can't imagine how hard it must be on you and the kids, but you *are* doing the right thing for Carson."

I nodded wearily. "Thanks for saying that, Brody."

I took the guys upstairs to Carson's room, and as we walked up the stairs, I thought of all the times that Carson had stayed downstairs because it was too hard for him to make it up the stairs. "At least Carson won't have to battle with these damn stairs anymore," I told Bill and Brody.

I'd totally forgotten about the broken mirror, or I would have explained it before we got up to the room. Brody walked around looking for things he could do, while Bill walked into the bathroom and asked, after a brief silence, "What happened in here?"

"Oh. I kind of lost it," I said in a flat voice.

Brody walked in to survey the damage. "I can fix that," he told me. "I'll clean it up right quick, then run and buy a new mirror and put it up."

That, more than anything, convinced me that Brody was a grown-up now, and frankly, it was a real shock. It was a full 180-degree reversal for him: he actually seemed pleasant to be around. As he returned from the bathroom, I told him, "I'm really not crazy, you know. I've never done anything like this before."

He shot me a little grin and said, "I have. But I completely understand. Strong emotions make us do weird things…and anyway, you don't have to explain yourself to anyone."

After setting things in motion with the guys, I told them I was going to run to the hospital and spend a little time with Carson before I had to pick up the kids. They were sympathetic, and told me to go, that they would start taking care of everything. When I saw Carson half an hour later, I was vastly relieved: he looked so much better, and the doctor assured me that he would be fine to leave soon. They'd like to watch him for the next 48 hours, but if everything stays the same, he could go home.

"I saw Brody today," I told Carson, once we were alone. "We got along just fine."

He nodded, as if to say, *Good.* I knew that Carson was probably worried about Brody and I being in the same house together, and I was quick to assure him that we'd both make an effort to co-exist; there would be no personality clashes, not at a time like this. I talked to him aimlessly for a while, then headed off to pick up the kids.

When we got home, I walked upstairs to find that all the glass from the mirror and jar had been cleaned up, and that Brody had in fact kept his promise and replaced the mirror. Bill had packed a couple of boxes, and pulled me aside and told me that he and Brody would take care of all of the moving. "Of course, if you want to help, you can; I don't want to step on your toes. But the option is open, if you just want to step back from it all and let us take care of it."

"You're right," I admitted. "It's probably a good idea that I step back for a while, if you're fine with doing it."

"Of course we are. I've already contacted a mover to come and move all the big stuff tomorrow and the insurance issues are already taken care of."

I was so glad I had Bill, because I just didn't know what I would have done without him. He was handling all the financial aspects of the affair; if it weren't for him, I'd probably just write a check to the facility every month so I wouldn't have to deal with any of the insurance stuff.

After talking to Bill, I went downstairs to check on the kids. They were sitting in the living room talking to Brody; he had Dylan cuddled by his side, with the girls sitting across from him on the couch while they told him all about what was new in their lives: their schools, their friends…and how they felt about their Dad's illness. I didn't want to deal with that, so I headed for the kitchen to prepare dinner. I'd already asked Brody and Bill if they would like to stay for dinner, and they had said that they would, so they could get done with the packing.

As I worked, I listened to the kids laughing with their "Uncle" Brody. Cousin, really, but Carson had introduced Brody to them as an uncle. I smiled to myself, shaking my head in surprise. I *never* thought I'd let Brody near my house…and now here he was, in my living room, playing with my children. It was a good thing, I thought; it was nice that the kids had someone so close to their father to talk to.

After awhile, Bill came in the kitchen and asked if I needed any help with dinner. "No," I told him, "but you can keep me company, if you wouldn't mind." I fixed him a soda and had him sit down at the table while I cooked.

He sat and listened to the kids talking with Brody, and after awhile he said quietly, "Kathryn, I know you and Brody don't really get along."

"That was when we were young, Bill." I stopped what I was doing and looked at him. "We're both grown-ups now, and at this stage of my life, I just don't have any room in my heart to hold grudges. I think it's great Brody is here, now, spending time with the kids. I…know this would make Carson very happy to see."

He laughed sharply. "I'm sure it would be a *shock* to Carson." He took a long swallow of his drink, and said, "Brody's going to be staying with me for awhile, Kathryn. He got laid off from his job…not because of his behavior, for once, but because the economy is so bad that no one's really building homes right now. I told Brody he could come work in the office until he found some work in his own field."

"I imagine you need a lot of help at the office with Carson gone," I said, as I slid a roast into the oven.

"I really do. We have just as big of a caseload as ever, and with everything going on with Carson, I can't seem to catch up with anything. There are some projects that I can only allow people that I really trust to touch, and with Carson gone, that pile of stuff is more than we can handle. So I thought Brody could help."

I cut my eyes in his direction. "You trust Brody?"

"Actually, I do. He's grown up Kathryn; you said it yourself. You haven't been around Brody for a long time, and I don't blame you; I understand why you avoided him. Like you, I'm surprised at how he turned out. We all know his younger years were a little…well, let's say 'rocky.' But he pulled himself together, and he's become a good man."

"That's good, Bill. I'm glad you have him, then."

He sat in silence for a few minutes as I worked, obviously trying to come up with a way to say something more. Finally he spit it out: "Kathryn are you and the kids going to be okay, being in this house alone?"

"We've been okay so far."

"Well, you know, I have enough room in my house for Brody, and I *am* excited to have the company. But if you need him to move in here for some peace of mind, that would be fine too, Kathryn."

I thought that was going a bit far, but what I said was, "Thanks, Bill—but we'll be fine, I think. I have you guys right down the way if I need anything. I'm glad Brody's here for you, but I'm still not too sure about how the two of us will be together. The last thing I need is to take on a roommate I'm not sure about. I really am fine by myself."

"Okay. Just know that the offer is always on the table. And, you know, I could come stay here for a while to if you need me to."

"Trust me, Bill I'm fine—but thanks for the offer."

A few minutes later, Bill went back upstairs to start packing again, and it wasn't long before Brody came into the kitchen and asked if I needed help with anything.

"I've got it." I told him. I wasn't used to so many hands trying to help me; I'd pretty much been handling everything myself, as far as the house was concerned, for a longtime now. Eventually, Brody went up to help Bill, while I sat the kids at the kitchen table and made them start doing their homework.

"It's fun to see Uncle Brody!" Selena said brightly, and Elisabeth echoed her enthusiasm.

"How long will Uncle Brody be here?" Dylan asked.

"Oh, I don't know," I said, as I looked over his math homework. "Your uncle will be moving in with Grandpa Bill for a while, so he'll be around a lot more." That made the kids really happy.

The next day was crazier than ever. The moving people showed up early to move all of Carson's stuff to the new place, and the place was a madhouse of shuffling furniture and stacks of boxes and too many people in too small a space. I stayed downstairs, mostly in the kitchen, because I couldn't bear to watch them move my poor husband's belongings out of his own house. When Bill came in and told me everything was done, I was relieved; now I could go up and start cleaning.

I headed up the stairs with a bucket of cleaning supplies, and when I walked into Carson's bedroom, I stopped short. Though it looked more or less the same, it felt empty; *I* felt empty. The room, once so full of warmth, was now so cold. Just four walls, a ceiling, and a carpet: no love, no personality. I started cleaning in the bathroom, working my way into the room. I wanted everything sparkling, because I knew that once I was done and I shut the door behind me, I probably wouldn't open it for a long time. I didn't want to see it again, not as it was now.

I was washing down the walls when Brody came in the room. At first, I didn't know he was there; I thought he had gone ahead to Greenbrier with the movers. I jumped when he spoke. "Hey, Kathryn. Are you okay?"

I spun to face him. "Of course I'm not okay! My husband's dying, and I can't take care of him anymore! I just want all of this cleaned up, so I don't have to come in here ever again."

Without a word, Brody got a rag and started to wash the walls with me, as I tried to hold in the tears. I was really good at crying my eyes out when I was by myself, but I didn't like doing it around other people. But I felt it building up in my chest, and I knew I wasn't going to be able to hold it in; so, finally, I gave up. I just sat on the carpet, back against the wall, and looked around…and the floodgates opened. Brody looked at me like a frightened kid; clearly, he wasn't sure what to do, as I sat there sobbing, I was sure he was wishing that he hadn't come into the room in the first place. But after the initial shock, he came over and sat next to me and, hesitantly, put his arm around my shoulders. I sank into his side and started sobbing hysterically.

Brody didn't say anything. He just sat there and held me.

When I finally calmed down, I stood up and apologized for the breakdown. Brody smiled crookedly and said, "Hey, we're family, Kat. I love Carson too." He levered himself to his feet, head hanging, and murmured, "More than you know." He looked up at me sharply. "I'm going to do anything and everything I can for you and the rest of the family now. Even if that means I have to help you through a breakdown here and there."

I laughed. "Thank you," I said, hugging him impulsively. After letting him go, I said, "Okay, I'm going to head over to Greenbrier to start to unpack. Carson's being released from the hospital tomorrow, and I want everything to be ready by then."

"Well, I can pick the kids up from school so you won't have to stop unpacking," he offered. "I can take them by the hospital to see Carson, and then bring them to you."

"That sounds perfect," I told him gratefully.

I swung by the hospital before I went to Greenbrier, and found that Carson was awake. He looked so much better! "Hey, handsome, how are you feeling?" I asked.

"Better," he murmured.

"You sure look better!"

"Kids?"

"They're at school right now—but they'll be coming by later with Brody. Your dad and I have something to take care of, so Brody will have them this afternoon. He said he was coming here as soon as the kids were out of school."

Carson had a half smile on his face, and I figured I knew what he was thinking. I'm sure he found it pretty amusing that I'd realized I was wrong about Brody.

I sighed. "Okay, okay, I guess I was a little too hard on Brody. He *has* been a big help with the kids. By the way, your Dad said he was moving in with him for the time being. He lost his job, so he's going to work in your office. I think it's good for Bill to have him around—I imagine he's pretty lonely, and I'm sure Brody is nice company for him. Speaking of your Dad, he is going to be so happy to see you. He's been so worried!"

Carson was finally starting to look like himself again, thank goodness. He was gaining color in his face, and I knew that Bill would be relieved to see the difference. After I told him about the kids and their day, I turned the TV on for Carson, and flipped the channels until he nodded his head to show that he wanted to watch the show that was on. Then I gave him a kiss goodbye: I kissed Carson on the lips, and for the first time in a while, he kissed me back.

I headed over to Greenbrier, where Bill was unloading boxes, and told him about Carson's progress—that he was even talking a little today. Bill headed straight to the hospital after hearing the news. I didn't begrudge him that: he wanted to spend every good opportunity he could with his only child. I picked up where Bill had left off, and soon realized that unpacking wasn't as bad, at least emotionally, as packing had been. Maybe it was because I knew Carson was going to be here for awhile, so it made it a happier place than the place he was leaving. I hung all the family pictures on the wall in places analogous to where they'd been back home, trying to keep the room as close as possible to the way his room had been at home, so he would feel comfortable here. In a few hours, I pretty much had the room done.

That's when Brody came bustling into the room with the kids. Selena put her hands on her hips and looked around, then said approvingly, "This looks just like Daddy's room at home!"

I hugged her and said, "Yep, that's what we were trying for."

"You hungry?" Brody asked. "I told the kids I would take them out for dinner."

"Are you kidding? I'm starving!"

After I took care of a few finishing touches, we left for dinner, and I called Bill on the way to have him meet us at the restaurant. He was just leaving the hospital, and sounded really happy; apparently, he'd gotten in some really good quality time with Carson. "I'm glad he's doing better," he confided. "We talked about the move a lot, and he seemed to respond pretty well. Of course, it probably wasn't his first choice, but he seemed at peace with it."

Sadly, what Carson was thinking was mostly a guess these days. We took various gestures and whatever we could understand of what he said, and put it together as best we could. I think we did a pretty good job; Bill and I knew Carson very well, so I was sure that most of the time, we were translating correctly. But I still wished he could look at me and tell me clearly that this was okay with him, or at least that he wasn't scared.

The next day, the doctor released Carson from the hospital, and I was a nervous wreck when we went to pick him up. I wasn't sure how he was going to respond to his new home, so I asked Brody if he would watch the kids while Bill and I took Carson to Greenbrier. As we drove to the care home, Carson just stared out the window with a blank look on his face. When we got there, we pulled out the wheelchair and carefully maneuvered him into it. He could usually walk with a walker, but since he had been down for the past week, the doctor had urged us not to let him walk right away. We introduced Carson to the receptionist at the front desk—we'd gotten to know her well, given all our comings and goings—and the owner came out and introduced himself to Carson. He told him that if there was anything he needed at all, to just call the front desk, and they could get it for him. He also gave us the schedule of the times Carson's room would be cleaned, along with the laundry days, and provided a menu of the meals that were going to be served that month. Of course, Carson also had a small refrigerator in his room that we filled with different drinks and snacks.

After Carson and I had met a couple of the very nice nurses who would be taking care of him, we took Carson to his room. We showed him all the different buttons by his bed and the chair: the TV controls, a button for emergencies, a button for the nurse, and a button for house services. They also had an emergency button in the bathroom; this place was set up for any emergency. There was always supposed to be someone popping in and out of the room, checking on him at regular intervals; I knew this would annoy him, but at this point it had to be done.

I'd purchased a 52-inch flat screen TV for his room, and I had the cable company come and set up every single channel I could—especially movie and sports channels. Since he'd be doing a lot of TV watching, it might as well be high quality.

I helped Carson out of his wheelchair and into the huge leather recliner I'd also picked up for him. I flipped on the TV, and gave him the remote so he could find what he wanted to watch while I talked to the nurse. I gave her all the prescriptions the doctor at the hospital had wanted him to be on, and then filled out the necessary ton of paperwork on all of those medications and the others that Carson was on, and when he was suppose to take them. When I was done, I went back to Carson's room to find him and Bill watching a football game on Sports Center. "I'm going to run and pick up the kids and bring them here," I told Bill. I looked at Carson and asked, "Honey, you up for some visitors?"

"Yes," he said clearly.

"Well, if you wanted to rest, that would be fine too." He didn't respond to that, so obviously, he wanted to see his kids.

I called Brody and asked him to have the kids ready, as I'd be there soon to pick them up. "How's Carson doing?" he asked quietly.

"I'm not sure, but he seems fine for now."

"Well, can I come along? I'd like to see him."

"Of course you can!"

When we all got back to Greenbrier an hour later, it was a tight squeeze: there were four adults and three kids packed into that tiny room. The girls laid on their Dad's bed while the rest of us, except for my son, sat in chairs around him: Dylan sat on the floor next to his Dad's chair, holding Carson's leg. Whenever Dylan got around his Dad, he instantly tried to find a way to attach himself to him. There was a special bond between those two, and always had been; Carson always seemed more at ease when Dylan was around him. We all sat and talked for a couple of hours, and after awhile, I noticed Carson fading, so I said brightly, "We'd better get going! It's time for the kids to eat dinner and get ready for bed." We all kissed Carson goodbye, and I asked Brody if he wanted me to take him home; but he said he'd just hang out and go home with Bill. So the kids and I left the three men there watching Sports Center. I knew that Carson was very happy to have Brody and Bill there.

A few weeks later, school let out for summer break. Now that the kids were older, I figured that this might be the last summer they all really wanted to be together, so I decided I'd plan a trip to Disneyland. I called Dad and Izzy and invited them to go, and of course I also invited Bill and Brody. They all responded eagerly, so I found us two two-bedroom suites and got us all day tickets in the park. There was a special going on—buy three days, get two free—so we got a great deal.

I couldn't wait to get out of town, and the kids were really excited about their vacation. Carson wasn't going to be able to make it, of course; I had talked to Dr. Callender about him going with us, and she didn't think it would be a very good idea, since the stress of Disneyland would probably be too much him. I still decided to ask him if that was something he wanted to do. I explained that it would probably be pretty crowded, with lots of people running around being crazy. I told him we all wanted him to go, but that if it was going to be too hard on him, we all understood if he couldn't. "Do you think you'll be able to go?" I asked gently.

He shook his head slowly, then looked down at his lap...and I felt a deep pain of sorrow and loss. I knew that Carson really *did* want to go; he used to have so much fun on our family vacations, running around and laughing and shouting with our kids, like a kid himself. But I had no doubt that the thought of going was overwhelming to him. I stood up and walked over to him, hugging him the best I could since he couldn't hug me back anymore, and told him, "I understand. I know it would be too much to handle. I'm sorry, honey." I ran my hands through Carson's hair, and then kissed him goodbye.

Vacation

Despite our deep, abiding concern for Carson, we all had a wonderful time in Disneyland, and I enjoyed spending time with Dad and Izzy: I really hadn't seen much of them for a while, considering everything else that was going on. Brody was also great to have around, if only because he went on all of the rides with the kids, and kept them company when I couldn't. I wasn't really a big ride person, so it was great that Brody took over that part for me—and the kids loved being with Uncle Brody. Brody was like Carson, in the sense that he was a big kid when it came to things like playing around with the kids.

In the California Adventure area of the park, there's a huge Ferris wheel. The kids all wanted to go on it, and begged me to go with them. I told them that the ride terrified me....and they pointed out that, hate it or not, I still went on it every summer. "Well, honey," I told Elisabeth when she pointed that out, "the only time I feel comfortable on the Ferris wheel is when I'm with your Daddy." In my heart, I knew I would probably never go on a Ferris wheel again.

"I'll take you kids on the Ferris wheel!" Brody spoke up. Luckily for the kids, the cars were enclosed, so I felt comfortable with them going on it. As I watched my kids get swept up into the sky, it brought me back to the night that Carson and I had ridden the Ferris wheel together, back in the carnival in Pollock. I remembered how special I felt to be sitting next to him, and how nervous I was when he grabbed my hand...and how the butterflies fluttered in my stomach when he kissed me. After all these years, that was still one of the best moments in my life. I couldn't believe how much had changed in the intervening years. Back then, we were young kids in love, with no worries in the world. Now look at us, weighed down with the weight of the Heavens like Atlas. It was insane how much time had changed us.

When Brody got off the wheel with the kids, we started walking to the next ride, and Brody piped up, "You know, Kat, I remembered Carson calling me and talking to me about how he was going to make a move on you that night you went to the carnival. He was so nervous."

I blinked and said, "Seriously?"

"Oh, yeah. He liked you so much that he was scared to death he'd do something wrong. He'd never liked a girl like that before, he said. He wasn't sure how he was going to do it, but he knew he was going to do it that night." He grinned fondly. "Yeah, I laughed at him, because I liked a lot of girls, and I asked him why he wanted to settle for just one. I was a little jealous."

That was something I'd never expected Brody to say.

"Yep, I remember how he called me the next day and told me about the Ferris wheel incident. I told him he took advantage of your weakness."

We both started laughing, thinking of Carson back then. "I have to say, he was pretty smooth back in those days," I said. "Here I thought he was just being a good friend, and the whole time he was trying to make a move on me!"

"Yeah." He looked at me. "So tell me: did you really like Carson back then as much as he liked you?"

"Are you kidding me? I probably liked him more."

"I find that hard to believe, because you were all he'd talk about to me. And he'd talk my ear off."

"I loved Carson from the first day I met him," I admitted. "There was some weird connection that we had for each other, I think. We were like magnets; no matter how hard people would try to pull us apart, we always found some way to snap back together. He was my perfect match, and I was his."

"Lucky stiff," he said fondly.

"I suppose." I winked. "Looks like I'll have to pick your brain about *other* things Carson and you talked about."

"Any time." We got in line for the next ride, and he said reflectively, "You know, it's kind of weird, you guys starting your relationship on a Ferris wheel."

"Because of the name?"

"Not just that, no. I guess I mean because you've had a lot of ups and downs in your lives together."

"I guess that *is* kind of how we've been," I agreed. "I...I just really wish we had another ride in us. I'd love to fly up in the air with him again. But I guess we can't always get what we want."

Brody said solemnly, "I learned that lesson a long time ago."

All day we'd been noticing signs all over the place for a performance at the local House of Blues. I had no clue who the band was, but Brody knew them and liked them. Late in the afternoon, he asked, "You want to go out with me tonight, after the kids go to bed, and see the band?"

"I don't think so, but maybe Bill will go with you."

"Nah, I'm pretty sure Bill wouldn't like the band." He shrugged.

"Sorry to interrupt," my Dad said, "but if you like, I'll watch the kids, if you want to go out."

"Um, no, that's okay," I told him.

"C'mon, girl, you never do anything for yourself. You should go out and have some fun."

Brody laughed and said, "Kat, I know you're in your thirties now, but you're not that old!"

I glared at him for a minute, and then started laughing. "Okay, fine. Let's see how I feel at the end of the day."

By the time we'd collected the kids from the next ride, dusk was falling. We watched the nightly fireworks display, then took the children back to the hotel to put them to bed. About an hour later, Brody knocked on my door to see if I was up for it or not. I decided what the hell: I might as well go and have a good time. "I'll meet you in your room when I'm ready," I told him, and his face lit up.

I'd brought some "going out" clothes with me, just in case, so that was covered. I put on a little more makeup than usual and curled my hair, which never happened nowadays, and the kids told me how pretty I looked. I gave them each a kiss good night and told them to have fun with Grandpa and Grandma, then walked over to Bill and Brody's room.

Bill opened the door. "Are you sure you won't go with us?" I asked hopefully.

"Nope, you need a night out with people your own age." He leaned over and kissed my cheek. "Now, try to have some fun."

About then Brody came out from the bathroom all dressed up, and I teased, "Wow, Brody, you actually smell good!"

We took a cab to the local House of Blues, and Brody went up to the bar and ordered us a drink. The band had already started, so I grabbed us a two-seat table pretty far back from everything. The place was really packed. When he arrived, Brody handed me my drink and nodded. This was perfect, because Brody and I couldn't talk too much—the music was so loud. To be honest, I was still scared of what was going to come out of his mouth, even though he'd been a perfect gentleman since he'd moved to town. He had helped me with so much, and I realized that I really shouldn't be so judgmental of him.

After a while, he said something to me and held out his hand. I looked at him, confused, and he leaned closer and asked, "May I have this dance?"

There were a ton of people dancing around in front of the band, where they'd cleared a space for it, so I grinned and grabbed his hand as I stood up. He swung me into motion—and it was so much fun! I couldn't remember the last time I'd had that much fun, in fact. During the course of the night, we danced and danced, and I drank far too much. I never got a chance to let my hair down anymore, so I think I went a little overboard.

After the band was done, we left the bar to find a cab back to the hotel. As I was stumbling in the parking lot, Brody grabbed my arm to help me walk and laughed, "Man, Kathryn, you don't do this too often, do you?"

I started laughing myself and replied, "Is it that obvious?"

"Oh, a little."

Brody hailed us a cab, and after we slid into the back, I found I could barely hold my head up. Brody pushed my wobbly head onto his shoulder, and I fell asleep there. Eventually, I felt the cab stop, and Brody said in a chipper voice, "Here we are, Sleeping Beauty, back at the castle!"

I had no idea how I was going to make it up to my room; I couldn't imagine walking right then. So after he paid the cab driver, Brody swooped me up in his arms and he carried me back to my room. He got the keycard out of my purse and opened the door, and very gallantly put me in my bed. Before he left, I saw him go over and kiss all three kids on the forehead; he was getting really close to them. I decided I'd have to thank him in the morning for taking care of me…but for now, I needed to go to sleep before I got sick from everything spinning.

The next morning, the kids got up bright and early to continue their raid on Disneyland; and as for me, well, I made myself get out of bed and put a smile on for the kids. When we walked downstairs to get breakfast, we found Bill and Brody already in the lobby, drinking coffee. "How ya doin', Kat?" Brody said loudly.

"Oh, I'm great," I replied, just a tad sarcastically, glaring at him. He showed no ill effects at all.

After I ate, I felt a little better. Once the kids took off with their grandparents to the entrance of the park, and Brody and I were alone, I thanked for taking care of me.

"No problem," he said with a genuine grin. "I had a lot of fun."

That was our last day in the park; after that, then it was back to reality. I was eager to go to see Carson once we got home; I missed him so much, and I knew the kids were excited to see him, too. We hadn't gotten any calls from the facility, so I assumed that everything was okay with him. The kids had a great day running from ride to ride, because they knew it was their last day to take advantage of it.

When we got back to our room I started packing things up, and when Brody came in to take our bags down to the car, he asked if he could take the kids swimming that night since it was the last night. "That'll be fine," I told him. "Please, wear them out so tomorrow will be easier for us all!"

After we got everything downstairs, I put on my bathing suit and decided to go meet them. I relaxed in the hot tub, and watched Brody play with the kids in the pool. The kids loved it, giggling and screaming and hanging onto Brody as he tossed them in the air and across the pool. I hadn't seen the kids have this much fun in a long time.

The next day, it really was back to reality: and when we got home, we went straight to Greenbrier to see Carson. He was about the same as he'd been before, and the kids were as excited as I was to see their Dad. We spent an hour sitting with him as the kids told him about their time in Disneyland. Dylan blabbed that he had to go on most of the rides with Uncle Brody, because Mom was scared! I saw Carson snicker; he knew how I was with rides. That made me feel a little better.

Shortly after, the nurse came in and asked if she could speak with me, so I walked out into the hall with her. "Mr. Ferris had a couple of…episodes while you were gone," she confided.

"What do you mean, 'episodes'?" I asked, my heart sinking.

"We had to give him some pretty strong medicine," she explained, "because he went into convulsions. We could tell that he was in a lot of pain, too."

"Oh." Swallowing hard, I said, "I'll talk to the neurologist about it."

When I went back into the room, Carson was shaking like a leaf, and I decided that this was probably far too much stimulation for him right now. "Time to go home and get to bed," I said brightly, ignoring the disappointed chorus from the kids, and ushered them out of the room. As we left, I told the nurse at the desk about him shaking, and asked her if she could watch over him closely, because I was very concerned.

That night, Carson was admitted into the hospital again. He had another horrible infection, so they had to hold him for a couple of weeks. What was worse, the doctor refused to allow visitors. I couldn't believe it! There were times that the doctors had told us that they wanted to keep his visits short, but I had *never* been told that we couldn't see him at all.

I felt so helpless. This disease had taken everything from us; it seemed to have won already, and now it had made it so that I couldn't even see my beloved husband. I couldn't go hold him, and I couldn't even let him see me to know that I was there and that he wasn't alone.

I hated the world.

Epilog

The next twelve months were more hellish than anything that had come before. My world seemed dark, even at high noon, there wasn't a flicker of light; if it hadn't been for the kids and our family, I had no idea how I could have survived. I closed myself off from the rest of world, because I couldn't handle any feelings whatsoever. I hated what I had become. When there was a lot going on, with moving Carson into the home and all, I was so overwhelmed that I never had a chance to mourn my situation. Now that the world had slowed down to normal pace again, and the shock had worn off, I really couldn't handle my life. I would basically go through my daily routine of waking up, visiting Carson, taking care of everything I needed to for the kids, and then I'd go to sleep. My days had no meaning, no substance. This life I was living without Carson almost wasn't worth living. If not for the kids, I would have become a hermit. They were the reason I got up in the morning; they were the *only* reason.

That year was especially hard on Carson; he was in and out of the hospital constantly, and sometimes the infections were so bad that they would put him into quarantine, which was difficult for all of us. Even when he wasn't quarantined, I could only let the kids visit him in very short increments; it upset them too much to see him, and sadly, it got to the point they didn't really *want* to see him anymore, especially the girls. They all loved him and claimed to want to see him, but the truth was that they were scared every time they went to Greenbrier. Finally, I told them that it was their call: they could go anytime I did, but if they felt like it would be too much that day, they didn't have to go. Fortunately, they were old enough to be alone without a sitter anymore, so they were able to make their own decisions about their dad. Their therapist told me, too, that it was a good idea to let them decide. Of course, I still went to see Carson every day. We were pretty good now with our situation; it had become our norm. For the most part life was going pretty smoothly, as much as I hated it.

Bill came over to talk to me one day, and got straight to the point. "I've been very worried about you, Kathryn. You used to have such a light in your eyes...and it seems to have gone out. You're doing everything right, but I can't help but think that you're just going through the motions. I'm worried about what's going on inside of you."

I tried to smile. "Thanks, Bill, for being concerned...but I'm fine. Really."

When Bill left he was clearly unconvinced, and I thought for a long time about what he'd said. I *was* doing everything right, I decided; in fact, it was almost like I was doing everything *too* right. I had the same daily routine, day in and day out, and that's what got me through my day. I would wake up and get the kids ready for school, then drop them off. I would go home and plan dinner, and do whatever cleaning needed to be done. Then I would go visit Carson till it was time to pick up the kids, and later I would do dinner, we'd eat, I'd do the dishes, and after that, it was bedtime. On the weekends, I shopped.

Like a robot, I never changed my routine; and I think I did this to protect myself. As far as what was going on inside of me, I had no idea. I didn't even remember my dreams anymore, so as far as I knew, there was nothing in there at all. No, that's not entirely true, I guess. I was empty and alone, but there were still some emotions there: worry and sadness. I suppose I blocked everything else out as a protective measure. I just didn't want to feel anything anymore. I tried my best to be excited about the things my kids were doing, the lives they were creating for themselves as they approached adulthood, but it was difficult to show any emotions now. I had very little emotion left in me; I felt like a stone statue. Oh, there were a few dull sparks when I'd learn of a new medicine or procedure that the Huntington's clinic was testing. But the pace of the research so glacial that I lost all hope of Carson ever being around to see the results from any of it.

That changed one day as I was cleaning the house after dropping the kids off at school. I had no idea how, but Dylan had become a dirt magnet, especially now that he was heavily involved in sports, and he had an amazing talent for tracking footprints all over the carpet. I was glad when I was interrupted in my scrubbing by the phone ringing, and pleasantly surprised when I realized it was Dr. Callender, Carson's neurologist. "Are you up for a meeting, Kathryn?" she asked brightly.

"I suppose," I replied. "What's this about?"

"I've got a colleague, Dr. Harrington, who's been approved to start human trials on Huntington's patients at the new stem cell facility here at the hospital," she said. "We've been compiling our list of candidates, and I'd like to put Carson on it. Interested?"

Of course I was! Two days later, I was sitting with Dr. Callender and Dr. Harrington at the clinic, listening to their proposal. They explained to me that progress had been made in applying stem cell therapies to people with Huntington's disease; so far, they'd been performing the procedures on primates, and it proved to be safe and effective. At the very least, they said, it would stop the progression of the disease; whether the effects could be reversed remained uncertain at this point.

I really didn't understand the scientific aspects of the treatment, but I did get the gist of it: if Carson was one of the candidates chosen, he would go in for brain surgery, and they would place stem cells into the brain. It sounded like the idea was that the stem cells would help the brain to repair itself. I really didn't understand how the whole process worked, but luckily I didn't have to. This amazing scientist, Dr. Harrington, did understand it, and she was ready to take it forward to human trials. There were a lot of applicants, though, and a panel was going to have to choose who would participate in the trials. It sounded like they were looking for people all over the spectrum of progression of Huntington's disease.

"So, Kathryn, do you think this is something that Carson and you would be interested in applying for?" Dr. Callender asked me.

Frankly, I was in shock. I'd stepped away from what was going on with the research for a couple of years; I'd gotten so frustrated because Carson's illness was progressing faster than anything was being done. I *had* to pull away from it, because even though I'd read about all of this stem cell stuff years ago and gotten really excited about it, I honestly didn't think anything was going to happen in Carson's lifetime. Maybe it still wouldn't…but then again, maybe he had a chance now.

Here I was, sitting and talking about it happening.

When I realized Dr. Harrington and Callender were looking at me, expectantly, I cleared my throat and said, "Where do I sign up?" I'd long since been entrusted with all of Carson's medical decisions.

They looked at each other, and Dr. Callender grinned. "Here's an application," she said, handing me a thick sheaf of papers.

"Great." When I left the doctor's office, I was still in shock. I called Bill right away, and told him he needed to come over for dinner. When he got to the house, I told him everything. We instantly got on the computer and started looking everything up, focusing over the last couple of years' worth of progress…and there was quite a bit. I couldn't believe that all this had been going on without us knowing! I felt a twinge of remorse, knowing I should have stayed in closer touch with the HDSA and kept up with the research, rather than letting myself become wrapped up in despair.

I think Bill felt the same way, because he had tears running down his face as he read the different articles about how stem cell therapy might slow or halt the progression of Huntington's disease. We sat down together at the kitchen table to fill out all the information the trial panel needed, and when we were done—hours later—I told Bill that I would send it out first thing in the morning.

I wanted to scream out loud with joy! I wanted to tell the kids that their Dad was going to be okay! But I knew better than to do anything like that, especially since I had become such a pessimist. The reality was that if Carson *wasn't* chosen for this trial, then that was it: all hope was gone. We would have to wait until the research was complete before they could perform the procedure on him…assuming it worked anyway. By then, Carson would certainly be gone.

Time was my worst enemy. I wanted to freeze Carson in time until they found a cure, but that wasn't going to happen, either.

A couple of months went by, and the whole time Bill and I were sitting on the edges of our seats, wondering if Carson would be selected for the trial. I felt like I was going to explode if I didn't hear soon, and as for Bill, he called to check everyday. He knew I would call him the second I heard anything…but he was on edge too. The weekends in particular seemed long, because we knew we wouldn't hear anything on the weekend.

It came when I'd stopped expecting it: one Friday, as I was getting ready to pull dinner out of the oven, the phone rang. It was Dr. Callender, and she had wonderful news: Carson had been chosen to participate in the stem cell trial! My knees started to shake, and all I could say to Dr. Callender was, "Thank you."

"I know you're probably in shock right now," she said kindly, "and I know you'll need a while for the news to sink in. So honey, you take all the time you need, and call me next week so we can start getting everything in order."

"Okay. Yes. Thank you!"

When she hung up, I immediately called Bill and gave him the news, and then Dad and Izzy. By then, I was so ecstatic that I could barely speak. I'd gone from one emotional extreme to another, and when I hung up with Dad, I just sat down and cried for awhile. I had been drowning in the darkest, the deepest water of despair; I had been in a vacuum chamber that had slowly sucked all of the life out of me for so long that now, I didn't know what to feel or even *how* to feel anymore.

I felt a feeling of warmth spread through my entire body, like the sun was starting to grace my darkened presence. Suddenly I seemed to be lifted from the earth; the gravitational pull on my soul was starting to let up! The only word I could use for the way I felt was *free*. I was becoming free from the darkness. I was becoming free from all of the pain I had suffered for so long; I had hope, and it felt *exhilarating*. I don't think anyone really knows the power of hope until it's all taken away from you, a piece at a time, and then for some reason, by the grace of God, it's given back to you in a flood. I felt whole again.

I took a huge breath of air. Carson was like oxygen to me; without him, I had slowly been suffocating. Now I felt like I could breathe again. I felt the blood rushing through my body, and I looked around and saw all of the warm magnificence of my home. It had felt so cold for so long without Carson in it; now, maybe, he could come back, if only in a limited way. Maybe he couldn't be the man I'd fallen in love with, but I'd take whatever part of him medical science could return to me.

Everything was better. I was coming back to life, after being dead for so long. Now I had stepped back into my consciousness…and I couldn't help but wonder how much I had missed.

But now I had hope again. And I felt *alive*.

Afterword

Living With Huntington's Disease

My name is Katie Jackson, and to me, Huntington's disease is more than just a plot device: like Kathryn in *Ferris Wheel,* I'm living with the consequences everyday...and wondering what the future holds for me and my family. As of this writing (early 2010), I'm a 29-year-old hairstylist. My husband Mike and I have two beautiful children, and Mike and I agree that our most important job is to be the best parents we can be for Madison and Cooper.

While *Ferris Wheel* isn't autobiographical, the experiences of the Ferris family often mirrors the experiences that my family has gone through over the past several years. Four years ago, our world was turned upside down by a single phone call. Like Carson in the novel, Mike was at a funeral when the news arrived; I was at home taking care of our children, so I took the call. Mike's father had passed away two months before from Huntington's disease, so Mike had recently gone in for a simple blood test to check whether he had it, too. The doctor gave me the devastating news that Mike had tested positive.

We immediately made an appointment with a neurologist in Sacramento to see what we should be doing for the disease, and it was a horrible experience. The neurologist seemed to care very little about the disease that we knew was going to change our lives forever, and like Kathryn in *Ferris Wheel,* I had a few choice words for him when we left his office. I instantly got on the phone and called the Huntington's Disease Society of America, which I'd learned about from a client at the salon. Years before, I'd overheard her telling someone else that her husband was ill with Huntington's, and when I revealed that my father-in-law had the same disease, she asked me if my husband had been tested yet. When I told her he hadn't, Judy advised me that if he ever decided to get tested, to contact the Huntington's Society for advice on what to do.

I let that conversation go, because I never thought in a million years that it was something we would have to deal with. By the time

Mike was diagnosed, I'd forgotten about what she had told me—so we just followed our primary care physician's referral to the neurologist in our health care group. I wish I had remembered that conversation before we made the biggest mistake of our lives! The neurologist knew *nothing* about Huntington's disease; he basically told us that all we could do was give up. Fortunately, the Huntington's Society of America Northern California Chapter was there to help us pick up the pieces. When I called their number, I talked to a woman who gave me the best advice I could have ever imagined: she directed us to a Huntington's clinic at UC Davis, right in our own backyard.

I was fortunate enough to have the nurse, Terri, answer the phone at the clinic. She was so wonderful to talk to! Terri and the fantastic people at the UC Davis clinic helped us through our shock, and we were gratified to learn that there was quite a bit of hopeful research going on with the disease. We made an appointment to see the neurologist at the clinic, who only worked with patients with Huntington's disease, and she was wonderful. The clinic was also participating in on-going clinical trials, and they were a wealth of helpful information on the subject. We got involved with the Society, and soon started taking part in local conferences, where we could learn more about the research undertaken by the brilliant scientists working toward a cure for this horrific disease.

It was exactly what we needed. Through the Society and the clinic, we now have hope that one day, there would be treatments for Huntington's disease. In fact, Tetrabenazine, the first drug designed to help chorea—the erratic movement that's one of the symptoms of Huntington's disease—has since been passed by the FDA. My husband is affected by chorea and is on now Tetrabenazine and it has helped him tremendously. I don't know if we would ever have found out about Tetrabenazine if we hadn't contacted the HDSA.

If you know anyone who's at risk for Huntington's disease, or has found out they have the disease and hasn't contacted the society, please advise them to do so as soon as possible. Knowledge is power; knowledge is hope. If nothing else, that's the service that the HDSA offers. And despite what our original neurologist said, there are many promising treatments for Huntington's disease that are currently undergoing testing. This is a disease that we *will* beat. While it's true that there's only one medication approved for Huntington's so far, there are many prospective therapies in the pipeline; if you go to a conference and just listen, you'll be amazed.

The people who are working to beat Huntington's are a dedicated, tight-knit group, as I've learned to my gratification. Even the non-scientists and non-physicians are fighting hard, and it's amazing what even the tiniest gesture can do to help. Here's an example: as I mentioned, I learned about the Society from overhearing a casual conversation years before. One day, at our very first conference in San Francisco, we were approached by a woman who said, "You look as scared and lost as I do." I told her this was our first conference, and that we weren't sure what to expect. She asked us where we were from, and we were surprised to learn that that we were all from Sacramento.

She said that she would introduce me to the president of the Northern California HDSA chapter when she arrived. When the president arrived, moments later, my jaw hit the ground. It was Judy Roberson, the woman I'd met in the salon years ago! I walked over to Judy and told her I wasn't sure if she remembered me…and she opened her arms and gave me a hug, as my eyes filled with tears. She asked if Mike had been tested yet, and I told her that he had been, and had tested positive.

Judy immediately introduced herself to Mike, and during the ensuing conversation, I was sad to learn her husband had passed away from Huntington's disease. Judy and I became friends, and she's helped me through so much over the past few years. I am truly thankful for her. Like so many others, Judy has dedicated her life to helping people dealing with this disease. I truly believe that we're all given certain things to help us through certain situations, and I feel blessed by the support I've gotten from Judy, and the Society, and the Huntington's clinic alike.

The neurologist at the clinic is hands down one of the most amazing women I've ever known. She has dedicated her career to treating Huntington's disease, and I'm so thankful to have Dr. Wheelock in our lives. That nurse I spoke to on the phone that first day, Terri, is also incredible. Together with their team at the clinic, they see and care for so many patients affected by this disease. They also run clinical trials that are conducted at UC Davis for the brave people who are willing to take part.

After Mike was diagnosed with Huntington's, I lived in a daze for the first couple of years. At that point, Mike wasn't showing very many symptoms—so I think I was in so much denial that I acted like it wasn't there. Of course, I wasn't *completely* in denial; I still attended the conferences, and we still went to our appointments at the clinic. When Mike started to show symptoms of the disease, though, I fell into a horrible depression. I tried anti-depressants, and they really didn't work for me; then I started to see a therapist, and that helped, but I still was in a terrible funk.

Ferris Wheel was my true therapy. One night after my kids went to bed, I picked up my laptop and started to write. An incredible thing happened: I felt better. I became addicted. Every night after my family went to bed, I would write. It was the best therapy I could imagine. A year later, *Ferris Wheel* was complete.

At first, I wasn't going to go any further with the book, because it was very personal to me. But after thinking about it for a while and talking it over with my husband, I decide to contact an editor; and soon, my novel was being professionally edited, in preparation for submission to publishers and agents! While my editor (who is brilliant) was going through the editing process, he suggested that I write an afterword —and I'm so glad he did.

I decided that if this story could give anyone hope, it was worth putting it out there. We've all been affected by having a loved one deal with some type of illness. It doesn't matter if it's Huntington's disease, cancer, Cystic Fibrosis, heart disease…the list goes on and on. But we can't give up hope! I believe we live in a whole new world of medicine. I think the key to dealing with any illness is hope and knowledge.

If *Ferris Wheel* can reach one person and help them, then all this work was worth it—every single minute of it.

For now, Mike and I live one day at a time. We're thankful for every minute we get to spend with our children. We live with the hope that one day, the dedicated researchers will find a cure for this disease, so Mike can watch our daughter walk down the aisle when she gets married, and see our son graduate high school and college. For now, we hope for tomorrow and live for today—and make every minute count.

227528LV00001B/3/P

LU00055584648